GILGAMESH

T0385494

A NEW TRANSLATION OF
THE ANCIENT EPIC

GILGAMESH

WITH ESSAYS ON
THE POEM, ITS PAST,
AND ITS PASSION

SOPHUS
HELLE

Yale
UNIVERSITY PRESS
NEW HAVEN & LONDON

Published with assistance from the Louis Stern Memorial Fund.

Copyright © 2021 by Yale University.
All rights reserved.
This book may not be reproduced, in whole or in part, including illustrations,
in any form (beyond that copying permitted by Sections 107 and 108 of the
U.S. Copyright Law and except by reviewers for the public press),
without written permission from the publishers.

Yale University Press books may be purchased in quantity for
educational, business, or promotional use. For information, please e-mail
sales.press@yale.edu (U.S. office) or sales@yaleup.co.uk (U.K. office).

Designed by Dustin Kilgore.
Set in Spectral type by Newgen North America.
Printed in the United States of America.

Library of Congress Control Number: 2020949520
ISBN 978-0-300-25118-0 (hardcover : alk. paper)
ISBN 978-0-300-26809-6 (paperback)

A catalogue record for this book is available from the British Library.

10 9 8 7 6 5 4 3

CONTENTS

INTRODUCTION

"*Gilgamesh* is tremendous!" the poet Rainer Maria Rilke exclaimed in 1916. "I hold it to be the greatest thing a person can experience."[1] Many modern readers have shared Rilke's enthusiasm for the epic. *Gilgamesh* will soon celebrate the 150th anniversary of its rediscovery in 1872, and since then the epic has swept like a flood through the literary world, captivating readers across the globe. Printed in millions of copies and translated into two dozen languages, including Klingon, *Gilgamesh* is an unlikely best seller. Who would have thought that a story written three millennia ago, in the dead language of a long-forgotten culture, could appeal so powerfully to modern readers?

Imagine a novel that came out today being read and appreciated in the year 5120. Our culture will be long gone by then, our digital files corrupted, our paper books crumbled. Will there even be humans in 5120? For a book to survive that long seems almost impossible, but this is the scope of *Gilgamesh*'s triumph. Composed around the eleventh century BCE, it has survived three thousand years of history, and may well survive three thousand more.

But *Gilgamesh* also feels strangely fresh. It reads less like the poetic Methuselah it is and more like its own young, hyperactive hero. One reason why the epic has not been worn down by age is that it reentered the literary world relatively recently, compared to the Greek and Roman classics that have been known and read since they were first composed. *Gilgamesh* comes to us unburdened by reception, open to new eyes. As the poet Michael Schmidt puts it, "It has not had time to sink in."[2] Impossibly ancient as it is, *Gilgamesh* can still be read as if for the first time.

The secret to *Gilgamesh*'s success lies in something else Rilke wrote about it: "It concerns me."[3] The poet felt that he could relate to the epic on a deeply personal level, and, again, many readers since have shared the sentiment. After all, that is literature's greatest trick: to tell the story of one person and make it feel like the story of everyone. It is a trick that *Gilgamesh* pulls off to perfection, leading the novelist Ali Smith to dub it "the original epic of human self-knowledge."[4] *Gilgamesh* appeals to our sense of fundamental humanity, but it does so in the strangest way possible. The hero is anything but an average human. He is two-thirds god and eighteen feet tall, an ancient despotic tyrant who goes in search of immortality. If Gilgamesh tells us anything about the human condition, he does so by embodying its farthest possible extreme. He is a litmus test for us all: what he cannot do, none of us can hope to, and this makes his failure to become immortal all the more poignant.

Rilke felt that *Gilgamesh* concerned him because he shared the hero's desire for immortality, but every age and every reader finds in the epic a new aspect to connect with. It is an existential struggle against death. It is a romance between two men. It is a tale of loss and grief. It is about finding peace in one's community. To *Star Trek*'s Captain Picard, *Gilgamesh* was about finding friendship in adversity. For the Palestinian poet Mahmoud Darwish, writing about the epic was a way "to escape our age," one marked by terrible disasters for the Arab world. To the psychoanalyst Carl Jung, the epic was about incestuous desire; to the German emperor Wilhelm II, it was about power. To the classicist Andrea Deagon, Gilgamesh is a fellow insomniac.[5] In a myriad of different ways, the epic continues to concern us.

In 2019, I had the pleasure of publishing a Danish translation of the epic with my father, the poet Morten Søndergaard. It was on our book tour that I truly realized the power and breadth of the epic's appeal. During a Q&A, a young woman whose partner had recently died asked me what the epic had to say about coping with loss. The next week a member of the audience teared up as I talked about the heroes' destruction of the Cedar Forest: that was the week of the Amazon wildfires. "It's just too real," he said. As a restless young man myself, I can't deny that I also feel a connection with Gilgamesh. When the book tour was over, my father said that *Gilgamesh* reminded him of a punching bag. "It just hangs there. You come up to it, spar with it. You push yourself and grow stronger, wiser. But the epic just hangs there, ready for the next reader. When you're done with it, it says, 'Is that all you've got?'"

One reason for the epic's appeal is that it lures the reader in with a mix of wild energy and sober reflection. Gilgamesh the hero is youthful and rash, but *Gilgamesh* the epic is much more melancholic, full of meditations on death and the burden of community. The hero's exploits move the plot forward from one scene of excitement to the next, but increasingly tragic realizations are woven into the text. The double perspective allows the epic to both concern and captivate its audience, turning it into a work of passionate philosophy.[6]

Gilgamesh confounds many of the expectations we bring to the epic genre, in part because those expectations were shaped by the later Classical tradition, and in part because the epic itself is bent on showing how Gilgamesh falls short of the heroic ideals he sets for himself. He weeps and worries, hugs and begs, mourns and dreams far more than he fights. He never quite becomes the hyper-masculine warrior we are told to expect in the opening pages. His greatest military success, defeating the monster Humbaba, is made possible only by the intervention of his mother. In the end, the most significant event in his life is not a heroic triumph but a resounding defeat: his failure to achieve immortality.

The not-quite-epic style gives the story a playful side. It is often ironic and subversive, poking fun at its hero or critiquing his society. But the playfulness is always balanced by the gravity of its themes. The epic tackles the darkest topics without flinching: death, the loss of a loved one, qualms about committing murder, catastrophe on an apocalyptic scale. These are disturbing topics but also topics that resonate forcefully across time and bring the epic alive. For all its bleakness, the theme of death is the most vivid of the story, that which makes it feel so quintessentially human.

There is a danger in projecting onto ancient poems our modern fascination with metanarrative and stories about stories, but *Gilgamesh* seems to welcome that projection. Its climax is not a battle or a kiss but an epic within the epic: the tale of the Flood recounted by the immortal sage Utanapishti. This autobiographical account is then mimicked by Gilgamesh himself when he writes down the story of his life. As he does so, he finally finds a semblance of solace: "He came back from far roads, exhausted but at peace, as he set down all his trials on a slab of stone."[7] The epic shows both the tremendous power of storytelling and the cost at which it is purchased. Through stories, the teller can achieve the next best thing to immortality: eternal life in literature. But to tell one's story is also to stop moving, surrender one's identity to the reader and become fixed as a character once and for all. In *Gilgamesh,* stories are both a kind of immortality and a kind of death.

However bleak, ironic, and meta-, *Gilgamesh* remains at heart a good story well told. It takes its readers through magical forests and lethal seas, dwelling on the pleasures of sex, beer, food, and friendship. The cast includes scorpion people, monkey mothers, a bull the size of a city, and the innkeeper of the gods. At times, the ambition of the epic almost seems encyclopedic. It works in an explanation for why snakes shed their skin, how sailing was invented, and why the city of Uruk celebrated New Year twice. The richness of detail makes the epic a source of constant fascination, but it is also a challenge for first-time readers, who can be left overwhelmed by the pure strangeness of the text.

Readers approaching *Gilgamesh* without any knowledge of the ancient Near East will find much to confuse them. The epic is written in a language that has been dead for over two thousand years, in a writing system that is richer and more complex than any alphabetic script can hope to be. Every attempt to describe the epic in a few words quickly runs into trouble. It is written in cuneiform and it is written in Akkadian—so what is the difference between them? It is a Babylonian story about a Sumerian king—or is it the other way around? Many say it is the oldest poem ever written—but is that true? (It is not.)

In the essays that follow the translation, I shall unpack the text in detail, but in this introduction, my aim is to lay out the basic knowledge necessary to understand it. Think of the introduction and the essays as need-to-know and nice-to-know, respectively. Here, I shall discuss the languages and writing system of the epic, the cultural world in which it was composed, the fragmentary state of the text, and the choices I have made in my translation.

Gilgamesh comes from ancient Iraq, a region often referred to as "Mesopotamia" or "the ancient Near East."[8] The terms denote not a single civilization but a number of interwoven cultural systems that waxed and waned over millennia. The most significant were the Sumerian, Babylonian, and Assyrian cultures, but they coexisted with cultures like the Hittite, Hurrian, Elamite, Eblaite, Amorite, Aramean, Kassite, Chaldean, Urartian, Ugaritic—and more. It is no coincidence that the Tower of Babel is an allusion to Babylon: ancient Iraq was always a cultural crossroad for endlessly shifting groups of peoples and languages.

What the Sumerian, Babylonian, and Assyrian cultures all have in common is the writing system they used, cuneiform.[9] The cuneiform script could be employed to represent a variety of languages, just as Latin letters can be used to write anything from Portuguese to Finnish. In the ancient world, cuneiform became a medium for cross-cultural exchange, as the scribes who learned it, from Turkey to Bahrain and from Egypt to Iran, were introduced to the world of cuneiform culture.[10]

Cuneiform is the world's oldest writing system, stemming from the middle of the fourth millennium BCE. The first texts were not literature or science but chartered accountancy: writing was invented by the Sumerian-speaking people to keep track of the goods they owed and owned.[11] Later, cuneiform was adapted to represent an ever-greater variety of information, growing into a complex system that could be used to write receipts as well as religious doctrines. The cuneiform script changed and grew over time, falling into disuse around 100 CE, some three and a half thousand years after its invention.[12]

The most remarkable aspect of the cuneiform script is how many meanings each sign can carry. Each of the roughly six hundred commonly used cuneiform signs has more than one meaning.[13] Most signs can also be used in more than one way: as either syllabograms representing a syllable or ideograms representing a whole word. The sign 𒌓, for example, can represent the sounds *ud, tam, par, pir, laḫ, liḫ,* and *ḫis,* but also the words "day," "sun," "white," "when," "bright," and "storm." Conversely, most syllables can be written with several different signs. Scholars assign each value a number, so the sound *u,* for example, can be written with the signs *u, u₂, u₃, u₄* (𒌓 again), *u₅, u₆,* and so on, ranging from the most to the least used.

All this makes cuneiform a vast semiotic system of many signs and meanings, one that is certainly complex but which also offered endless possibilities for creative expression and clever interpretation.[14] Rather than simplifying their script, the ancient scholars relished its complexity, exploring its every crevice and connotation. While it was always possible to use cuneiform in straightforwardly prosaic ways as well, the scholars saw a wealth of meanings hidden in every sign, ready to be unpacked.

If *Gilgamesh* has survived the passing of time, this is largely because of the material on which it was written. Though cuneiform could be carved into rock, inscribed on wax, or even inked, it was mostly written by pressing a reed stylus into wet clay. The stylus leaves a wedge-shaped impression in the clay—*cunei-form* literally means "wedge-shaped"—and each sign consists of a sequence of such impressions. Cuneiform is thus a three-dimensional script, as the signs become visible only when they are brought into relief by the play of light and shadow. When light falls on a cuneiform tablet from its upper left corner, what seemed a mishmash of gray on gray arranges itself into row upon row of neatly written signs, often just a tenth of an inch in height.

Clay is a peculiar medium for poetry to survive on, because it combines two seemingly opposite properties: it is both durable and frail. Clay can survive the passing of time virtually unaffected. Unlike the papyrus of the Egyptians, it neither rots nor crumbles, and it cannot be eaten by vermin. As a result, archaeological excavations have yielded a cornucopia of cuneiform. Around half a million cuneiform texts have been excavated, a larger corpus than Classical Latin, though many remain unread and unpublished, as the world has only a few hundred scholars with the expertise needed to decipher them.[15] Even more tablets remain in the ground, awaiting excavation.

However, clay can also be shattered with frustrating ease. The vast majority of cuneiform texts have not reached us intact, but as the splinters of a tablet: the excavated sources are basically a jigsaw puzzle of gigantic dimensions. Scholars have been working to solve this puzzle since the middle of the nineteenth century, and that is the essence of the discipline known as Assyriology: studying the cultures of ancient Iraq through their numerous but fragmentary written remains.

Assyriology is closely allied to, and often overlaps with, the archaeological study of those same cultures.[16] Archaeologists are focused on material culture, meaning physical artefacts shaped by humans, whereas Assyriology is a philological discipline, focused on the reading and interpretation of ancient writings. Cuneiform tablets are photographed, drawn by hand or on a computer, transliterated into Latin letters, translated, annotated, and interpreted. When parts of a tablet are broken away, philologists try to reconstruct what is missing. When multiple versions of the same text exist, philologists compare their differences and merge them into a composite text.[17] When the text is unclear—because the signs are damaged or badly written, because the ancient scribe has made a mistake, or because the meaning is obscure—philologists debate how the signs should be identified and read. It is challenging, painstaking work, but as *Gilgamesh* shows, it can be enormously rewarding.

Of the many languages that cuneiform was used to write, two concern us here: Sumerian and Akkadian.[18] The languages were brought into close contact during the third millennium BCE, but in linguistic terms they could hardly be farther apart. Akkadian is a Semitic language like Arabic and Hebrew, while Sumerian is a linguistic isolate, meaning that it is unrelated to any other known language. Think of it as akin to a meeting between an Ethiopian and a Greenlander. But the two languages coexisted for millennia and became thoroughly intertwined, exchanging loanwords and grammatical features. Cuneiform culture was thus bilingual from the start, and *Gilgamesh* is no exception: Gilgamesh's story is found in both a Sumerian cycle and an Akkadian epic.

Sumerian died out as a spoken language sometime around 2000 BCE, but it continued to be used for the next two thousand years as the language of scholarship and religious rituals, much like Latin in Europe or Sanskrit in India.[19] Meanwhile, Akkadian split into two varieties: Babylonian in the south and Assyrian in the north (the dividing line ran roughly where Baghdad lies today). Although the two languages share a basic grammar and vocabulary, they differ in pronunciation and some verbal forms. Again, *Gilgamesh* straddles the two. The Akkadian epic was composed in Babylonian, but it is best preserved in manuscripts copied by Assyrian-speaking scholars, who slipped in the occasional "Assyrianism."

In what follows, I cite Akkadian words in transcription, a system that attempts to reproduce the original sound of the word with Latin letters, however imperfectly. For example, the word *destiny* in Akkadian would be *šīmtu*, to be pronounced (roughly) *sheemtu*. The other system used to write Akkadian words is transliteration, which reproduces not the sound of the words but their spelling in cuneiform: in this case, *ši-im-tu*, or *ši-im-tu₂*, or *šim-tu*, or the ideographic NAM-*tu*, or any other of the many possibilities that cuneiform affords. In both systems, a number of special characters are used: *š* for *sh*, *ḫ* for *kh*, and ' for the glottal stop (think of the Cockney pronunciation of *bottle* as "bo'-le"). One set of consonants is known as emphatic—that is, a somehow "heavier" version of *k*, *s*, and *t*: their emphatic variants are written *q*, *ṣ*, and *ṭ*, respectively.[20] Finally, long vowels are marked with either a macron (*ī*) or a circumflex (*î*), if the vowel resulted from two vowels being contracted into one. So in Assyriology, we literally have to dot the *ṭ*'s and cross the *ī*'s.

Both Assyrian and Babylonian changed over time, and they are today divided into linguistic phases: Old Babylonian and Old Assyrian, Middle Babylonian and Middle Assyrian, Neo-Babylonian and Neo-Assyrian, and Late Babylonian. (There is no Late Assyrian, because Assyrian culture had disappeared by that time.) Last, Standard Babylonian, a literary version of

Akkadian, was used to write poetry and royal inscriptions; it has a free word order, an archaizing grammar, and a rarefied vocabulary. As I return to in the essays, *Gilgamesh* existed in many different versions, which are today classified by language and findspot. There is an Old Babylonian version and a Standard Babylonian version, abbreviated OB and SB, respectively, as well as a Sumerian cycle, a version found in Ugarit, an Assyrian version, and a translation into Hittite and Hurrian.

The best-preserved of these is the Standard Babylonian version, and that is the one I translate here. (Watch out for a common confusion: it is not the Standard, Babylonian version, but the Standard-Babylonian version. The language is standard; the version is not.) But even the Standard Babylonian version has not survived in its entirety—again, cuneiform tablets are numerous but broken. When translating the epic, it is customary to fill some of the holes by inserting passages from an older version in which the scene survives. For example, Enkidu's dream midway through the story is preserved only in the Hittite version, Gilgamesh's gigantic measurements are found in the Ugaritic version, and much of Tablet II comes from the Old Babylonian version.

Inserting material from another version is a risky affair, however, since they are far from identical. To continue the jigsaw metaphor, it is like filling the gaps left by missing pieces with an older, slightly different edition of the same puzzle: not ideal, but perhaps better than leaving the gaps blank. In this translation, the shift from one version to another is noted in the right-hand margin.[21] Note also that the names of some characters changed between versions: in the Old Babylonian version, the monster Humbaba is called Huwawa, and the priestess Shamhat is called Shamkatum. For the sake of clarity, I have standardized their names, so that Shamhat is called Shamhat even in passages that have been inserted from the Old Babylonian version.

The Standard Babylonian version of *Gilgamesh* was divided into twelve Tablets. The standard citation for a line from the epic is the number of the Tablet in uppercase Roman numerals followed by the line number in Arabic figures: for example, the line "All the past has turned to clay" would be XI 119. Scholars refer to these Tablets with an uppercase *T*, to avoid a potential confusion between the sections of the text, the Tablets, and the physical medium on which the text is preserved, the tablets. *Gilgamesh* is divided into twelve Tablets, but exists on hundreds of tablets.

Cuneiform tablets come in many shapes and sizes, but the gold standard for philologists are those found in Nineveh, modern Kuyunjik, the last capital of the great Assyrian Empire. The tablets belonged to the royal library of King Ashurbanipal (r. 669–627 BCE), who gathered literary and scholarly texts from throughout his empire, and these library tablets evince remarkable care and elegant writing.[22] The tablets are rectangular clay blocks with rounded edges, like pillows, often about an inch thick and the size of A5 paper (roughly 6 x 8 inches). Their front side (obverse) is flat, their back side (reverse) slightly curved. The Kuyunjik manuscripts of *Gilgamesh* are six-column tablets, arranged in a landscape format with three columns on either side, separated by vertical rulings. There is no textual formatting to speak of on cuneiform tablets, no commas or capitals, no meaning-bearing difference in color or spacing. All punctuation in the translation, including quotation, exclamation, and question marks, reflects our modern interpretation of the text.

A text consisting of multiple Tablets such as *Gilgamesh* was called a series, Akkadian *iškaru*. Tablets that belong to a series end with a catchline—the first line of the next Tablet—that strings the series together. After the catchline comes a colophon, giving various pieces of information about the tablet: its title and length, the date it was made, the scribe who copied it, and the scholar who owned it.[23] From these colophons we know how ancient readers referred to *Gilgamesh*: like most cuneiform compositions, the epic was known by its first few words, called the incipit of the text. For the Standard Babylonian version, the incipit was "Who saw the deep" (*ša naqba īmuru*); for the Old Babylonian version, it was "Surpassing all kings" (*šūtur eli šarrī*).

The verses of the epic have no fixed rhyme, but they often use alliteration and assonance, which I have done my best to re-create in translation.[24] The verses are often divided into half-lines and arranged into matching couplets, as in the opening sequence:

He discovered a secret,	revealed a hidden matter,
and brought home a story	from before the Flood.[25]

It is unclear whether the epic follows any kind of meter, since Akkadian prosody is an unsolved problem—different systems have been proposed, but none has reached universal agreement.[26] As a result, it is also unclear how the characters' names are to be stressed. They are generally pronounced with a stress on the penultimate syllable (SHAM-hat, hum-BA-ba), with the exception of GIL-ga-mesh and EN-ki-du. In these cases, the pronunciation is a modern convention, and we are not sure how the Babylonians would have pronounced them. As first noticed by the Assyriologist Benno Landsberger, almost all Akkadian verses end in a trochee—a stressed syllable followed by an unstressed one—so we may assume that names found at the end of a line were pronounced that way as well: gil-GA-mesh, en-KI-du.[27]

Though the epic consists of twelve Tablets, the main narrative fills just eleven. Tablet XII is a direct translation of an older Sumerian narrative, and it tells a separate story about Gilgamesh and Enkidu, unlinked to preceding events. This is simply another story, set among the same characters but impossible to reconcile with the main epic. After his tragic death in Tablet VII, Enkidu is alive again, married and a father, and he travels into the underworld to retrieve a wooden ball that Gilgamesh has lost.[28] The bulk of the story consists of Enkidu's report of how people fare in the underworld depending on how they lived and died on earth. Scholars have been divided on how to understand Tablet XII. Some insist that it is an extraneous addition, others that it should be read as an integral, though disjointed part of the epic. The majority view is that Tablet XII is an appendix that was rather mechanically tacked on, linked to the rest of the epic by the theme of death but separate in style and storyline.[29]

So far, I have been referring to *Gilgamesh* as an epic, and, indeed, that is how most readers today approach it: as an epic to be read alongside the *Odyssey*, *Beowulf*, and the *Ramayana*. However, there is no exact definition of what can and cannot count as an "epic," and ancient Babylonian readers would not have used this term, which is a much later Greek invention (*épos* literally means "word"). In the essays that follow, I return to the topic of how *Gilgamesh* combines and toys with multiple genres, but it is worth pausing at the basic question of whether the epic is, in fact, an epic.[30]

Despite the lack of a precise definition, the word *epic* still summons a cluster of characteristics in the minds of modern readers, most of which are found in *Gilgamesh*. An epic is usually a narrative poem. It usually tells the story of one or more superhuman figures, either gods or humans made exceptional by their exploits. It is usually set in the distant past but directly tied to a community in the present. It is usually focused in large part, if not entirely, on a military conflict or a battle against a monstrous opponent. All these descriptions apply to *Gilgamesh.*

However, most definitions of epics also include the requirement that it be long, and *Gilgamesh* is quite short: in its original form, it was around 3,000 lines, slightly shorter than *Beowulf* (3,182 lines) but much shorter than Homer's *Iliad* (15,693 lines), not to mention the Persian *Shahnameh* (about 50,000 lines) or the Sanskrit *Mahabharata*, which is in a league of its own (about 200,000 lines). Dwarfed as it is by these cross-cultural siblings, *Gilgamesh* is still much longer than the average lyric poem, and roughly three times as long as the second-longest Babylonian poem, *Enuma Elish* (about 1,000 lines). So *Gilgamesh* is still long enough to be an epic.

But more important for most modern readers, *Gilgamesh* has an epic *feel*. It may be difficult to define a genre, but it is virtually impossible to define a feel. All the same, when they hear the word *epic*, audiences today expect something grand, heroic, action-packed, and so pathetic as to verge on the camp: in short, an escape from the quotidian into the exceptional, the excessive, the emotional. And on all those counts, *Gilgamesh* delivers in spades. Its drama is enormous and its emotions unrestrained. To steal a word from modern slang, Gilgamesh is *extra* ("over the top, excessive, dramatic, inappropriate, doing more than what the situation calls for"), and this dramatic excess is what makes him, in our modern eyes, an epic character, even though Babylonian audiences would not have used any of those words about him.[31]

At the heart of the epic is the city of Uruk. In this, *Gilgamesh* is typical of its time: cuneiform cultures were first and foremost urban cultures. The invention of writing took place during what archaeologists call the Uruk Phenomenon, an explosive historical process that created the first major cities, the first states, and the first complex social hierarchies.[32] Alongside Uruk, major urban centers began to spring up across the ancient Near East, and from then on, Sumerian and Akkadian cultures would be forever tied to cities. Each city had its own local identity, its own dialect and deity, its own claim to importance. The history of ancient Iraq was always defined by its most important cities: Babylon, Ur, Uruk, Ashur, Nineveh, Nippur, Sippar, Eridu, and so on.[33]

In the beginning of the third millennium BCE, southern Iraq consisted of a series of independent city-states that were embroiled in a complex network of alliances and conflicts. The cities remained largely independent of one another until the twenty-third century BCE, when King Sargon of Akkad brought them all under a single rule and so created the world's first empire.[34] For the next two millennia, Mesopotamian history would consist of an alternation between large empires that united the cities into one state, and a political collapse that reverted them to local self-governance.[35] But even as they were subjugated by far-reaching empires, the cities retained their sense of local identity. Though king after king attempted to standardize their rule, cities like Babylon and Nippur still saw themselves as the center of the universe—ancient, unique, and not to be forgotten. This is certainly the case for Uruk in *Gilgamesh*. Our hero twice travels to the edges of the world, first east to Humbaba, then west to Uta-napishti, but he always comes back to Uruk in the end. Placed midway between two symmetrical journeys to the ends of the earth, Uruk is effectively made the center of the cosmos.

The epic opens and closes with a description of Uruk, stating that the city, orchards, and clay pits are one *šār* each, and that the Temple of Heaven is half a *šār*. A *šār* was roughly two thousand acres—epics like to use big round numbers, and the real Uruk was much smaller.[36] The lines strike many modern readers as odd: why bother giving us the measurements of Uruk, when it is the adventures of its king that concern us? But the lines are a key example of the importance of cities in Babylonian culture.

The city is the natural frame of the epic, the logical beginning and end of the story. When the epic lifts its gaze from the individual travails of its hero, what it sees is the city.[37] Within the walls of the city, one could find all the comforts and conveniences of life: the temple was Uruk's crowning glory, the orchards were its economic lifeblood, while the clay pits provided building material for the houses and writing material for the scribes. The measurements that enclose the epic show us a city bustling with activity—planting, building, worshipping, and writing—in short, a living city.

The description of Uruk also reveals how closely the identity of the city was tied to its temple. In the religious world of cuneiform cultures, each god was connected to a city. Though the gods could be worshipped anywhere by anyone, they retained a special connection to the city (or sometimes cities) in which their main temple stood. The sun god, Shamash, had a special connection to Sippar and Larsa, the moon god, Sîn, to Ur, the wise god Ea to Eridu, and so on. Uruk had two local deities: Anu, lord of the skies and grandfather of the gods, and Ishtar, the most complex and unpredictable deity in the Babylonian pantheon, patron goddess of sex, destruction, paradox, and transformation.[38]

Ishtar is a central character in Babylonian poetry, and with good reason—her poetic potential is endless. Some hymns portray her as a naive young girl smitten with the shepherd boy Dumuzi, others as a savage warrior devouring the corpses of her enemies. She is always changeable and always changing everything around her, turning mountains into valleys, men into women, and weaklings into warriors. She does nothing that ought to be done and everything that should not be.[39] Given the link between gods and cities, her character in turn reflected on Uruk, which was associated with frequent festivals and the ritual performance of activities that were otherwise taboo.[40]

The link between gods and cities also meant that when the political balance between cities shifted, so did that between gods. When Babylon rose to political prominence during the second millennium BCE, its previously minor god Marduk became the king of the universe, ousting the former ruler Enlil. The shift had already taken place when the Standard Babylonian version of *Gilgamesh* was composed, but the epic retained the older theology, with Enlil as the ruler of the gods and Marduk all but absent.[41]

The Babylonian pantheon was a motley and messy affair, and nowhere is that clearer than in *Gilgamesh.* The gods were not expected to act in unison, a fact that the epic employs to great dramatic effect. The gods in *Gilgamesh* furiously disagree with one another, repeatedly change their minds, and make any number of shortsighted decisions. They are selfish, spiteful, trigger-happy, and vain. But the epic is not universally critical of the divine order, though readers could easily be left with that impression. In the end, it seems to favor one god in particular: as noted by the Assyriologist Martin Worthington, the god Ea plays an intriguingly central role in the epic, even when he hides at the margins of the story.[42]

Ea, god of wisdom and city god of Eridu, is a trickster figure, a sly and calculating character who in Babylonian poetry is often called upon to resolve the problems caused by others, or to protect the humans against his fellow gods.[43] Ea lives in the Apsû, a mythical underground lake from which rose the groundwater that nourished the fertile land of ancient Iraq. Gilgamesh descends to the Apsû at the end of the epic, and it is implied that he gains great wisdom by the mere proximity to Ea.[44]

Hints about Ea's importance are strewn throughout the epic. The second word of the text, *naqbu*, can mean "totality" or "depth," recalling Gilgamesh's journey into the Apsû, but it was also one of Ea's many names.[45] Another hint at Ea's importance is the repeated mention of the fraction "two-thirds" (for example, the name of the character Ur-shanabi means "servant of two-thirds").[46] Each god in Babylonian mythology was assigned a number: the Moon God was thirty, Ishtar was fifteen, Shamash was twenty, and Anu was sixty. The Babylonian number system was base sixty (as opposed to the current Western system, base ten), and two-thirds of sixty is forty: the number of Ea.[47]

Despite his importance, Ea evades the spotlight of the epic, appearing very rarely outside Uta-napishti's story in Tablet XI. Gilgamesh never talks to him in person, as he does with Ishtar and Shamash. Instead, Ea enters the story as a muffled whisper through the cracks of a wall, warning Uta-napishti to flee the coming Flood. Ea's words are retold to Gilgamesh centuries later by the now immortal Uta-napishti. Nested in Gilgamesh's story, the words have defied all odds in reaching our ears as well. They have been passed from scribe to scribe for centuries, buried for millennia, unearthed and pieced together by philologists, so that we too can hear the echo of a divine whisper telling us to listen.

The story of the Flood and of Ea's whispered words is one of the most important myths in Babylonian culture.[48] The background of the story is only hinted at in *Gilgamesh*, but we may safely assume that all Babylonian scribes would have known it from countless retellings. Today it is best preserved in an older epic, *Atra-hasis*, in which it goes as follows:[49] Thousands of years ago, humans had grown so numerous that the gods could not sleep for their noise, and Enlil, ruler of the gods, was furious. He tried to cull the human population with famines and plagues, but each time Ea (who is there called Enki) broke ranks and showed the humans a way out of their predicament. In the end, Enlil decided on a truly catastrophic solution: he would unleash the Flood and exterminate all humans. The gods swore an oath not to warn the humans of the coming destruction—this time, there would be no help.

Enter Uta-napishti. His name literally means "He Found Life," but this seems to be an honorific he earned after achieving immortality: he was first called Atra-hasis, "He Is Very Wise."[50] In the eponymous epic *Atra-hasis*, we are told that he had a special bond with Ea: he could speak to his god and his god would speak back. Sensing that something was afoot, Atra-hasis asked Ea for advice—but of course, Ea had been bound not to reveal the gods' plans. However, Ea managed to circumvent the oath of silence by communicating with him indirectly, through a coded speech passed on through the wall of his house. Ea's speech, especially as reported in *Gilgamesh*, is a masterpiece of misdirection and ambiguity.[51] Luckily, Atra-hasis understood Ea's coded words and built a ship on which to escape the Flood.[52] After the cataclysm, the gods realized the true extent of their mistake: without the humans to feed them with regular offerings, they starved, swarming like flies to Atra-hasis's sacrifice.

The story of the Flood gives the mythical background for two central elements of Babylonian culture: omens and offerings. Without offerings, the gods would go hungry, meaning that they were dependent on humans. Conversely, the humans were dependent on the gods' every whim, however ill-considered, and their only way of deducing those whims was through omens. In *Atra-hasis* it seems that before the Flood gods and humans had been able to communicate directly, but after the oath of silence, the gods would rely on the subterfuges devised by Ea, speaking through dreams and objects, like the wall through which Ea whispers to Atra-hasis: the first omen. One possible (if not fully certain) reading of the Flood myth is thus as an etiology of omens, explaining why the gods began to speak in codes.[53]

In ancient Iraq, omens were everywhere. Omens could be found in the path of planets, the entrails of sacrificed sheep, the movement of oil in water, malformed births, and bizarre events, but also in seemingly everyday occurrences. The series *Shumma Alu*, "If a City," collected omens relating to city life: cats of various colors crossing the street, ants crawling on a wall, pigs dancing in the city square, and the number of thieves, scholars, idiots, tall men, short men, deaf men, and blind men who lived in the city. (Too many scholars was a bad omen.) Even human behavior could be an omen: there were omens to be found in the way a person looked, spoke, walked, woke up, built a house, got divorced, and had sex.[54]

The post-Flood system of human-divine communication involved a sequence of offerings and omens.[55] A person would give an offering to the

gods—such as a white lamb if the donor were rich, or sesame oil if poor—
and pose a question. The gods would consume the offering and give their
answer in the liver of the sheep, or the pattern formed by the oil as it was
poured into a bowl of water, or in any of the other divinatory media. If the
answer was negative, revealing that the gods were ill-disposed, the humans
could attempt to change their minds with yet more offerings, accompanied
by prayers and incantations designed to glorify the gods' power and pacify
their angry hearts. New omens would then be taken to see if the attempt
had been successful—and the process was repeated until the result came
out positive.

The characters in *Gilgamesh* are no different. Throughout the epic, the
heroes are constantly making sacrifices to the gods: they pour out sacred
flour and fresh water, they offer trophies after their victories in battle. In
return, they seem not to sleep a single night without receiving an ominous
dream.[56] The dreams are among the most vivid scenes in the epic, but as
with all omens, their meaning is far from straightforward, and the interpretations given by Enkidu and by Gilgamesh's mother are anything but
intuitive. The system of communication instituted by Ea relied on ambiguity and interpretation: dreams and omens were like knots to be untied. The
Akkadian word for "interpret," *pašāru*, literally means "to unknot."[57]

The logic of indirect communication also shaped ancient medicine.
Diseases were thought to be caused by divine displeasure, so Babylonian
physicians had to both allay the patient's symptoms and identify their underlying cause: which god was angry and why.[58] We see this logic at work
in Tablet VII. The gods announce their decision that Enkidu must die
through an ominous dream, and he immediately falls ill. Gilgamesh says
that he will pray and sacrifice to the gods in order to change their minds,
as per the usual system. But here the normal order is interrupted, since
Enkidu explains that Enlil's stubborn mind will not be swayed, and that
there is no escape from him. Enlil's verdict was the ancient equivalent of a
terminal disease.

For Babylonian and Assyrian citizens, the back-and-forth between gods
and humans was an all-important part of life. Omens, offerings, prayers,
and incantations were a mainstay of the ancient world, and the vast majority of texts held in ancient libraries were related to this system of communication.[59] Cuneiform scholarship consisted of enormous omen collections,
ritual incantations, hymns and prayers, instructions for the performance of

offerings, lists of symptoms and their diagnoses—all texts that were meant to deduce and then sway the will of the gods.

The system allowed humans to claim just a sliver of influence on the wild cosmic forces that ruled their lives. The Flood story that appears in *Gilgamesh* is told in no small part to explain this order of things, linking gods and humans through ciphers and sacrifices, and so demonstrating the full extent of their mutual dependency. It also reminds us of the importance of being on the lookout for omens: our every dream could hold a warning of the next Flood.

The story of the Flood is remarkably well preserved, but all the epic's Tablets are incomplete: *Gilgamesh* comes to us as a broken echo. The ancient song was silenced long ago, and today it survives only as the fragment of a transcript. There is not one, complete manuscript of *Gilgamesh*, as there is of *Beowulf* or *Sir Gawain and the Green Knight*. In translation the epic appears to be a coherent text, but in fact it is a tapestry of broken pieces, overlaid to fill one another's holes. When Andrew George completed his magisterial edition of *Gilgamesh* in 2003, there were a total of 184 fragments of the Standard Babylonian version.[60] From that heap of shards, philologists forge a single text.

However, the multitude of manuscripts is not distributed equally across the epic. Some parts have more copies than others, and, conversely, there are many sections for which not a single copy survives. These holes in the text are called lacunae, literally "little lakes": they are the missing sections we cannot reconstruct. In 2003, George assessed the epic's preservation:

> The grand total for the eleven-tablet epic, leaving aside the appended Tablet XII, yields a survival rate of almost 2,400 lines out of an original line-count that fell just short of 3,000. On these figures, 20 per cent of the poem is still completely missing; taking into account the fact that many lines counted as present are damaged to some degree, it is probably fair to write that so far we have about two-thirds of the poem at our disposal. As new manuscripts are found this fraction will steadily grow. Several centuries hence there will surely come a day when the text is once again complete.[61]

George's hope is already being fulfilled. Since 2003, several new sections have come to light. The largest discovery came in 2014, when George and

Farouk al-Rawi published a new manuscript that added a long section to Tablet V. The publication of new pieces from older versions of the epic has also added to our understanding of *Gilgamesh* as a whole, and our knowledge of its literary history grows with every passing year.[62]

A project titled Electronic Babylonian Literature (eBL), headed by Enrique Jiménez, is assembling an online repository of literary manuscripts that will make the jigsaw puzzle of Assyriology much easier to solve by using digital tools to identify even the tiniest fragments: these can be less than half an inch in height and contain no more than four signs.[63] Minute as they are, these pieces can be used to fill in holes that still remain in *Gilgamesh* and other works of Babylonian literature, one sign at a time. In 2021, the database will be made freely available, accompanied by translations in English and Arabic, so that anyone with Wi-Fi can follow the latest discoveries of *Gilgamesh*.

Add to this the ongoing archaeological discovery of new tablets, and the text of *Gilgamesh* is likely to remain in flux for the foreseeable future. New pieces can be expected to appear with regular frequency over the next decades. This is another feature that makes *Gilgamesh* unique in the literary canon: no other ancient classic is so frequently updated. While we cannot hold out hope for a new passage from the *Odyssey*, a new scene of *Gilgamesh* appeared as recently as 2018.

About that scene. It was a small fragment that made George rearrange the beginning of Tablet II.[64] We can now follow Enkidu's transformation from beast to man in more detail, tracking the stages that led him to humanity: despite being no more than two inches high, the fragment shed new light on what it meant to become human in ancient Babylonia. It also showed that Enkidu's marathon of sex with Shamhat lasted twice as long as previously thought, and this was the aspect that the media latched on to: the *Times* reported the discovery under the headline, "Ancient Sex Saga Now Twice as Epic."[65]

At the time, I was working on the Danish translation of *Gilgamesh* with my father. When the new fragment came to light, we had to go back and change our translation to reflect the latest philological developments. Likewise, a tiny piece of Tablet III was published just two weeks before I submitted the final manuscript for the present book, including a lovely line where Gilgamesh's mother asks the Sun God to "open the road and ready the mountains" for her son.[66] This is a bizarre experience for a translator—

to see the text you are working on, especially one as ancient as *Gilgamesh,* change shape before your eyes. It is like trying to paint a model who refuses to sit still.[67]

With the steady trickle of new texts, perhaps the epic will one day be complete. I feel both optimistic and wistful about the prospect. I think I will miss the blanks when they are gone. In one sense it is obviously preferable to have a complete story: many readers find the breaks frustrating, and every addition brings new and exciting perspectives to the epic. All the same, I cannot escape the feeling that the fragments are beautiful in their own way. The scatter of words sometimes reads like a modernist poem: "... gods ... made ... gift ... throw ... his heart ... provide ... humanity."[68] There are also moments when the breaks feel like deliberate reticence. The last section of Tablet VII is missing, as if to spare us the pain of witnessing Enkidu's death, or perhaps to give him a last moment of privacy—like a nurse pulling the curtain to hide a dying man.

In the blank spaces, readers can get a sense of the epic as it really is. They show the seams of a story that has been stitched together from multiple manuscripts, none of which holds the entire text. The blanks remind us of the ultimate inaccessibility of ancient poetry. The story as it was experienced by a Babylonian audience has disappeared once and for all, leaving us only with fragmentary remains. We cannot possess the ancient text, we cannot grasp it and make it ours, since the original form that was sung in ancient Uruk will forever escape us. The missing sections show the unsurmountable distance that remains between us and the epic, and that distance can be engaging. "I don't know if it would be as intriguing," the playwright Yusef Komunyakaa says about *Gilgamesh,* "if there weren't a hundred ellipses. There are these great silences in the piece. So we can negotiate within those silent spaces. We can imagine within those spaces."[69]

There is also another, grimmer reason why the discovery of new fragments should not always be met with celebration. Some new discoveries are made through legitimate means: scientific excavations or the study of overlooked tablets in museum archives. But sometimes, as with the large fragment of Tablet V published in 2014, texts come to light because they were dug up through illegal looting and bought on the black market.

Looting is calamitous for archaeology.[70] It destroys the structure of an archaeological site, depriving us of vital information about the original context of ancient artefacts. Often the looters are desperate Iraqi citizens, impoverished by the many waves of war and disaster that have rolled over their country for decades. But the black market's chain of supply is naturally difficult to divine, and some middlemen probably have ties to terrorist organizations. When a new discovery of a cuneiform tablet is widely advertised and celebrated, it raises the stakes for the looters, who now have more incentive to find new pieces. More archaeological sites are disturbed and more cash injected into a shadowy, potentially dangerous economy. That cash often comes from private collectors in the West, who have no scruples about the pedigree of the artefacts they acquire. When it is done right, the discovery of new cuneiform tablets can be serendipitous, adding new lines to ancient literature, even shedding new light on what it meant to be human in Uruk. (And yes, doubling already impressive sex marathons.) But when it is done wrong, the consequences can be disastrous.

Whether or not *Gilgamesh* will ever be reconstructed in its entirety, for now we must read it as it is: broken. While some translators fill in the gaps with their best guesses, most prefer to leave them blank. The usual way of indicating a break is with ellipses enclosed in square brackets: [. . .]. I find this convention unbearably ugly. The bulky, sharp-cornered brackets are like barbed wire in my eyes. So when making the Danish translation, my father and I were determined to find a new way of representing fragments. The designer Åse Eg and the team at Wrong Studio came up with what I think is a brilliant solution: a raised dot. Like so:

The mountain ·   · the skies ·   ·
The beasts of the wild ·   · your crimson sheen.[71]

I have used this method to indicate missing sections in the translation below. When more than one line is missing, I have left the corresponding number of lines blank, so if philologists estimate that the text had twenty lines that are no longer there, you will find twenty empty lines in my translation. The raised dots are still a bit of an experiment—I hope you like them.

Faced with a medley of fragmentary manuscripts, each of which poses its own problems and often deviates from the others, readers would be at a complete loss on how to approach the text were it not for philologists, who turn those messy manuscripts into a readable text edition. Luckily, *Gilgamesh* has been graced with an exceptionally good edition, that by Andrew

George.[72] George's book is a master class in philological precision and inge-nuity, giving a transliteration of the original Akkadian and a faithful trans-lation into English, as well as a series of illuminating essays on the epic's history and meaning. It is a benchmark not just for the study of *Gilgamesh* but for philology as such.

My translation of Gilgamesh, like many others, is thoroughly indebted to George's reconstruction and interpretation of the Akkadian text. George also published a slightly freer translation with Penguin in 1999, and it was soon joined by Benjamin Foster's translation of the epic in 2001 and his updated version in 2019.[73] George and Foster take similar approaches to the text: they stay close to the original and seek to re-create the archaizing quality of the text. When the Standard Babylonian version was composed, a little more than three thousand years ago, it was already meant to sound old, and George and Foster reproduce this *altmodisch* effect in their trans-lations. But the translations remain first and foremost scholarly endeavors, whose primary aim is philological faithfulness.

Based on these and other translations, poets across the world have retold the epic—to convey its beauty, like David Ferry and Jenny Lewis, or to bring out its immediacy and clarity, like Nancy Sandars and Stephen Mitchell.[74] These retellings have much to commend them, but they are not based on the Akkadian original—they are translations of translations. Here, I stake out a middle way, engaging with the text in its original form but also try-ing to stay true to the poetic power and extraordinary vividness of the epic, which often leads me to depart from philological exactitude.

The translations by Foster and George indicate words that are missing but which have been reconstructed by enclosing them in square brackets, and words that are only implied in the Akkadian by setting them in pa-rentheses. George also indicates words that are problematic or somehow obscure by setting them in italics. I do none of this. Words that are am-biguous, implicit, emended, or reconstructed appear in regular typeface, giving my best guess at what the text once said (mostly following George's edition). The reader who would like to know exactly what is in the original manuscripts and what modern philologists have emended should consult George's edition or go to the eBL website.

I stick as close as I can to the original structure of the text, by letting most verses be self-standing phrases, but occasionally I break up overly long lines by turning each half-verse into its own verse. A major challenge in translating Akkadian poetry is to render how wonderfully succinct it is. In a line like "he smeared himself in oil and turned into a man," English needs ten words where Akkadian has four (*šamnan iptaššaš-ma awīliš īwe*).[75] Instead of the archaisms highlighted by George and Foster, I focus on alliterations and aural patterning, another important quality of the text. Lines that appear unimpressive in a literal translation often hide a vivid verbal game in Akkadian. For example, the dull-looking sentence "If your hand can reach this plant" does no justice to the amazing and alliterative verse *šúmma šámma šášu | ikáššadá qatáka*.[76] So in my translation, I echo the alliteration, however faintly, by letting Gilgamesh's hand not just reach but "pluck this plant." While I cannot always match verbal games in the Akkadian with an English counterpart in the same line, I have done my best to re-create the sinuous and sonorous pleasure of the poem.

Like all translations, this approach has its pros and cons. Consider the following literal translation of the epic's opening passage:

Who saw the depth (or: the totality), the foundations of the land,
who knew the ways, understanding everything:
Gilgamesh, who saw the depth (or: the totality), the foundations of the land,
who knew the ways, understanding everything.
He examined each of the (or: the matching) throne-daises,
and grasped the sum of knowledge about everything.
He saw the secret and opened the covered,
he brought back a report from before the Flood,
he came a distant road and so was exhausted, but (or: and) given peace,
all (his) hardships being set on a stele.
He built the wall of Uruk, the sheepfold,
of holy Eana, the pure storehouse.
See its wall, which is like a thread of tufted wool (or: like the shining of copper?),
look at its parapet, which no one will equal.
Take the threshold (or: stairway), which is of former times,
and draw near to Eana, Ishtar's dwelling,
which no future king whatsoever will equal.[77]
Go up on top of the wall of Uruk and walk around,
examine the foundation base, inspect the brickwork,
(check) if its brickwork is not oven-baked bricks,

and if the seven sages did not lay its foundation.

One *šār* is city, one *šār* is orchard, one *šār* is clay-pits, half a *šār* is Ishtar's temple:

Three and a half *šār* is Uruk, (its) measurements.

Even a faithful translation like this obscures more problems than it reveals. What looks like one text is in fact a composite of six different manuscripts (named B, F, d, o, h, and g), which have been woven together in George's edition.[78] They differ from each other in relatively minor ways: manuscripts from the first millennium BCE are notoriously flippant about case endings, so in line 6, the word "everything" is variously rendered *kalāmu, kalāmi,* and *kalāma,* but the sense is the same. In line 9, one manuscript has "he comes" in the present tense while the other has a past tense, "he came" (*illakam* and *illikam,* respectively); the latter is more appropriate in the context.[79] In George's edition, the first five lines were highly fragmentary; they were restored later thanks to the discovery of a Middle Babylonian manuscript from Ugarit, which, however, deviates from the Standard Babylonian text in all sorts of other ways.[80]

Having established what the text says, we come to the question of what it means. The prologue is far from the most problematic passage in the epic, but it does have its difficulties—starting with the second word of the epic, *naqbu,* which can mean either "depth" or "totality."[81] Most translators opt for the former, which is more evocative, but that leads to the question of what depth is meant: might it be the Apsû, the underground lake that Gilgamesh visits in Tablet XI, or perhaps a more metaphorical profundity? In line 13, we come to a particularly tricky phrase, which has bedeviled philologists since 1933: *kīma qê nipš[u],* or, perhaps, *kīma qê nibṭ[i].*[82] The two current proposals are to read "like a thread of tufted wool" or "like the shining of copper." The word choice of the former is strange, the grammar of the latter is unusual, and the meaning of both is obscure. How is a wall like a thread, and how is it like copper? In my translation, I assume that it was "white as wool," but other options are equally possible. Such problems are found throughout the text.

Then we have the question of how to render words whose meaning may be obvious to philologists but not to anyone else. This is the case with Eana in the passage above. Eana is Ishtar's temple in Uruk, but since it is metaphorically called a pure storehouse, the modern reader could easily be confused: does Ishtar live in a clean storage room? In my translation, I follow the original Sumerian meaning of Eana, which is literally "house of heaven," turning it into "Temple of Heaven" and so allaying doubt.

By that same principle—making the text as clear and easily accessible as I can—I have clarified phrases whose meaning would be knotty in a literal translation. In the phrase "all (his) hardships being set on a stele," the Akkadian text does not include the word "his," but it is clearly implied, so it is common practice to restore it. Such implied words are often given in parentheses, but I feel that this would clutter the text, so in my translation the phrase becomes "he set down all his trials on a slab of stone."[83] I likewise transform the phrase "he examined each of the throne-daises" into "he sought out rulers everywhere," because the "throne-dais" is here used as a metonym for the ruler who sat on it—referring, I believe, to Gilgamesh's visits to the two rulers at either end of the earth, Humbaba and Uta-napishti.[84]

Finally, we come to the end of the passage, the list of Uruk's measurements. This couplet is extremely compressed in Akkadian: it is literally just "šār city, šār orchard, šār clay-pit," and so on. In English, something must be done to keep the list from killing the epic mood before the story has even started. Here I break the couplet into five separate lines, to emphasize the rhythmic, rigid structure of the list. Further, in order to bring out the shift in focus that invites the audience to consider not just Gilgamesh's achievement, but the glory of Uruk as a whole, I have inserted the word "Look" at the beginning of the list. It is not there in Akkadian, but I feel that it reflects the thrust of the text, which does ask its audience to summon Uruk in their mind's eye. Some readers may feel uncomfortable with such liberties, but luckily, more faithful translations of *Gilgamesh* are readily available. What follows is merely my take on this ancient masterpiece.

GILGAMESH

TABLET I

Who saw the deep

There was a man
who saw the deep, the bedrock of the land,   1
who knew the ways and learned all things:
Gilgamesh saw the deep, the bedrock of the land,
he knew the ways and learned all things.

He sought out rulers everywhere   5
and came to grasp all wisdom in the world.
He discovered a secret, revealed a hidden matter,
and brought home a story from before the Flood.
He came back from far roads, exhausted but at peace,
as he set down all his trials on a slab of stone.   10

He built the wall around Uruk the Sheepfold
and around that holy treasury, the Temple of Heaven.
See that wall—white as wool!
Behold the bulwark that cannot be rivaled.

Step across the ancient threshold and up   15
to the Temple of Heaven, home of Ishtar,
that no king will ever outdo.

Climb the wall of Uruk, walk its length.
Survey the foundation, study the brickwork.
There—is it not made of oven-baked bricks?   20
Did the Seven Sages not lay its cornerstone?

Look: Two thousand acres for the city,
two thousand acres for the orchards,
two thousand acres for the pits of clay,
and one thousand acres for the temple of Ishtar.
Seven thousand acres is the size of Uruk.

Now look for the cedarwood box,
undo its locks of bronze,   25
open the door to its secrets,
take up the tablet of lapis lazuli and read aloud:

read of all that Gilgamesh went through,
read of all his suffering.

He surpassed all kings, that splendid man of muscle,
heroic son of Uruk, the goring aurochs.[1]   30
When he marched at the front, he was the leader of his army,
when he marched at the back, the trust of his troops.

A mighty riverbank, the shield of his soldiers,
and a furious flood that crushes walls of stone.
The calf of Lugalbanda, superb in strength,   35
nursed by Ninsun, the holy aurochs!

Gilgamesh the great, magnificent and terrible!
He cut passes through the mountains,
he dug wells in the hillsides,
he traveled toward sunrise, crossing sea after sea,   40
he searched in all directions for life without end,
he reached, through his toils, the faraway Uta-napishti,
he rebuilt the temples that the Flood had destroyed
and established the right rituals for vast humankind.

Who can compete with him in kingship   45
and claim, like Gilgamesh, "I am the king"?
From the day that Gilgamesh was born and named,

he was two-thirds god and only one-third human.

The mother goddess Belet-ili designed his body,
the wise god Ea brought his figure to perfection   50
so that he brimmed with strength and shining beauty.

He was a giant in height, eighteen feet tall,
and his chest was six feet broad.   55
His feet were five feet long, and twice that his leg,
and the length of his stride was the same.
His beard, too, was five feet long.   58

UGARITIC VERSION

His locks curled thick like ears of corn, Ug_1 31
his teeth glistened like the rising sun,
his hair glowed dark like lapis lazuli.   33

STANDARD BABYLONIAN VERSION

He grew up to be superb in charm,   61
as stunning as any mortal can be.
But he was stomping through Uruk the Sheepfold
with head held high, overbearing like an aurochs.

He was unmatched when the weapons were unsheathed,   65
and the swing of his bat kept his team on their toes.[2]
He darkened the youth of Uruk with despair,
Gilgamesh let no son go home to his father.

Day and night, he stormed around in fury,
King Gilgamesh, leader of the many.   70
This is how he tended to the Sheepfold of Uruk!
Gilgamesh let no daughter go home to her mother.

Month after month, the women prayed to their goddesses,
again and again, they gave voice to their sorrows:
that powerful, splendid, clever king!   75

Gilgamesh let no bride go home to her groom.

The warriors' daughters and the young men's wives:
the goddesses listened to their sorrows.

The gods of heaven, lords of words,
said to Anu, the god of the skies: 80
"Why did you unleash this savage aurochs in Uruk?

"He is unmatched when the weapons are unsheathed,
and the swing of his bat keeps his team on their toes.
He has darkened the youth of Uruk with despair,
Gilgamesh lets no son go home to his father.   85

"Day and night, he storms around in fury,
this is how he tends to the Sheepfold of Uruk!
King Gilgamesh, leader of the many,
meant to be their shepherd and protector.

"This powerful, splendid, clever king!   90
Gilgamesh lets no bride go home to her groom."
The warriors' daughters and the young men's wives:
Anu listened to their sorrows.

They summoned the mighty Aruru:
"You, Aruru, created this man,   95
now create his counterpart!
Let him be a match for the storm of his heart,
let them rival each other and leave Uruk at peace."

When Aruru heard this,
Anu's idea found form in her heart.   100
Aruru washed her hands,
she took a lump of clay and threw it down into the wild.

In the wild she created the hero Enkidu,
a son of silence, woven for war.

All his body was covered with fur,   105
his hair was as long as a woman's,
and his locks curled thick like ears of corn.
He knew no people and no country.

Naked like an animal,
with the gazelles he grazed on grass,   110
with the herd he rushed to drink,
with the beasts he quenched his thirst.

One day by the waterhole,
he locked eyes with a hunter, a woodsman.
One day, and a second, and a third,   115
Enkidu and the hunter locked eyes by the waterhole.
The hunter looked at him and froze with fear,
then he headed home with his catch.

The hunter was troubled, speechless, and still,
his heart was heavy, and his face full of gloom.
There was sorrow in his mind,   120
and he looked like one who had traveled far.

The hunter worked his words, saying to his father:
"Father, there was a man by the waterhole,
a man all muscle, the mightiest in the land,
as mighty as a meteorite fallen from the sky.[3]   125

"I see him roaming through the mountains,
always grazing with the herd,
always standing by the waterhole.
I am afraid to go near him!

"Each pit I dig he fills,   130
each trap I set he breaks.
He helps his herd escape my grasp,
he will not let me do the work of the wild."

His father worked his words, saying to the hunter:
"My son, ·   · to Gilgamesh, king of Uruk.   135
·   · before him,
for he is mighty as a meteorite fallen from the sky.

"Take the road and head toward Uruk,
·   · a man's muscles.
Go, my son, and bring back a priestess of Ishtar,   140
·   · as strength.

"When the herd comes to the waterhole,
make her strip and show her charms.
He will see her and run to her,
then he will abandon the herd of his youth."   145

The hunter listened to the advice of his father,
and went to ·   ·
He took the road and headed toward Uruk.

He said to King Gilgamesh:
"There is a man by the waterhole,   150
a man all muscle, the mightiest in the land,
as mighty as a meteorite fallen from the sky.

"I see him roaming through the mountains,
always grazing with the herd,
always rushing to the waterhole.   155
I am afraid to go near him!

"Each pit I dig he fills,
each trap I set he breaks.

He helps his herd escape my grasp,
he will not let me do the work of the wild."   160

Gilgamesh said to him, to the hunter:
"Go, my hunter, and bring with you Shamhat, a priestess of Ishtar.
When the herd comes to the waterhole,
make her strip and show her charms.
He will see her and run to her,   165
then he will abandon the herd of his youth."

The hunter went and brought with him Shamhat, a priestess of Ishtar.
They took the road and set out on the journey;
after three days they reached their destination.
The hunter and the priestess sat down to wait.   170

One day and a second they sat by the waterhole,
then the herd arrived at the waterhole.
The beasts came and quenched their thirst,
and so did Enkidu, child of the mountains.

With the gazelles he grazed on grass,   175
with the herd he rushed to drink,
with the beasts he quenched his thirst.

Shamhat saw him, the man of the wild,
this brute born in the wasteland's womb.

"There he is, Shamhat! Bare your breasts   180
and spread your legs, work your charm!
Be brave and smell his scent,
he will see you and run to you,
throw off your clothes and bring him down.

"Show this wild man what women can do,   185
and his lust will wrap him around your body.
Then he will abandon the herd of his youth."

Shamhat untied her skirt,
spread her legs and worked her charm.
She was brave and smelled his scent,   190
threw off her clothes and brought him down.

She showed the wild man what women can do
and his lust wrapped him around her body.
For six days and seven nights Enkidu was aroused
and made love to Shamhat.

When he had had his fill of her delights,   195
he turned back to the herd.
But the gazelles saw him and ran,
the herd of the wild fled from him.

Enkidu had sullied his spotless body.
The herd was running, his knees were stuck;   200
Enkidu was weakened and could not keep up,
but now he could reason and think.

He came back to sit at the priestess's feet,
he looked at the priestess's face
and heard what she had to say.   205

The priestess said to him, to Enkidu:
"You are beautiful, Enkidu! You look like a god.
Why do you roam the wild with the beasts?

"Come, I will take you to Uruk the Sheepfold,
to the holy temple where Anu and Ishtar live   210
and where Gilgamesh is superb in strength,
overbearing like an aurochs among the young men."

The words she spoke agreed with him;
his wise heart told him to find a friend.
Enkidu said to her, to the priestess: 215

"Come, Shamhat, take me with you,
to the holy sacred temple where Anu and Ishtar live
and where Gilgamesh is superb in strength,
overbearing like an aurochs among the young men.

"I will be the one to challenge him, subdue him by force,   220
I will stand in Uruk and cry out: 'I am the greatest!'
·   · I will change ·   · the fight
Those born in the wild are mighty, full of muscle."

"No ·   · let him see your face,
I know ·   · that exist.   225

"Come, Enkidu, to Uruk the Sheepfold,
where the men are dazzlingly dressed,
where every day is a party,
where the drums thunder on
and the priestesses are ravishing,   230
their faces full of charm and hearts full of joy,
so that even old men are lured into the night.

"Enkidu, you know nothing of life!
Let me show you Gilgamesh, this man about town.
Look at him, see that face: 235
the dignity he has, the beauty of youth!

"His whole body is full of charm,
his strength is greater than yours.
He never sleeps, day or night—
oh Enkidu, forget your wicked plan!   240

"Gilgamesh is the darling of the Sun God,
and Anu, Enlil, and Ea have made him wise.
Long before you came down from the mountains,
Gilgamesh was dreaming of you.

"One day, Gilgamesh got up to interpret his dream   245
and said to his mother:

"'Mother, in my dream tonight
the stars of the skies blazed up
and one of them fell to the ground like a meteorite.
I tried to pick it up, but it was too heavy,
I tried to push it over, but it would not budge.   250

"'All of Uruk was there.
The whole country flocked to it,
they thronged around in crowds.
The young men rushed
to kiss its feet, like a baby's.   255

"'I wrapped my arms around it
and loved it like a wife,
then I picked it up and set it at your feet.
And you declared it my equal!'

"Gilgamesh's mother was clever and wise,
she knew everything. She spoke to her son.
The goddess Ninsun, the aurochs, was clever and wise,   260
she knew everything. She spoke to Gilgamesh:

"'The stars of the skies blazed up
and one of them fell to the ground like a meteorite.
You tried to pick it up, but it was too heavy,
you tried to push it over, but it would not budge.

"'You picked it up and set it at my feet,   265
and I declared it your equal.
You wrapped your arms around it
and loved it like a wife.

"'A strong ally is coming, a friend in times of need,
a man all muscle, the mightiest in the land,

as mighty as a meteorite fallen from the sky.   270

"'You will wrap your arms around him
and love him like a wife,
and mighty as he is, he will save your life.'

"He had another dream. He got up
and went to his mother, the goddess.
Gilgamesh said to her, to his mother: 275

"'Mother, I've had another dream!
In the streets of Uruk the Marketplace
there was an ax, and people gathered round.

"'All of Uruk was there.
The whole country flocked to it,   280
they thronged around in crowds,
and the young men rushed to it.

"'I picked it up and set it at your feet,
I wrapped my arms around it
and loved it like a wife.
And you declared it my equal!'   285

"Gilgamesh's mother was clever and wise,
she knew everything. She spoke to her son.
The goddess Ninsun, the aurochs, was clever and wise,
she knew everything. She spoke to Gilgamesh:

"'My son, the ax you saw is a man.
You will wrap your arms around him
and love him like a wife,
and I will declare him your equal.   290

"'A strong ally is coming, a friend in times of need,
a man all muscle, the mightiest in the land,
as mighty as a meteorite fallen from the sky.'

"Gilgamesh said to her, to his mother:
"'Oh mother, let it be so! By the will of Enlil!   295
I will have a friend and adviser,
a friend and adviser all mine.'

"That is what he saw in his dreams."
When Shamhat had told Enkidu about Gilgamesh's dreams,
the two of them began to make love again.   300

TABLET II

Enkidu was sitting

OLD BABYLONIAN VERSION

Enkidu was sitting at the priestess's feet,   P 45
and the two began to make love again.
Enkidu forgot the wild of his youth:
for six days and seven nights he was aroused
and made love to Shamhat.   50

The priestess said to him, to Enkidu:
"When I see you, Enkidu, you look like a god.
Why do you roam the wild with the beasts?   55

"Come, I will take you to Uruk the Marketplace,
to the holy temple where Anu and Ishtar live   60
and where all men can ply their trade: you, too,
human as you are, will find a place for yourself.
Leave the wild that the herdsmen fear!"   65

The words he heard agreed with him,
the woman's wisdom landed in his heart.   67

STANDARD BABYLONIAN VERSION

Shamhat tore her clothes in two,   34
put one half on herself and dressed him in the other.   35
She took his hand and led him, like a god,[4]
to the herdsmen's huts and the pens of their sheep.

The herdsmen's camp gathered round him
·   · and said to themselves:

"That man—he looks just like Gilgamesh!   40
His figure looms large, proud as a rampart.
This must be the child of the mountains
who is as mighty as a meteorite fallen from the sky."

They served him bread,
they served him beer.   45
Enkidu ate no bread, but stared and gaped.
No one had taught him how to eat bread,
he did not know how to drink beer.   48

OLD BABYLONIAN VERSION

The priestess said to him, to Enkidu: 95
"Enkidu! Eat the bread, life's essence,
drink the beer, the people's pleasure."

Enkidu ate the bread until he was full,   100
and drank the beer—seven jugs of it.
His mind unwound and he broke into song,
his heart was happy and his face resplendent.   105

The barber shaved the fur on his body.
He smeared himself with oil and turned into a man;
he put on clothes and looked like a bridegroom.   110
Then he picked up his weapons to fight off lions.

While the herdsmen lay down for the night,
he butchered wolves and battled lions.   115
When the old shepherds slept,
he was their guardian and watchman.

There was a man who had been invited to a wedding.   120

 .   .
 .   .
 .   .
 .   .

.   .

.   .

.   .

Enkidu was enjoying himself with Shamhat,   135
when he looked up and saw the man,
and said to the priestess:
"Shamhat, bring that man over,   140
I want to hear his reason for coming here."

The priestess called to the man,
he came over and Enkidu asked him:
"Young man, why do you hurry?   145
Where does your tiring journey take you?"

The man worked his words, saying to Enkidu:
"I've been invited to a wedding:
all men are fated for marriage.   150
I am to load the family altar
with heaps of delightful food for the feast.

"But the curtains of the wedding bed will open   155
for one last suitor: the king of Uruk.
The curtains of the wedding bed will open
for one last suitor: Gilgamesh, king of Uruk.

"He will make love to the wife-to-be,
first him, the groom later.   160
In their wisdom the gods decreed it so:
the bride is his birthright."

When Enkidu heard this, his face went white.   165

.   .

.   .

.   .

.   .

.   .
.   .
.   .

Enkidu went off, with Shamhat behind him.   175

He stepped into Uruk the Marketplace,
and a crowd gathered round him.
He stood in the street of Uruk the Marketplace,   180
the people gathered round him and talked:

"He looks just like Gilgamesh,
but shorter and stouter.   185
This must be the child of the mountains
who was brought up by the beasts."

Uruk never forgets a festival.   190
The young men made merry and chose their champion:
for Gilgamesh, the youth with chiseled features,
a partner was chosen, as if he were a god.   195

A bed was made for Ishara, the goddess of love:
that night Gilgamesh would lie with the bride.
But then *he* stepped forth and stood in the street,   200
blocking Gilgamesh's path to the wedding house.

.   · discussed him.
.   .
.   .
.   .
.   .

Gilgamesh ·   .
In front of him ·   .   210
Angry ·   .

Enkidu went up and stood before him,
the two men locked eyes in the street of the land.

Enkidu blocked the door with his foot   215
and would not let Gilgamesh into the wedding house.

They took hold of each other, butting like bulls:
the door broke, the walls shook.   220
Gilgamesh and Enkidu took hold, butting like bulls:
the door broke, the walls shook.   225

Gilgamesh put his knee to the ground,
he ended the fight, his anger dispelled.[5]   230
When Gilgamesh ended the fight,
Enkidu said to him, to Gilgamesh:

"Your mother Ninsun, aurochs of Uruk,
has given birth to a man without equal.   235
You are superb among warriors!
Enlil has made you the ruler of men.   240

.   .
.   .
.   .
.   .
.   .
.   .

.   · throbbing.   Y 10
What drives you to do this?
Anything ·   · want it so much?   15
Let me ·   ·
a feat that no one has ever attempted."

They kissed and became friends.
Discussing ·   · sat down.   20
.   ·

"I have a friend and adviser,   Schø₁ 1'
just as I saw in my dreams!"

— 19 —

Enkidu said to her, to the priestess:
"Come, Shamhat, let me give you a gift
for leading me to Uruk the Marketplace,
and showing me this great man—my friend!

".   · Uruk the Marketplace,
·   · entered.   Schø₁ 8'
·
·
·
·
·
·
·
·
·
·
·
·
·
·
·
·
·
·   ·
·   ·
·   ·
·   ·
·   ·
·   ·
·   ·
·   ·
·   ·
·   ·
·   ·
·   ·
·   ·
·   ·
·   ·
·   ·

"He is a man all muscle, the mightiest in the land,   162
as mighty as a meteorite fallen from the sky.
His figure looms large, proud as a rampart."

Gilgamesh's mother worked her words, saying to her son,   165
the aurochs Ninsun worked her words, saying to her son:

"My son, ·   ·
Bitterly ·   ·

.   .
.   .

You hold ·   .
In his gate ·   .
Bitterly he will weep ·   .
Enkidu has no ·   .   175
.   · shaggy hair ·   .
He was born in the wild, he has no family."

Enkidu stood there listening to her words,
he thought about it and sat down to cry.
Tears filled his eyes,   180
his arms lost strength,
his power disappeared.

They took hold of each other, together ·   .
their hands ·   · like ·   .
Gilgamesh ·   .
and spoke to Enkidu, saying: 185

"Why, my friend, did tears fill your eyes,
your arms lose strength,
your power disappear?"

Enkidu said to him, to Gilgamesh:
"My friend, my heart burns ·   .
.   · shakes with sobs.   190
Fear has stepped into my heart,
grief has tied knots in my neck."⁶

Gilgamesh worked his words, saying to Enkidu:
"My friend, if only ·   .
.   · imminent ·   .   195
But we ·   · brawl
.   · the days ·   .
.   · at your side

Now, my friend ·   ·
·   · in the land ·   ·   200
·   · Humbaba ·   ·   201
·   ·
·   ·
·   ·
·   ·
·   ·
·   ·

OLD BABYLONIAN VERSION

".   · the savage Humbaba,   Y 97
let us kill him, crush his mind!
Let us destroy Humbaba in his home,   100
in the Cedar Forest where he lives."

Enkidu worked his words, saying to Gilgamesh: 105
"I knew him, my friend, in the mountains,
when I roamed there with the herd.
The forest is empty for a thousand miles around him
—who would dare to go near him?

"Humbaba: his howl is a flood,   110
his voice is fire, his breath is death.
What drives you to do this?
In the home of Humbaba, all hope is lost."   115

Gilgamesh worked his words, saying to Enkidu:
"My friend, I will climb the slopes of the forest
·   ·
·   ·
·   ·

The home of the Anunnaki gods.[7]
An ax ·   ·
May you ·   ·   125
May I ·   ."   126

STANDARD BABYLONIAN VERSION

Enkidu worked his words, saying to Gilgamesh: 216
"My friend, how could we travel to the Cedar Forest?
To keep the cedars safe from harm,
Enlil has made him the terror of men.

"This journey cannot be made,
this creature cannot be seen.
The guardian of the cedars is ·   ·   220
Humbaba: his howl is a flood,
his voice is fire, his breath is death.

"He hears every whisper for a thousand miles around him.
Who would dare to go near him?
Humbaba is the greatest, second only to the Storm God. 225
Would even the gods defy him?

"To keep the cedars safe from harm,
Enlil has made him the terror of men.
Despair strikes all who step into his forest."   229

OLD BABYLONIAN VERSION

Gilgamesh worked his words, saying to Enkidu: Y 138
"My friend, who has ever climbed to the skies?   140
Only gods live in endless sunlight.

"But the days of men are numbered,
all that we do is nothing but wind.
And there you are—afraid of death!
What then is the use of your valiant might?   145

"I will go first. You can stand behind me
and shout: 'Be brave and march on!'
If I die, I will only have made a name for myself:
'Gilgamesh battled the brutal Humbaba!'   150

— 23 —

"You were born and grew up in the wild,
you've fought with lions—you've seen it all!
Young men flee from you,
   ·   · evening.   155

"But now, you speak like a coward.
Your words have gone soft, and you trouble my heart.
I want to get started! I want to cut down the cedar
and make for myself an everlasting name.   160

"Come, my friend, let us go to the forge,
let them make mighty axes for us."
They took each other's hands and went to the forge
where the blacksmiths sat, deep in discussion.

They forged great axes: 165
axes of one hundred and twenty pounds each.[8]
They forged great swords:
their blades alone weighed one hundred and twenty pounds,
thirty pounds weighed their cross-guards,
and their hilts were thirty pounds of gold.   170
Gilgamesh and Enkidu were armed with six hundred pounds of metal.

He closed the seven gates of Uruk,
he summoned the assembly, and a crowd gathered round him.

·   · in the street of Uruk the Marketplace,
Gilgamesh sat down on his throne   175
and the crowd sat down before him,
in the street of Uruk the Marketplace.   176

STANDARD BABYLONIAN VERSION

"Men of Uruk! Hear me.   260
Men of Uruk, who know how to fight!

"My mind is made up. I will walk
the far road to the home of Humbaba.

I will face an unknown battle,
I will tread an unknown path.

"Give me your blessing! Then I will go.   265
Unharmed may I see your faces again,
triumphant may I step through Uruk's gate.

"When I return, I will hold New Year twice,
from now I will always hold New Year twice.
Let us celebrate the festival, let us sing in joy,   270
let the drums thunder for Ninsun!"

Enkidu gave counsel to the elders,
to the men of Uruk, who know how to fight:
"Tell him not to go to the Cedar Forest!
This journey cannot be made,   275
this creature cannot be seen.

"The guardian of the cedars is ·   ·
Humbaba: his howl is a flood,
his voice is fire, his breath is death.

"He hears every whisper for a thousand miles around him.   280
Who would dare to go near him?
Humbaba is the greatest, second only to the Storm God.
Would even the gods defy him?

"To keep the cedars safe from harm,
Enlil has made him the terror of men.   285
Despair strikes all who step into his forest."

The old councilors rose to their feet
and spoke their mind to Gilgamesh:
"You are young, Gilgamesh. Your heart carries you away,
you do not understand the things that you say.   290

"Humbaba: his howl is a flood,
his voice is fire, his breath is death.
He hears every whisper for a thousand miles around him,
and despair strikes all who step into his forest.

"Who would dare to go near him?   295
Would even the gods defy him?
Humbaba is the greatest, second only to the Storm God.
To keep the cedars safe from harm,
Enlil has made him the terror of men."   299

ASSYRIAN VERSION
When Gilgamesh heard this,   Y 16'
he looked at Enkidu and laughed:
"Look, my friend, how scared I am,
I am so scared I will not go! Bah!

"I will walk the far road to the home of Humbaba,
·   · Humbaba like a lion.
I will make a raft of cedar, cypress, and juniper,   20'
and there I will gather ·   ·
I will cut Humbaba's head off and sail it down the river."

The old councilors rose to their feet,
and said to Gilgamesh: 23'

OLD BABYLONIAN VERSION
"May he ·   · you!   Y 211
May your god ease your path.
May he ·   · your journey.
Come back unharmed to Uruk's dock."   215

Come back unharmed

"Come back unharmed to Uruk's dock.
Gilgamesh, do not rely on your strong arms alone:
let your eyes take aim and your sword strike home!

"They say: 'Go first and you help an ally,
know the road and you save a friend.'   5
So let Enkidu go first.

"He knows the way to the Cedar Forest,
he is skilled in battle and versed in war.
Enkidu shall save his friend, shield his ally,
and bring him back to the fields of his city.   10

"Enkidu! The assembly entrusts the king to your care.
You will bring him home and entrust him back to us."

Gilgamesh worked his words, saying to Enkidu:
"Come, my friend, let us go to the Great Palace,   15
and stand before Ninsun, the mighty queen.
Ninsun is clever and wise, she knows everything.
She will lay a path of good ideas at our feet."

They took each other's hand,
Gilgamesh and Enkidu went to the Great Palace   20
and stood before Ninsun, the mighty queen.
Gilgamesh got up and stepped before Ninsun.

Gilgamesh said to her, to Ninsun:
"My mind is made up, Ninsun. I will walk

the far road to the home of Humbaba.   25
I will face an unknown battle,
I will tread an unknown path.

"Please, will you bless me? Then I will go.
Unharmed may I see your face again,
triumphant may I step through Uruk's gate.   30

"I will return and hold New Year twice,
from now I will always hold New Year twice.
Let us celebrate the festival, let us sing in joy,
let the drums thunder for you!"

The holy aurochs Ninsun listened in pain   35
to the words of Gilgamesh and Enkidu.

She went seven times into the chamber of cleansing
and took baths infused with tamarisk and soapwort.
She put on a dress worthy of her body,
and chose a jewel worthy of her breasts.   40

·   · was in place, the crown was on her head.
Priestesses ·   · the ground ·   ·

She climbed the staircase and went up to the roof.
She went up to the roof and lit a censer for the Sun God.
She lit incense for the Sun God and lifted her arms: 45
"Why, Shamash, did you burden my son with so restless a heart?

"Now you have touched him, and so he will walk
the far road to the home of Humbaba.
He will face an unknown battle,
he will tread an unknown path.   50

"For every day of his journey there and back again,
every day until he reaches the Cedar Forest,
every day until he kills the brutal Humbaba,

and destroys the evil creature you hate,
while you travel round the edges of the world,   55
may Aya, your bride, not fear to remind you:
'Bring him unharmed into the care of the night.'

"At night ·   ·
·   ·
·   ·
·   ·
·   · light.

"Shamash, you opened ·   · the herd comes out,
·   · you ride out to the land.
The mountain ·   · the skies ·   ·   65
The beasts of the wild ·   · your crimson sheen.
·   · wait ·   · them.
The animals ·   · you.
·   · offerings to you.
The dead ·   · life.   70
For ·   · your head.

"Crowds flock to see your sunbeams flare,
even the Anunnaki gods long for your rays.
May Aya, your bride, not fear to remind you:
'Bring him unharmed into the care of the night.'   75

"Lay a path of safety at his feet,
touch Enkidu so that he goes first,
for he knows the road to the Cedar Forest.
Open the road and ready the mountains,
and in his hand ·   · of the road.   80

"While Gilgamesh travels to the Cedar Forest,
lengthen the days and shorten the nights.
Make sure that his weapons are ready, his gear girt,
and that he pitches a camp to sleep in for the night.
To sleep ·   · lie down.   85

"May Aya, your bride, not fear to remind you:
'When Gilgamesh and Enkidu face off with Humbaba,
unleash, Shamash, your mighty storms against him.'

"South wind, north wind, east wind, west wind, gust, and gale,
tempest, blizzard, wind of evil, demon blast,   90
thunderstorm, whirlwind, and hurricane: let thirteen winds
    rise!
Darkness will fall on the face of Humbaba
and Gilgamesh's weapons will bring him down.

"When your light flares up, turn,
Shamash, to the man who reveres you.   95
Then let your fast mules take you to ·   ·

"A bed shall be laid out for you, a place of rest,
while the gods, your brothers, serve you delightful food
and Aya wipes your brow with the fringe of her dress."

The holy aurochs Ninsun repeated her instruction: 100
"Shamash! Will Gilgamesh not join the gods one day?
Will he not stand in the skies with you?
Will he not share the scepter of the Moon God?
Will he not grow wise with Ea in the Apsû?
Will he not rule with Irnina in the underworld?   105
Will he not live with Ningishzida in the Land of No Return?

"Shamash, let me ·   ·
He must not ·   · must not ·   · the Cedar Forest.
He must not reach ·   ·
        ·   · your great godhead.   110
        ·   ·
        ·   ·
        ·   · ·
        ·   · like the people,
        ·   · like ·   ·
You are leading him into the ·   · of Humbaba."   115

When the holy aurochs Ninsun had stated her wish,
Ninsun, clever and wise, who knows everything,
·   · Gilgamesh ·   ·
She put out the censer and came down from the roof.

She summoned Enkidu to announce her intent: 120
"Strong Enkidu, you were not born from my womb.
But now your family will be Gilgamesh's temple:
the temple girls, the votaries, and the holy women."

She placed the amulet around Enkidu's neck:
"The temple girls have found a foundling,   125
the holy daughters will foster the foster child.
I hereby take Enkidu as my beloved son,
let Gilgamesh treat him with brotherly love.

·   ·

"And ·   ·   130
While you travel with Gilgamesh to the Cedar Forest,
let the days be long and the nights be short.
Make sure that your weapons are ready, your gear girt,
and that you pitch a camp to sleep in for the night.
·   · protect."   135
·   ·
·   ·
·   ·
·   ·
·   ·
·   ·
·   ·
·   ·
·   ·
·   ·

Gilgamesh ·   ·
·   ·

The gate of cedar ·   ·
Enkidu in the temple of ·   ·   150
and Gilgamesh in the temple of · ·
Juniper, incense ·   ·
Sons of ·   ·
·   ·
·   ·
·   ·
·   ·
·   ·
·   ·
·   ·
·   ·
·   ·
·   ·
·   ·

By the will of Shamash, you will have your wish.
In the gate of Marduk ·   ·
On the water's breast ·   ·
·   ·

In the gate of cedar ·   ·   170
Gilgamesh ·   ·
And Enkidu ·   ·

After one hundred miles ·   ·
·   ·
·   ·
·   ·
·   ·
·   ·
·   ·
·   ·
·   ·
·   ·
·   ·

·   ·
·   ·
·   ·
·   ·
·   ·
·   ·
·   ·
·   ·
·   ·
·   ·
·   ·
·   ·
·   ·
·   ·
·   ·
·   ·
·   ·
·   ·

"For every day of our journey there and back again,
every day until we reach the Cedar Forest,
every day until we kill the brutal Humbaba,
and destroy the evil creature Shamash hates,   205
·   ·

"You will have no ·   ·
·   · must not assemble the young men in the street.
Instead, set straight the lawsuits of the poor, find ·   ·
until we get our wish, like little children,   210
until we plant our weapons in Humbaba's gate."

His governors stood there and blessed him,
while a crowd of Uruk's men ran behind him
and the lords of the land fawned at his feet.

"Come back unharmed to Uruk's dock.   215
Gilgamesh, do not rely on your strong arms alone:

let your eyes take aim and your sword strike home!

"They say: 'Go first and you help an ally,
know the road and you save a friend.'
So let Enkidu go first.   220

"He knows the way to the Cedar Forest,
he is skilled in battle and versed in war,
·   · to the mountain passes.
Enkidu shall save his friend, shield his ally,
and bring him back to the fields of his city.   225

"Enkidu! The assembly entrusts the king to your care.
You will bring him home and entrust him back to us."

OLD BABYLONIAN VERSION

Enkidu worked his words and said to Gilgamesh: Y 272
"You have set your mind on this place, so go.
Allow no fear into your heart. Follow me,
for I know where Humbaba lives in the forest   275
and the paths that he takes.

"Speak to the crowd, send them back.
·   ·
·   · should not go with me.
·   · you."   280

The crowd ·   · glad at heart.
·   · heard what he said.
The young men ·   ·
"Go, Gilgamesh ·   ·
May your god go ·   ·   285
May Shamash lead you to triumph."

Gilgamesh and Enkidu ·   ·
·   ·

Between ·   ·

They stopped to eat

They stopped to eat after a hundred miles,
they pitched camp after two hundred miles more.
In a single day they had walked three hundred miles,
by the third day it was more than a month's march.
They were getting closer to Mount Lebanon.

They dug a well toward the setting sun,   5
and poured fresh water into their flasks.
Gilgamesh went up to the top of the mountain,
and offered sacred flour to its peak:
"Bring me a dream, mountain! Show me a good omen."

Enkidu built him a house for the Dream God,   10
with a windbreak against the storm.
He had Gilgamesh lie in a circle of sacred flour,
while Enkidu slept like a snare in the doorway.

Gilgamesh rested his chin on his knees
and was struck by sleep, which fills the minds of men.   15
But at midnight he ran out of sleep
so Gilgamesh got up to talk with his friend.

"My friend, did you call me? Why am I awake?
Did you touch me? Why am I anxious?
Did a god walk by? Why are my limbs numb?   20

"My friend, I've had a dream,
and the dream I had was all confused.

"At the foot of a mountain ·   ·
The mountain fell ·   ·
and we, like ·   ."   25

The child of the wilderness was the right man to ask.
Enkidu showed him the meaning of his dream:
"My friend, your dream is a good omen,
your dream is precious, ·   ·

"My friend, the mountain you saw is Humbaba.   30
We will capture Humbaba and kill him,
and leave him unburied in the wasteland.
When morning comes, the Sun God will send us a sign."

They stopped to eat after a hundred miles,
they pitched camp after two hundred miles more.   35
In a single day they had walked three hundred miles,
by the third day it was more than a month's march.
They were getting closer to Mount Lebanon.

They dug a well toward the setting sun,
and poured fresh water into their flasks.
Gilgamesh went up to the top of the mountain,   40
and offered sacred flour to its peak:
"Bring me a dream, mountain! Show me a good omen."

Enkidu built him a house for the Dream God,
with a windbreak against the storm.
He had Gilgamesh lie in a circle of sacred flour,   45
while Enkidu slept like a snare in the doorway.

Gilgamesh rested his chin on his knees
and was struck by sleep, which fills the minds of men.
But at midnight he ran out of sleep
so Gilgamesh got up to talk with his friend.   50

"My friend, did you call me? Why am I awake?
Did you touch me? Why am I anxious?
Did a god walk by? Why are my limbs numb?

"My friend, I've had another dream,
and the dream I had was all confused.   55

OLD BABYLONIAN VERSION

"I carried a mountain on my shoulders,   Schø$_2$ 5
but it crumbled and crushed me down.
Despair chained my legs, awe shook my arms.

"But there was a man. He came to me, lionlike,
and lit up the land with his beauty.   10
He took hold of my arm
and pulled me out of the rubble."

Enkidu spoke to Gilgamesh and interpreted his dream:
"My friend, the man we now travel to,
that monstrous creature, is he not the mountain?   15
Humbaba, to whom we now travel,
that monstrous creature, is he not the mountain?

"You will be the first to meet him in battle,
and do what men do: the work of warriors.
His rage will batter you,
fear will chain your legs.   20

"But the man you saw was Shamash.
He will take your hand when you need him."   22

STANDARD BABYLONIAN VERSION

They stopped to eat after a hundred miles,   79
they pitched camp after two hundred miles more.   80
In a single day they had walked three hundred miles,

— 37 —

by the third day it was more than a month's march.
They were getting closer to Mount Lebanon.

They dug a well toward the setting sun,
and poured fresh water into their flasks.
Gilgamesh went up to the top of the mountain,   85
and offered sacred flour to its peak:
"Bring me a dream, mountain! Show me a good omen."

Enkidu built him a house for the Dream God,
with a windbreak against the storm.
He had Gilgamesh lie in a circle of sacred flour,   90
while Enkidu slept like a snare in the doorway.

Gilgamesh rested his chin on his knees
and was struck by sleep, which fills the minds of men.
But at midnight he ran out of sleep
so Gilgamesh got up to talk with his friend.   95

"My friend, did you call me? Why am I awake?
Did you touch me? Why am I anxious?
Did a god walk by? Why are my limbs numb?

"My friend, I've had a third dream,
and the dream I had was all confused.   100

OLD BABYLONIAN VERSION
"The storm howled, the earth roared,   Schø₂ 34
daylight hid, darkness spread,   35
lightning flashed, fires blazed,
flames shone and death rained down.

"I was stunned by the howl of the storm,
the day went dark and I lost my way.
But then the blaze faded, the fires died down,   40
they slowly burned out and dimmed into embers.

— 38 —

The darkness turned bright, a god came out
·   · he led us here ·   ·"

Enkidu interpreted the dream,
saying to Gilgamesh:

".   · the storm howled,   45
·   · will batter you.
·   · your eyes will shine.
·   · the bright fire that blazes for you,
·   · flames, and turn his weapons into ashes.   50

"Your dreams are good. Luck is on our side,
and soon you will reach your reward."   53

STANDARD BABYLONIAN VERSION

They stopped to eat after a hundred miles,   120
they pitched camp after two hundred miles more.
In a single day they had walked three hundred miles,
by the third day it was more than a month's march.
They were getting closer to Mount Lebanon.

They dug a well toward the setting sun,   125
and poured fresh water into their flasks.
Gilgamesh went up to the top of the mountain,
and offered sacred flour to its peak:
"Bring me a dream, mountain! Show me a good omen."

Enkidu built him a house for the Dream God,   130
with a windbreak against the storm.
He had Gilgamesh lie in a circle of sacred flour,
while Enkidu slept like a snare in the doorway.

Gilgamesh rested his chin on his knees
and was struck by sleep, which fills the minds of men.   135
But at midnight he ran out of sleep
so Gilgamesh got up to talk with his friend.

"My friend, did you call me? Why am I awake?
Did you touch me? Why am I anxious?
Did a god walk by? Why are my limbs numb?   140

"My friend, I've had a fourth dream,
and the dream I had was all confused.   142

OLD BABYLONIAN VERSION

"I watched a Thunderbird soar to the skies,   Ni 11
gliding above us like a cloud.
·   · and its face was strange,
its voice was fire, its breath was death.

"There was a man. He looked strange,   15
·   · standing in my dream.
He bound its wings and took my arm,
·   · and threw it at my feet.
·   · on it."

·   ·

·   ·

"You watched a Thunderbird soar to the skies,
gliding above us like a cloud.   r. 1'
·   · and its face was strange,
its voice was fire, its breath was death.

"It glowed with frightful light, and you were scared,
but I ·   · its foot, and lifted you up.   r. 5'
The man you saw was the great Shamash."   r. 6'

STANDARD BABYLONIAN VERSION

They stopped to eat after a hundred miles,   163
they pitched camp after two hundred miles more.
In a single day they had walked three hundred miles.   165

They dug a well toward the setting sun,
and poured fresh water into their flasks.
Gilgamesh went up to the top of the mountain,
and offered sacred flour to its peak:
"Bring me a dream, mountain! Show me a good omen."   170

Enkidu built him a house for the Dream God,
with a windbreak against the storm.
He had Gilgamesh lie in a circle of sacred flour,
while Enkidu slept like a snare in the doorway.

Gilgamesh rested his chin on his knees   175
and was struck by sleep, which fills the minds of men.
But at midnight he ran out of sleep
so Gilgamesh got up to talk with his friend.

"My friend, did you call me? Why am I awake?
Did you touch me? Why am I anxious?   180
Did a god walk by? Why are my limbs numb?

"My friend, I've had a fifth dream,
and the dream I had was all confused.   183

OLD BABYLONIAN VERSION

"I had taken hold of an aurochs,   Har₁ 4
but it bellowed and split open the earth,   5
thrusting dust into the skies,
and I threw myself in front of it.

"But a figure took hold of me ·   · around my arm,
·   · pulled me out ·   ·
My cheek ·   ·
and gave me water from his flask."

"My friend, the man we now travel to,   10
that monstrous creature, is he not the aurochs?

But the figure you saw is shining Shamash,
he will take your hand when you need him.

"The one who gave you water from his flask
is the god who looks after you, Lugalbanda.   15
We will be the first to meet Humbaba in battle,
a feat no one has ever attempted."   17

.   .
.   .
.   .
.   .
.   .
.   .
.   .
.   .
.   .
.   .
.   .
.   .
.   .
.   .
.   .
.   .
.   .
.   .
.   .
.   .
.   .
.   .
.   .
.   .

There they stood

There they stood, staring at the forest.
They saw how tall the cedars were,
they saw a way into the woods.
Where Humbaba walked, there was a track,
the trail was clear and the path well worn.   5

They gazed on the Cedar Mountain,
home of gods, throne of goddesses.
Sumptuous cedars grew along the mountainside
and cast their pleasant, joyful shades.

The forest was snarled up in branches, tangled with thorns,   10
they blocked the path through the cedars and *ballukku* trees.
For six miles around the forest grew new shoots of cedar,
for four miles around it grew new shoots of cypress.

The trees were webbed with creepers a hundred feet tall,
and the resin that oozed from them fell like raindrops   15
to be swallowed by the ravines.

The song of a bird went through the forest,
calls came back and song became clamor.

A single cicada set off a chorus,
·   · sang, ·   · chirped,   20
pigeons sobbed, doves answered.

The stork clattered, filling the forest with joy,
the rooster crowed, filling the forest with resounding joy.

Monkey mothers sang, baby monkeys cried:
this was the concert of songs and drums   25
that always thundered for Humbaba.

Then a cedar cast its shadow
and terror fell on Gilgamesh.
His arms went stiff,
despair struck his legs.   30

Enkidu worked his words and said to Gilgamesh:
"Let us go into the forest.
It's time, let us sound the battle cry!"

Gilgamesh worked his words and said to Enkidu:
"My friend, why do we tremble like cowards?   35
Was it not us who crossed all those mountains?
·   · before us
·   · see the light."

"My friend, you know war.
You've been in battle and fear not death,   40
you've bathed in blood and fear not death.

"Now rage! Let your mind run wild like a prophet,
let your cry ring loud like the drum of a temple.
Let despair leave your legs and stiffness your arms!"

"My friend, take hold of me. We will go as one.   45
Let your heart speak war!
Forget death, chase life.

".   · the careful man.
'Go first and you help an ally, you save a friend!'
That is how you make a lasting name for yourself."   50

The two of them arrived at the distant ·   ·
They stopped their conversation and stood

·   · staring at the forest.

·   ·

The swords ·   · straight away,   55
and unsheathed ·   ·
Axes smeared in ·   ·
swords and hatchets ·   ·
One ·   ·
Crept ·   ·   60

Humbaba conversed with his heart, saying to himself:
"Didn't ·   · go by?
Didn't ·   · go by?
Why ·   · scared?
Why ·   ·   65

"In terror ·   ·
So how ·   ·
In my own bed ·   ·
That must be Enkidu ·   ·

"In peace ·   ·   70
If a word ·   ·
Enlil damn ·   ."

Enkidu worked his words, saying to Gilgamesh:
"My friend, Humbaba is ·   ·
One man stands alone, but two count for double: 75
though weak on their own, together they are strong.

"Icy peaks cannot be climbed alone, only teams reach the top.
Two triplets ·   ·
Just as a two-ply rope is not easily snapped,
and a pair of pups brings down the big dog.   80
So stand your ground ·   ."

— 45 —

"My friend, an arrowhead ·   ·
The road you walk ·   ·
As we have ·
    ·   · held up ·   ·   85
    ·   · two ·   ."

"My friend, ·   · the winds of Shamash,
with winds in his face and storms at his back.
Speak to Shamash, ask him to unleash the thirteen winds!"

Gilgamesh looked up to Shamash and wept,   90
shedding his tears in the light of the sun:
"Shamash, remember the day I put my trust in you!
Stand by me now ·   ·
Come to the aid of Gilgamesh, the sapling of Uruk."

Shamash heard the words he spoke,   95
and straight away a battle cry boomed from the skies:
"Be brave, stand firm! He must not get to his lair,
he must not get to his glade, ·   ·
before he is wrapped in his seven cloaks of dread.[9]
He has taken six off, he has only one left!"   100

They ·   ·
Like a goring aurochs, ready to ·   ·

He let out a single, terrifying scream.
The guardian of the forest screamed,
·   ·

Humbaba roared like the Storm God.   105

·   ·
·   ·
·   ·
·   ·
·   ·
·

.   .
.   .
.   .

Humbaba worked his words, saying to Gilgamesh: 115
"Fools will take advice from half-wits.
Gilgamesh, what is it you want here?

"And you, Enkidu! Fish that never knew its father,
turtle spawn that never drank its mother's milk!
I watched you when you were young, but I let you be.
.   · filled my belly.   120

"Why did you lead that evil Gilgamesh to me?
You stand there like a stranger, an enemy!
I will split his throat and gullet
and feed his flesh to bugs, eagles, hawks, and vultures."

Gilgamesh worked his words, saying to Enkidu: 125
"My friend! Humbaba is changing shape.
We were brave enough to reach his home,
but now my fearful heart can find no peace."

Enkidu worked his words, saying to Gilgamesh:
"My friend, why do you speak like a coward?   130
Your words have gone soft, and you trouble my heart.

"My friend, we have only one chance now!
What do smiths do to get copper from the mold?
It takes an hour to get the furnace hot—then you strike!

"To unleash a flood, you must crack the whip.   135
Do not pull back your foot, do not turn around!
.   · strike with all your strength.

.   .
.   .

.   .
.   .
.   .
.   .
.   .
.   .
.   .
.   .
.   .
.   .
.   .
.   .
.   .
.   · banished."

Shamash heard them from afar.
He struck the ground and ·   · against him   155
and the earth split open under their feet:
Mount Lebanon and Hermon broke apart in the battle.[10]
White clouds turned black
and death fell like fog.

Then Shamash unleashed his mighty storms: 160
south wind, north wind, east wind, west wind, gust, and gale,
tempest, blizzard, wind of evil, demon blast,
thunderstorm, whirlwind, and hurricane.

Thirteen winds rose. Darkness fell on the face of Humbaba
—he could not ram ahead, he could not kick back—   165
and Gilgamesh's weapons brought him down.

Humbaba begged for his life, saying to Gilgamesh:
"You are young, Gilgamesh, still your mother's boy!
You are the son of the holy aurochs Ninsun,
and by the will of Shamash, these mountains ·   ·   170
King Gilgamesh, the sapling of Uruk!

"Gilgamesh, the dead man serves no lord,
but the living slave works for his master.
Gilgamesh, spare my life ·   ·
Let me stay here, in your service ·   ·   175

"As much timber as you command ·   ·
For you I will guard the myrtle, the ·   ·
Timber worthy of a palace ·   ·"

Enkidu worked his words, saying to Gilgamesh:
"My friend, do not listen to him,   180
·   · his prayers ·   ·
·   ·
·   ·
·   ·
·   ·
·   ·
·   ·
·   ·
·   ·"

Humbaba worked his words, saying to Enkidu:
"You know the mind of the forest, the mind of ·   ·   190
You know all that is said there.

"I should have hanged you on a tree outside the forest
and fed your flesh to bugs, eagles, hawks, and vultures.
But now, Enkidu, only you can release me.
Speak to Gilgamesh, spare my life!"   195

Enkidu worked his words, saying to Gilgamesh:
"My friend! Humbaba, the guardian of cedars:
Destroy him, kill him! Crush his mind!
Humbaba, the guardian of cedars:
Destroy him, kill him! Crush his mind—
before Enlil hears of it, the leader of gods!   200

"The great gods will grow angry with us,
Enlil in Nippur, Shamash in Larsa, ·   ·
So make for yourself an everlasting name:
how Gilgamesh killed the brutal Humbaba."

Humbaba heard what Enkidu said.   205
He looked up to Shamash and wept,
shedding his tears in the light of the sun:

UGARITIC VERSION

"When Enkidu slept with his beasts, I never called him   Ug$_2$ 13'
or sullied the cedar-bearing mountains with his blood.

"Shamash, be my king and my judge!   15'
No mother gave birth to me, no father brought me up:
the mountain gave birth to me, you brought me up!

"Enkidu, only you can release me.
Speak to Gilgamesh, spare my life!"   18'

·   ·
·   ·
·   ·
·   ·
·   ·
·   ·
·   ·
·   ·
·   ·
·   ·

OLD BABYLONIAN VERSION

".   · Humbaba   Isch 1'
·   · weeping ·   ·
I look at ·   ·
·   · took hold of us,
·   · before us."   5'

Enkidu said to him, to Gilgamesh:
"Kill Humbaba ·   · your god hates!

·   ·

My friend, why have mercy on him?"

Gilgamesh said to him, to Enkidu: 10'
"My friend, now is the time to secure our victory:
his cloaks of dread flee into the forest,
his frightful light fades into the mist."

Enkidu said to him, to Gilgamesh:
"My friend, catch a bird and where go the chicks?   15'
Let us find the cloaks of dread later,
they are like chicks running wild in the forest."   17'

STANDARD BABYLONIAN VERSION

Humbaba heard what Enkidu said.   255
He looked up to Shamash and wept,
shedding his tears in the light of the sun:

"Enkidu, you came into ·   ·
A king ·   · in the clash of weapons,
but hatred ·   · for those who live in the palace.   260

"You sit at his feet, like sheep and shepherd,
like a hireling ·   ·
But now, Enkidu, only you can release me.
Speak to Gilgamesh, spare my life!"

Enkidu worked his words, saying to Gilgamesh: 265
"My friend! Humbaba, the guardian of cedars:
Destroy him, kill him! Crush his mind!
Humbaba, the guardian of cedars:
Destroy him, kill him! Crush his mind—
before Enlil hears of it, the leader of gods!

"The great gods will grow angry with us,   270
Enlil in Nippur, Shamash in Larsa, ·   ·
So make for yourself an everlasting name:
how Gilgamesh killed the brutal Humbaba."

Humbaba heard what Enkidu said.
He looked up to Shamash and wept,
shedding his tears in the light of the sun: 275

·   ·

·   ·

"May they not ·   ·
May they not grow old together!
May Enkidu have no one but Gilgamesh to bury him."   280

Enkidu worked his words, saying to Gilgamesh:
"My friend, I speak to you, but you do not listen!
Until the curse ·   ·
·   · to his mouth."

Gilgamesh heard the words of his friend   285
and drew the sword from his side.

Gilgamesh struck him in the neck,
Enkidu cut open his chest and pulled out his lungs.
·   · jumped up,
and as a trophy, he tore the tusks off his head.   290

·   · fell on the mountains,
·   · fell on the mountains.

·   ·

·   ·

·   ·

·   ·

·   ·

·   ·

.   .

.   .

Gilgamesh ·   ·   300
they gathered resin from the cedars as incense for Enlil.

Enkidu worked his words, saying to Gilgamesh:
"My friend, we have turned the forest into wasteland.
What will we say if Enlil asks us in Nippur:
'You used your strength to kill the guardian!   305
What wrath sent you trampling through the forest?'"

After they had killed his seven sons
—the Cicada, the Growler, the Blizzard, the Loudmouth,
the Wise Man, Kappah, and the Demon—
they cut off their ·   ·

Their axes weighed one hundred and twenty pounds each
and each of their blows struck six feet deep.   310
Gilgamesh cut down the trees
while Enkidu found the best timber.

Enkidu worked his words, saying to Gilgamesh:
"My friend, we have felled a mighty cedar,
whose topmost branches touched the skies.   315

"Make a door of it: one hundred and twenty feet tall,
forty feet wide, and two feet thick.
It will all be one piece—pole, pivot, and swivel.
Let the Euphrates carry it to Enlil in Nippur,
let it fill the temple of Nippur with delight."

They gathered branches of cedar, cypress, and juniper,   320
and made a raft, loading it with ·   ·
Enkidu sailed on the raft ·   ·
and Gilgamesh sailed on the head of Humbaba.

TABLET VI

He washed his filthy hair

He washed his filthy hair, cleaned his dirty gear
and shook his hair down over his shoulders.
He took off his tatters and put on clean clothes,
wrapped in a cloak and tied it with a belt.

Then Gilgamesh put on his crown,   5
and Ishtar caught sight of his beauty.

"Come, Gilgamesh! Marry me,
give me the fruit of your body!
Be my husband, make me your wife!

"Let me ready for you a chariot of lapis lazuli and gold,   10
with golden wheels and caps of amber,
drawn by demons—big mules indeed!

"Step into my cedar-scented house,
and as you step into my house,
the threshold and throne will kiss your feet.   15

"Kings, lords, and nobles will bow down before you
and bring you tribute from mountains and plains,
while your goats bear you triplets and your ewes twins.

"Your donkey will be fastest with its freight,
your horse will gain glory in the chariot,   20
your ox will be unmatched at the plow."

Gilgamesh worked his words, saying to Ishtar:
"As if I would ever marry you!
Who would wash my clothes and body,   25
who would give me food and fare?

"Would you serve me bread that is fit for a god?
Would you pour me beer that is fit for a king?
·   · obliged
·   · heap high   30
·   · cloak
·   · marry you?

"You are a winter too warm to freeze ice,
a half-door that blocks no wind or draft,
a palace that crumbles and kills its heroes,   35
an elephant that throws off its rider,
a lump of pitch that stains the hand,
a flask of water that soaks the cloak,
a block of limestone that weakens the wall,
a ram that wrecks our walls for the enemy,   40
a shoe that bites the foot of its owner.

"Tell me, did any of your lovers last?
Did any of your lovebirds fly to the skies?
Come, let me count out your conquests.

"There was the man who ·   · his arm.   45
Your childhood lover Dumuzi
you damned to sorrow, year after year.

"You loved the bright-dyed roller bird,
but then you struck it, breaking its wing.
Now it sits in the forest and cries: 'My wing!'[11]   50

"You loved the lion, superb in strength,
but dug seven pits for it, and seven more.

"You loved the stallion, eager for battle,
but damned it to whips, lashes, and pain.
You damned it to fifty miles of gallop,   55
you damned it to drink muddied water,
and its mother, Silili, you damned to sorrow.

"You loved the shepherd—the herdsman, the drover—
who always baked fresh bread for you
and slaughtered a goat for you day after day.   60

"But you struck him and turned him into a wolf.
Now his own shepherd boys chase him away
and his own sheepdogs bite at his thighs.

"You loved Ishullanu, your father's gardener,
who always brought you dates in his basket   65
and every day set for you a sparkling table.

"You caught sight of his beauty and went straight to him:
'Ishullanu! Let's have a taste of your work:
Stretch out your hand and pluck my fruit!'

"Ishullanu said to you: 70
'Me? What do you want me for?
I've already eaten what my mother baked,
should I eat slander and insults instead,
with reeds as my only cover in the cold?'

"You heard what he said,   75
so you struck him and turned him into a weevil.
You let him live in his garden,
but he cannot climb ·   · or go under ·   ·

"And now you would love me and treat me the same?"

When Ishtar heard this,   80
the furious goddess flew to the skies.

Weeping she went before Anu, her father,
shedding her tears before Antu, her mother.

"Father! Gilgamesh keeps insulting me.
He keeps spouting slander about me—   85
slander about me and insults against me!"

Anu worked his words, saying to Queen Ishtar:
"Ah, but did you not goad King Gilgamesh
into spouting slander about you—   90
slander about you and insults against you?"

Ishtar worked her words, saying to her father, Anu:
"Father! Give me the Bull of Heaven,
so I can kill Gilgamesh in his home.   95

"If you do not give me the Bull of Heaven,
I will raze all the houses of the underworld
and open the gates to the land below.
I will raise the dead to eat the living,
—the living will be outnumbered by the dead!"   100

Anu worked his words, saying to Queen Ishtar:
"If you really want the Bull of Heaven,
first Uruk's widows must gather seven years of fodder
and the farmers of Uruk must grow hay."   105

Ishtar worked her words, saying to Anu:
"I already stored ·   ·
I already grew ·   ·
Uruk's widows gathered seven years of fodder   110
and the farmers of Uruk grew hay.
I will kill him with the fury of the Bull!"

Anu heard what Ishtar said
and gave her the reins to the Bull of Heaven.
Ishtar led it down to earth.   115

When it reached the land of Uruk,
the forest, marsh, and canebrake dried up.
As it went down to the river,
the water level fell twelve feet.

The Bull snorted, a pit opened up,
and a hundred men of Uruk fell in.   120
It snorted again, a pit opened up,
and two hundred men of Uruk fell in.
It snorted a third time, a pit opened up,
and Enkidu fell in, up to his waist.

He jumped out and took   125
the Bull of Heaven by the horns,
but it spat froth in his face
and threw him off with its tail.

Enkidu worked his words, saying to Gilgamesh:
"My friend, we prided ourselves ·   · in our city,   130
now what shall we say to the gathering crowd?
My friend, I have tested the strength of the Bull,
measured its might and learned its aim.
Now I will test its strength once more.

"I will sneak up behind the Bull   135
and grab the tuft of its tail.
With my foot on its hock,
I will ·   ·
Then you, like a butcher, brave and deft,
thrust in your sword between neck, horns, and spine."   140

Enkidu sneaked up behind the Bull
and grabbed the tuft of its tail.
With his foot on its hock,
he ·   ·
Then Gilgamesh, like a butcher, brave and deft,   145
thrust in his sword between neck, horns, and spine.

— 58 —

After they had killed the Bull of Heaven,
they cut out its heart and gave it to the Sun God.
They stepped back and bowed before Shamash,
then the two of them sat down together.   150

Ishtar went up on the wall of Uruk,
stamped her feet in anger and cried:
"Woe to Gilgamesh, who disgraced me
and killed the Bull of Heaven!"

Enkidu heard what Ishtar said,
tore off the Bull's member and hurled it at her: 155
"I would do the same to you, if only I could catch you,
and drape your arms in its guts!"

Ishtar convened her devotees, her temple girls and priestesses.
Around the Bull's member she began the lamentation.

Gilgamesh called for the craftsmen and smiths of the city,   160
and they all praised the size of the horns.

Each horn was thirty pounds of pure lapis lazuli
and their cases were two fingers thick.
They could hold three hundred gallons of oil.
Gilgamesh dedicated them to his god Lugalbanda;   165
he picked them up to hang them in his bedroom.

They washed their hands in the Euphrates,
then took hold of each other and went.
They rode through the streets of Uruk,
and Uruk's people thronged to see them.   170

Gilgamesh called to his servant girls:
"Who is the most beautiful youth?
Who is the most splendid of men?"

"Gilgamesh is the most beautiful youth!
Gilgamesh is the most splendid of men!"   175

".   · we knew in our wrath
·   · in the streets no one disgraces him
·   · way ·   ."
In his palace, Gilgamesh began the celebration.

When the young men went to sleep in their beds,   180
Enkidu too went to bed, and had a dream.
Enkidu got up to interpret his dream
and said to his friend:

TABLET VII

Why, my friend

"Why, my friend, were the great gods in council?"

HITTITE PROSE VERSION

"My brother, what a dream I had tonight! Anu, Enlil, Ea, and the heavenly Sun God were assembled, and Anu said to Enlil: 'Because they killed the Bull of Heaven, and because they killed Humbaba, who kept the mountains thick with cedar,' said Anu, 'one of them must die.' And Enlil said: 'Enkidu will die, but Gilgamesh will not die.'

"Then the heavenly Sun God answered the hero Enlil: 'Was it not at my order they killed them, the Bull of Heaven and Humbaba too? And now innocent Enkidu must die?' Enlil grew angry with the heavenly Sun God: 'And how come you marched with them like a comrade in arms?'"

Enkidu lay down before Gilgamesh, shedding streams of tears. He said: "My brother! How dear to me is my brother! No one will bring me back from the dead to be with my brother. I will sit with the shades, I will cross the threshold of death. Never again will I see my dear brother!"

STANDARD BABYLONIAN VERSION

Enkidu worked his words, saying to Gilgamesh:		28
"Come, my friend! ·	·	
In ·	·	30
The door ·	·	
Because ·	·	
·	·	
·	·	
In ·	."	

Enkidu looked up, as though at the door,
he spoke to the door as if it were human:
"Door of the woods! You cannot hear me,
you lack the reason I have gained.   40

"Through a hundred miles of forest I sought out
the best timber, until I found a mighty cedar
whose topmost branches touched the skies.

"I made you from a matchless tree,
one hundred and twenty feet tall,
forty feet wide, and two feet thick.
You are all one piece—pole, pivot, and swivel.   45
I made you, I carried you to Nippur, I fixed you in place.

"Had I only known, oh door, how you would repay me!
Had I only known, oh door, how you would reward me!

"I would have grabbed my ax, I would have cut you down,
and sailed on you to Sippar, to the Shining Temple.   50
I would have brought you to the temple of Shamash
and planted you in the gate of the Shining Temple.

"I would have stationed Thunderbirds by the gate,
I would have ·   · by the entrance.
I would have ·   · the city ·   · Shamash.   55
and in Uruk ·
because Shamash listened to my words
and lent me a weapon in times of need.

"But now I have made you, oh door, and fixed you in place.
Can I break you up again? Can I tear you down again?   60

"Instead, may a future king loathe you,
·   · hide you,
may he scratch out my name and inscribe his own!"
Enkidu tore off his clothes and threw them to the ground.

He was listening to his words, 65
and soon his tears began to drop.
Gilgamesh listened to Enkidu's words,
and soon his tears began to drop.

Gilgamesh worked his words, saying to Enkidu:
"My friend, ·   · apparent.
You, who learned to think and reason, now speak nonsense! 70
My friend, why does your heart speak nonsense?

"Your dream was strange indeed, and very troubling.
Your sleeping lips were trembling like flies.
·   · great, your dream was odd.

"But grief is left to the living: 75
the dead leave, the living grieve.

"So let me pray and plead to the mighty gods for you,
let me seek out Shamash and turn to your god,
let me supplicate Anu, the father of the gods!
May my plea for you reach Enlil, adviser of gods, 80
Ea ·   · I will implore for you!

"I will make for you a statue of untold gold,
·   · silver."

"No, my friend! Spend no silver, waste no gold.
Enlil's decrees are different, he is not like other gods. 85
What he decrees, he does not change.
What he declares, he does not change.

"No, my friend, my fate is carved:
some people die before their time."

At the first flood of daylight, 90
Enkidu looked up and cried out to Shamash,

shedding his tears in the light of the sun:
"I call on you, Shamash, for the little life I have left!

"The hunter, the woodsman:
he did not let me be a match for my friend,   95
so let the hunter not be a match for his friend!

"Destroy his catch, cut his gains,
may his wealth shrink before your eyes!
Let luck fly out of the room that he enters."

He cursed the hunter till his heart was full.   100
It then told him to curse Shamhat as well.

"Come, Shamhat, I will fix a fate for you,
a fate that will last forever.
A mighty curse I will work on you,
may it catch you straight away!   105

"You will never build a happy home,
or be surrounded by your children,
or sit with the girls in their room.

"Dust will soil your pretty clothes
and drunkards drag your dress through the mud,   110
so that you have no beautiful ·   ·

"The potter ·   ·
You will never have ·   ·
and no merry feasts will happen in your house!

"Your love nest will be a doorway   115
and your home a highway crossing.
You will make a bed in ruins
and find cover beneath a wall.

"Thorns and spines will flay your feet,
drunk men and sober will slap your cheek.

". · will sue you,   120
the builder will not fix the hole in your roof.
Owls will roost in your ·
No banquets will be ·

".
·
·
· purple ·
· sullied thighs ·
· thighs sullied ·

"Because you weakened my untouched body,   130
my untouched body you weakened in the wild!"

The Sun God Shamash heard the words of Enkidu,
and straight away a warning boomed from the skies:

"Why, Enkidu, do you curse the priestess Shamhat,
who served you bread that is fit for a god,   135
poured you beer that is fit for a king,
dressed you in dazzling clothes,
and led you to Gilgamesh, your great friend?

"Now Gilgamesh, your friend and brother,
will lay you on a mighty bed,   140
will lay you on a bed of glory.
You will sit at ease by his left hand
while the lords of the underworld kiss your feet.

"He will make Uruk weep for you, wail for you,
the merry he will fill with misery for you.   145
When you are gone, he will wander unwashed
through the wild, wearing only the skin of a lion."

Enkidu heard the words of Shamash the hero,
·   · his angry heart found peace,
·   · his furious heart found peace.   150

"Come, Shamhat, I will fix a fate for you,
the mouth that cursed you will now bless you.

"You will be loved by lords and governors!
Men will slap their thighs six miles away,
and shake out their hair twelve miles away.   155
No soldier will be slow to undo his belt for you
or to give you gold, lapis lazuli, and obsidian.

"You will be given elaborate earrings,
and Ishtar, the cleverest goddess, will lead you   160
to a man with wealth in his vault, grain heaped high.
He will leave his wife for you, a mother of seven!"

But Enkidu's mind was ill.
Lying by himself, he thought back and forth.
He told his friend what went on in his mind:

"My friend, what a dream I had last night!   165
The skies screamed, the earth called back,
and I stood there, caught in the middle.

"There was a dark-faced man.
His head was like a Thunderbird,
his hands were like lion paws,   170
his nails were like eagle claws.

"He grabbed my hair and broke my strength.
I knocked him down, but he sprang back like a sling,
he knocked me down, and I keeled over like a raft.
Like a fierce aurochs, he crushed me underfoot,
·   · poison in my body.   175

"'Save me, my friend!' ·   ·
But you were scared of him and ·   ·
You ·   ·
·   ·
·   ·
·   ·

"He struck me and turned me into a dove.
He bound my arms like a bird's and carried me captive
to the house of darkness, the home of Irkalla:

"to the house that no one leaves,   185
to the road of no return,
the home of those who long for light,
who eat dust and live on clay.

"Wrapped like birds in feather cloaks,
they see no light but dwell in darkness.   190
Dust lies thick on door and bolt,
silence drowns the house of dust.

"I entered the house of dust
and saw the crowns stashed away.
There sat the kings, who ruled the land in days long past, 195
who once served meat at the tables of Anu and Enlil,
who once served the gods bread and poured cold water.

"I entered the house of dust:
there were the high priests and the *lagar* priests,
there were the *išippu* priests and the *lumaḫḫu* priests, 200
there were the *gudapsû* priests of the great gods.
There was old king Etana, there the wild god Shakkan,
and there was Ereshkigal, queen of the underworld.

"Before her sat Belet-seri, scribe of the underworld,
she was holding a tablet and read out to Ereshkigal. 205
Then Belet-seri looked up and saw me:

"'Who brought this human here?
Who took this man to us?'

".   · prepared
·   · tomb   210
·   ·
·   ·

·   · me
·   · Ereshkigal
·   · the flood   215
·   ·
·   ·
·   ·
·   ·
·   ·
·   ·
·   · I saw his body
·   ·
·   ·
·   ·
·   ·
·   ·
·   ·
·   ·
·   ·
·   ·
·   ·
·   ·
·   ·
·   ·
·   ·
·   ·
·   ·
·   ·
·   ·
·   ·

.   .
.   .
.   .
.   .
.   .
.   .
.   .
.   .
.   .

"Me, who went through every danger with you.
Remember me, my friend,
do not forget what I went through."

"My friend had a dream that will not ·   ·
On the day of that dream, his strength disappeared!"

Enkidu lay ill for one day, and a second.   255
In his bed, Enkidu ·   ·
A third day and a fourth, Enkidu ·   ·
A fifth, sixth, and a seventh day, an eighth, ninth, and a tenth day,
Enkidu's illness ·   ·
An eleventh and a twelfth ·   ·   260
In his bed, Enkidu ·   ·

He called out to Gilgamesh and ·   ·
"My friend, I have been cursed to ·   ·
When in battle ·   ·
I feared war ·   ·   265
My friend, those who in war ·   ·
I, who in war ·   ."

.   .
.   .
.   .
.   .
.   .
.   .
.   .

TABLET VIII

At the first flood of daylight

At the first flood of daylight,
Gilgamesh wept for his friend:

"Enkidu! Born to a gazelle
and an onager, your parents,
you were brought up by donkeys   5
and led to pasture by the beasts!

"Enkidu, may the tracks of the Cedar Forest
ceaselessly weep for you, day and night.
May the elders of Uruk the Sheepfold, the vast city, weep for you.
May the crowds who blessed our departure weep for you.   10

"May the peaks of hills and mountains weep for you.
May the pure ·   · weep for you,
may grasslands wail like mothers for you.

"May boxwood, cypress, and cedar weep for you,
the trees we crept through in our wrath.   15
May the bear, hyena, leopard, cheetah, deer, jackal, lion,
aurochs, stag, ibex, beast, and herd of the wild weep for you!

"May the holy river Ulay weep for you,
along whose banks we sauntered.
May the sacred Euphrates weep for you,
whose water we poured out in sacrifice.   20

"May the young men of Uruk the Sheepfold weep for you,
who watched us do battle and kill the Bull of Heaven.

May the plowman in his field weep for you,
who will cherish your name in his work song.
May the ·   · of Uruk the Sheepfold, the vast city, weep for you,   25
who will cherish your name ·   ·

"May the herdsman of Uruk the Sheepfold weep for you,
who filled your mouth with milk and *ayran*.[12]
May the shepherd boy of Uruk the Sheepfold weep for you,
who covered your lips with ghee.   30
May the brewer of Uruk the Sheepfold weep for you,
who filled your mouth with beer.

"May the priestesses of Uruk the Sheepfold weep for you,
who rubbed your head with scented oil.
May ·   · of the wedding house weep for you,   35
who ·   · a wife ·   ·

"May ·   · weep for you!
May ·   · weep for you like brothers.
May they walk with untied hair, as if they were your sisters.
May they weep for you, Enkidu, your mother and your father!   40

"Now I too will weep for you.

"Hear me, young men, hear me!
Hear me, elders of vast Uruk, hear me!
I weep for my friend Enkidu,
I cry as bitterly as a weeper woman.   45

"Ax at my side, strength of my arm,
sword in my belt, shield in my hand!
My festival dress, my belt of joy!
An evil wind rose and robbed me of you.

"My friend, you hounded mule,   50
highland donkey, leopard of the wild!
Enkidu, you hounded mule,

highland donkey, leopard of the wild!

"It was we who joined forces, climbed mountains,
grappled and killed the Bull of Heaven,
and crushed Humbaba, who lived in the Cedar Forest.

"What sleep has seized you now?   55
Come back! You do not hear me."

But he did not turn his head.
He touched his heart—it beat no more.

He veiled the face of his friend like a bride's,
like an eagle he circled around his corpse,   60
like a lioness forced to abandon her cubs
he paced back and forth, before and behind him.

He pulled out heaps of curly hair
and cast his clothes off in disgust.

At the first flood of daylight,   65
Gilgamesh sent out a call across the land:
"Smiths and stonecutters, coppersmiths and goldsmiths, jewelers!
Make a statue of my friend ·   ."

·   · he shaped the statue of his friend:
"My friend, your limbs are ·   ·   70
Your eyebrows are lapis lazuli, your chest is gold,
your body is ·   ·

·   ·

·   ·

·   ·

·   ·

·   ·

·   ·

·   ·

·   ·
·   ·
·   ·
·   ·

"I will lay you on a mighty bed,
I will lay you on a bed of glory.   85
You will sit at ease by my left hand
while the lords of the underworld kiss your feet.

"I will make Uruk weep for you, wail for you,
the merry I will fill with misery for you.
When you are gone, I will wander unwashed   90
through the wild, wearing only the skin of a lion."

At the first flood of daylight,
Gilgamesh got up and went to his treasury.
He broke the seal and surveyed the jewelry:
obsidian, carnelian, lapis lazuli, alabaster,   95
·   · made ·   ·

He gave his friend ·   ·
He gave his friend ·   ·
He gave his friend golden ·   ·
He gave his friend golden ·   ·   100
He gave his friend golden ·   ·
He gave his friend golden ·   ·
He gave his friend ·   ·
He gave his friend ·   · set in thirty pounds of gold.
He gave his friend ·   ·   105
He gave his friend ·   ·
·   · thick.
He gave his friend ·   ·
·   · wide.
He gave his friend ·   ·   110
·   · for his waist.
He gave his friend ·   ·

He gave his friend ·   ·
He gave his friend ·   ·
He gave his friend ·   ·   115
He gave his friend ·   ·
He gave his friend ·   ·
He gave his friend ·   · for his feet,
·   · pounds of ivory.
He gave his friend a ·   · with a golden handle.   120
He gave his friend a mighty ·   · for his arm.
He gave his friend a ·   · quiver,
whose handle was sixty pounds of gold.
An ivory mace in his hand ·   ·
He gave his friend a ·   ·
whose handle was forty pounds of gold.
·   · five feet long.   125
He gave his friend ·   · thick.
·   · of pure gold,
·   · of carnelian and ·   · of iron,
·   · shaped like an aurochs,
·   · for his friend.   130

He slaughtered big bulls and fat sheep,
and heaped up the meat for his dead friend.
".   · of my friend!"
They bore the meat to the underworld lords.

·   · for Ishtar, the mighty queen.[13]
A weapon of *kallirê*, the sacred wood,   135
he offered in the sun to Ishtar, the mighty queen.
"May Ishtar, the mighty queen, accept my gift.
May she welcome my friend and walk by his side!"

·   ·

he offered in the sun to Belet-ili, the mighty queen.   140
"May Belet-ili, the mighty queen, accept my gift.
May she welcome my friend and walk by his side!"

A flask of lapis lazuli ·
                                     ·
·
he offered in the sun to Ereshkigal, queen of the underworld.   145
"May Ereshkigal, queen of the underworld, accept my gift.
May she welcome my friend and walk by his side!"

A flute of carnelian ·
he offered in the sun to Dumuzi, Ishtar's shepherd lover.
"May Dumuzi, Ishtar's shepherd lover, accept my gift.   150
May he welcome my friend and walk by his side!"

A throne of lapis lazuli ·
and a staff of lapis lazuli ·
he offered in the sun to Namtar, minister of the underworld.
"May Namtar, minister of the underworld, accept my gift.   155
May he welcome my friend and walk by his side!"

·   ·
·   ·
he offered in the sun to Hushbishag, manager of the underworld.
"May Hushbishag, manager of the underworld, accept my gift.   160
May she welcome my friend and walk by his side!"

·   · he had made,
silver clasps, copper bracelets ·   ·
he offered in the sun to Qassi-tabat, sweeper of the underworld.
"May Qassi-tabat, sweeper of the underworld, accept my gift.   165
May he welcome my friend and walk by his side!
Let not my friend be sad or sick at heart."

·   · of alabaster, inlaid with lapis lazuli and carnelian,
in the shape of the Cedar Forest,
·   · inlaid with carnelian,   170
he offered in the sun to Ninshuluh-hatumma, cleaner of the
    underworld.
"May Ninshuluh-hatumma, cleaner of the underworld, accept my gift.
May she welcome my friend and walk by his side!

·   · before my friend.
Let not my friend be sad or sick at heart."

A double-edged sword with a hilt of lapis lazuli   175
in the shape of the sacred Euphrates
he offered in the sun to Mouflon, butcher of the underworld.
"May Mouflon, butcher of the underworld, accept my gift.
May he welcome my friend and walk by his side!"

A flask of alabaster ·   ·   180
he offered in the sun to Dumuzi-abzu, scapegoat of the underworld.
"May Dumuzi-abzu, scapegoat of the underworld, accept my gift.
May he welcome my friend and walk by his side!"

·   · with a top of lapis lazuli,
·   · inlaid with carnelian,   185
he offered in the sun to ·   ·
"May ·   · accept my gift.
May he welcome my friend and walk by his side!"

·   ·
·   ·
·   ·
·   ·
·   ·
·   ·
·   ·
·   ·
·   ·
·   ·

"May he welcome my friend and walk by his side!"

·   · cedar   200
he offered in the sun to the great ·   ·
"May the great ·   · accept my gift.
May he welcome my friend and walk by his side!"

"·

· cedar

· that we ·
· their names ·
· the judge of the Anunnaki gods."   210

When Gilgamesh heard this,
the idea of the river found form in his heart.[14]

At the first flood of daylight,
Gilgamesh opened the city gate,
and brought out a mighty table of *elammaku* wood.   215
He filled a carnelian bowl with honey,
he filled a lapis lazuli bowl with ghee.
· he adorned and offered in the sun.
· offered in the sun.

.   .
.   .
.   .
.   .
.   .
.   .
.   .
.   .

As he wandered

As he wandered through the wild,
Gilgamesh wept bitterly for his friend Enkidu:
"I too will die. Am I not like Enkidu?
Grief has stepped into my heart.

"Afraid of death, I wander through the wild   5
toward Uta-napishti, son of Ubara-tutu.
I have taken the road, I walk it fast.

"One night, I reached a mountain pass
and found lions there. I was scared,
so I looked up and prayed to Sîn.   10
My prayer went to the moon, lamp of gods:
'Sîn ·   · protect me!'"

Gilgamesh woke up: it was a dream.
In the moonlight, he was happy to be alive.

He took his ax in hand   15
and drew the sword from his side.
He fell on the lions like an arrow,
he struck, killed, and scattered them.

And ·   ·
He threw ·   ·   20
He drew ·   ·
The name of the first ·   ·
The name of the second ·   ·

He looked up and prayed to Sîn,
his prayer went to the moon, lamp of gods: 25
"Sîn ·   ·
May ·   ·
How ·   ·"   28
·   ·
·   ·
·   ·

                                                        OLD BABYLONIAN VERSION
·   · aurochs and wisents ·   ·   VA+BM i 1'

He wore their skins and ate their flesh.
Gilgamesh dug wells where there were none,
he drank their water as he chased the winds.

Shamash was worried. He bent down   5'
and said to Gilgamesh:
"Gilgamesh, where are you going?
You will not find the life you seek."

Gilgamesh said to him, to Shamash the hero:
"After I have walked and wandered the wild,   10'
will I lack rest in the underworld?
All those years of lying down!

"Now my eyes will see the sun, till I am full of light.
The dark of death is far away—look at all the sun!
When do the dead ever see daylight?"   15'

·   ·
·   ·
·   ·
·   ·

The name of the mountains was Twin Peaks.   37

He reached the Twin Peaks,
that guard the rising sun each day,
the peaks whose tops touch the firmament,   40
whose roots reach down to the netherworld.

The gate was guarded by scorpion people,
whose visage was dread, whose eyes were death,
and whose frightful light engulfed the mountains.
They guard the sun when it rises and sets.   45

When Gilgamesh saw them, his face went dark with dread.
But he took hold of himself and went up to them.

The scorpion man called to his wife:
"That man over there, in him is the flesh of gods!"
The scorpion woman answered back: 50
"He is only two-thirds god and one-third human."

The scorpion man called out,
saying to King Gilgamesh, the flesh of gods:

"How did you cover the far road that leads here?
How did you make your way into my sight?   55
How did you cross the dangerous passes?

"I want to know ·   ·
·   · where you are headed,
I want to know your reason for coming here."

·   ·
·   ·
·   ·
·   ·
·   ·
·   ·

.   .
.   .
.   .
.   .
.   .
.   .
.   .
.   .
.   .
.   .

"I seek the way to my ancestor, Uta-napishti,   75
who found eternal life in the gathering of gods.
He will tell me the secret of life and death."

The scorpion man worked his words, saying to Gilgamesh:
"Gilgamesh, there never was ·   · like you,   80
and no one has ever passed through the mountains.
Twenty-four hours ·   · inside,
the dark is dense and void of light.

"At sunrise ·   .
At sunset ·   .   85
At sunset ·   .

".   · out
.   .

But how will you ·   .
Will you enter ·   ."   90
.   .
.   .
.   .
.   .
.   .
.   .
.   .
.   .

·   ·
·   ·
·   ·
·   ·
·   ·
·   ·
·   ·
·   ·
·   ·
·   ·
·   ·
·   ·
·   ·
·   ·
·   ·
·   ·
·   ·
·   ·
·   ·
·   ·
·   ·
·   ·
·   ·
·   ·
·   ·
·   ·
·   ·

".   · by grief,   125
my face is scorched by frost and sun.
·   · exhausted.
Now, you ·   ."

The scorpion man worked his words,
saying to King Gilgamesh, the flesh of gods: 130
"Go, Gilgamesh! ·   ·

"May the Twin Peaks ·   ·
The hills and mountains ·   ·
Unharmed ·   ·

The gate of the mountains ·   ."   135

When Gilgamesh heard this,
the speech of the scorpion man, ·   ·
He took the path of the sun through the mountains.

When he had walked for two hours,
the dark was dense and void of light,   140
there was no way of looking back.

When he had walked for four hours,
the dark was dense and void of light,
there was no way of looking back.

When he had walked for six hours,   145
the dark was dense and void of light,
there was no way of looking back.

When he had walked for eight hours,
the dark was dense and void of light,
there was no way of looking back.   150

When he had walked for ten hours,
the dark was dense and void of light,
there was no way of looking back.

When he had walked for twelve hours,
the dark was dense and void of light,   155
there was no way of looking back.

When he had walked for fourteen hours,
the dark was dense and void of light,
there was no way of looking back.

After sixteen hours, he was running like a ·   ·   160
The dark was dense and void of light,
there was no way of looking back.

After eighteen hours, he felt the north wind,
·   · his face.
The dark was dense and void of light,   165
there was no way of looking back.

After traveling twenty hours,
·   · was near.

After twenty-two hours, there were just two hours left,
and after twenty-four hours of darkness,
he walked out into the sun.   170

·   · full of light.
He went straight to look at the trees of the gods.

One tree bore fruits of carnelian,
it was laden with grapes and lovely to look at.
Another tree bore leaves of lapis lazuli,   175
it was blooming and beautiful to see.

·   ·
·   ·
·   ·
·   ·
·   ·
·   ·
·   ·

·   · cypress ·   ·
·   · cedar ·   ·   185
fronds of *pappardilû* stone and ·   ·
coral ·   · *sāsu* stone,
its thorns and spines were shards of crystal.

Gilgamesh touched a carob—it was *abašmu* stone,
agate and hematite ·   ·   190

Instead of ·   ·

instead of ·   · turquoise,
·   · mother of pearl,
it had ·   ·

As Gilgamesh walked around and gaped,   195
she looked up and saw him.

Shiduri was an innkeeper

Shiduri was an innkeeper who lived by the seashore.
There she lived ·   ·
with racks full of cups and golden vats for brewing.
She was wrapped in a shawl; her face was veiled.

Gilgamesh roved around ·   ·   5
covered in pelts and spreading fear.
In him was the flesh of gods,
but his mind was full of grief.
He looked like one who had traveled far.

The innkeeper watched him at a distance.   10
She conversed with her heart, speaking to herself,
taking counsel in her own mind:
"That man must be an aurochs-killer!
Why is he making straight for my door?"

The innkeeper eyed him and locked her door,   15
she locked the door and went up on the roof.
But Gilgamesh heard ·   ·
He raised his head and turned to her.

Gilgamesh said to her, to the innkeeper:
"Innkeeper, why did you lock the door when you saw me?   20
You locked the door and went up on the roof,
but I will shatter the door and break the bolt.
·   · my ·   ·
·   · in the wild."

The innkeeper said to him, to Gilgamesh: 25
".   · I locked the door,
·   · I went up on the roof.
I want to know ·   ."

Gilgamesh said to her, to the innkeeper:
"Enkidu and I ·   ·   30
It was we who joined forces, climbed mountains,
grappled and killed the Bull from the skies,
crushed Humbaba, who lived in the Cedar Forest,
and butchered lions in the mountain passes."

The innkeeper said to him, to Gilgamesh: 35
"If you really killed the guardian with Enkidu,
crushed Humbaba, who lived in the Cedar Forest,
butchered lions in the mountain passes,
grappled and killed the Bull from the skies—

"what hollowed your cheeks, bowed your head,   40
wrecked your heart, and broke your body?
Why is your mind full of grief?

"Why, looking like one who has traveled far,
with your face scorched by frost and sun,
do you wander the wild, dressed as a lion?"   45

Gilgamesh said to her, to the innkeeper:
"How could my cheeks be full, my head held high,
my heart not wrecked, my body not broken?
How could my mind be full of anything but grief?

"How could I not look like one who has traveled far,   50
with my face scorched by frost and sun?
How could I not wander the wild dressed as a lion?

"My friend, a hounded mule,
highland donkey, leopard of the wild!

My friend Enkidu, a hounded mule,
highland donkey, leopard of the wild!

"My friend, whom I loved so much,   55
who with me went through every danger!
My friend Enkidu, whom I loved so much,
who with me went through every danger!

"The fate of humankind caught up with him.
For six days and seven nights, I wept for him.
I would not let his body be buried,
until a maggot fell from his nose.   60

"I grew scared of ·   ·
Afraid of death, I wander the wild.
The story of my friend wears me down,
so I wander the wild on far-off roads.
The story of Enkidu wears me down,   65
so I wander the wild on far-off roads.

"How could I be quiet? How could I stay silent?
My friend, whom I loved, has turned to clay.
My friend Enkidu, whom I loved, has turned to clay.
Am I not like him? I too will lie down   70
and never get up, for all of eternity."

Gilgamesh said to her, to the innkeeper:
"Now, innkeeper, what is the way to Uta-napishti?
What landmarks should I follow? Tell me,
tell me what landmarks to follow!   75
If it can be done, I will cross the ocean,
if not, I will keep roaming the wild."

The innkeeper said to him, to Gilgamesh:
"Gilgamesh, there never was a way across,
and no one has ever crossed the ocean.   80

Only Shamash the hero crosses the ocean,
who could ever cross it except the sun?

"The crossing is dangerous, the route full of peril,
and the Waters of Death block the way ahead.
So, Gilgamesh, even if you do cross the ocean,   85
what will you do when you get to the Waters of Death?

"But Gilgamesh! There is Ur-shanabi, Uta-napishti's boatman,
trimming cedar in the forest with the Stone Ones.[15]

"Go to him, let him see your face.
If it can be done, cross the ocean with him,   90
if not, turn back and go home!"

When Gilgamesh heard this,
he took his ax in hand
and drew the sword from his side.

He crept up and stormed at them,   95
falling on them like an arrow.
His cry resounded in the forest.

Ur-shanabi saw the shining ·   ·
he took his ax in hand and charged at him.
But Gilgamesh struck his head and ·   ·   100
he took his arm and ·   ·

The Stone Ones that sealed the boat,
that did not fear the Waters of Death,
that ·   · the wide ocean,
·   · and threw them in the water.   105
He crushed the Stone Ones and threw them in the river.

·   · the boat.
·   · the beach.

Gilgamesh said to him, to the boatman Ur-shanabi:
"·   · you tremble.   110
.   · you."

Ur-shanabi said to him, to Gilgamesh:
"What hollowed your cheeks, bowed your head,
wrecked your heart, and broke your body?
Why is your mind full of grief?   115

"Why, looking like one who has traveled far,
with your face scorched by frost and sun,
do you wander the wild, dressed as a lion?"

Gilgamesh said to him, to the boatman Ur-shanabi:
"How could my cheeks be full, my head held high,   120
my heart not wrecked, my body not broken?
How could my mind be full of anything but grief?

"How could I not look like one who has traveled far,
with my face scorched by frost and sun?
How could I not wander the wild dressed as a lion?   125

"My friend, a hounded mule,
highland donkey, leopard of the wild!
My friend Enkidu, a hounded mule,
highland donkey, leopard of the wild!

"It was we who joined forces, climbed mountains,
grappled and killed the Bull of Heaven,
crushed Humbaba, who lived in the Cedar Forest,   130
and butchered lions in the mountain passes.

"My friend, whom I loved so much,
who with me went through every danger!
My friend Enkidu, whom I loved so much,
who with me went through every danger!

"The fate of humankind caught up with him.
For six days and seven nights, I wept for him.   135
I would not let his body be buried,
until a maggot fell from his nose.

"I grew scared of ·   ·
Afraid of death, I wander the wild.
The story of my friend wears me down,   140
so I wander the wild on far-off roads.
The story of Enkidu wears me down,
so I wander the wild on far-off roads.

"How could I be quiet? How could I stay silent?
My friend, whom I loved, has turned to clay.   145
My friend Enkidu, whom I love, has turned to clay.
Am I not like him? I too will lie down
and never get up, for all of eternity."

Gilgamesh said to him, to the boatman Ur-shanabi:
"Now, Ur-shanabi, what is the way to Uta-napishti?   150
What landmarks should I follow? Tell me,
tell me what landmarks to follow!
If it can be done, I will cross the ocean,
if not, I will keep roaming the wild."

Ur-shanabi said to him, to Gilgamesh: 155
"Gilgamesh, your own hands are holding you back.
You crushed the Stone Ones and threw them in the river.
The Stone Ones are crushed and the cedar not trimmed.

"Gilgamesh, take your ax in hand and go to the forest.   160
Cut three hundred punting poles, a hundred feet long.
Sand them smooth and give them a handle,
then bring them to ·   ·"

When Gilgamesh heard this, he took his ax in hand,
drew the sword from his side and went to the forest.   165

He cut three hundred punting poles, a hundred feet long.
He sanded them smooth and gave them a handle,
then brought them to ·   ·

Gilgamesh and Ur-shanabi boarded the boat,
they launched the ferry and sailed away.   170
By the third day they had sailed more than a month's voyage,
then they came to the Waters of Death.

Ur-shanabi said to him, to Gilgamesh:
"Careful, Gilgamesh! Take the first punting pole.
Do not touch the water, your hand will go lame.   175

"Take a second punting pole, Gilgamesh, a third and a fourth,
take a fifth punting pole, Gilgamesh, a sixth and a seventh,
take an eighth punting pole, Gilgamesh, a ninth and a tenth,
take an eleventh punting pole, Gilgamesh, and a twelfth!"

After thirty miles, Gilgamesh ran out of punting poles,   180
so Ur-shanabi untied his belt.
Gilgamesh took off his clothes
and held them up to make a sail.

Uta-napishti was watching them at a distance.
He conversed with his heart, speaking to himself,   185
taking counsel in his own mind:

"Why are the Stone Ones of the boat broken,
and why is it mounted with this new rigging?
He who comes there is no mere man,
but at his side stands Ur-shanabi.   190

"I look at him, and he is no mere man.
I look at him, he is no ·   ·
I look at him ·   ·
       ·   · me ·   ·
       ·   ·

No man of mine ·   ·

·   ·

The boatman ·   ·
The man I see ·   ·
The man I see is no ·   ·   200
Perhaps the wild ·   ·

·   ·

The cedar ·   ·"

Gilgamesh neared the dock ·   ·
He sent down ·   ·   205
He went up ·   ·

Gilgamesh said to him, to Uta-napishti:
"Long live Uta-napishti, son of Ubara-tutu!
·   · after the Flood that ·   ·   210
What ·   · the Flood?"
·   ·

Uta-napishti said to him, to Gilgamesh:
"What hollowed your cheeks, bowed your head,
wrecked your heart, and broke your body?
Why is your mind full of grief?   215

"Why, looking like one who has traveled far,
with your face scorched by frost and sun,
do you wander the wild, dressed as a lion?"

Gilgamesh said to him, to Uta-napishti:
"How could my cheeks be full, my head held high,   220
my heart not wrecked, my body not broken?
How could my mind be full of anything but grief?

"How could I not look like one who has traveled far,
with my face scorched by frost and sun?
How could I not wander the wild dressed as a lion?   225

"My friend, a hounded mule,
highland donkey, leopard of the wild!
My friend Enkidu, a hounded mule,
highland donkey, leopard of the wild!

"It was we who joined forces, climbed mountains,
grappled and killed the Bull of Heaven,
crushed Humbaba, who lived in the Cedar Forest,   230
and butchered lions in the mountain passes.

"My friend, whom I loved so much,
who with me went through every danger!
My friend Enkidu, whom I loved so much,
who with me went through every danger!

"The fate of humankind caught up with him.
For six days and seven nights, I wept for him.   235
I would not let his body be buried,
until a maggot fell from his nose.

"I grew scared of ·   ·
Afraid of death, I wander the wild.
The story of my friend wears me down,   240
so I wander the wild on far-off roads.
The story of Enkidu wears me down,
so I wander the wild on far-off roads.

"How could I be quiet? How could I stay silent?
My friend, whom I loved, has turned to clay.   245
My friend Enkidu, whom I loved, has turned to clay.
Am I not like him? I too will lie down
and never get up, for all of eternity."

Gilgamesh said to him, to Uta-napishti:
"I thought to myself: I will go and find   250
the faraway Uta-napishti, of whom people talk.
So once more I traveled through the lands,

passing through dangerous mountains,
crossing sea after sea.

"My eyes longed for sweet sleep.
I wrecked myself with restlessness,   255
I filled my sinews with pain.
What has all this toil accomplished?

"I had not even reached Shiduri when my clothes gave out,
so I killed the bear, hyena, lions, leopard, cheetah,
deer, ibex, beast, and herd of the wild;   260
I ate their meat and flayed their skins.

"Now let the door of grief be closed,
seal its gate with pitch and tar!
No more will dances stop for my sake,
no more will the lively ·   ."   265

Uta-napishti said to him, to Gilgamesh:
"Why, Gilgamesh, do you always chase grief?
You, fashioned from the flesh of gods and men,
made to be like your mother and father!

"Gilgamesh, when were you ever mindful of the fool?   270
They placed a throne in the assembly and told you: 'Sit!'
But the fool is fed not fresh ghee but dregs of beer,
he lives on bran and chaff, not ·   ·

"He is dressed in a sack, not ·   ·
it's tied with a threadbare string, not a fine sash.   275
Because he has no councilors ·   ·
because he hears no good advice ·   ·

"Gilgamesh, be mindful of him ·   ·
·   · their lord ·   ·
·   ·

·   · the moon and the gods of the night.

— 97 —

At night, the moon travels ·   ·
The gods do not rest ·   ·
Alert, awake ·   ·
Since ancient times ·   ·   285

"Now you! Consider ·   ·
·   · your help
Gilgamesh, if the temples of the gods ·   ·
The temples of the goddesses ·   ·
·   · gods ·   ·   290
·   · made   ·   ·
·   · gift ·   ·
·   · throw ·   · his heart
·   · provide ·   ·
·   · humanity,   295
·   · they took to his fate.

"You never rest, and what do you get for it?
You have exhausted yourself with ceaseless toil,
you have filled your sinews with pain
and hastened the day of your death.   300

"Humans! Your lines snap like reeds.
The beautiful youth, the beautiful girl
—abducted by death in their prime!

"No one sees death.
No one sees the face of death,   305
no one hears the voice of death.
But it is savage death that snaps mankind.

"One day, we build a house,
one day, we found a home.
One day, the heirs divide it,   310
one day, the sons grow bitter.

"One day, the river rose and brought high water,
a mayfly drifting down the river,
its face turned toward the sun.
But even then it could see nothing.   315

"How similar are death and abduction,
and one cannot draw the image of death.
Yet no one has ever greeted a dead man.

"The Anunnaki were assembled, the great gods.
Mami, maker of destinies, fixed fates for them: 320
The gods gave humans life and death,
but did not reveal which day you will die."

Gilgamesh said to him

Gilgamesh said to him, to the faraway Uta-napishti:
"I look at you, Uta-napishti,
and your body is no different, you are just like me.
You are no different, you are just like me!

"My heart was all set on fighting with you,   5
but now that I see you, my arm falls limp.
Tell me, how did you find eternal life in the gathering of gods?"

Uta-napishti said to him, to Gilgamesh:
"I will tell you a secret, Gilgamesh,
and reveal what the gods keep hidden.   10

"You know the city of Shuruppak,
the city that lies on the banks of the Euphrates.
That city was old, and the great gods were there
when their hearts led them to unleash the Flood.

"They swore an oath of silence: Father Anu,   15
the hero Enlil, adviser of gods,
their throne-bearer, young Ninurta,
and Ennugi, watchman of the waterways.

"Lord Ea was also sworn to silence,
but he repeated their words to a wall: 20
'Fence, fence! Wall, wall!
Hear me, fence! Heed me, wall!

"'Man of Shuruppak, son of Ubara-tutu!
Raze the house, build a boat,
leave wealth, look for life,   25
forget your goods, save yourself!
And bring on board the seed of all life.

"'The ship you will build:
let her measures match up,
make her as wide as she is long,   30
and roof her over, like the Apsû.'

"I understood and said to Ea:
'Master, I have received your order,
I heard what you said, I will do it.
But how should I answer the city, the crowds, and the elders?'   35

"Ea worked his words, saying to me, his servant:
'You will say to them this:

""Surely, Enlil must hate me!
I can no longer live in your city   40
and set my feet on Enlil's land.
I will go down to the Apsû,
to live with my lord Ea.

""On you he will rain
a shower of birds, a windfall of fish,
you will reap a deluge of riches!   45

""At dawn sweets,	""*At dawn dark,*
at dusk wheat	*at dusk death*
in downpours he	*for all he will*
will rain on you."'	*let fall on you.* "'[16]

"At the first flood of daylight,
the city gathered at the gate of Atra-hasis.[17]

— 101 —

"The carpenter brought his ax,   50
the thatcher brought his stone,
the shipwright brought his adze.

"The young men came with ·   ·
the old men brought ropes,
the rich came with pitch,   55
the poor brought whatever they had.

"By the fifth day, I had laid out the hull of the ship:
her area was an acre, her sides two hundred feet tall,
and her deck was the same, two hundred feet wide.

"Then I drew the design and laid out her frame: 60
Six times I decked her over,
dividing her into seven decks,
each deck I divided into nine cabins.
I drove water plugs into her belly,
found poles and mounted the tackle.   65

"I poured ten thousand gallons of tar into the furnace
and coated the boat with ten thousand gallons of pitch.
The water boys brought ten thousand gallons of oil:
one-third of it was poured out in sacrifice,
and the boatman stowed the rest away.   70

"I butchered oxen for the workmen,
and every day I slaughtered sheep.
I let all my ale, beer, oil, and wine
flow like rivers for the workmen,
they drank like it was New Year's!   75

"At dawn I began to oil the wood,
by sundown the ship was finished.

".   · difficult.

We kept carrying rollers for the slipway back and forth,
until two-thirds of the ship was in the water.   80

"I brought everything I had on board:
I brought on board all the silver I had,
I brought on board all the gold I had,
I brought on board the seed of all life.

"I sent on board all my family and kin,   85
the herds and the creatures of the wild,
and the experts of all kinds of crafts.

"The sun had set me a deadline:

"'At dawn sweets,   "'At dawn dark,
at dusk wheat   at dusk death
in downpours he   for all he will
will rain on you.   let fall on you.

"'Go on board and seal the hatch:
the time has arrived.   90

"'At dawn sweets,   "'At dawn dark,
at dusk wheat   at dusk death
in downpours he   for all he will
will rain on you.'   let fall on you.'

"I watched the weather,
the storm was terrifying.
So I went on board and sealed the hatch.
I gave my palace and all its treasure to Puzur-Enlil,   95
the shipwright who caulked the hatch from outside.

"At the first flood of daylight,
a black cloud rose on the horizon.

"Adad the Storm God was roaring inside it,
Thunder and Lightning marched at the front,   100
bearing his throne over mountains and plains.

"Erra, god of war, ripped out the moorings,
the dikes overflowed as Ninurta walked by.[18]
The Anunnaki gods came bearing torches,
burning the land with their frightful light.   105

"The Storm God's silence covered the skies,
and all that was bright turned dark.
Like an ox, he trampled on the land,
and it shattered like a pot of clay.

"For a full day, the wind blew,   110
it stormed from the east and brought the Flood
that spread like war over the country.

"Brothers looked in vain for each other:
men all looked the same in the slaughter.

"Even the gods grew afraid of the Flood;
they fled to the skies, they flew up to Anu;   115
the gods curled up like dogs in the cold.
The goddess wailed like a woman giving birth,
the sweet-voiced Belet-ili screamed:

"'All the past has turned to clay,
because I spoke evil in the gathering of gods.   120
How could I speak evil in the gathering of gods?

"'I declared a war to destroy the human people,
but I am their mother—the people were mine!
Now like fish they fill the sea.'

"The Anunnaki gods wept with her.   125
The gods slumped and sat in tears,
while fever parched their lips.

"For six days and seven nights, the wind blew.
The storm and the Flood flattened the land.

"When the seventh day arrived,   130
the storm relented ·   ·
The sea, which had fought like a woman in labor,
found peace, the wind stilled, the Flood ended.

"I watched the weather; it was quiet,
but all the people had turned to clay.   135

"The flooded land was flat as a rooftop.
I opened a hatch and felt the sun on my face.
I fell to my knees and wept,
the tears streaming down my cheeks.

"I looked for land, for an end to the sea,   140
and found fourteen peaks rising from the water.
The ship ran aground on the Mountain of Secrets,[19]
the mountain held on to it and would not let go.

"One day and a second, the mountain held on and would not let go.
A third day and a fourth, the mountain held on and would not let go.   145
A fifth day and a sixth, the mountain held on and would not let go.

"When the seventh day arrived,
I brought out a dove and set it free.
The dove flew off, but then it returned.
It found nowhere to land, so it came back.   150

"I brought out a swallow and set it free.
The swallow flew off, but then it returned.
It found nowhere to land, so it came back.

"I brought out a crow and set it free.
The crow flew off and saw the sea ebb away,   155
it pecked, hopped around, and did not come back.

"I brought out a sacrifice to the four winds
and offered incense to the mountain peak.
I laid out seven offering bowls, and seven more,
with sweet reed, cedar, and myrtle underneath.   160

"The gods smelled the scent,
the gods smelled the sweet scent,
the gods swarmed to the sacrifice like flies.

"As soon as Belet-ili arrived,
she held up the mighty jeweled flies   165
that Anu had made to seduce her:
'Gods! I will hang these flies like beads round my neck,
to remind me of these days—I must never forget![20]

"'Now let the gods all come to the sacrifice.
Only Enlil is not welcome at the sacrifice,
because he caused the Flood, acting without counsel,   170
consigning my people to the slaughter.'

"As soon as Enlil arrived,
he saw the ship and was furious.
He grew angry with the Igigi gods:[21]
'How did this living creature escape?   175
No one was to survive the slaughter!'

"Ninurta worked his words, saying to Enlil the hero:
'Who could have done this, if not Ea?
There is nothing Ea cannot do.'   180

"Ea worked his words, saying to Enlil the hero:
'You, the hero, the sage of the gods!
How could you cause the Flood, acting without counsel?

"'Only culprits should bear the crime,
only the guilty should bear the guilt!   185
Slacken the rope so it does not snap,
or pull it taut so it does not slacken!

"'Instead of the Flood you unleashed,
lions could have come to cull humankind.
Instead of the Flood you unleashed,   190
wolves could have come to cull humankind.
Instead of the Flood you unleashed,
famine could have come to cull humankind.
Instead of the Flood you unleashed,
war could have come to cull humankind.   195

"'I did not reveal the secret of the great gods to Atra-hasis,
I only let him see a dream, where he heard the gods' secret.
Now, decide what to do with him.'

"Enlil came aboard my boat,
he took my hands and led me out,   200
he led out my wife and made her kneel by my side.
He stood between us and touched our brows, blessing us:

"'In the past, Uta-napishti was human,
now he and his wife will be like us gods!
Uta-napishti shall live far away, where the rivers rise.'   205
They took me far away and made me live where rivers rise.

"But now, what will convene the gods for your sake,
Gilgamesh, so you too can find the life that you seek?
Come, try to stay awake for six days and seven nights!"

But as soon as Gilgamesh squatted down,   210
sleep blew over him like a fog.

Uta-napishti said to her, to his wife:
"Look at that young man, who wants eternal life!
Sleep blows over him like a fog."

His wife said to him, to the faraway Uta-napishti: 215
"Touch him, let the man wake up!
By the road that he came, let him go home unharmed,
let him go back through the gate that he crossed."

Uta-napishti said to her, to his wife:
"Humans are deceitful, he too will deceive you.   220
Come, bake his daily bread and set it by his head,
and make a mark on the wall for each day he sleeps."

She baked his daily bread and set it by his head,
and made a mark on the wall for each day he slept.

His first bread was all dried out,   225
the second was tough as leather,
the third had some moisture left,
the fourth had turned white,
the fifth was showing spots,
the sixth was still fresh
and the seventh was on the coals   230
when he touched and woke up the man.

Gilgamesh said to him, to the faraway Uta-napishti:
"Sleep seems to have seized me a moment,
but straight away you touched and woke me!"

Uta-napishti said to him, to Gilgamesh:
"Come, Gilgamesh, count out your daily bread,   235
and realize how long you slept.

"Your first bread is all dried out,
the second is tough as leather,

the third has some moisture left,
the fourth has turned white,
the fifth is showing spots,   240
the sixth is still fresh
and the seventh was on the coals
when you woke up."

Gilgamesh said to him, to Uta-napishti:
"How can I go on, Uta-napishti? Where should I go?
The Thief of Life has a hold on my heart.
Death is sitting in my bedroom,   245
and wherever I turn, there too is death."

Uta-napishti said to him, to the boatman Ur-shanabi:
"Ur-shanabi! May the dock disown you, the ferry detest you!
You, who used to walk this shore, shall long for it.

"The man you led here,   250
whose body is covered with filthy hair,
whose beauty is spoiled by dirty pelts:

"Take him, Ur-shanabi, bring him to the bathtub.
Wash his hair with water, as clean as it can be,
take off those pelts and throw them in the sea.   255

"Bathe his beautiful body!
Find a new scarf for his head,
give him a royal mantle worthy of his dignity.

"Until he arrives home in his city,
until he reaches the end of his road,   260
the mantle will stay new and unblemished."

Ur-shanabi took him and brought him to the bathtub.
He washed his hair with water, as clean as it could be,
he took off the pelts and threw them in the sea.

He bathed his beautiful body, 265
found a new scarf for his head,
and gave him a royal mantle worthy of his dignity.

Until he arrived home in his city,
until he reached the end of his road,
the mantle would stay new and unblemished. 270

Gilgamesh and Ur-shanabi boarded the boat,
they launched the ferry and sailed away.

His wife said to him, to the faraway Uta-napishti:
"Gilgamesh struggled and strained to come here,
and what did you give him to bring back home?" 275

Then Gilgamesh raised the punting pole
and brought the boat back to shore.

Uta-napishti said to him, to Gilgamesh:
"Gilgamesh, you struggled and strained to come here,
and what did I give you to bring back home? 280

"I will tell you a secret, Gilgamesh,
and reveal what the gods keep hidden.

"There is a plant that looks like a thistle,
whose thorns, like a wild rose, hurt your hands.
If you can find and pluck this plant, 285
you will win back your life force."

When Gilgamesh heard this,
he dug a shaft down to the Apsû ·   ·
He tied heavy stones to his feet,
they pulled him down to the Apsû ·   · 290

He grasped and plucked the plant, it hurt his hand,
then he cut the heavy stones from his feet
and the sea threw him back on the beach.

Gilgamesh said to him, to the boatman Ur-shanabi:
"Ur-shanabi, this is the plant of the pulsing heart,   295
the man who finds it will win back his life force.

"I will bring it home to Uruk the Sheepfold
and try it out, I will make an old man eat from it.
If the old man grows young again,
I will eat it too, and return to my youth."   300

They stopped to eat after a hundred miles,
they pitched camp after two hundred miles more.
Gilgamesh found a pool with cool water,
he went down to swim in the pool.

A snake smelled the scent of the plant,   305
it slid up in silence, it snatched it away
and shed its skin as it slithered back.

Then Gilgamesh sat down crying,
tears streaming down his cheeks.
·   · and said to the boatman Ur-shanabi: 310

"Ur-shanabi, I have worn out my arms—and for whom?
For whom did I spill the blood of my heart?
I got my reward, but not for myself,
I gave it instead to this underground lion!

"Now all around us the tide has been rising.   315
When I dug the shaft, I threw away the tools.
And if I went back, how could I find the same spot?
I even left the boat on the beach."

They stopped to eat after a hundred miles,
they pitched camp after two hundred miles more.   320
They arrived at Uruk the Sheepfold,
and Gilgamesh said to him, to Ur-shanabi:

"Climb the wall of Uruk, Ur-shanabi! Walk its length.
Survey the foundation, study the brickwork.
There—is it not made of oven-baked bricks?   325
Did the Seven Sages not lay its cornerstone?

"Look: Two thousand acres for the city,
two thousand acres for the orchards,
two thousand acres for the pits of clay,
and one thousand acres for the temple of Ishtar.
Seven thousand acres is the size of Uruk."

TABLET XII

Had I only left

The eleven Tablets of the epic were accompanied by a twelfth, an appendix translated directly from an older Sumerian tale. Tablet XII tells a separate story about the same characters, throwing another light on the theme of death. Here, Enkidu is alive again, apparently a father and a widower.

"Had I only left the ball with the carpenter today!
His wife is like my mother—had I only left it there.
His daughter is like my sister—had I only left it there.
For today my ball fell down to the underworld,
today my bat fell down to the underworld."[22]   5

Enkidu answered Gilgamesh:
"My lord, why do you weep? Why is your heart troubled?
Today, I will fetch your ball from the underworld myself,
I will fetch your bat from the underworld myself."

Gilgamesh answered Enkidu: 10
"If you are to descend to the underworld,
you must pay attention to my instructions!

"You must not wear clean clothes,
for they will see that you are a stranger.
You must not smear yourself with sweet oil,   15
for they will gather around the scent.
You must not throw a stick through the underworld,
for you will be surrounded by those it strikes.
You must not carry a cudgel in your hand,
for the spirits will tremble before you.   20

"You must not wear sandals on your feet,
you must not raise your voice in the underworld.
You must not kiss the wife you love,
you must not hit the wife you hate.
You must not kiss the son you love,   25
you must not hit the son you hate,
lest the outcry of the underworld overwhelm you!

"Ereshkigal is lying down, lying down, lying down.
Her pale shoulders are uncovered,
her bare breasts sag like jars of stone."   30

Enkidu descended to the underworld,
but did not heed Gilgamesh's instructions.

He wore clean clothes,
and they saw that he was a stranger.
He smeared himself with sweet oil,   35
and they gathered around the scent.
He threw a stick through the underworld,
and he was surrounded by those it struck.
He carried a cudgel in his hand,
and the spirits trembled before him.   40

He wore sandals on his feet,
he raised his voice in the underworld.
He kissed the wife he loved,
he hit the wife he hated.
He kissed the son he loved,   45
he hit the son he hated,
and the outcry of the underworld overwhelmed him.

Ereshkigal was lying down, lying down, lying down.
Her pale shoulders were uncovered,
her bare breasts sagged like jars of stone.   50

Then Enkidu could not come back up from the underworld.
He was not taken by the God of Death, or by a demon,
he was taken by the underworld.
He was not taken by the merciless bailiff of Nergal,
he was taken by the underworld.
He did not fall in the field where men do battle,
he was taken by the underworld.

Then King Gilgamesh, son of Ninsun,   55
went off alone, weeping for his servant Enkidu,
to the Temple of the Mountain, home of Enlil.

"Father Enlil, today my ball fell down to the underworld,
today my bat fell down to the underworld.
Enkidu, who went down to get it, was taken by the underworld.

"He was not taken by the God of Death, or by a demon,   60
he was taken by the underworld.
He was not taken by the merciless bailiff of Nergal,
he was taken by the underworld.
He did not fall in the field where men do battle,
he was taken by the underworld."

But Father Enlil did not answer,
so he went alone to Ur, the home of Sîn:

"Father Sîn, today my ball fell down to the underworld,   65
today my bat fell down to the underworld.
Enkidu, who went down to get it, was taken by the underworld.

"He was not taken by the God of Death, or by a demon,
he was taken by the underworld.
He was not taken by the merciless bailiff of Nergal,
he was taken by the underworld.
He did not fall in the field where men do battle,   70
he was taken by the underworld."

But Father Sîn did not answer,
so he went alone to Eridu, the home of Ea:

"Father Ea, today my ball fell down to the underworld,
today my bat fell down to the underworld.
Enkidu, who went down to get it, was taken by the underworld.   75

"He was not taken by the God of Death, or by a demon,
he was taken by the underworld.
He was not taken by the merciless bailiff of Nergal,
he was taken by the underworld.
He did not fall in the field where men do battle,
he was taken by the underworld."

Father Ea listened to his prayer,
and said to the young hero Shamash: 80
"Young hero Shamash, son of Ningal, ·   ·
if you can open a hole to the underworld,
you can bring Enkidu's spirit back, like a ghost!"

The young hero Shamash, son of Ningal, ·   ·   85
listened to the words of Father Ea.
He opened a hole to the underworld
and brought Enkidu's spirit back, like a ghost.

They hugged, they kissed,
they talked, they asked:

"Tell me, my friend, tell me, my friend,   90
tell me the laws of the underworld you saw!"

"I will not, my friend, I will not.
For if I tell you the laws of the underworld I saw,
you would break down crying!"
"So let me break down crying!"   95

"My friend, my penis, which you touched to please your heart,
is being eaten by a moth, like a threadbare cloth.
My friend, my crotch, which you touched to please your heart,
is filled with dust, like a crack in the ground."

"Woe," cried the king, and threw himself in the dust.   100
"Woe," cried Gilgamesh, and threw himself in the dust.

"Did you see the man with one son?"[23]
"I saw him. He weeps bitterly, for his house belongs to the creditor."

"Did you see the man with two sons?"
"I saw him. He sits eating bread on top of two bricks."   105

"Did you see the man with three sons?"
"I saw him. He drinks water from the saddlebag."

"Did you see the man with four sons?"
"I saw him. He is as happy as if he owned a team of donkeys."

"Did you see the man with five sons?"   110
"I saw him. His hand is as skilled as an expert scribe's;
he can go straight into the palace."

"Did you see the man with six sons?"
"I saw him. He is as happy as a plowman."

"Did you see the man with seven sons?"   115
"I saw him. He sits on a throne with the lower gods,
listening to the proceedings of the court."

"Did you see the eunuch of the palace?"
"I saw him. He is propped in the corner like a fine banner,
like a ·   ."

"Did you see the woman who never gave birth?"[24]   273–74
"I saw her." "How does she fare?"
"She is thrown aside like a broken pot,
no man finds joy in her."

"Did you see the young man who never   275–76
unclasped his wife's underclothes?"
"I saw him." "How does he fare?"
"He ties endless ropes, weeping."

"Did you see the young woman who never   277–78
unclasped her husband's underclothes?"
"I saw her." "How does she fare?"
"She ties endless mats of reed, weeping."

"Did you see the man eaten by a lion?"   279–80
"I saw him." "How does he fare?"
"He cries bitterly: 'My hand! My foot!'"

"Did you see the man who fell from a roof?"   281–82
"I saw him." "How does he fare?"
"They cannot fix his broken bones."

"Did you see the man who was drowned by the Storm
    God?"   283–84
"I saw him." "How does he fare?"
"He twitches like an ox as maggots eat him."

"Did you see the man who suffered from leprosy?"   285–86
"I saw him." "How does he fare?"
"His food is kept apart, his water is kept apart.
He eats uprooted grass, he drinks bitter water.
He lives outside the city."

"Did you see the man who did not pay heed   295–96
to the words of his father and mother?"
"I saw him." "How does he fare?"
"He constantly cries out: 'My body! My limbs!'"

"Did you see the man who was doomed   297–98
by a curse from his father and mother?"
"I saw him." "How does he fare?"
"He has no heir, his spirit is restless."

"Did you see the man who profaned the name of his god?"   299–300
"I saw him." "How does he fare?"
"His ghost eats bitter bread and drinks bitter water."

"Did you see the stillborn babies   303–4
who did not even know their name?"
"I saw them." "How do they fare?"
"They eat honey and ghee
at tables of gold and silver."

"Did you see the man who burned to death?"   305–6
"I did not see him. His ghost is not there,
his smoke went up to the skies."[25]

STANDARD BABYLONIAN VERSION
"Did you see the man who was impaled on a mooring pole?"   144
"I saw him. His poor mother and father!   145
When a peg is pulled out, he wanders about."

"Did you see the man who died a natural death?"
"I saw him. He lies on the bed of gods, drinking pure water."

"Did you see the man who was killed in battle?"
"I saw him. His father and mother hold up his head,
his wife weeps for him."

"Did you see the man who was left unburied in the steppe?" 150
"I saw him. His ghost has no rest in the underworld."

"Did you see the man who has no one to give him offerings?"
"I saw him. He eats scraps from the pot,
and breadcrumbs strewn in the streets."

ESSAYS

A Poem for the Ages

Toward the end of his story, Gilgamesh steps out, dazzled by the light after many miles of darkness, into the garden of the gods. Here grow the most curious trees. On their branches hang precious stones: leaves of lapis lazuli, grapes of carnelian, thorns of crystal. Gilgamesh wanders among them, bewildered by their splendor. In disbelief, he reaches out to touch a carob, finding it made of agate and hematite. Then the epic becomes fragmentary, as it so often does. When it is again readable our hero has moved on, relentless in his pursuit of what he hopes to find beyond the garden: immortality. We are left with the brief image of Gilgamesh touching the fruit, wondering about the odd gem he has stumbled upon, perhaps turning it this way and that to admire the otherworldly light that shines on its surface.

Gilgamesh's wonder is an apt analogue for what many modern readers feel when they first come across his story. They are dazzled, surprised, and confused. What is this gem, how was it made, where does it come from? But after the initial wonder, they are often forced, like the hero himself, to hurry on, pressed by the pursuits of everyday life. In the essays that follow I try to stop readers in their tracks, offering them a chance to spend a little more time turning the text this way and that, as I guide them through the epic and its world, helping them to make more sense of what seems at first mere marvel and mystery.

Each of these essays builds on vast amounts of Assyriological scholarship: the readings I present draw on and summarize the long labor of philologists who have read, reconstructed, and translated the text, traced its patterns, and thrown light on its details. An introductory book like mine cannot hope to mention all the scholars who deserve credit for their work on *Gilgamesh*—the notes would swell to the size of shelves—so the reader must bear in mind that this book is but the tip of an academic iceberg, a brief glimpse into the world of Assyriology.[1]

That world is worth stepping into, but it is also in dire need of funding and attention. Philological departments worldwide are being shut down or reduced, and with them precious insights into the past and its poetry are disappearing.² As an introduction to *Gilgamesh*, these essays are naturally and joyously indebted to the discipline that made it possible for me to write a book on *Gilgamesh*, for without philology, ancient texts would remain lifeless and confounding. This would be a disastrous loss.

"It has torn through time like a literary fireball, full of passion and despair."³ That is how the novelist Naja Marie Aidt sums up the history of the epic. Its ability to tear through time makes *Gilgamesh* a prime example of what is known as world literature, books that circulate across cultures and centuries.⁴ *Gilgamesh* has done so exceptionally well, making it an ideal starting point for understanding how literature moves through time—and how it changes with time.

Over the past century, *Gilgamesh* has been read, retold, and reimagined in countless ways. It has been reworked into novels, plays, paintings, operas, sonnets, comic books, and anime.⁵ There are two bands and three albums named after the hero, ranging from heavy metal to jazz fusion. A restaurant in London and a crater on Ganymede share his name. Gilgamesh is a recurring character in the *Final Fantasy* video-game universe, and he fights alongside Thor in the Marvel comics. Stanislav Lem, sci-fi author of *Solaris* fame, reviewed a nonexistent book called *Gigamesh* as a parody of James Joyce's *Ulysses*. A Japanese softcore porn show bore the title *Gilgamesh Night*—and the list goes on.

In *Batman: The Animated Series*, we learn that the villainous Bane was a test subject in *Project Gilgamesh*, a secret research project to develop a drug that would turn its subjects into super-soldiers. In a bizarre instance of life imitating art, "Project Gilgamesh" is now used as a catchword for experimental strands of bioengineering that aim to radically expand the human lifespan, honoring the hero's quest for immortality.⁶ And again, the list goes on.

Gilgamesh is also the name of a geolocation software developed by the U.S. National Security Agency (NSA) that is used to guide drones to their victims. Placed on the drone's wing, the Gilgamesh equipment acts as a fake cell tower. When the target's mobile phone tries to connect with the signal, the software latches on to the connection and uses it to lead the drone to its destination.⁷ I have no idea what drove NSA engineers to name so horrid a device after Gilgamesh (did they run out of Greek heroes?), but once more, the list goes on.

With so wide a range of adaptations, we may well ask what it is about the epic that makes it so appealing to modern readers. One reason is that it is displaced in time: it feels both old and new, an ancient classic as well as an exciting discovery. The epic is a found foundation. It is found in the sense that, unlike other classics, it became widely available relatively recently, so it has not been weighed down by centuries of interpretation. New readers can still discover it for themselves and make up their own minds about it. But it is also foundational, an ancient text from the bottommost layers of history. When the world around us seems hopelessly caught in crisis after crisis, shaken by endless waves of turmoil, returning to the deepest foundation of culture can offer a sense of solidity and reassurance.

The epic's foundational role is one reason why it is so often dubbed "the world's first poem" or "the oldest epic." The notion has clung to the text with dogged determination, but it is simply wrong. A typical claim is that *Gilgamesh* is four thousand years old, and although its earliest forerunners do date to the early second millennium BCE, the Standard Babylonian version that most people read today is about a millennium younger. But even granting the anachronism, *Gilgamesh* is still not the first anything. The oldest-known poems date to some six centuries before the earliest versions of Gilgamesh, and depending on how we define an epic, *Atra-hasis* or the *Cycle of Aratta* are likelier candidates to be the first epic.[8]

But although *Gilgamesh* may not be the *first* poem, it is still unbelievably old. Following its literary history is like diving into a rabbit hole of giddying depths.[9] We do not know when stories about Gilgamesh first began to circulate, but the earliest mention of his name dates to the twenty-first century BCE. Some two centuries later, an unknown hand crafted the stories about him into an epic. For the next two millennia, the epic would be retold and revised, expanded and adapted, memorized by schoolchildren and studied by the scholars at King Ashurbanipal's library. But over the course of the first millennium BCE, Ashurbanipal's empire crumbled, the Akkadian language died out, and the cuneiform tradition became obsolete. Sometime around 130 BCE, a man named Bel-ahhe-usur made the last known cuneiform copy of *Gilgamesh,* and soon the epic would be all but forgotten. Today, Bel-ahhe-usur seems like a figure of the ancient past, but he may actually be closer in time to us than to the person who first recited a story about Gilgamesh.

The distance in time can be dizzying to contemplate. The Old Babylonian version of *Gilgamesh* is about twice as old as Virgil's *Aeneid* or Ovid's

Metamorphoses. But the dizziness grows more acute when we consider that even for the Babylonians, Gilgamesh was a figure of great antiquity. According to a historical chronicle known as the *Sumerian King List,* Gilgamesh lived around 7800 BCE.[10] This is certainly not true (if he ever lived, it would have been much later), but it does show that even four thousand years ago, Gilgamesh was thought to have lived more than four thousand years before that.

As if this were not enough, Gilgamesh himself travels even farther back in time, to meet what was even for *him* a figure of great antiquity: Uta-napishti. According to the *Sumerian King List,* the Flood took place more than twenty-five thousand years before Gilgamesh became king, that is, thirty-five thousand years ago from now. Uta-napishti belonged to Gilgamesh's ancient history, just as Gilgamesh belonged to Ashurbanipal's ancient history, Ashurbanipal to Bel-ahhe-usur's and Bel-ahhe-usur to ours.

When Gilgamesh meets Uta-napishti, we might be forgiven for thinking that we have at last reached the oldest past possible. But the epic makes us think again. Uta-napishti begins his story with the words:

> You know the city of Shuruppak,
> the city that lies on the banks of the Euphrates.
> That city was old, and the great gods were there
> when their hearts led them to unleash the Flood.[11]

"That city was old": *ālu šû labir* in Akkadian. With three short words, Uta-napishti hints at the long stretch of time before even his ancient lifetime. When it comes to *Gilgamesh,* there is always an older story.

The history of the epic begins in total darkness. The earliest preserved versions of the story probably date to the reign of Shulgi (r. 2094–2047 BCE), a Sumerian king who boasted of being able to read, write, and compose poetry. Shulgi proclaimed himself brother to Gilgamesh, and perhaps it was the king's vanity that prompted the scholars at his court to copy out poems about the hero.[12] But Gilgamesh must already have been famous for the king to want to claim him as his brother, so stories about the hero must have been circulating for some time—perhaps for decades, perhaps for centuries.

A related question is whether there ever was a historical Gilgamesh, whose exploits were embellished to reach the epic proportions we know today.[13] Again, it is impossible to say. The only shred of evidence we have are two alabaster vases that bear the name of King Enmebaragesi, who in a Sumerian tale is the father of Gilgamesh's enemy Akka. Enmebaragesi *may* have been a real person, but even if he were, it would not prove that Gilgamesh was real too.[14] It is fully possible that the literary tradition mixed stories based on actual events with pure invention. But if Gilgamesh did exist, he probably lived in what is known as the Early Dynastic period, in the first centuries of the third millennium BCE.

The Sumerian stories about Gilgamesh were not a single composition but a cycle of five poems. The first, part of which was excerpted to become Tablet XII in the Standard Babylonian version of *Gilgamesh*, tells of Enkidu's journey to the netherworld and what he found there—though in the Sumerian version he returns not as a ghost but as a living body. The second tells of Gilgamesh and Enkidu's encounter with Humbaba (or Huwawa, as he is called there), and the third of their battle with the Bull of Heaven. The fourth recounts Gilgamesh's confrontation with Akka, king of Kish, and the fifth describes Gilgamesh's death and funeral. Each poem preserves an interlinked piece of the hero's mythology, but they are separate compositions. The Gilgamesh cycle was in turn part of a larger group of stories about a heroic dynasty in Uruk that also included tales about Lugalbanda and Enmerkar, and their epic struggle against the rival city of Aratta.[15]

The Sumerian stories about Gilgamesh were studied in the schools of the Old Babylonian period, in the early second millennium BCE.[16] At the time, Sumerian had died out as a vernacular spoken language, becoming instead a learned language of scholarship and religious ritual, much like Latin was later to be in Europe. The schools taught the future priests and civil servants how to read cuneiform and understand Sumerian, as well as mathematics, law, and administration. It is because the Old Babylonian students were made to write out copy after copy of the Sumerian poems that they survive today: the schools kept the old tradition alive. But when the curriculum was restructured in the sixteenth century BCE, the stories about the kings of Uruk were left out, consigning them to oblivion.[17]

The Sumerian version might have died out, but Gilgamesh's story survived, now in an Akkadian version. The oldest manuscripts of the Akkadian *Gilgamesh* also date to the Old Babylonian period, and it appears that, unlike the five Sumerian poems, the Akkadian version was a single epic, stitching the stories about Gilgamesh into one connected tale.[18] As noted by

Jeffrey Tigay, the author of a pioneering study on *Gilgamesh*'s historical development, two main changes separate the Akkadian story from its Sumerian forerunners.[19] In the Sumerian poems, Enkidu had been Gilgamesh's servant, but in the Akkadian he became his intimate friend. At the same time, Gilgamesh's fear of death was given a far more central position in the Akkadian story. The two changes are related: Gilgamesh's love for Enkidu is matched by his grief at Enkidu's death, leading to his desperate attempt to gain eternal life. In the Old Babylonian epic, Gilgamesh's story snaps into focus as a tale of love and loss.

By the fourteenth century BCE, the Akkadian language had become an international lingua franca, much like English today. Scribes throughout the ancient Near East sought to learn Akkadian and cuneiform, which involved learning about the cultural baggage that came with them.[20] *Gilgamesh* was part of that baggage, so copies of the epic have been found far afield, in what are now Syria, Israel, and Turkey. The epic was also translated into Hittite and Hurrian, the two main languages of ancient Anatolia, showing that interest in the epic went beyond the practical need to learn Akkadian.

But at that time the epic did not have a fixed form. Its development is not a simple sequence of improvement after improvement; rather, *Gilgamesh* existed in many different versions at any one time, all of which told the same basic story, but each in its own way. One manuscript even replaces the names of Gilgamesh and Enkidu with those of the gods Sîn and Ea, and we do not know why.[21]

From this mess of conflicting variants, at the end of the second millennium there emerged the Standard Babylonian version. Around the eleventh century BCE, cuneiform scholarship underwent a major overhaul. Texts that had previously been in flux, circulating in several conflicting versions, were brought together, standardized, and arranged into a fixed sequence of Tablets.[22] The Babylonian medical author Esagil-kin-apli described his work as the "weaving anew of tangled threads," and the metaphor perfectly applies to *Gilgamesh* as well.[23] The creator of the Standard Babylonian version rewove the old threads of the story into a form that would remain unchanged for the next millennium.[24]

Some eight centuries had passed since the Old Babylonian version was composed, and the Akkadian language had changed substantially. The poem was revised into the literary language we now call Standard Babylonian, which would probably have sounded to Babylonian audiences much like Shakespeare sounds to modern theatergoers: poetic and old-fashioned, but not unintelligible. As part of the process, the names of some characters changed as well: Huwawa became Humbaba, Shamkatum became Shamhat, Sursunabu became Ur-shanabi.

The epic was also made longer, but mainly through the addition of long word-for-word repetitions.[25] The Old Babylonian version is generally snappier: shorter, to the point, and much less repetitive. When the Old Babylonian version describes the same situation more than once, it often adds subtle changes for the sake of variation. But the Standard Babylonian version bulldozed that variation into a stiffer, more monotonous form, padding the text with long repeated sequences.

What the new version lost in pace it made up for in depth, as the epic became far more complex and philosophical. The Old Babylonian version is a straightforward tale of heroic adventure and loss. To this the Standard Babylonian version added the prologue that opens the epic and the story of the Flood that closes it, giving the epic a focus on self-reflection, storytelling, and wisdom. The epic grew more pessimistic, but also more profound. What had been a romantic legend became a philosophical tragedy.[26]

In its Standard Babylonian version, *Gilgamesh* went on to become one of the most famous stories of the cuneiform world: second only to *Enuma Elish*, the Babylonian myth of creation, *Gilgamesh* was the most frequently copied cuneiform poem.[27] We can safely assume that any Babylonian scholar worth his salt would have been able to recite favorite lines of *Gilgamesh* by heart. At the height of its fame, the epic even became a model for the most powerful man the ancient world had ever seen: King Sargon II, emperor of Assyria.

In the Assyrian galleries of the Louvre Museum stands a relief of a muscular man with bulging eyes, holding a lion to his chest.[28] The immediate reaction most people have when they see him is, "What a tiny lion." The lion does seem strangely small, barely the width of the man's chest. But the lion is perfectly lion-sized. It's the man who is very big.

The relief comes from the royal palace in the city of Dur-Sharrukin, modern Khorsabad. It was built as the new capital of the Assyrian Empire during the reign of Sargon II (r. 721–705 BCE). Under Sargon's rule, Assyria had become an enormous empire, reaching from its heartland in northern

Iraq into Turkey, Jordan, Iran, and the Arabian Peninsula.[29] Sargon named the new capital after himself—Dur-Sharrukin means "Sargon's Fort"—and planned the city with geometrical perfection. The royal palace at the center of the city was decorated with splendid reliefs, including that of the man holding a lion.

In the nineteenth century, the relief was excavated by Paul-Émile Botta and brought to Paris. While many scholars assumed that it represented Gilgamesh, it bears no inscription that might prove its identity, so in the Louvre catalogue the relief is simply titled "Hero overpowering a lion." But the philologist Amar Annus noticed that the relief was, in fact, eighteen feet tall, very near Gilgamesh's height as given in the epic. Close to that relief stood another, also of a man holding a lion, but he is shorter and stouter than the first: this must be Enkidu.[30] Separated by death, the two heroes were reunited in Sargon's palace and brought together again in the Louvre. The deceptively small lions only emphasize how gigantic the heroes were. Even today, visitors are daunted by Gilgamesh's monstrous height, and taken aback by his stone-stiff eyes.

The relief shows that ancient kings like Sargon wanted to be associated with Gilgamesh. Gilgamesh may have been a tyrannical and unjust ruler, but he was also remembered as a formidable warrior. When the Assyrian kings recounted their military triumphs, inscribing them on the walls of their palaces, they worked in allusions to legendary heroes, including Gilgamesh, thus subtly comparing themselves to these famous figures.[31] Sargon's account of his campaign against the land of Urartu (now eastern Turkey) is the pinnacle of Assyrian royal literature, vividly describing the army's march through the mountains. At times it seems as if Sargon is fighting not the people of Urartu but the landscape itself: the mountains rise up like swords and spears to oppose his advance, including Mount Simirriu, "whose topmost peaks touch the skies, and whose roots reach down to the netherworld depths."[32] An Assyrian audience would probably have been reminded of the Twin Peaks in *Gilgamesh*, which are described in similar terms, and the implication is clear—Sargon faced dangers no less epic than his legendary predecessor did.

Despite its opulence, Dur-Sharrukin was abandoned by the king's court shortly after it was finished. In 705, Sargon died in battle, and the army was unable to recover his corpse. The Assyrian court was thrown into chaos, and the shock would plague the reign of his successors for decades to come.[33]

Sargon's son Sennacherib moved the capital to nearby Nineveh, and modern scholars have been puzzled by that decision. After all, Dur-Sharrukin was a brand-new city built expressly to house the Assyrian court, so why abandon it? According to an intriguing theory put forth by the Assyriologist Eckart Frahm, a tablet of *Gilgamesh* may hold the answer.[34]

The tablet in question is a manuscript of Tablet XII, copied by Nabu-zuqup-kenu, a top-ranked scholar at Sargon's court and one of the most accomplished cuneiform scribes who ever lived. A few weeks after Sargon's dramatic death, Nabu-zuqup-kenu copied out Tablet XII, including its long description of the afterlife, perhaps as a way of meditating on the traumatic event. What he might have been looking for comes at the end of the Tablet. Gilgamesh asks Enkidu about the man killed in battle, and Enkidu replies: "His father and mother hold up his head, his wife weeps for him." Gilgamesh asks about the man left unburied: "His ghost has no rest in the underworld." Gilgamesh asks about the man who cannot be provided with funerary offerings: "He eats scraps from the pot and breadcrumbs strewn in the streets."[35]

Nabu-zuqup-kenu must have been stunned. The text describes Sargon's fate with eerie precision. Because the king's corpse could not be recovered, his spirit could not be provided with funerary offerings. A miserable destiny lay in store for him: his ghost was to be forever restless and hungry, his death rewarded only by the tears of his widow. But for Nabu-zuqup-kenu, Sargon's fate would also have introduced an acute practical problem. A restless ghost meant trouble under the best of circumstances, but Sargon was no ordinary man. This may have been one reason why Dur-Sharrukin was abandoned: Sargon's son could not hold court in a palace plagued by the hungry and furious spirit of a once mighty emperor.

Despite the move, Sargon's death left his descendants with plenty of other problems to deal with. His successors lived through one of the most turbulent periods in Mesopotamian history.[36] The empire kept growing larger, but its kings grew no safer. Sargon's son Sennacherib (r. 705–681) was assassinated in a court conspiracy, and his grandson Esarhaddon (r. 681–669) suffered from a terrible disease throughout his life. Increasingly paranoid, Esarhaddon spent the last years of his reign purging the court of suspected conspirators before dividing the empire between his sons: Ashurbanipal would rule Assyria, Shamash-shum-ukin would rule Babylonia. But tension flared up between the two brothers, culminating in a catastrophic civil war in which Shamash-shum-ukin was defeated and Babylon brought back under Assyrian rule.

Ashurbanipal took great interest in literature, claiming not only that he could read and write (which may well have been true) but also that he was an accomplished scholar and poet (which he certainly was not).[37] The king used the war with his brother as an occasion to assemble an enormous library in Nineveh. Plundering the defeated cities in Babylonia, his army sent all tablets worthy of the king's interest to the capital.[38] The king's love of lore led to the creation of what was at the time the world's largest library, the Alexandria of its day: H. G. Wells called it "the most precious source of historical material in the world."[39] With thousands of tablets carefully copied by expert scholars, the library included omen collections, ritual instructions, astronomy, astrology, lexicography, mathematics, medicine, and epic poetry. In a postscript added to many of the library's tablets, Ashurbanipal claimed to have read and copied all the texts himself.[40]

The best-written manuscripts of *Gilgamesh* come from this library; they complement those that came out of the ancient school system, where would-be scribes were made to copy literary texts so as to learn cuneiform and Akkadian grammar.[41] There are more school texts than there are library copies, but the school texts are often full of blunders. In the first millennium BCE, scribal education had two phases, basic and advanced, and *Gilgamesh* was read in both. In the basic phase, students read small selections from the start of the epic to whet their appetite for learning. The opening description of Gilgamesh, the famous king who "discovered a secret, revealed a hidden matter, and brought home a story from before the Flood," fostered a love of ancient and secret knowledge that became part of the students' budding sense of scholarly identity.[42]

The second phase was reserved for students who would go on to become true scholars, not mere bureaucrats in the empire's civil service. In this phase, *Gilgamesh* was studied in greater detail, and again it served an important ideological purpose. Many scholars would go on to seek a position at the king's court, and *Gilgamesh* offers a vision of kingship that is not unreservedly positive. Kings are portrayed as necessary leaders but also as dangerous hotheads whose whims must be reined in by their advisers. The epic gives a terrifying example of what happens when royal power is unchecked by wisdom: Enlil, king of the gods, is said to have acted "without counsel" in unleashing the Flood. The disaster would have been even worse if Ea, counselor of the gods, had not warned Uta-napishti and saved humanity. We have every reason to believe that Assyrian scholars would have picked up on the moral: kingship was all well and good, but it could turn catastrophic without the counsel of wise men.[43] *Gilgamesh* explained why their job mattered.

Today we take it for granted that behind every book there is an author, but this was not always the case. The oldest-known literature is anonymous, and Akkadian poetry stayed that way for centuries: our earliest datable sources about the authors of literary works in Akkadian come from the seventh century BCE. It seems that during the height of the Assyrian Empire, the scholars began to think with new concertedness about the person behind the poem.[44] A catalogue from the library of Ashurbanipal goes through cuneiform literature work by work, attributing each one to a named author. Some attributions are correct, but many are unreliable. In the catalogue, *Gilgamesh* is said to have been written by a man named Sîn-leqi-unnenni, but the claim raises more questions than it answers.

If Sîn-leqi-unnenni existed, he probably lived around the eleventh century BCE, but the sources that credit him as the author of *Gilgamesh* were written several centuries later. It is indeed possible that his memory survived that long, carried by an oral tradition or inscribed on lost tablets, but it is also possible that he was invented by the Assyrian scholars when they became interested in authorship. (The same is true of the medical author I mentioned earlier, Esagil-kin-apli.) Either way, we know next to nothing about Sîn-leqi-unnenni. The catalogue of authors only states that he was an *āšipu*, an incantation priest: these were scholars and ritual performers whose job it was to banish evil forces and reconcile their clients with the gods they had angered.[45]

Because Sîn-leqi-unnenni would probably have lived around the time the Standard Babylonian version was composed, some Assyriologists have claimed that he was not the author of the epic but the editor of its final version. That may be, but it is not how the ancient scholars thought of him. In fact, they might not even have known that *Gilgamesh* had gone through different versions. As far as our sources suggest, to them *Gilgamesh* was a complete text, and Sîn-leqi-unnenni was its author. This is not to imply that the Assyrian and Babylonian scholars were not interested in their own past or knew nothing about it—they were keenly invested in it, but they understood it differently from the way modern historians do, and we must bear that difference in mind.

A text from the final period of cuneiform culture makes clear that at least one Babylonian scholar thought of Sîn-leqi-unnenni as not only the author of the epic's earliest version but a contemporary of Gilgamesh himself. In 165 BCE, a man named Anu-belshunu wrote a list of the most important kings and scholars of cuneiform history, and according to that list, Sîn-leqi-unnenni served as Gilgamesh's chief scholar.[46] This is certainly not true in historical terms, but it does show that according to Anu-belshunu, Sîn-leqi-unnenni was the author of the earliest story about Gilgamesh, not an editor of its later version.

Anu-belshunu placed Sîn-leqi-unnenni at the top of his list of scholars, and he had a good reason for doing so: he saw Sîn-leqi-unnenni as his own ancestor. It was common for cuneiform scholars to claim descent from a famous figure of the past, and authors in particular were often invoked as mythical ancestors.[47] The "Sîn-leqi-unnenni family," a group of priests from Uruk in the last centuries BCE, drew great pride from their association with the famous king and with the scholar who wrote down his story.

As *Gilgamesh* became a central part of Babylonian and Assyrian culture, ancient writers could refer to the epic safe in the knowledge that educated readers would pick up on the allusion.[48] Echoes of *Gilgamesh* are found in many texts, including a magical incantation to quiet a crying baby and an elegy for a woman who died in childbirth. Several omens refer to Gilgamesh, often alluding to his outstanding size. One omen collection states that the diviner should examine the heart of the sacrificed sheep: "If the heart is massive, it is an omen of Gilgamesh, who had no equal."[49]

In a spoof letter supposedly written by Gilgamesh himself, the hero threatens a neighboring ruler and demands truly outrageous amounts of tribute: vast quantities of gems and metal for the building of Enkidu's statue, to be carried by half a million donkeys and horses.[50] Gilgamesh also appears in the *Ballad of Early Rulers*, among other ancient kings who did great deeds but are no longer with us. Faced with the realization that time passes and takes even the best of men with it, the ballad concludes that the only right thing to do is to hail Nisaba, goddess of beer, and drink up.[51]

The most cunning allusion to *Gilgamesh* comes in *The Dialogue of Pessimism*. The *Dialogue* is the story of an indecisive master and his clever servant.[52] The master proposes to go to the palace, and the servant eloquently argues that this is an excellent idea. The master then changes his mind. The servant just as eloquently argues that it would have been a terrible idea anyway. The master says that he will have dinner, the servant agrees; the master says that he will not have dinner, the servant agrees again. And so on. The text ridicules just about every activity that an Assyrian gentleman could possibly contemplate: to go hunting, start a family, make offerings to the gods, commit a crime, serve one's country, become a loan shark, fall in love. Having exhausted all options, the master asks the servant what he should do. The servant proposes suicide.

The *Dialogue* repeatedly hints at *Gilgamesh*, and always with a cruel twist. When the master decides not to make an offering, the servant argues that by withholding sacrifices, "you teach your god to follow you like a dog," recalling the Flood story, in which the starving gods are also compared to dogs.[53] When the master decides not to start a family, the servant argues that a man with wife and child is "one-third sound and two-thirds a fool (*lillu*)," meaning that the family consists of one sane man and two idiots. The misogynist comment is also a jab at Gilgamesh, who is "two-thirds god (*ilu*) and one-third human." The part of him that is not a man is flipped from *ilu* to *lillu*, god to fool.[54]

The servant outdoes himself in spite when the master decides not to serve his country. Why should he, the servant asks, when our lives and achievements come to naught anyway. "Climb the ancient ruin mounds and walk around, look at the skulls of the poor and the great. Which of them did evil and which great things?" The servant here hints at the opening lines of *Gilgamesh*: "Climb the wall of Uruk, walk its length . . ."[55] In the epic, the walls represent the grand achievements by which humans may gain a kind of immortality, transcending time by the greatness of their deeds. The *Dialogue* disagrees: as the servant sees it, even the greatest monument will one day be a ruin, and the greatest king a hollow skull.[56]

For a while, it seemed that the poetic achievement of *Gilgamesh* would defy the servant's pessimism. The epic was copied for century after century, passing the memory of its hero on to new generations of scholars and schoolchildren. But by the end of the first millennium BCE, time had caught up with it. The Akkadian language was dead and the once mighty wall of Uruk had become exactly the ruin mound prophesized by the servant. Gilgamesh himself was all but forgotten, and the *Dialogue,* it seemed, had been proven right. But then the tables turned again.

The fortunes of the epic have always been closely tied to the cuneiform script. In the ancient world, the epic traveled to Turkey, Israel, and Syria, but at no point did it move beyond what we might call the cuneiform cosmopolis—the group of scribes who, dispersed across the Middle East, could communicate with one another in cuneiform. *Gilgamesh* was translated into other languages, but as far as we know not into other writing systems: it remained throughout a cuneiform text.[57] So when cuneiform died, the epic died with it. Some modern scholars have tried to show that the story continued to be told after the death of cuneiform, but no convincing link has been found.[58] The cuneiform world had provided the epic with an infrastructure of circulation and cultural authority, and Gilgamesh's fame could not survive without it.

After the disappearance of cuneiform, only garbled traces of the epic remain. The Roman writer Aelian tells the story of Gilgamos, an ancient Babylonian king whose mother was held captive in a tower. She threw the infant out of the window, but he was rescued by an eagle—a story entirely unrelated to the Babylonian epic. Gilgamesh also appears in the apocryphal *Book of Giants,* where he is an evil monster created by the fallen angels, and as the demon Jiljamish in the Arabic incantations of Jalal al-Din al-Suyuti. In these faint echoes, Gilgamesh is remembered either as an ancient king or as an enormous and therefore evil creature, but no other aspect of the epic survived.[59]

One of the most pressing questions about the epic's afterlife is whether it had any influence on the Hebrew Bible or the Homeric epics. Tablet XI is of course remarkably similar to the biblical story of the Flood, and various other parallels and allusions to *Gilgamesh,* as well as other works of Babylonian literature, have been detected throughout the Hebrew Bible.[60] Copies of *Gilgamesh* have been found at Megiddo, so the scribes of ancient Canaan clearly knew of it—if not always firsthand, then through the scribal community at Ugarit to the north, which was well acquainted with cuneiform literature. Perhaps an oral account of the Flood also circulated across the ancient world, one that may well have reached the Hebrew scribes irrespective of its cuneiform versions. However it circulated, the story of the Flood was not simply lifted from *Gilgamesh* and dumped into Genesis: the two texts reworked the same basic plot for their own ends. The Hebrew Bible made the Flood a story of human sin and subsequent covenant with God, while cuneiform works like *Atra-hasis* and *Gilgamesh* used it to explain the origin of omens and the necessity of death.

The question of whether *Gilgamesh* influenced the *Iliad* and the *Odyssey* is likewise unclear.[61] The friendship between Achilles and Patroclus resembles that between Gilgamesh and Enkidu in many ways, and Odysseus's journey to the underworld has several parallels in *Gilgamesh.* But does that mean that the Homeric bards heard *Gilgamesh* directly, or did stock tropes of epic poetry make their way from Nineveh to Homer's Smyrna without direct contact? Scholars have long been divided on the issue, but personally I lean toward the latter: the similarities seem to me too vague to prove a link, though I would love to be convinced otherwise. But even if *Gilgamesh* and the Homeric epics were composed independently, that does not mean that one cannot compare them—on the contrary, I recommend it.

Even if Greek poets did draw on *Gilgamesh,* the influence would soon have become invisible to ancient audiences. Readers of the *Iliad* in fifth-century Athens knew nothing of *Gilgamesh* and would not have recognized an allusion to it. The confused glimpses in Aelian and al-Suyuti could easily have been all we knew about Gilgamesh, had it not been for the serendipitous survival of the clay tablets. Just as it took the death of cuneiform to put an end to *Gilgamesh*'s fame, it took the rediscovery of the script to bring it back. This was no easy task, but when cuneiform was deciphered, the epic soon followed.

The rediscovery of *Gilgamesh* stunned Victorian Britain. George Smith, assistant curator at the British Museum, came upon fragments of the epic in 1872, and immediately suspected that the story resembled the biblical account of the Flood. The tablet was encrusted with "a thick whitish lime-like deposit" and largely unreadable, so he gave it to a curator named Robert Ready to have it cleaned—but Ready went away on other business. The Egyptologist Wallis Budge tells us what happened next:

> Smith was constitutionally a highly nervous, sensitive man; and his irritation at Ready's absence knew no bounds. He thought that the tablet ought to supply a very important part of the legend; and his impatience to verify

his theory produced in him an almost incredible state of mental excitement, which grew greater as the days passed. At length Ready returned, and the tablet was given to him to clean. . . . Smith took the tablet and began to read over the lines which Ready had brought to light; and when he saw that they contained the portion of the legend he had hoped to find there, he said, "I am the first man to read that after more than two thousand years of oblivion." Setting the tablet on the table, he jumped up and rushed about the room in a great state of excitement, and, to the astonishment of those present, began to undress himself![62]

The story must be taken with a grain of salt, but if Smith really did start to take off his clothes in the British Museum, he may have been imitating Archimedes, who upon discovering the principle now named after him ran naked through the streets of Syracuse shouting "Eureka!"[63]

Naked or not, Smith was hugely excited by the discovery, and the rest of Victorian England followed suit. In these clay fragments lay the potential to either prove or disprove the historical truth of the Hebrew Bible. When Smith announced his discovery at the Society for Biblical Archaeology on December 3, 1872, he was received with cheers by the assembled scholars, and no less a figure than the sitting prime minister, William Gladstone, was in the audience. When Smith had finished his lecture, Gladstone rose and declared, "I assure you I did not come into this room for the purpose of delivering a speech," before doing exactly that.[64]

Gladstone had two things to say. First, he dashed Smith's hope that the government might provide the funds for further archaeological excavations in Iraq, appealing to the supposed British tradition of accomplishing great things through "individual effort," meaning private funding. Gladstone did offer to join the society, though, and was welcomed on the spot. But the prime minister also had another point to make. He noted that the discovery was monumental not only because of the story's parallel to the Bible but also because of the light it shed on the Homeric epics. The prime minister then launched into a panegyric on Homer—"the friend of my youth, the friend of my middle age, the friend of my old age"—that duly impressed his learned audience.

Gladstone's speech reveals something fundamental about literature: new works are always understood in relation to works we already know.

When we read a poem, we make sense of it by comparing it to poems that are more familiar to us. So from the first day of its modern life, *Gilgamesh* was read comparatively, in relation to both Homer and the Bible.[65]

While Gladstone's government was disinclined to fund further excavations, help arrived from an unlikely source. In January 1873, the *Daily Telegraph* announced that the newspaper would finance a new expedition to Iraq, so that Smith could recover more cuneiform accounts of the Flood. Improbable as the scheme may sound, it worked only too well, for when Smith uncovered a tablet of *Atra-hasis,* which also includes the story of the Flood, the *Daily Telegraph* immediately retracted its support, leaving the dig half-done. Smith would later return to Iraq for two more excavations, now more reliably funded by the British Museum, but his third trip proved fatal, and he died of dysentery in Aleppo in 1876.[66]

These were exciting times in ancient history. Archaeological excavations were uncovering a forgotten world: in the 1840s, excavations by Paul-Émile Botta and Austen Henry Layard had brought to light the magnificent ruins of the Assyrian Empire. Layard struck philological gold in 1851 when he found the library of Ashurbanipal and its treasure trove of tablets. Layard was first assisted and then succeeded as director of the excavations by Hormuzd Rassam, an Assyrian-Chaldean archaeologist who discovered the tablet that shocked Smith into undress.[67]

The wealth of material found at Nineveh gave a huge boost to the decipherment of cuneiform, which had been progressing slowly since the mid-eighteenth century. The Irish clergyman Edward Hincks worked on the tablets found by Layard and Rassam, and finally began to tease out the mysteries of cuneiform, including its complex system of multiple meanings—though Hincks's discoveries were soon plagiarized by the British officer Sir Henry Rawlinson, who would go on to claim credit for deciphering cuneiform.[68]

In 1857, the inventor Henry Fox Talbot felt confident enough in Hincks's and Rawlinson's theories to put them to the test. Rawlinson, Hincks, Talbot, and the French Orientalist Julius Oppert were asked to produce independent translations of a newly discovered inscription, under a strict injunction not to communicate with one another in any way. If they gave irreconcilable translations of the text, the proposed system allowed for too much ambiguity. On May 29, the sealed envelopes containing the translations were opened, and the Royal Asiatic Society convened to judge their similarity. To the judges' relief, they found the four translations to be sufficiently alike: cuneiform had been deciphered.[69]

The decipherment of the script was only the first step in the arduous and still ongoing process of actually reading and translating the many cuneiform tablets with which European and American museums found themselves enriched. It was this painstaking work that led to the discovery of *Gilgamesh* and the commotion it caused.

According to the historian Vybarr Cregan-Reid, one reason for the epic's dramatic reception was that it forced Victorian readers to reconsider their relation to the past.[70] Cregan-Reid argues that *Gilgamesh* was seen as unsettling in part because the Victorians were caught between two ways of thinking about time. Geological discoveries in the early nineteenth century had shown that the earth was billions of years old, but the much shorter biblical perspective, which held that the world had been created some six thousand years ago, still lingered. The discovery of *Gilgamesh* and its account of the Flood exposed the gap between the theories: the epic was older than the biblical frame of history, but younger than the geological one, pressing the sore question of how they related to each other.

Another key reason for the excitement caused by the epic was the theological questions it raised. Did the epic bolster the Bible's claim to historical truth by giving an independent account of the same event? Or did it undermine the truth of the Bible, by showing that it derived from Babylonian myth? The religious anxiety continued into the following century, igniting what became known as the "Bibel-Babel" controversy.[71] In 1902, the Assyriologist Friedrich Delitzsch gave a lecture in which he claimed that the Old Testament was not the true word of God, but a mere retelling of Babylonian tales. The theological opposition was immense, and Delitzsch was pressured into recanting. Once more, the highest political authority of the time was involved, as Emperor Wilhelm II took a deep personal interest in the debate.

The emperor did not forget this encounter with Babylonian literature. When the declaration of the Weimar Republic in 1918 forced Wilhelm into exile, he settled in a small manor house in the Netherlands and devoted himself to the study of ancient history. In 1938 he wrote a short treatise on Mesopotamian kingship, claiming that there was an unbroken lineage in spirit between the Babylonian and Prussian empires, and that the stories about Gilgamesh reflected an ideal that he himself had tried (and failed) to uphold: "the idea of a universal monarchy spanning heaven and earth."[72]

The shock and controversies that swirled around the epic gave it an early fame that would become the foundation for its current popularity. But soon the nature of that fame changed: the epic was seen no longer as simply a parallel to the Bible but as a work of literature in its own right. Many hurdles had to be cleared before *Gilgamesh* could be read with any real appreciation, beginning with the issue of its name. Smith had originally read Gilgamesh's name as "Izdubar," though he acknowledged that this was incorrect. Since cuneiform signs have many different meanings, it was not clear how to understand the sequence GIŠ-GIN$_2$-MAŠ, and IZ-DU$_5$-BAR was as good an option as any (by the same logic, Enkidu's name was read "Heabani"). Numerous readings were proposed until Theophilus Pinches in 1890 published a half-page essay with the dramatic title "Exit Gištubar!" in which he finally gave the correct answer: "It has been found at last, the long wished-for read'ing of the name of the well-known hero, and it is neither Gištubar, nor Gišdubar, nor Gišdubarra, nor Izdubar, nor finally, Namraṣit, but GILGAMEŠ."[73]

One year later, the American Assyriologist Paul Haupt published a series of hand-drawn copies of all manuscripts of *Gilgamesh* known at the time, and this in turn allowed his German colleague Peter Jensen to complete the first edition of the epic in 1900. Jensen's edition was a tremendous achievement for its time, and soon the epic was translated into several European languages.[74] Of course, fewer manuscripts were known than today, and the Akkadian language was still poorly understood, but at least in broad outlines *Gilgamesh* had become available to a wider audience.

In Germany, a scholarly translation by Arthur Ungnad appeared in 1911, and a free version by Georg Burckhardt followed five years later. These were the translations that so excited Rainer Maria Rilke. But while Rilke found the story captivating, he was unsatisfied with Burckhardt's rendering and much preferred Ungnad's scholarly version. If the story were to be freely retold, Rilke wrote to his editor, he felt that he could do so better himself.[75] With these words, the epic had once and for all crossed into the public sphere. No longer the sole purview of a small group of academics, *Gilgamesh* now belonged to a larger audience who would judge new translations not only by philological standards but by literary criteria as well.

* * *

Rilke may have been an early fan of the epic, but many more would follow, as artists and authors across the globe retold and reacted to the epic. To name but a few, Thomas Mann wove the story into his monumental tetralogy on the ancient Near East, *Joseph and His Brothers,* Anselm Kiefer and Willi Baumeister each made several paintings based on the epic, and Ted Hughes was working on a dramatic adaptation of *Gilgamesh* at his death.[76]

In *Gilgamesh Among Us,* the literary critic Theodore Ziolkowski follows these and other encounters with the epic. Though he limits himself to the epic's reception in the West, Ziolkowski catalogues more than eighty works of art that respond to *Gilgamesh* in one way or another. What is striking about the epic's reception is the variety of media that have been used to retell the story, and the variety of themes that these retellings have focused on. Surveying the epic's modern retellings, Ziolkowski concludes that "if we compare this phenomenon to the reception of other masterpieces of world literature, it is difficult, if not impossible, to find anything remotely analogous."[77] Works like Ovid's *Metamorphoses* have of course had a much deeper impact on Western art history; what is exceptional about *Gilgamesh* is the intensity of its reception. While a comparable list of adaptations could be drawn up for many other classics, *Gilgamesh* is unique in having achieved its influence so quickly.

As noted above, *Gilgamesh* comes to us unfixed, open to new readings. Our cultural understanding of the epic, our shared sense of what it means, is still fluid, so the story can be presented as being about any number of topics. Ziolkowski calls the epic a "cultural seismograph" for the modern world, as it registers the tremors of society through the ways in which it is retold.[78] The themes highlighted in the epic's reception are a prism through which we can view the cultural developments of the West over the past century and a half.

According to Ziolkowski, the epic was initially read as a "secular myth," a religious tale that lay outside the world of the Bible, having been written before it. As such, "it encountered an increasingly secularized public that was eager to find surrogates for its lost religious faith."[79] *Gilgamesh* was both mythological and nonbiblical enough to fill that role. The combination also made it appealing to Sigmund Freud and Carl Jung, who saw myth as a powerful illustration of subconscious structures: for them, *Gilgamesh* was proof that their new theories could reach across vast expanses of history. The letters they exchanged in 1911 show that they both took an active interest in *Gilgamesh*, and the epic is repeatedly mentioned in the second part of Jung's *Symbols of Transformation*.[80]

After the world wars, the emphasis naturally fell on the themes of loss and death. The German author Hermann Hesse was fascinated by *Gilgamesh*, calling it "the most powerful poem I have read in a long time" and "a treasure of gold, lately drawn to light again from mankind's most ancient crypts." For Hesse, *Gilgamesh* was first and foremost a story about a hero raging against mortality. His enthusiasm was shared by another German Nobel laureate, Elias Canetti, who recalled that "Gilgamesh's lament on the death of his friend Enkidu struck me in the heart."[81]

But as the wind of culture changed again, the interpretations of *Gilgamesh* changed with it. There were homoerotic readings of *Gilgamesh*, such as Henrik Bjelke's avant-garde novel *Saturn*, which crosscuts between passages from the epic and exuberant, otherworldly descriptions of anal sex. There were feminist readings of *Gilgamesh*, such as the retelling by Zeynep Avcı, which gave voice to the previously neglected character Shamhat. There were ecocritical readings of *Gilgamesh*, including Thomas Mielke's *Gilgamesc: König von Uruk*, which focused on the heroes' devastation of the Cedar Forest.[82]

And once more, the list goes on—the epic is a source of unending fascination. But the history of *Gilgamesh* is far from over, and just as its interpretation has changed over and over again for the past four millennia, it will undoubtedly change again in the future. Cultural shifts and crises we cannot even imagine will bring us back to *Gilgamesh* with new eyes.

There is no doubt that *Gilgamesh* should be hailed as a global human heritage, but all too often readers forget that it is also a specifically Iraqi heritage. World literature rightly celebrates the cross-cultural circulation of literature, and the epic is an important exemplar of that circulation, but the movement of historical heritage from Iraq to the West also carries dark echoes of the country's colonial past. There is a reason why manuscripts of *Gilgamesh* are scattered across museums all over the Western world: in the early days of excavation, archaeologists brought all significant finds back to their home countries.[83] When countries like Iraq and Syria became independent, they introduced laws regulating the export of antiquities, but by then most cuneiform tablets had already been excavated and shipped off to Europe and North America.

Apologists of the colonial past might well argue that this was a fortu-itous misdeed, since the cuneiform collection of the Iraq Museum was hor-rifically damaged by looters during the 2003 invasion of Iraq. But in *The Rape of Mesopotamia,* the cultural critic Lawrence Rothfield argues passion-ately that the looting of the Iraq Museum was the direct result of colonial prejudice in the U.S. military.[84] This does not mean that Western readers should refrain from engaging with *Gilgamesh,* only that they should remem-ber that the epic is not just a global legacy—it is also an Iraqi legacy with an Iraqi history.

The epic's reception in Iraq is tied to the modernist movement of the 1950s.[85] After World War II a vibrant modernism sprang up in the recently autonomous nation of Iraq. This modernist movement celebrated artistic innovation but was also deeply aware of the country's ancient heritage. The old and the new were not to be counterpoised; rather, the modernist move-ment was to be "an explosive continuation of the past."[86] It was against this cultural background that Taha Baqir published the first Arabic translation of *Gilgamesh* in 1962. Tellingly, the translation was reissued three years later with drawings by the young Dia al-Azzawi, who would go on to become a towering figure in Iraqi modernism.[87] The epic thus became associated with what the art historian Zainab Bahrani calls the "modern antiquity" embodied by Azzawi, and it continued to influence later Iraqi painters such as Suad al-Attar and Faisel Laibi Sahi.

In Iraq, *Gilgamesh* was seen as an intimate newcomer: both a new arrival and an integral part of the country's history. This combination made it a natural fit for the optimistic mood of the sixties. Mesopotamia became the hallmark of all that was distinctly Iraqi, and the ancient cultural heritage was seized upon by the Ba'ath regime to promote its nationalist agenda.[88] But *Gilgamesh* was also used to criticize that nationalism. In 1964, just two years after Baqir's translation, the playwright Adil Kadhim published *The Flood,* in which he used the tyrannical Gilgamesh as a thinly veiled allu-sion to President Abdul Salam Arif and explicitly called for revolt against dictatorship.[89]

Since Gilgamesh is a constant traveler, forever journeying through for-eign landscapes, his story is especially resonant with Iraqi artists who have been forced into exile. In *Gilgamesh's Snake* (2016), the London-based poet Ghareeb Iskander engages with the epic to reflect on loss, war, history, and nostalgia. Likewise, Walid Siti's graphic series *Rites of Passage* (2014) transforms Gilgamesh's journeys into a line that winds and wends in a continuous circular motion, with no beginning or end, reflecting the painful experience of diaspora in the twenty-first century.[90]

Ever since Baqir's translation, *Gilgamesh* has been a source of constant creative impulses for Iraqi artists. Even today the epic retains the historical ambiguity it held in the sixties, being associated with both innovation and antiquity. Tellingly, the painting *The Path Ahead* (2003) by Leila Kubba shows Gilgamesh and Ur-shanabi crossing the Waters of Death, one of them looking forward, the other looking back.[91] For Iraqis searching for a way forward, *Gilgamesh* points in two directions at once. A dramatic example of this is the play *Waiting for Gilgamesh* (2014) by Amir al-Azraki, which asks difficult questions about how complicit Iraqis themselves have been in the unraveling of their country. The complex polemic unfolds between a mural of Iraq's recent history on the right side, and images from *Gilgamesh* on the left side. The title's reference to *Waiting for Godot* places the epic squarely in the modernist tradition, pointing both back to the sixties and forward to an unknown future. In a nasty twist of fate, the play premiered one day before the Islamic State declared its short-lived independence—a reminder of just how uncertain that future can be.[92]

In this essay, I have tried to do justice to Aidt's description of the epic as a fireball tearing through time. I have followed the epic down the arches of the years, seeking to understand what has allowed it to move so confidently across the centuries. My conclusion should already be clear. *Gilgamesh* has been successful not because it appeals to some universal truth or because it gives us a resounding answer that is as valid now as it was in ancient Uruk. Rather, *Gilgamesh* has been successful because it interweaves an extraordinary number of threads and themes and topics, allowing new ages and new readers to use it to ask their most pressing questions. The epic survives because it can adapt—because it is a poetic kaleidoscope that can be shaken endlessly into new forms.

But that is only part of the answer. Aidt's metaphor of the fireball describes not only the epic's survival through time but also the intensity of the poem. It is that intensity, the immediacy of its language and the power of its emotions, that makes it so touching to so many—and so frustrating to others. As the Assyriologist Thorkild Jacobsen points out, *Gilgamesh* asks a thousand questions and answers none, ending with an abrupt, unsatisfying turn: "The Epic of Gilgamesh does not come to a harmonious end; the emotions which rage in it are not assuaged; nor is there, as in tragedy, any sense of catharsis, any fundamental acceptance of the inevitable. It is a jeering, unhappy, unsatisfying ending. An inner turmoil is left to rage on, a vital question finds no answer."[93]

To me, this is one of the great things about the epic: it rages on. The fact that it finds no answer means that it can go on asking questions. Jacobsen's unresolved turmoil and the passionate despair described by Aidt are two sides of the same coin. But Jacobsen does make a fair point—the ending of the epic *is* strange. Gilgamesh points Ur-shanabi to the city wall of Uruk, and then the story stops. What are we to do with the scene? In the next essay, I examine what we can take away from that ending.

Study the Brickwork

When we finish reading *Gilgamesh,* we suddenly find ourselves back at the beginning. In the last lines of the epic, Gilgamesh says to Ur-shanabi: "Climb the wall of Uruk. . . . Walk its length. Survey the foundation, study the brickwork."[1] We are reminded of the prologue, in which the narrator had told us to do the same thing. The repetition brings us back to Tablet I, and we cannot help reflecting on how much has happened since we read it. As we stand on the walls and look out over the story, the sequence of events that has unfolded at breakneck pace comes into view as a coherent whole.

The wall surrounds both Uruk and the story. It marks the outer edges of the city just as it marks where our reading starts and ends: a border between the fictional world of the epic and the real world of the audience. As noted by the Assyriologist Annette Zgoll, the prologue draws a close connection between the wall and the epic itself.[2] They are woven together in the text, as we are first told of how the epic was made—"he set down all his trials on a slab of stone"—and in the very next line of how the wall was made: "He built the wall around Uruk the Sheepfold." We are then told to look at the wall and, finally, to read the epic. The prologue winds back and forth between the creation and the inspection of these two objects, interweaving them in our minds and so suggesting that they are connected, that one is a metaphor for the other. Both are impressive works of art, both are ancient and long-lasting, both were created by Gilgamesh and now stand as a monument to his memory.

So when the narrator tells us to walk the length of the wall, the implication is clear. We are not only to go around the city, we are to circumambulate the story, following its circular path in our mind.[3] The word for "walk" is set in a special verbal form, the iterative imperative, which implies that the task should be done not once but in a continuous ongoing motion. Many readers are confused by the abrupt ending of the epic, uncertain what to take away from the story, but that is precisely the point.[4] *Gilgamesh* lends itself not to easy summary but to repeated consideration.

*   *   *

Though the instructions of the beginning are repeated word for word at the end, they are not the same. Something has changed, and our understanding of the epic will change with it: the words spoken by the narrator in the prologue are now spoken by Gilgamesh, and we are made to realize that the two are one and the same. The prologue had told us that Gilgamesh "set down all his trials on a slab of stone."[5] What he set down was the epic itself, though he wrote it in the third person. An autobiography in the third person is a curious thing, but it is clear from other cuneiform texts that this is what *Gilgamesh* is.[6]

The closest parallel to the epic is *The Cuthean Legend of Naram-Sîn*, which tells the story of the Old Akkadian emperor Naram-Sîn, who was punished by the gods for his impatience and impiety.[7] He did not wait to receive a favorable omen from the gods before embarking on war, and as a result his land was overrun by a horde of monstrous enemies. At the climax of the story, Naram-Sîn writes down what happened to him as a warning for future rulers to obey the orders of the gods, inviting kings and scholars to read his story and learn from his mistakes.

Just like *Gilgamesh*, Naram-Sîn's story begins with an invitation to "open the tablet box and read out the stele."[8] The word for "stele" is *narû* in Akkadian—this is the word I translate as "slab of stone" in the prologue. The stele gives its name to the genre that modern scholars call *narû* literature: the autobiographical account of an ill-fated king that purports to be the king's own words inscribed on a stone stele and kept in a box.[9] The similarities between the two texts show they are to be understood the same way, and that we can read *Gilgamesh* as the king's own story as told by himself. As the philologist Christopher B. F. Walker puts it, "The impression is deliberately created that the whole epic was written down in antiquity by Gilgamesh himself, just as the Naram-Sin Legend purports to have been written down by Naram-Sin."[10]

However, since it is told in the third person, we gradually forget over the next eleven Tablets that the narrator is Gilgamesh himself. We are reminded of it only in the final lines, where his voice and the narrator's merge into one. The ending is no ending at all but a new beginning. The epic ends as Gilgamesh begins to tell his story, and the epic starts over: "Climb the wall of Uruk. . . . Walk its length."[11] The text is like a snake biting its own tail, telling the story of its own creation, eager for one more spin around the walls, propelling itself through time and so carrying Gilgamesh's name into eternity.

A cruel symmetry bisects the epic. The poem tells of Gilgamesh's love for Enkidu, then brings out the pain of Enkidu's death. It tells of Gilgamesh's victories over Humbaba and the Bull of Heaven only to tell of the hero's failure to find immortality and regain youth. *Gilgamesh* begins as adventure but ends as tragedy. The turning point comes at the end of Tablet VI, and the epic can be neatly divided into two mirroring halves, before and after the dream in which Enkidu witnesses the gods sentencing him to death.[12]

The entire story is organized around this symmetry. Gilgamesh first travels west to reach the Cedar Forest, then east to reach the garden of Jeweled Trees.[13] Gilgamesh goes on the first journey to bring death to Humbaba and on the second to retrieve eternal life from Uta-napishti. In the first part, Gilgamesh is approached by Ishtar, who attempts to seduce him, in the second he approaches Shiduri, who is revolted by him.[14] Gilgamesh's original problem is that he cannot find rest, but in the end he is unable to stay awake, failing Uta-napishti's test and so forfeiting immortality. When Aruru creates Enkidu, we are told that "Anu's idea found form in her heart"; when Gilgamesh builds a tomb for Enkidu, we are told that "the idea of the river found form in his heart," linking Enkidu's birth and burial in a neat reversal.[15] Enkidu's tragedy in the first half of the poem is that the gods convene to decree his death; Gilgamesh's tragedy in the second half is that the gods will not convene to decree eternal life for him, as they had for Uta-napishti. Though the problems are symmetrical, the outcome is the same: both must die.

Often, the symmetry involves some form of expansion in the second case. At the end of Tablet V, the heroes look back at the destruction they have wrought on the Cedar Forest and wonder if they have done the right thing. At the end of Tablet XI, the gods do the same after unleashing the Flood: they question their own motives and regret their lack of forethought. The symmetry is clear, but the scale of the destruction is also massively expanded, from a single forest to the entire world.[16] The epic delights in imperfect symmetries of this kind: many more examples can be found, large and small.

And at the center of the entire structure, at the turning point of it all, we find once more the wall of Uruk. When the heroes have defeated the Bull of Heaven, they offer its heart to Shamash, subtly indicating that we have here reached the heart of the story. The furious Ishtar then climbs the wall of Uruk and cries out, "Woe to Gilgamesh!"[17] Ishtar's wish comes true the very next day, as Enkidu wakes up from his nightmare and knows that he will die. With just two words (*allû Gilgāmeš*), Ishtar has turned the epic around, from glory to gloom.

After Ishtar's curse, the women of Uruk gather to mourn around the Bull's member, which Enkidu hurled in Ishtar's face.[18] Meanwhile, the men of Uruk gather to admire the horns—a protuberance, as it were, sticking out from the other end of the animal. Again, the epic is playfully showing us how it is structured. It takes a limb from either end of the Bull, front and back, and puts them next to each other, marking the transition from the story's beginning to its end.

The first half of the epic is a tale of triumph, the second a tale of sorrow, and the structure is again reflected in the two groups that gather around Gilgamesh and Ishtar. While the women carry out a ritual lament, the men throw a party: Ishtar "began the lamentation," Gilgamesh "began the celebration."[19] In short, this scene is a miniature mirror of the entire epic. The long story of Gilgamesh's triumphs is followed by a tiny mourning, then by a tiny celebration, then by the long mourning of Enkidu's death.

Crucially, Ishtar is standing on the wall of Uruk when she declares her curse on Gilgamesh. In the text as preserved, the wall makes only three appearances in the story. It is mentioned in the prologue, it is mentioned at the end, and it is mentioned here, at the turning point of Tablet VI. To understand the structure of the epic, we must follow the wall of Uruk: it traces out a circle split in two.

After the men have held their party, they all go to bed. The last lines of Tablet VI read: "Enkidu got up to interpret his dream and said to his friend:" And there the Tablet ends.[20] So what did Enkidu say? What was his dream? To learn the answer, modern readers can simply turn the page, but for the ancient scribes things would not have been so simple.

When we read the epic today, it can be deceptively easy to treat the twelve Tablets as chapters in a novel—bits of the book that could not stand on their own. But that is not how the ancient scribes saw them. To them, each Tablet was an individual object, a separate piece of clay that could be read and appreciated on its own. The collection of an average scribe did not hold the entire epic, only select Tablets: one scribe might have had Tablets I, V, and VIII, while his neighbor had Tablets II, VI, and XI.[21]

Rather than chapters of a novel, the Tablets were more like the episodes of a modern television series. Each Tablet contains a separate story, a rounded episode. Of course, the Tablets still combine to form a larger story, just as today we can be captivated by a single episode of a series while also following the overall story arc. The parallel is surprisingly precise, because the Akkadian scribes, having no word for "epic," referred to the story as "the series of Gilgamesh" (*iškār Gilgāmeš*).

The epic often marks the division between Tablets by letting them coincide with physical borders of the story. Just as the epic is surrounded by the wall of Uruk, so are the individual Tablets marked by other kinds of thresholds in time and space. For example, Tablet V begins with the heroes standing at the entrance of the Cedar Forest and ends with them sailing out of it. When Gilgamesh enters the forest, we enter the Tablet, when he leaves the forest, we leave the Tablet. Likewise, Tablet X begins at the inn of Shiduri, "who lived by the seashore," and ends on another shore, that of Uta-napishti. The plot of the Tablet unfolds between those beaches, as Gilgamesh struggles to cross the Waters of Death. Tablet III is marked not by borders in space but by the repetition of speech: it begins with the elders of Uruk giving advice to Gilgamesh and ends with that advice restated word for word.[22]

Reprinting the epic on paper changes how we read it. What were once separate episodes are literally glued together to make a book. The story may be easier for us to read this way, but we would do well to pause after every Tablet and consider the episode by itself. If we do, the ending of Tablet VI becomes much more poetically effective: we realize that the text breaks off mid-couplet, leaving us suspended in uncertainty and eager to know about Enkidu's dream, in the ancient equivalent of an end-of-season cliffhanger.

Reading the epic as a series of clay tablets changes our understanding of the story, but that understanding changes again when we consider that in the ancient world the epic could also be appreciated in another way—as a performance. In Christian Hess's delightful phrase, Akkadian epics were "songs of clay."[23]

When the prologue invites us to find the tablet box, pick up a tablet, and start reading, it tells us specifically that we should "read aloud" (Akkadian *šasû*). Today, silent reading has become the norm outside children's bedrooms, but that was not the case in antiquity, where communal reading was common: one person would read aloud for an audience, who would afterward discuss what they had heard. When the Babylonian epic *Enuma Elish* imagines how it will be received in the future, it specifically asks that "the wise and the learned should discuss it together."[24] Of course, ancient readers were perfectly capable of reading silently and alone, and frequently did so, but communal reading was far more widespread than it is today.[25]

Gilgamesh was no different: it is likely that when it was read, it was most often recited for an audience. But the question of *how* this was done is much more difficult to answer. Archaeologists can dig up a tablet, but they cannot dig up a performance. When it comes to the oral quality of the story, we have many questions and few answers. Was the epic originally an oral story that was later put down in writing? Probably, but we cannot be sure. Was the epic sung or spoken? Or perhaps chanted, or rapped? Was it recited by a single performer or a cast of singers? Was the performance accompanied by instruments, and if so, which ones? Was it always performed the same way, or did the text allow for improvisation? Unfortunately, we just do not know.[26]

Despite these uncertainties, modern scholars have done their best to re-create how the text would have sounded. Since the Akkadian language has been dead for over two thousand years we must rely on guesswork, but leading philologists have recorded their best guess at soas.ac.uk/baplar/recordings/ (I especially recommend the one by Nathan Wasserman).[27] One need not be fluent in Akkadian to appreciate a performance of *Gilgamesh*. The professional storyteller Fran Hazelton has worked tirelessly for the past two decades to bring Sumerian and Akkadian literature back to life through oral storytelling, founding the Enheduanna Society to take over her work. Recordings of their performances in English and Arabic are available at their website, zipang.org.uk.

The question of how the epic would have sounded is not mere curiosity. Some aspects of the story would work differently if they were heard rather than read. The many repetitions in the epic can be numbing to modern readers, who are easily bored and skip ahead to find new information.[28] But a listening audience cannot skip ahead—they must hear the story from one end to the other. And when they are sat through for their full duration, the repetitions can become a way of building up suspense by delaying the resolution of the plot: the listening audience waits, hearts in their throats, to hear how the quest turns out, and each repetition keeps them suspended in the dramatic uncertainty.

The Assyriologist Selena Wisnom argues that repetitions in *Gilgamesh* may have worked like a musical chorus.[29] Though readers today are easily put off by written repetition, we generally do not mind hearing the chorus of a song repeated. Our mind is pleased to come across a familiar sound, which it can more easily enjoy knowing what will follow. Musical repetition is most effective when it is mixed with some measure of variation, to keep it from getting dull: the verse varies while the chorus stays the same. This is essentially what happens in Tablet IV of *Gilgamesh*. Long repeated passages describe the heroes' journey to the Cedar Forest, but the repetition is offset by the vivid description of Gilgamesh's nightmares. Heard as a piece of music, the repetitions of the epic might have sounded less like a dull litany and more like a catchy refrain, nestling in the mind of the audience with the charm of an incantation.[30]

As Gertrude Stein pointed out, there is no such thing as repetition in poetry, there is only insistence. The words of the poem grow more intense with each repetition, as Stein shows with her famous phrase, "a rose is a rose is a rose." Even the same exact words spoken again will be different because the emphasis will always be different. As it happens, Stein goes on to illustrate her point with an example from Assyria:

> When you first realize the history of various civilizations, that have been on this earth, that too makes one realize repetition and at the same time the difference of insistence. Each civilization insisted in its own way before it went away. I remember the first time I really realized this in this way was from reading a book we had at home of the excavations of Nineveh.[31]

If Stein is right to argue that every culture insists in its own way, we have to ask—How did Babylonian poetry insist? That is, I think, a question that deserves a longer answer than the present book can contain.

Though the oral epic is lost to us, we can still recover some of its *aural* quality—that is, how it sounds even in silent reading, how the words of the text become voice in our minds. The epic teems with verbal games, puns and assonances, rhythm and alliteration, metaphors and similes, contrasts and parallels.[32] To read *Gilgamesh* in its original language is to enter a landscape not unlike the Cedar Forest—dense and richly scented, ill-lit but alluring, full of shadows and echoes.

In my translation, I have emphasized the alliterations that give the epic its rich texture. The play of consonants is everywhere in *Gilgamesh,* and I will mention only a few of my favorite examples. The common stock formula used to introduce direct speech, "he worked his words," is in Akkadian the lovely phrase *pāšu īpuš*, literally, "he made his mouth," perhaps to be taken as "he did his speech." At the end of Tablet III, the dignitaries of Uruk bid farewell to Gilgamesh as he leaves for the Cedar Forest: we are told that the young men ran behind him "and his governors kissed his feet," which in Akkadian is the stunning line *u šakkanakkūšu unaššaqū šēpīšu*, interweaving the vowels *u* and *a* and the consonants *š*, *n* and *k/q*. (I did my best in the translation: "the lords of the land fawned at his feet").

A particularly beautiful line comes in Tablet XI, when Belet-ili scolds Enlil for unleashing the Flood: "Now let the gods all come to the sacrifice. Only Enlil is not welcome at the sacrifice." The Akkadian has a wonderful play on the sound *l* and the sequence *k-n*: *ilu lillikūni ana surqenni / ellil ayy-illika ana surqenni*.[33] Even better is the description of the mountain that is guarded by the scorpion people. Most translations give its name as Mount Mashu, but since *māšu* means "twin," I have honored both the original text and the fans of David Lynch by rendering it "Twin Peaks." When we are told that "the name of the mountains was Twin Peaks," the line may be unimpressive in English, but the Akkadian has a glorious tongue-twister: *šá ša-dú-u šu-má-šu ma-šú-ma*.[34]

Equally difficult to translate are the puns of the epic.[35] A complex sequence of puns comes in Tablet VI, when Ishtar propositions the gardener Ishullanu. As I understand it, the exchange goes as follows. Ishtar says to Ishullanu: "Let's have a taste of your work: stretch out your hand and touch my *ḫurdatu*."[36] The word means "vagina" (one ancient scribe glossed it as *ḫur dādī*, "hole of love"), but it can also be used to describe date palms and tamarisks, so Ishtar is flirting with Ishullanu by asking him to do what he does best: plucking dates and tending trees.[37] But Ishullanu, fearful of the goddess's reputation, pretends not to understand the double entendre and acts as if she had offered him actual fruit: he says that he has already eaten. Ishtar avenges herself by transforming Ishullanu into a garden pest, always eating plants without ever being full. Just like the shepherd who is turned into a wolf, Ishullanu is turned against his former profession.[38]

Puns are especially abundant in speeches by Ea, who, as described in the introduction, speaks in code to circumvent the oath of silence imposed on him by the other gods. There are too many wordplays in his speech to describe in full, but one example comes from his first instruction to Uta-napishti. A literal translation would be:

Property *scorn, life* seek!
Board all *seed of living things* onto the boat.[39]

The clever couplet revolves around the phrase *zēr napišti*, which in the first line means "scorn, life" and in the second means "seed of living things." In the first line, the words are to be read separately; in the second line, they are brought together.[40] But that is just the beginning of Ea's speech.

Ea's first message to Uta-napishti orders him to build a boat and explains how to do so, but not why: he only tells the sage to flee, not what it is he is fleeing from. Technically, Ea has still not broken his oath or revealed anything about the coming Flood. But Uta-napishti presses him on the matter: "How should I answer the city, the crowds, and the elders?" The word "answer" (*apālu*) can also mean "pay," so as noted by Martin Worthington, Uta-napishti may be asking both how he should remunerate the people of his city for their work and how to explain this apparently madcap project.[41] Ea replies with a stunt of eloquence, in a couplet that can be read in two ways at once: either as a promise of cakes and wheat for the builders of the boat or as a warning of darkness, demons, and death.

Worthington has dedicated an entire book to untangling the wordplay in Ea's message, teasing out its multiple, hidden, contradictory meanings.[42] For example, when Ea tells Uta-napishti to say, "Enlil must hate me," this is technically true, but he omits to mention that Enlil has grown to hate not just Uta-napishti but the entire human race.[43] The most tightly packed set of puns comes in the last two lines of Ea's speech. They form a rhyming couplet, a rare thing in Akkadian poetry, which otherwise seldom uses end rhymes. The lines read as follows:

ina šēr kukkī ina lîlâti
ušaznanakkunūši šamût kibāti[44]

As Worthington shows, every one of these words can be read in several ways at once. There is a surface positive meaning, promising the citizens of Shuruppak a rich reward for their labor, as well as not one but two hidden meanings, which adumbrate their deaths. Following Worthington's argument, we could read the lines in at least three ways:

Meaning 1: "At dawn there will be cakes, in the evening
he will provide you with a shower of wheat."

Meaning 2: "At dawn there will be darkness; in the (thus created) evening
he will rain on you a shower (thick) as wheat."

Meaning 3: "With magical incantations, with wind-demons,
he will rain on you death for the 'wheat' (that is, for humanity)."[45]

The third meaning is achieved in part because there are no spaces between words in cuneiform writing, so a sequence of signs can be read as forming one or more words, depending on the context. The Akkadian phrase *ina šēr kukkī* can mean "at dawn, cakes"; but if it is read as two words, *ina šerkukkī*, it means "with magical incantations." Likewise, *šamût kibāti* means "a shower of wheat"; but if it is read as three words, *ša mūt kibāti*, it means "that (which will cause) the death of wheat," with stalks of wheat being a commonly used metaphor for the human race.[46] Ea's coded message spells death for everyone, if spelled correctly.

As Worthington also notes, this passage is a crucial example of how oral performance could have changed the meaning of the poem.[47] The couplet is repeated a total of three times, so it is possible that a performer might have introduced subtle differences in pronunciation along the way, perhaps to highlight first its positive, then its negative senses, bringing the ominous undertone into still clearer view. It would only take a brief inflection to emphasize the crucial difference between *šamût* and *ša mūt*, "shower" and "of death."

Faced with so complex a series of puns, what is a translator to do? I wanted to convey both the many meanings and the compact, rhyming structure of the original couplet. So I resorted to the ultimate translator cop-out, giving different versions side by side:

At dawn sweets,	*At dawn dark,*
at dusk wheat	*at dusk death*
in downpours he	*for all he will*
will rain on you.	*let fall on you.*

Today, the word *pun* connotes a fun and lighthearted play with double meanings, but that is not the case for this couplet. The puns in Ea's speech are not frivolous wordplay—they are a matter of life and death. Those who understand the message will have a chance to save themselves; those who do not will die in the Flood. In other words, the scene can be read as a cruel lesson in literary criticism. By having us ponder over Ea's ambiguous message, the epic reminds us to pay close attention to language and the layers of meaning encoded in poetry. In *Gilgamesh*'s world, reading the cosmos with an eye for hidden messages can mean the difference between salvation and disaster.

In a previous section, I compared the sound of the epic to the scenery of the Cedar Forest, full as it is of echoes, rhythms, and shadowy figures. But according to Selena Wisnom, the soundscape of the Cedar Forest contains a hidden, discordant note. She argues that the description of the forest alludes to traditional Akkadian descriptions of the underworld, hinting at the illness and death that would strike most mortals who ventured into Humbaba's lair. For example, when the epic says that the trees are "webbed" with creepers, it uses a word that is rare in epic poetry but common in medical texts, where it seems to be used to describe the scar tissue caused by an infectious disease.[48]

But that is not the only way of reading the scene. The Assyriologist Gösta Gabriel argues that the description of the Cedar Forest alludes not to death and the underworld but to the religious rituals of Uruk, presenting the forest as a dark mirror of the civilized city: for example, the band of monkeys "thundered for Humbaba" just as the drums of Uruk "thunder for Ninsun."[49] The scene uses not only the terminology of medical diagnosis but also that of religious worship, as when Enkidu tells Gilgamesh: "Let your mind run wild like a prophet, let your cry ring loud like the drum of a temple!"[50]

The description of the Cedar Forest can thus be read as an allusion to both Uruk and the underworld, to worship and illness. One set of allusions is positive, the other negative, but we do not have to choose between them. The rich language of the epic makes room for multiple and even contradictory allusions at once, just as the same couplet can offer both a warning and a promise. However, the allusions that are folded together in the description of the Cedar Forest also illustrate another aspect of the epic—namely, its tendency to refer to other kinds of texts, using the tropes and clichés of other genres in surprising ways, such as medical phrases for trees or temple terms for battle cries.

Rather than being a straightforwardly epic narrative, *Gilgamesh* plays with several literary forms at once, leading Andrew George to dub it "an anthology of genres."[51] There is, for example, the opening hymn that exalts the hero, the proverbs quoted by the characters, Ninsun's prayer to Shamash, the folktale of Ishallanu, the curses and blessing spoken by Enkidu, Gilgamesh's eulogy for his friend, and the dream accounts that in Akkadian literature were a genre unto themselves. Perhaps most noteworthy is the epic inside the epic, Uta-napishti's story of the Flood. By weaving together so many styles and genres, *Gilgamesh* gives its readers a taste of the richness and variety of Babylonian literature.

The epic's use of other genres is rarely a matter of simple inclusion—often the genres come with a surprising twist. To understand how the epic uses genre, we must first understand that genres are, in essence, made of expectations. Every genre embodies a set of assumptions about what a text will do, assumptions that the text can either follow or overturn. Take the story of a murder that goes unsolved. Such a narrative would fit well into a realist novel, because the genre relies on the expectation that the plot will be a grim, unvarnished image of real life, where murders go unpunished all the time. But the same story would be incongruous in a detective novel, because that genre is defined by the expectation that murderers are eventually found out and (often) brought to justice.[52]

When *Gilgamesh* refers to other genres, it thus also refers to their generic expectations, and it often does so to undermine them. Take Enkidu's speech to the door in Tablet VII: "May a future king loathe you . . . may he scratch out my name and inscribe his own!"[53] This is an example of a formal curse in Akkadian literature, but it also reverses the logic of the curses found on most royal inscriptions. In a normal inscription, a king would put his name on the building he had made, and then curse any king who dared to remove that name and replace it with his own. But Enkidu *wants* a future ruler to obliterate his memory from the door, which failed to protect him. The epic alludes to a common trope of royal inscriptions, then uses the trope against itself.

Another example of this dynamic is the folktale of Ishullanu. Gilgamesh recounts how Ishullanu was punished for his rejection of Ishtar, but he does not realize that by telling the story he is failing to learn from it. By offending Ishtar, Gilgamesh repeats Ishullanu's mistake and will soon be punished too. The story of Ishullanu carries a clear moral, as folktales often do: the gods are not to be denied. But in the epic, the moral falls on deaf ears, as Gilgamesh fails to understand the meaning of the fable he tells.[54] Even worse: if the moral is that one should not offend the gods, telling Ishullanu's story specifically to offend a goddess is a spectacularly bad use of it.

Finally, we might argue that Ninsun's prayer also plays with the genre to which it belongs. It has many of the hallmarks of a traditional Akkadian prayer. Gilgamesh's mother, the "holy aurochs," goes up to the roof of her temple accompanied by her priestesses, makes an offering of incense, and glorifies the power of the Sun God, before stating what she wants him to do in return. In many ways, the sequence makes this a typical prayer.[55] But the situation is also unique, because Ninsun is herself a goddess. The temple on whose roof she prays is *her* temple—she is not its priestess but its deity. As a result, her exchange with Shamash also twists the usual genre of prayers, because it is not a request from a desperate mortal to an almighty god, but an exchange between deities in which their respective power and status are at stake. Ninsun seeks to cajole and convince Shamash in flattering terms, but at the end of the day she is not afraid to boss him around.

When she turns to the second half of the prayer, the text tells us that "the holy aurochs Ninsun repeated her instruction," with the last word, Akkadian *ûrtu,* literally meaning "order" or "command," such as a king might give his subjects. What begins as a simple petition is shown, halfway through, to also be something else and far more unusual, as Ninsun hovers elegantly between flattery and firmness, prayer and command. The epic uses the style and the ceremonials of prayer, and so summons the assumptions that come with that genre—but then upends them, as it becomes increasingly clear that Ninsun is not a mere supplicant praying to Shamash, as one would expect from a conventional prayer, but a goddess giving orders.[56]

* * *

Gilgamesh also plays with multiple voices. The characters often speak in a voice that is wholly their own: as Benjamin Foster puts it, the epic "differentiates the speech of some characters, including their style, diction, grammar, and even pronunciation."[57] Ea's speech is full of puns, Uta-napishti's is dignified and old-fashioned, Ishtar's is crude and blunt. These voices are juxtaposed to bring out their differences, responding and adding nuance to one another.

In the opening hymn, the narrator states that Gilgamesh is two-thirds god and one-third human. In Tablet IX, the scorpion man tells his wife that Gilgamesh has the flesh of gods in his body, but she disagrees, stating that he is two-thirds god and one-third human.[58] The narrator had originally used the phrase to glorify the godlike Gilgamesh, but the scorpion woman uses it to argue that Gilgamesh is not fully divine, shifting the emphasis from the first part of the line to the second. The two voices, the narrator's and the scorpion woman's, say the same words, but with opposite intents.

Crucially, the meaning of the scorpion woman's words becomes apparent only when they are read as a reply to her husband. It is because she disagrees with him that her words take on a negative inflection. That is, it is the dialogue between them that gives their words meaning: the statements make sense in the context of the dialogical exchange. That fact is central to the epic, which is heavily focused on dialogue. Reported speech takes up most of the text, at the expense of action.[59]

Take the relatively brief battle with Humbaba, which is enclosed in speech after speech. The battle is narrated in about twenty lines, but it is preceded and followed by a long string of dialogues. Gilgamesh announces his decision to fight Humbaba to Enkidu and the elders, who then present their counterarguments, to which Gilgamesh responds. Then come the elders' advice, Ninsun's prayer, Gilgamesh's dream reports, Enkidu's interpretations, the two friends' mutual encouragements in the forest, the threats and taunts between Humbaba and the heroes, Humbaba's pleas for mercy and his dying curse, Enkidu's troubled reflection on his victory—and so on. The action itself is resolved briskly, while dialogue is used at great length to prepare for that action and reflect on its consequences.

One particularly important voice in the epic is that of the narrator. Although we are given to understand that the narrator is Gilgamesh himself, telling his own story in the third person, this premise leads to a range of complications: in the words of the literary critic Keith Dickson, "Difficult and impertinent questions follow on the assumption that Gilgamesh himself is the author of the tablet."[60] Take Gilgamesh's decision to launch the quest against Humbaba. In that scene, we hear the words of the youthful character Gilgamesh, full of optimism and self-assurance, but the scene is supposedly being narrated by an older, wiser Gilgamesh. As a narrator, he is looking back on his decision, knowing the tragic consequences to which it will lead. The two Gilgameshes must have very different views of the situation.

In a strange twist, at one point Gilgamesh the character and Gilgamesh the narrator seem to contradict each other. In the opening lines of Tablet IX, we are told by the narrator that Gilgamesh "wept bitterly for his friend Enkidu," but in the next line, Gilgamesh says, "I too will die. Am I not like Enkidu?"[61] According to himself, he is no longer weeping for his friend, but bemoaning his own mortality. Grief and fear clearly mingle in his heart, but the narrator highlights one emotion and the character the other.[62]

"I too will die. Am I not like Enkidu?" Tellingly, the question finds no answer. Gilgamesh is not talking to anyone in particular in this scene, so the question is surely rhetorical, but the way it is phrased still leaves an unanswered note, as if the hero were waiting for an outside authority to step in and tell him what fate awaits him. The question is simple enough, almost banal, but it strikes at the heart of Gilgamesh's anxiety: "*Am* I like Enkidu?" The question may be unanswered, but so is almost every other question in *Gilgamesh.* Hardly any question in the epic receives a direct answer. This is not for a lack of questions, of which there are plenty, though many are rhetorical: the speakers seem to pause for a moment, however theatrically, to allow for answers that never come.[63]

Some questions are answered with other questions. On his journey to Uta-napishti, Gilgamesh is repeatedly asked to account for his decrepit condition: "What hollowed your cheeks, bowed your head, wrecked your heart, and broke your body?" Gilgamesh replies: "How could my cheeks be full, my head held high, my heart not wrecked, my body not broken?"[64] Gilgamesh repeats the questions he hears, redoubles and turns them against the questioners, stressing that his worn-out state is the only logical result of an event he cannot explain—the loss of Enkidu. The real question, to Gilgamesh, is not why he is mourning, but why Enkidu had to die.

Granted, much of the epic is missing, but in the text that survives, I can find only a handful of questions that receive an answer, if we can call them answers. Take Gilgamesh's rock-star welcome on his return to Uruk. He asks, "Who is the most splendid of men?" and the servant girls reply, "Gilgamesh is the most splendid of men!" This is an answer, but only technically. Another exception is the story of the Flood. Gilgamesh asks Uta-napishti, "How did you find eternal life in the gathering of gods?" and Uta-napishti replies at length. In his narrative, Uta-napishti asks Ea what he should answer if the people of his city ask where he's going, and Ea does reply. But in both cases—the story of the Flood and Ea's cryptic message—the answers pose far more riddles than they solve.[65]

The abundance of unanswered questions is one of several literary techniques that give the dialogues of the epic their open-ended quality. The voices of the characters come together, disagree with one another, and give us different perspectives on the same events. The epic is what literary critics call "polyphonic": it blends and juxtaposes a variety of voices and perspectives rather than flattening them into a single worldview.[66]

Perhaps the most telling example is the scene in Tablet VII in which Enkidu curses the priestess Shamhat: he accuses her of having set in motion the sequence of events that led to his death. But Enkidu is rebuked by the sun god, Shamash, who reminds him that Shamhat's seduction led not only to his death but also to his friendship with Gilgamesh.[67] Enkidu relents and replaces the curse with a blessing, giving us a dual perspective on Shamhat's role and the meaning of her actions. Her seduction of Enkidu set off a chain of events with many different outcomes, none of which she could have predicted at the time. From this mess of actions and consequences, the Sun God and Enkidu draw different conclusions, focusing on a positive and a negative link, respectively.

The scene of seduction is emplaced in two story arcs, acquiring a different meaning in each. Enkidu tells the story of how Shamhat seduced him and so made him human, so that he was weakened and sullied, and so died. The Sun God tells the story of how Shamhat seduced him and so made him human, so that he came to Uruk, and so became friends with Gilgamesh, who will now honor his memory.

There is an important lesson to be learned from this scene: moral judgments rely on storytelling. To decide whether a given action is worthy of blame or blessings, one must draw a connection between that action and its consequences—but things are rarely so simple. In the complex world we live in, every action brings about a whole sequence of unpredictable consequences, whose significance can change from one moment to the next.

When we make a judgment, we use the structure of a story to highlight one set of connections: this person did X, which led to Y. But often, those same events could easily have been shaped into other stories too: what about W or Z?[68] The takeaway is not that judgments are useless, but that stories matter. The way we tell our life stories can make a big difference; they are all that stand between justice and vitriol. The scene of Enkidu's curse reminds us to critically consider the narratives we use to make sense of our lives.

The epic begins by telling us to study the brickwork of the story, and as we do so, we come to realize why this is important. Ea's tricky message shows that we must pay attention to the double meanings that lie buried in poetic language, if we are to understand the hidden codes and warnings that surround us. Likewise, Shamhat's double judgment reveals how storytelling shapes the way we make sense of our lives and make judgments about others.

As we think of the epic as a work of literature, Jacobsen's "jeering, unhappy, unsatisfying ending" seems perhaps less unsatisfying now than it did at first.[69] The wall of Uruk encircles the text and splits it into a symmetrical tale of triumph and mourning, while the final words bring us back to the beginning, tying it together in a neat circular structure that invites us to consider the narrative anew.

But Jacobsen's dissatisfaction also concerned the *emotional* aspect of the ending, the sense of resolution that one expects from the closure of a story. As he puts it, "An inner turmoil is left to rage on." What, then, is that turmoil? What feelings rage in the epic? Understanding the nature of the powerful force that drives Gilgamesh may help us realize how that force does, after all, find some kind of closure by the end of the epic.

The Storm of His Heart

Gilgamesh's superhuman forces have been all but spent as he finds himself adrift on otherworldly waters. His search for immortality has led him through strange lands, but now he is stuck. As always, the problem is of his own making. Had he not met everyone with thoughtless aggression, smashing the Stone Ones that used to guard Ur-shanabi's boat, he would not have found himself stranded on the Waters of Death, out of punting poles and out of luck. But Gilgamesh has energy left for one last feat. He strips off his shirt and raises it up to form a sail. With sore and outstretched arms, he becomes a human mast.[1]

This is a powerful image—it hurts. When I first read the passage, I struggled to make sense of it, but it eventually became for me the clearest image of who Gilgamesh is as a person. Throughout the story, he is always driven onward, as a sail bearing the brunt of his own desire. There is a storm in his heart, as the gods say when they create Enkidu.[2] The disquiet in his mind makes him exceptional, but it also brings him much pain, often the result of his own thoughtless fury. Buffeted by winds both within and without, Gilgamesh is led to glory and grief, love and undoing.[3]

Unlike Greek heroes who are half man and half god, Gilgamesh is an uneven fraction, two-thirds god and one-third human: he is, in a word, unbalanced.[4] The opening line of the epic's Old Babylonian version is "He surpassed all kings," in Akkadian *šūtur eli šarrī*. The word *šūturu* means "to exceed, to overdo" and this is the hero's defining trait, both the ideal to which he aspires and his main problem. Eager to excel, he is unable to rest. Gilgamesh goes where none has gone before, and often he goes too far. He outdoes all rivals and is too much to bear.

The epic begins with the key problem of Gilgamesh's excessive desire. His surplus energy makes Gilgamesh a tyrant who subjects his people to constant demands. It is not made clear how he exploits the citizens of Uruk—sexual abuses? constant athletic games? forced labor on the wall of Uruk?—but manifestly he asks too much of them.[5] His ambition drives him to extremes and them to exhaustion. Later that same restlessness will lead him to magnificent quests, such as the expeditions to kill Humbaba and to find eternal life, but where does it come from? What is the force that urges him on to new exertions? Why can't he just find peace in the luxury of his palace? The epic is anything but clear on the question.

Take the expedition against Humbaba. The epic gives several reasons for it, but the actual motive is much more muddled.[6] That Humbaba is evil and should be killed, that precious cedar should be brought back to Uruk, and that Gilgamesh wants to establish a name for himself are all presented as excuses for a quest whose actual origin is surprisingly ambiguous. Gilgamesh first proposes the quest because Enkidu is sad. The passage is fragmentary, but it seems that Ninsun has made Enkidu realize that because he has no family, he will have no one to honor his memory after his death.[7] Gilgamesh's solution is simple: do what no one has done before, become famous, and you will be remembered forever, with or without a family. But if the mission is for Enkidu, it is also despite him, since Enkidu opposes the idea at every turn. Enkidu's sadness may be the occasion for the quest, but it does not sit easily as its cause.

Gilgamesh's idea meets with disapproval from Enkidu, Ninsun, and the elders of Uruk, and to each he explains his plan by saying, "My mind is made up. I will walk the far road to the home of Humbaba."[8] He presents the quest as stemming from nothing but his will, letting the royal resolution "my mind is made up" (literally "I have grown massive," *agdapuš*) eclipse any argument for why it should be a good idea.

Ninsun is dismayed by her son's plan. On the roof of her palace she appeals to the Sun God, asking with palpable despair, "Why, Shamash, did you burden my son with so restless a heart? Now you have touched him, and so he will walk the far road to the home of Humbaba."[9] With these words, Ninsun effectively explains why Gilgamesh wants to go: it is because of his restless spirit, literally, "the heart that does not sleep" (*libbu lā sālila*). But in the same breath, Ninsun also complicates Gilgamesh's motive. She repeats Gilgamesh's words but gives them a crucial spin, saying that he will walk the far road to the home of Humbaba, not because his mind is made up, but because the Sun God set him off in that direction. Her description of the quest is the same, but the underlying cause is not, blurring the distinction between internal desire and external influence. So which is it? Did Gilgamesh make up his mind, or did the god make him go?[10] The epic leaves the question—like most of its other questions—unanswered.

However, the quest to the Cedar Forest still seems relatively straightforward. Regardless of its motive, at least the righteousness of the mission appears to be beyond doubt. Humbaba is evil, Shamash hates him, he should be killed. But things become increasingly complicated as the quest nears its end, in an arc that leads from clarity through confusion to disaster.

Our suspicion that the quest might not be blessed by the gods is first awakened by Gilgamesh's dreams. Every night, the heroes build a dream house and pray for a favorable omen, but each dream turns out to be a nightmare. Still, Enkidu manages to interpret Gilgamesh's hellish visions as signs of certain success, and the heroes march on. They exchange constant encouragements, taking turns to egg each other on to glory. But when glory comes, it is not as sweet as they had hoped. Humbaba's evil nature is thrown into doubt just when the heroes are about to kill him. With Humbaba defeated and pleading for his life, Enkidu urges Gilgamesh to finish him off, "before Enlil hears of it, the leader of gods! The great gods will grow angry with us."[11] The gods seem not to hate Humbaba so much after all. Far from an evil ogre, Humbaba turns out to be a sacred guardian they installed to protect the forest.

When the heroes do kill Humbaba, murder his sons, and fell his trees, they begin to wonder whether they have done the right thing. Enkidu turns to Gilgamesh and asks,

> My friend, we have turned the forest into wasteland.
> What will we say if Enlil asks us in Nippur:
> "You used your strength to kill the guardian!
> What wrath sent you trampling through the forest?"[12]

Enkidu pictures himself being questioned by the ruler of the gods, and asks Gilgamesh what they should say if they are taken to task for their actions. But the thought experiment reduces him to silence. Neither he nor Gilgamesh can give a satisfactory account of his own motives. As so often in the epic, the question (and the question inside the question) goes unanswered. The heroes use Enlil as an imaginary mirror to look at themselves and examine their own motives but find only an anger they cannot explain.

* * *

The same unclear desire also drives Gilgamesh's quest for immortality in the second half of the epic. Again, at the outset matters seem relatively straightforward. Enkidu's death has confronted Gilgamesh with his own mortality, and he desperately wants to avoid sharing that fate. But once more, the quest soon grows more complicated. It turns out that Gilgamesh wants to travel to Uta-napishti not so much because he has a clear goal in mind but because he cannot stay still.

On his way to Uta-napishti, Gilgamesh is asked three times: "What hollowed your cheeks, bowed your head, wrecked your heart, and broke your body?" To which he replies: "How could my cheeks be full, my head held high, my heart not wrecked, my body not broken?"[13] As always in the epic, when the heroes' motives are interrogated, questions are answered by yet more questions, which obscure as much as they explain. Gilgamesh goes on to tell the story of his adventures with Enkidu, but in so doing he demonstrates that his grief is not the only reason for his journey to Uta-napishti. The story he tells places that journey next to many others, including the quest to the Cedar Forest and his aimless wandering in the wild after he left Uruk.[14]

By his own account, Gilgamesh is always on the move. Now he is in search of immortality, but beneath that search lies a deeper, more fundamental restlessness. In the end, Uta-napishti must disappoint him: he cannot give Gilgamesh eternal life. In despair, Gilgamesh asks,

> How can I go on, Uta-napishti? Where should I go?
> The Thief of Life has a hold on my heart.
> Death is sitting in my bedroom,
> and wherever I turn, there too is death.[15]

Here Gilgamesh finally reckons with the inevitability of death, staring mortality straight in the eye—but he does not confront his own restlessness. He asks Uta-napishti for a new direction, a way to go on traveling, not a way to *stop* traveling. Gilgamesh cannot describe the solace he seeks as anything but more wandering, even as he himself says that wandering would hold no relief for him. No road to which he might turn can give him consolation, since death is everywhere. But he cannot rest, either, for death sits in his bedroom too. Fear of death makes Gilgamesh travel to the ends of the earth, but traveling in no way dispels that fear. Though Gilgamesh finally accepts that death is inevitable, his acceptance means that he has nowhere to go; it does not release him from his restlessness.

In his conversation with Uta-napishti, Gilgamesh offers a rare flash of self-awareness, but most of the time he cannot account for his own motives in explicit terms. When he proposes the quest against Humbaba, the elders of Uruk cry out in frustration, "You are young, Gilgamesh. Your heart carries you away, you do not understand the things that you say."[16] Gilgamesh's desire tears him away from himself, so that he fails to understand even the meaning of his own words.

Enkidu is not much more self-aware. When Shamhat invites him to come to Uruk, where she will show him the splendid King Gilgamesh, the narrator notes that "the words she spoke agreed with him; his wise heart told him to find a friend." But in the very next lines, Enkidu proclaims, "I will be the one to challenge him, subdue him by force."[17] His heart and his words have him looking for two opposing things: a friend and a rival. Again, a deceptively simple journey ends up revealing an underlying ambiguity of motive.

Enkidu's journey to Uruk illustrates another aspect of the heroes' stormy hearts. As he travels to the city, Enkidu is transformed from an animal-like creature that cannot eat bread to a fully human being who can act as adviser to King Gilgamesh himself, the paragon of urban life. The journey to Humbaba and back that follows will transform him yet again, eventually leading to his death. Likewise, Gilgamesh may be constantly restless, but his restlessness is the only constant thing about him. He is not only driven but also reshaped by his restlessness. Here is where the metaphor of the human sail breaks down: unlike a mast, Gilgamesh does not bear the weight of the winds with wooden indifference. He is completely worn down by them, arriving exhausted at Uta-napishti's island and sleeping for a week at the first chance he gets.

Keith Dickson argues that in *Gilgamesh*, journeys and especially the confrontation with strange people and places along the way always lead to change: "Seeing the other is transformative; it always brings with it a risk of oneself no longer being the same. . . . The traveller who is gone for long and whose journey takes him far afield, returns home to his kin a changed man because of the labour of travel and also because of what he has seen along the way."[18] When Shiduri, Ur-shanabi, and Uta-napishti are shocked by the sight of Gilgamesh's wasted body, this is precisely what they say: that Gilgamesh looks "like one who has traveled far."[19] Such a person must, they assume, be worn down in body and mind. This is what journeys do to the traveler according to the logic of the epic: they lead to change and hardship. The restlessness that besets the hero drives him to his own undoing.[20] In the end, the journeys prove fateful to both characters. Enkidu dies, and Gilgamesh succumbs to an all-consuming grief. Had the heroes been content with the luxury that Uruk had to offer, they would have been spared their pain. The tragedy of Gilgamesh lies, as with all tragic characters, in the self-destructive force of his own desire.

More often than not, the storm in Gilgamesh's heart leads him to truly idiotic acts of aggression. When he meets Uta-napishti, he exclaims, "My heart was all set on fighting with you."[21] Was it, though? And why would it be? It is as if Gilgamesh has forgotten why he went looking for Uta-napishti in the first place, perhaps confusing the quest to kill Humbaba with the quest to learn Uta-napishti's secret. But the explanation is much simpler: Gilgamesh meets everyone with hostility.[22] When he meets Ishtar, he not only rejects her; he heaps abuse on her. When he meets Shiduri, he threatens to break down the door of her house. When he meets Ur-shanabi, he smashes the Stone Ones. But as Ur-Shanabi then points out, Gilgamesh's aggression does most harm to himself—as the boatman dryly puts it, "Your own hands are holding you back."[23] Without the Stone Ones, Gilgamesh has no way of crossing the Waters of Death.

Nowhere is Gilgamesh's self-destructive character clearer than in his rejection of Ishtar. Why does he turn down her offer of marriage? Surely, the insatiable hero must have been tempted by the goddess of sex. Scholars have proposed various reasons for the rejection: perhaps it was considered unacceptable for women to be so forward, and Gilgamesh's reply suggests that, while she might be a great sex partner, Ishtar would not have provided him with the basic comforts he expected from a wife in a patriarchal household—food and clothes.[24] But what is striking about it is the spite with which it is delivered. Even if Gilgamesh had good reasons to decline Ishtar's offer, it was hardly a tactful way to do so, and Enkidu only adds to the insult by throwing the Bull's penis in her face.

Their behavior once again betrays a deep instinct for aggression, and again that aggression backfires, as Enkidu is sentenced to death by the gods. The only time this knee-jerk hostility does the heroes more good than harm is when they meet each other. They instantly fly at each other's throats, winning a mutual respect.[25] For once, their aggression is reciprocated.

It is not only the heroes who act combatively; the gods do the same. They act with thoughtless aggression, unable to foresee the consequences of their actions, as shown most powerfully by the story of the Flood. Watching the storm they unleashed grow out of control, Belet-ili wails, "How could I speak evil in the gathering of gods?"[26] Like the human heroes at the end of Tablet V, she cannot explain why she chose to wreak such massive destruction. She looks inward for an answer but finds only a passionate confusion. In the Cedar Forest, Enkidu looked to Enlil as an upholder of morals, but in the story of the Flood, Enlil is placed in the opposite role.[27] Belet-ili expels him from the assembly of the gods "because he caused the Flood, acting without counsel," and Ea berates him at length for choosing the Flood over a less cataclysmic solution.[28] Thoughtless aggression is not only a problem for bored young men; even the ruler of the gods has the same bent.

The gods' behavior does not excuse Gilgamesh's; rather, it warns us that the violent storm raging in his heart is not his alone. If it can afflict even Enlil, it can afflict mortal readers of the epic as well. Like the heroes and gods, we too must interrogate our motives, preferably before and not after doing something catastrophic. As noted by the Assyriologist Karen Sonik, the epic repeatedly emphasizes the importance of taking counsel with others and listening to the words of advisers and friends.[29] Had Gilgamesh listened to Enkidu, he would not have incurred the wrath of the gods. Had Enlil listened to Ea, he would not have made the single biggest mistake in Babylonian mythology—unleashing the Flood. Only conversation offers a check on the destructive instincts in our hearts.

And yet for all their violence and obscurity, Gilgamesh's passions are not solely to blame. No matter how violent the storm in his heart, no matter how idiotic, short-sighted, and self-destructive it makes him, at the end of the day the force of his passion is also his redeeming quality. For better and worse, Gilgamesh feels more than most mortals.[30] Although the power of his emotions brings him much pain, it also leads him to a love of epic dimensions. Gilgamesh is at his best when he channels his superhuman strength into the one thing that matters to him: his friendship with Enkidu.

As long as they are both alive, the heroes never speak each other's name, referring to the other only as "my friend." Other characters call them Enkidu and Gilgamesh, and they in turn call others by their name, so—as first noted by Martin Worthington—it is only when talking to each other that they avoid using names.[31] It is as if names would introduce an unwanted difference between them: without names to separate them, they slip into the shapeless intimacy of "my friend" and "my friend." Similarly, for as long as they are together, they do not name their bond as "love." After Enkidu's death, Gilgamesh calls him "my friend, whom I love so much," and before meeting him he dreams of a meteor and an ax that he "loves like a wife."[32] But for the duration of their friendship, they do not explicate the nature of their feelings for each other. Again, it is as if they want to leave their bond undefined by words, shapeless in all its intensity.

The heroes' unwillingness to describe their bond is one reason for the controversy that now surrounds it. Had they been more forthcoming about their feelings, the ambiguity of the text might not have provoked so much debate. The controversy was ignited as early as 1930 by Thorkild Jacobsen, who first labeled their love homosexual, at a time when the English word *homosexual* had been in use for just forty years.[33] But Jacobsen's suggestion was not universally accepted, and the debate has gone back and forth ever since.[34] The problem is that there is not much evidence either way. In Tablet XII, the relationship between the heroes seems to be explicitly sexual— Enkidu tells Gilgamesh about the decrepit condition of "my penis, which you touched to please your heart"—but in the main part of the epic, their relation is studiedly ambiguous.[35]

Even if a new fragment of the epic comes to light that does clearly show the heroes having sex, *homosexual* might not be the right word for it. It is a recent invention, and before the nineteenth century homosexuality was not part of a person's identity in the same way it is today: it did not come with the same stereotypes and expectations. Men could have sex with each other, but that did not make them homosexual, in the same way that today, touching yourself does not make you a masturbator: it is not an identity or a fixed role in our society.[36] If we could bring Enkidu's ghost back from the dead one more time to ask him if he was gay, he would not understand the question. But—and this is the clincher—if the heroes cannot be homosexual, they cannot be heterosexual, either.[37] Both identities are a modern construction. Neither the epic's ambiguity nor the modern invention of homosexuality precludes a reading of the heroes' love as erotic.

But at the end of the day, whether they have sex does not matter. The heroes are said to *râmu* each other, and the Akkadian term covers both erotic and platonic love: the difference between them is not central to the vocabulary of the epic. As the Assyriologist Joan Goodnick Westenholz puts it, to a Babylonian audience emotional love and sexual attraction "were not perceived as two separate forces. The physical and emotional sides of love were different reflects of the same relationship."[38] What does matter is that their love is one of the epic's most powerful themes. Whether sexual or platonic, their friendship is the emotional core around which the epic turns. The cuneiform sign for love, RAM, shows a human body with a flame inside it, and in Gilgamesh's body, that flame burns with unmatched power.

In his book *Desire, Discord, and Death,* the philologist Neal Walls spells out the simple but important premise that one can appreciate the fiery love between Gilgamesh and Enkidu without having to label it with modern terms. Walls reminds us not to look for the "true nature" of their relationship (they are fictional characters anyway) but rather to understand how the epic describes bodies and attraction on its own, Babylonian terms.[39]

The most important of those terms is *kuzbu.* I translate it as "charm," but the Akkadian word is much stronger, more like a magnetic sexual allure that pulls people to those who wield it. Walls calls it "an energy that emanates from the possessor to arouse the observer." The logic of *kuzbu* is summarized by the hunter, who tells Shamhat to reveal her body to Enkidu: "he will see you and run to you." The very sight of her body is enough to draw the wild man to her—that is what *kuzbu* does.[40]

After seducing Enkidu, Shamhat redirects his gaze from her own body to Gilgamesh. Enkidu's first glimpse of his future friend is through Shamhat's eyes, as she uses her words to summon Gilgamesh out of thin air and tell Enkidu to examine his body:

Let me show you Gilgamesh, this man about town.
Look at him, see that face:
the dignity he has, the beauty of youth!
His whole body is full of charm (*kuzbu*).[41]

It is thus not only women whose body can hold *kuzbu;* on the contrary, male bodies are often shown to be powerfully attractive. Another example of *kuzbu* in the epic is when Ishtar "caught sight" of Gilgamesh's beauty and instantly proposes to him.[42] His body works the same kind of magnetic pull on Ishtar that Shamhat's had worked on Enkidu.

The relationship of Gilgamesh and Enkidu is thus wrapped in *kuzbu,* but the exact nature of the attraction is less clear. Enkidu wants a friend, then a fight. When they meet, their inborn hostility has them fighting from the moment they lay eyes on each other, but the fight is soon followed by friendship. They seem to go back and forth between attraction and aggression, but as Walls points out, perhaps there is no real difference between the two in the world of the epic. In both cases, the heroes' feelings for each other are intense and physical, to the point that rage and lust merge into one.

This is especially clear in the scene of the fight: "The intimate bodily contact of wrestling, the implied grunts and groans of physical exertion, and the threshold symbolism of the doorway all contribute to the scene's sexual symbolism."[43] Once more, the terms of the epic are revealing. We are told that when the fight begins, the heroes "took hold of each other" (*iṣṣabtū*) to wrestle, but later, when Enkidu breaks down crying and Gilgamesh comforts him, the heroes "took hold of each other" (*iṣṣabtū* again) in an affectionate embrace.[44] The same verb can denote both comfort and combat, friendship and aggression because in *Gilgamesh* they are not clearly distinct.

Tellingly, the fight between the heroes takes place on a threshold—they break its frame and shake the walls. As noted by the Assyriologist Jean-Jacques Glassner, it is a threshold of great symbolic importance. On one side of it is the wedding house (*bit emūti*), a private and intimate space, on the other lies "the street of the land" (*rēbit māti*), a public space visible to all.[45] The heroes' friendship is forged on that threshold, and it retains the ambiguity throughout—Enkidu is both Gilgamesh's official adviser and his intimate companion.

Because their friendship is founded on aggression, aggression is necessary for its survival. As John Bailey puts it, "Once friends, all there is for them to do is to seek out (one could almost say, create) an enemy and destroy it; violence is what binds them."[46] The campaign against Humbaba is a natural reflex for this very male form of friendship, in which love is never fully separate from violence. What is striking about the quest is how easily the militaristic heroic ideals of the epic can be an occasion for intimate affection. Walls writes that the quest against Humbaba is "a type of heroic honeymoon. The couple flees the crowded city for the privacy of the wilderness where, like Achilles and Patroclos, they sleep together in the same tent."[47] What they do in that tent is not the point. The point is that, whether they fuck or fight, the heroic ideal they live by keeps throwing them into each other's arms.

During World War I, the writer Lytton Strachey—a figure whom today we would call a gay icon—applied to be treated as a conscientious objector. The tribunal that assessed his application, seeking to test the resolve of his pacifism, asked, "Mr. Strachey, what would you do if you saw a German soldier trying to violate your sister?" To which Strachey replied, "I would try to get between them."[48] Strachey's joke works because it assumes that the hypermasculine German soldier would be just as willing to have sex with Strachey as with his sister—and that Strachey would relish it. That is the assumption at work in *Gilgamesh* too, where Enkidu does pretty much exactly what Strachey suggests. Seeing Gilgamesh on his way to the unwilling bride, he gets between them, substituting himself as the object of Gilgamesh's desire, and relishing it. The strategy works. Gilgamesh, preoccupied with his new friend, forgets all about the woman he was on his way to violate.

The parallel highlights an important aspect of the heroes' friendship: it always involves a third person. Their love has the shape of a triangle, but the third point of that triangle keeps changing. In the scene of the fight, the third party is the bride. When the heroes become friends, she is quickly replaced by Humbaba: the heroes are now joined by their common quest against the monster. With Humbaba dead, Ishtar steps into the same role as the heroes form a common front against her and the Bull of Heaven. But the original third party in the heroes' triangle is Shamhat. As David Damrosch notes, the epic "goes out of its way" to show Gilgamesh approving the hunter's plan of having Shamhat seduce Enkidu.[49] As a result, the sexual encounter between Enkidu and Shamhat is framed by the overarching relation between Gilgamesh and Enkidu, showing how difficult it can be to categorize ancient sex according to modern terms: an unarguably heterosexual marathon of love is used to bring two men together.

The presence of a third party allows the heroes to project their emotions outward. Their wild and mixed feelings for each other can be channeled through the third person, whether it is the erotic attraction that Enkidu feels for Shamhat or the aggression that the heroes bring to bear on Humbaba and Ishtar. Projecting their mutual feelings onto someone else allows them to be much more evasive about what they feel for each other. Without names to separate them, and without the word *love* to define their bond, their friendship slips into an amorphous tide of passion, tears, kisses, hugs, wrath, and *kuzbu*. But this formlessness cannot last. Other characters of the epic repeatedly try to shoehorn the heroes' feelings into a more definite form—and in the end, they succeed.

Whereas Walls shows how fluid the bonds between men can be, the Assyriologist Ann Guinan and the screenwriter Peter Morris examine how that fluidity is forced to conform to the strict logic of a militarized society. Walls's keyword is *kuzbu*; Guinan and Morris's is *meḫru*. The word means something like "match" in its broadest possible sense. Two equally long lines of a geometrical diagram are each other's *meḫru*, a tablet copied from an original is the *meḫru* of that original. Among humans, a *meḫru* can be a social peer but also a rival. As Guinan and Morris put it, "'Meeting one's match' means very different things to a soldier engaged in single combat or a single person responding to a personals ad."[50]

Those shades of meaning are all present when Enkidu is made Gilgamesh's *meḫru*. The gods create him "to be a match (*māḫir*) for the storm of his heart," and in the dreams that presage his arrival, Ninsun declares him Gilgamesh's equal, again using a form of the word *meḫru*. The epic repeatedly stresses how similar the two men are: the shepherds exclaim that Enkidu "looks just like Gilgamesh," and the phrase "his locks curled thick like ears of corn" is used to describe them both. When Enkidu is on his deathbed, his dying regret is that he can no longer live up to this role, as he curses the hunter "who did not let me be a match (*meḫru*) for my friend."[51]

Tellingly, when Enkidu first arrives in Uruk, the young men elect him as their champion in the fight against Gilgamesh: "For Gilgamesh, the youth with chiseled features, a partner (*meḫru*) was chosen, as if he were a god."[52] This could mean one of two things. The epic may be alluding to mythological stories of a god meeting a monster in battle: as the *meḫru* of such a god, Enkidu would be Gilgamesh's rival. Or the epic may be alluding to the ritual of the Sacred Marriage, where a priestess was chosen to sleep with the god of the city: as a *meḥru* in that sense, Enkidu would be Gilgamesh's lover.[53] The term has both meanings, and Enkidu has both roles—Gilgamesh has met his match in every sense.

Not only are they physically similar; after Ninsun's adoption of Enkidu, they are also social equals. But as Guinan and Morris point out, that perfect equality is a challenge to the cultural order of the time. The love between social equals was an unusual thing in cuneiform cultures.[54] The love between men and women was an inherently unequal affair, because men held a higher social rank, and the love between two men typically involved an asymmetrical relation of power, with the penetrator being automatically superior to the penetrated. The love between Gilgamesh and Enkidu does not conform to that pattern because they are equal in every way, and so it must be resisted.

To understand how that resistance works, Guinan and Morris compare the epic to other cuneiform texts about male homosexuality. One of those texts is an omen from the series *Shumma Alu*. As noted in the introduction, Babylonians found omens not only in the errancy of planets or the entrails of sheep but in human behavior as well, including the way people had sex. One omen states that "if a man has anal sex with a social peer (*meḥru*), that man will become foremost among his brothers and colleagues."[55] The outcome is positive, and, as often in cuneiform cultures, the prediction relies on a hidden link between the two parts of the omen: here between "anus," *qinnatu,* and "colleague," *kinātu.* According to the logic of cuneiform omens, the similarity in sound indicated a connection in content.

But to Guinan and Morris, the crucial point is that even when the omen describes sex between two social equals, that equality is instantly collapsed into hierarchy, between the man who goes foremost and the colleagues who follow. The idea of male equals having sex with each other irrespective of power is simply not entertained: their social relations to each other, to their colleagues, and to their family will always be central to the act. (As Oscar Wilde is said to have said, "Everything is about sex, except sex, which is about power.")

In cuneiform cultures, sex between equals was a puzzling thing, and the omen supplies a solution to that puzzle, resolving it into the more familiar pattern of unequal positions in social space—the penetrator gains power and gets to go in front. "An inexorable, almost geometric logic governs Mesopotamian imaginings of sex between male social equals. Any possibility of mutuality and eroticism instantly is collapsed into positionality, and reinscribed with hierarchy and power."⁵⁶ Sex between men is a public concern; it involves not them alone but their colleagues and brothers too.

Guinan and Morris argue that the same hierarchical impulse is also at work in *Gilgamesh*. When the elders advise the heroes as they embark on their quest, they stress that the two should conform by the logic of unequal roles: "'Go first and you help an ally, know the road and you save a friend.' So let Enkidu go first!"⁵⁷ The logic is clear: Enkidu should go ahead, Gilgamesh should go behind. Again, the relation between two male equals is a public concern, and it must abide by what Guinan and Morris call the logic of positionality. A shapeless, mutual love between equals is molded into hierarchy, with one person in front and the other behind.

In short, the epic exposes a tension in the military logic of cuneiform cultures, which both celebrated the camaraderie between soldiers and insisted on a hierarchical order between leaders and followers. Gilgamesh and Enkidu resist that hierarchy. As they travel toward Humbaba, they take turns leading and being led. First Enkidu is afraid, and Gilgamesh chides him for his cowardice. Then the exchange is reversed, and Enkidu speaks the same words to Gilgamesh. To them, it does not matter who leads and who follows, because they see each other as perfect equals who can equally well take on either role.

Resisting the demand for a fixed position in social space, the two heroes constantly blur their differences, especially by refusing to use each other's name. Over the course of the epic, it becomes increasingly difficult to tell them apart. The confusion is especially strong in their conversation at the beginning of Tablet V, as they stand at the entrance of the Cedar Forest. The stock formula normally used to introduce direct speech, "he worked his words," is absent from this passage, so it is not clear which of them is speaking at any one point. The quotation marks used in the translation are a modern convention; they do not appear in cuneiform. The only hint that a change of speaker has taken place is the phrase "my friend," which, according to Andrew George and Farouk al-Rawi, indicates that one or the other has taken over.⁵⁸ But of course, that phrase is ambiguous too, as it could refer to either one of them.

In this scene, it seems as if the two friends really have achieved the perfect equality they wanted. They truly are each other's match, so much so that we cannot tell which one is speaking. At the end of the conversation,

Gilgamesh (or is it Enkidu?) says, "My friend, take hold of me. We will go as one."[59] The terms that define their relationship—"my friend," "take hold"—come together, and for a moment it seems that they have successfully resisted the logic of hierarchy and fixed positions, merging into one, insisting on a love between equals.[60] But their unity is not to last.

The epic cannot escape the dictates of its time. The heroes must fit into the hierarchy that was demanded of love in the cuneiform world, one way or the other. If they will not listen to the advice of the elders, the gods will force them to obey: the gods decide that one must die and the other must live. They are not to "go as one" into death and be together in the afterlife: "One goes first, another is left behind. This is not only the logic of military hierarchy and social position, it is the logic of life and death," as Guinan and Morris grimly conclude.[61] The friends do abide by the elders' instruction, but not in the way any of them had imagined: grieving for Enkidu, Gilgamesh paces "back and forth, before and behind him."[62] The line is a poignant reminder of the demand for sequences and fixed positions, which has now been met in the most tragic way possible. Just as the elders told him to, Enkidu went first. Gilgamesh must try to go on without him.

Having insistently avoided each other's names throughout their friendship, Gilgamesh begins his eulogy in Tablet VIII by crying, "Enkidu!" It is the first time he speaks his friend's name, and the first word he speaks after Enkidu's death.[63] The heroes' avoidance of names had helped them efface the distance between themselves, but now that distance can no longer be ignored: Enkidu rots while Gilgamesh weeps.[64]

Gilgamesh is utterly undone by his grief. In Enkidu he has lost both a friend and a part of himself. As Walls puts it: "Having achieved a complete union in their heroic friendship, Gilgamesh must now face an equally complete separation from his beloved companion."[65] Who is Gilgamesh outside that union? The relation with Enkidu transformed who he was, so now he must find out who he is without him. Having constantly striven to be like Enkidu, to be a match for his friend in every respect, Gilgamesh realizes the flip side of that likeness: "I too will die. Am I not like Enkidu?"[66] Having seen the corpse of his all-too-human partner rot away, Gilgamesh understands what the match he so ardently wished for entails. Now he no longer wants to be like Enkidu; instead he fears for his own life and decides to seek immortality.

Some scholars have argued that Gilgamesh is being narcissistic in these lines, too quick to forget Enkidu and think only of himself.[67] But I do not think that the two feelings—grief over Enkidu's death and fear for his own life—are all that separate. Rather, I would argue that Gilgamesh's search for immortality constitutes a way for him to mourn. Mourning entails finding a way to continue living after loss, and to do so, we must discover who we are when those who have shaped us are no longer with us. What part of our being survives the loss of a loved one?[68] As he had achieved a near-perfect union with Enkidu, for Gilgamesh the task is especially difficult, but in these lines he finds a way to be different from his dead friend: he will be immortal. In short, Gilgamesh's quest for eternal life is a coping strategy of the most impossibly ambitious, over-the-top heroic kind.

As his identity crumbles in Enkidu's wake, Gilgamesh becomes less of a man in several ways. First, he becomes more of an animal.[69] He leaves Uruk behind and travels into the wilderness, the land of wild beasts. He eats their flesh and wears their skin; in Tablet X he is asked why he is "dressed as a lion."[70] Just as Enkidu could not move from the steppe to the city without becoming human, learning to eat bread and put on clothes, so Gilgamesh cannot move from city to steppe without becoming nonhuman, devouring raw flesh and dressing in pelts.

In addition, Gilgamesh tries to become more of a god. His ambitions go from the heroic to the divine.[71] It is one thing to seek eternal fame— any hero worth his salt will do that—and quite another to seek eternal life. Gilgamesh had always been two-thirds god, but now he wants to dispense with the human element entirely. Again, his transformation is reflected in the physical landscape through which he travels. He moves from the city, where humans live, through the steppe, where animals live, to the land beyond the Tunnel of Darkness, where gods live.[72]

Gilgamesh's final change is to become more of a woman. The metaphors that describe his grief are insistently gendered. Gilgamesh weeps "as bitterly as a weeper woman," he circles the corpse of his friend "like a lioness" and covers Enkidu's face "like a bride."[73] There seems to be a general association between mourning and women in cuneiform cultures, so when he is flung into all-consuming grief, it follows that Gilgamesh also becomes somehow less male.[74] The triple transformation is wonderfully captured in the painting *Gilgamesh and Enkidu* (2001) by the Iraqi artist Suad al-Attar, which shows Enkidu fading into darkness while Gilgamesh is left behind, turned into a hybrid creature with the body of a bull, the wings of an angel, and the face of a woman.[75]

No longer fully a man, no longer fully himself, Gilgamesh goes in search of eternal life, but what he is really looking for is a person to be and a road to take. The only thing that is left of his usual self is the storm in his heart, the constant force that drives him on, and on, and on.

In one of the older Sumerian poems about Gilgamesh, *The Death of Gilgamesh*, the hero breaks down crying when he realizes that he must die—indeed, that everyone must die, for as the text puts it, "Gilgamesh grieved for all humanity." The gods have little sympathy for him, replying:

> You must have been told that this
> is what it means to be human.
> You must have been told that this
> is what it means to have your umbilical cord cut.
> The darkest day of humanity awaits you now.
> The loneliest place of humanity awaits you now.[76]

The poem describes death as a uniquely human problem. Gods do not care, because they will not die. Animals do not care, because they do not know that they will die.[77] Only humans live with death. Death is the essence of "what it means to be human"; death is our darkest and loneliest moment, the negation of all that matters to us.

The Babylonian *Gilgamesh* inherited the notion of death as a specifically human problem and added a cruel twist. The epic first shows Enkidu becoming human; only later does it remind us that becoming human also means becoming mortal—"this is what it means to be human." That is why Enkidu lashes out with such spite at the people who humanized him, the priestess and the hunter: by making him a man, they also chained him to death.

The irony is especially clear in the lines that describe Enkidu's humanization: "he smeared himself with oil and turned into a man; he put on clothes and looked like a bridegroom."[78] For all of Enkidu's joy of life in the lines, death hangs in the air like a false note. If the word for bridegroom, *mutu*, is pronounced with a long first syllable, *mūtu*, it means death.[79] When

Enkidu turns into a man, looking like a happy human bridegroom, he also lets death into his bedroom.

The epic returns to the pun and adds a further twist when Gilgamesh covers the face of his friend "like a bride." The metaphor has us thinking back to Gilgamesh's dream, in which he prophesied that he would come to love his new friend "like a wife." But we also think back to the moment when Enkidu looked like a bridegroom, and the eerie echo between the human and the mortal. When Gilgamesh covers his face like a bride, both premonitions come true at once: Gilgamesh did love his friend, and Enkidu did die.

This sequence of echoes and repetitions brings together the play of passions I have traced out in this essay—the enlacement of love and grief, transformation and desire, humanity and death that unfolds over the course of the epic. *Gilgamesh* shows that we cannot want without changing, love without losing, or live without dying. The storm in Gilgamesh's heart does eventually find peace, however, and his confrontation with death, this supremely human problem, is eventually resolved into a form of immortality.

Dying to Be Read

Gilgamesh revolves around the phrase "six days and seven nights." As noted by William Moran, this stretch of time keeps recurring in the text, guiding the audience to what may be the epic's most important theme: the extreme limits of the human condition.[1] The first time it appears is when Shamhat makes loves to Enkidu, turning him into a human being, as he abandons his herd and learns to think. The second is in the week during which Gilgamesh weeps for Enkidu, moving from the human to the inhuman, as he decides to seek a godlike immortality. The third is in the week when Gilgamesh sleeps, failing Uta-napishti's test and so losing his shot at immortality, forcing him back to a human fate. The three weeks thus bring the heroes back and forth across the threshold of humanity. Sex, grief, and sleep are all events that bring us out of ourselves, and we may return to find a different self from the one we left.

Enkidu is the focus of the first week, and Gilgamesh is the focus of the third week, but in the second week they undergo the transformation together. Gilgamesh becomes inhuman in the sense that he begins to strive for immortality, while Enkidu becomes inhuman in the sense that his body is given back to the animal domain: he rots away until a maggot drops from his nose. This is their last moment together, the moment in which their perfect equality gives way to difference.

The third week is the most elaborately described, as Uta-napishti's wife marks the passage of time by baking a loaf of bread each day. The text lists their various states of decay at the moment when Uta-napishti "touched and woke up the man."[2] The word "man," Akkadian *amēlu*, is placed at the end of the line, an unusual position for a noun in Akkadian, whose sentences usually end with a verb. In the poetic Standard Babylonian, the normal word order can be reversed for a number of reasons, including to emphasize words that are uncommonly placed. By putting the word "man" at the end of the sentence, the epic shows that this is the end result of the last week of transformation: Gilgamesh has become irrevocably human. This, according to the logic of the epic, is the same as irrevocably mortal—Gilgamesh wakes up to the realization that he must die.

The phrase "six days and seven nights" makes one last appearance. Uta-napishti says that "for six days and seven nights, the wind blew. The storm and the Flood flattened the land."[3] But this is a different story altogether, not the story of Gilgamesh but the story of the Flood that is nestled inside it. The repetition cuts across two layers of storytelling, inviting us to think about the relation between them. The story of the Flood is what literary critics call a *mise en abîme,* that is, a story within a story. Often, literary works will use a mise en abîme to reflect on themselves. The smaller story makes a statement about how literature works, and the reader is then invited to consider how that statement might apply to the larger story as well. Likewise, by including an epic inside the epic, *Gilgamesh* asks us to consider what storytelling does, to both those who tell the story and those who hear it.

This essay is about the links joining these three themes: being human, facing death, and telling stories. According to *Gilgamesh,* there is no escape from death—but there may still be a way to transcend it.

The monologue that closes Tablet X, where Uta-napishti muses on the nature of death, is one of the most striking passages in all of Babylonian poetry:

Humans! Your lines snap like reeds.
The beautiful youth, the beautiful girl
—abducted by death in their prime!

No one sees death.
No one sees the face of death,
no one hears the voice of death.
But it is savage death that snaps mankind.

One day, we build a house,
one day, we found a home.
One day, the heirs divide it,
one day, the sons grow bitter.

One day, the river rose and brought high water,
a mayfly drifting down the river,
its face turned toward the sun.
But even then it could see nothing.

How similar are death and abduction,
and one cannot draw the image of death.
Yet no one has ever greeted a dead man.

The Anunnaki were assembled, the great gods.
Mami, maker of destinies, fixed fates for them:
The gods gave humans life and death,
but did not reveal which day you will die.[4]

The monologue begins with a simple metaphor, the snapping of the reed. The death that Uta-napishti is about to describe is not the gradual fading of age or sickness but a sudden gash that cuts down young and old alike.[5] However, its furious suddenness is the only quality that Uta-napishti is willing to ascribe to death. All its other aspects he leaves undescribed. For a monologue on death, the text says surprisingly little about death itself, because no attribute can be attached to something we always experience as absence. Death takes away but is nothing in itself, so it can only be described through denial. It is that which has no face or voice, that whose image we cannot draw, whose coming we cannot predict.

This insistent denial makes death almost impossible to describe, yet Uta-napishti succeeds in doing so in the third stanza of the monologue. He tells the story of a family home being built and torn apart. In the Akkadian original, the small tale is told in no more than fourteen words. Not one of those words is "death," yet death stays at the center of the stanza. Somebody must die halfway through, because in the third verse the brothers are dividing the family fortune that was built up in the first two verses. Death is not shown directly because it cannot be shown directly; instead it emerges as an implication from the sequence of events. Death is nothing but a pause in the structure of the stanza, as the readers stop for breath between couplets, and somebody dies. One cannot draw the image of death; it can only be painted with silence.

The division of the inheritance in turn leads to bitterness between brothers, which might lead to more deaths, which might lead to more feuds, which might lead to more deaths, and so on.[6] The monologue contrasts the death of a single person with the larger flow of time in which the story repeats itself, again and again, as emphasized by the repetition of "One day . . ."

This contrast becomes even clearer in the following stanza, which depicts mayflies floating on a sunlit river. Every spring, as the snow on the mountain peaks melted, the Tigris would swell and the insects that had settled on its surface would be swept along, making the water glitter with their wings.[7] That is the image Uta-napishti summons, and as Andrew George notes, the stanza "makes clear the distinction between the fragile brevity of a man's life (the mayfly) and the infinite repetition of mankind's generations through past and future time (the flooding river)."[8] Each man must die, but men live on, just as the river will carry more mayflies downstream. But Uta-napishti also points to the brutal reality that lies beyond the metaphor. Even as the dead mayflies lie on the river, faces turned toward the sun, they see nothing—for death is nothingness.[9]

The monologue (and with it, Tablet X) ends with a couplet that describes two decisions made by the gods. They decreed that humans would be fated to die but also that they would not know when it would happen. By setting the two decisions next to each other, Uta-napishti reveals the central paradox that defines humanity's relation to death. Death is at one and the same time completely certain and completely uncertain.[10] The gods have decreed that we must die, so die we must: death is the one certainty we have in life. But the gods also left us in painful ignorance of when our death will occur. Remember that, according to Uta-napishti, we do not slowly fade but suddenly snap: death is a single moment, unknown to us. As a result, the certainty of death is an entirely hollow certainty. We know that we must die, but not when, where, or why, how it will come about, or how it will feel, because no one sees death or hears its voice. We know nothing about death except its certainty.

Uta-napishti's monologue is a poetic feat, but it is not the only perspective on death found in the epic. Gilgamesh's emotional journey from bravado at the story's beginning to despair at the end can be mapped through his changing relation to death.[11] Given the link between death and humanity, it follows that Gilgamesh, who is two-thirds god, also has an ambiguous relation to mortality, one that matures over the course of the story.

In the first Tablets, Gilgamesh exhibits the disdain of death that we expect of epic heroes. He wants to achieve eternal fame through epic deeds, but he does not care whether he survives those deeds. He says to Enkidu, "Forget death, chase life," but he is not telling his friend to flee danger. The life Enkidu must chase is the metaphorical kind, the eternal life of fame, and to achieve it he must set aside the fear of facing death. The heroes talk big at this point: "You've bathed in blood and fear not death."[12] But that is clearly not true. In fact, they are full of fear, and must take turns comforting each other.

Enkidu's death comes as a rude awakening to the not at all metaphorical reality of death. Having seen what death actually looks like, Gilgamesh loses all disdain for it. The image of a maggot dropping from Enkidu's nose is as sobering as images get. After Enkidu's death, Gilgamesh leaves the epic ideals of the first Tablets behind to pursue more concrete goals. Gone is the dilemma of Achilles and his ilk: of whether to purchase immortal fame at the price of literal death. Instead, we find an all-devouring obsession with avoiding death itself.

When Gilgamesh realizes that this cannot be done, he says to Uta-napishti, "The Thief of Life has a hold on my heart. Death is sitting in my bedroom, and wherever I turn, there too is death."[13] The couplet paints a very different picture of death from the one in Uta-napishti's philosophical musing. For Gilgamesh, death is not a sudden snapping, but a constant presence. Death is everywhere. The defining uncertainty of death described by Uta-napishti has grown into full-blown paranoia. Because we cannot know when and where death will strike, it is potentially around every corner and inside every room.

One final perspective on death comes from the epic's Old Babylonian version. Here, the innkeeper Shiduri tries to soothe Gilgamesh's pain, telling him to return to a quieter, happier life. The passage was cut from the Standard Babylonian edition, to be replaced by Uta-napishti's much grimmer monologue, but recently it has attracted a cult following of its own.[14] Shiduri's point is simple: since immortality is not possible, we must enjoy the time we have.

Gilgamesh, where are you going?
You will not find the life you seek.

When the gods created humankind,
they decreed death for the humans,
eternal life they kept for themselves.

So, Gilgamesh, fill your belly,
and be happy night and day.
Let all your days be merry,
dance and play day and night.

Let your clothes be clean,
wash your head in water.
Look at the child holding your hand,
and let your wife delight in your lap.
This is the fate of humankind![15]

Shiduri tells us to enjoy our brief lives, and as with the carpe diem of Horace, the joys she recommends are not a hedonistic frenzy but everyday pleasures. The fear of death, she says, can be dispelled with a good bath. Her speech also includes a rare Babylonian celebration of female sexual pleasure, as she calls for Gilgamesh to let a woman enjoy his body.[16] Shiduri's monologue begins with the same assumption as Uta-napishti's, that mortality and humanity define each another, but she reaches a very different conclusion. For Shiduri, mortality is a reason to enjoy ourselves all the more.[17] The fate of humankind is not gloom and paranoia, but sex, food, and dance.

The epic gives us an array of perspectives on death, from disdain through pleasure to despair, but what comes after death is shown only through hints and glimpses. What is the fate that Gilgamesh so desperately wants to avoid? The clearest description of what happens after death is the sight of Enkidu's body rotting away, but what of the afterlife? On that question, the first eleven Tablets are stubbornly shy.

The first glimpse of the afterlife comes in Ninsun's prayer to Shamash. The prayer stands as a stunning moment in the epic; it is as if the poem steps out of the story to give the reader a bird's-eye view of the narrative. We leave the perspective of our main character to follow that of his all-knowing mother, who goes up to the roof of her palace to talk with a fellow deity about the fate of her son. Ninsun explains why Gilgamesh acts as he does (pointing to his restless heart) and tells Shamash how he can help him, revealing the outcome of the battle against Humbaba long before it begins. Not content with this, Ninsun prays to (or, rather, instructs) Shamash again, and again reveals what will happen later:

> Shamash! Will Gilgamesh not join the gods one day?
> Will he not share the skies with you?
> Will he not share the scepter of the Moon God?
> Will he not grow wise with Ea in the Apsû?
> Will he not rule with Irnina in the underworld?
> Will he not live with Ningishzida in the Land of No Return?[18]

According to the popular Babylonian belief, Gilgamesh would indeed go on to "rule with Irnina in the underworld."[19] The Babylonians believed that Gilgamesh was a judge in the realms of the afterlife, ruling the souls of the dead, and they might even have expected to meet him after death, as Catholics expect to meet Saint Peter. Gilgamesh's role as underworld judge is explained in the Sumerian poem *The Death of Gilgamesh* as a compromise. He was too human to live forever, but too divine to die like other mortals, so he became a god, but only in death.[20]

That is the fate that Ninsun's prayer foreshadows.[21] She gives us a glimpse of Gilgamesh's future, and a Babylonian audience would not have been surprised by her comment. But in the context of the epic, it is a striking interruption of the narrative sequence. Ninsun reveals that Gilgamesh's quest for immortality will fail long before it has even entered his mind to undertake it: at this time, he is still focused on the quest against Humbaba. But Ninsun already knows his destiny (though she has apparently not told him about it), and now readers know it too.

Revealing as it is, Ninsun's comment is no more than a short glimpse of the afterlife. Enkidu offers a more detailed description when he recounts the dream in which he is taken to the underworld. Enkidu describes a land of dust and darkness, with clay for food and silence everywhere. Even the once-mighty kings sit in misery, their crowns stashed away in a corner. This is the place Gilgamesh fears. Babylonian mythology contains no paradise: what Enkidu describes was all that mortals had to look forward to. As Tablet XII shows, our fate in the underworld could be made better or worse depending on how many children would provide our soul with regular offerings. But the Babylonians had no positive image of life after death, unlike the Egyptians, who believed that a lavish tomb and the right combination of spells would secure bliss in the hereafter. (A Babylonian omen states, "If a man thinks every day about building a tomb, he will be constantly anxious," and I can't help but read that as a puzzled comment on ancient Egyptian culture.)[22]

However, Enkidu's description of the underworld is thrown into doubt before it even begins. It is easy to take the dream as a factual account of what the afterlife consists of according to the Babylonians, but the epic undermines its vision from the start, as the passage begins with the words "Enkidu's mind was ill."[23] As I read it, the verse warns us that what we are about to hear is not a clear-headed account of a prophetic vision but the confused reverie of a dying and deranged mind. Even as it offers us a peek at the underworld, the epic immediately retracts and disowns it.

Over the course of the epic's eleven Tablets, these few descriptions are all we hear of the fate that Gilgamesh tries to escape. These glimpses evoke the afterlife but do not show it directly. We do not follow Enkidu on his journey into the underworld; the perspective of the epic is firmly bound to this side of the mortal chasm. But then, just as the story has ended, we suddenly find a vivid and detailed account of the afterlife.

Tablet XII tells a separate story about Gilgamesh and Enkidu, translated directly from one of the five Sumerian poems. Not only is the plot disjointed from the rest of the epic, but, as noted in my introduction, the style is also markedly different: it reads less like an epic and more like a fable. After the high drama of the Flood, a lost ball appears to be a *very* surmountable problem. But different as it is from the rest of the epic, Tablet XII was included in the "series of Gilgamesh" by the ancient scholars, so they saw it as belonging to the story as a whole. What does it then tell us about the afterlife? From Enkidu's answers, we learn the principles by which our fate after death is decided.[24] These principles are not ethical—this is not Dante's *Divine Comedy*—rather, our fate depends on the manner of our death, and on how many people remain to provide our souls with offerings. It is not a question of how we lived in the world but of how we leave it and whom we leave behind.

The monotonous list of questions and answers may not be exciting to read, but their structure is important all the same. Tablet XII uses a common format of cuneiform culture, arguably its most important format—namely, a list of conditions and consequences: if this, then that. This is the format that Babylonian scholars used to organize most of their knowledge about the world; it was their default mode for structuring information.[25] It could be used for omens: "If a man's door is open, he will become rich; if a man's door is closed, he will be sick at heart." It could be used for laws: "If a man commits a robbery and is caught, he will be killed." And it could be used for medicine: "If the head of a man is hot but his nose, hands, and feet are cold, he is suffering from the 'mountain seizure' disease."[26] If this, then that: the format could be used for all kinds of knowledge. Crucially, the lines did not stand on their own, though that is how I quote them here. Instead, each sentence was one entry in a potentially endless list of possibilities. The link between "if" and "then" became meaningful when it was read as part of a larger context, as shown by the first example: open was good, closed was bad. The reader had to consider the contrast between the two omens to get the point. The entries only make sense as part of a list.

Philologists refer to this format as *Listenwissenschaft*, "list science."[27] The Babylonian scholars did not express their knowledge though abstract generalizations, but through a list of examples and counterexamples. Of course, Babylonian scholars were more than capable of abstract thought, as shown by their skill in mathematics, but they expressed abstractions differently from the way modern scholars do.[28] For example, in omens, the right side was considered favorable and the left side unfavorable, but the principle is never stated in so many words.[29] Rather it becomes apparent from a long list of "ifs" and "thens" in which the right side is always connected with a good outcome and the left side with a bad one.

The same logic underlies the Q&A of Tablet XII.[30] There the afterlife is described through a list of examples. The text does not say that having many children leads to a good fate in the underworld. Instead it says that if a man has one child he fares poorly, if he has two he fares better, and so on, all the way up to the man with seven sons, who sits with the gods. If this, then that. Babylonian scribes would have recognized the structure of Tablet XII as the standard format of knowledge. It is the equivalent of footnotes and references today: the format imbued the text with authority.[31] Though Tablet XII begins as a fable, it ends as a scholarly treatise on the afterlife. In the most scientific language of its time, it reveals what death has in store for human beings. Including, despite his superhuman efforts, Gilgamesh.

In the end, Gilgamesh fails to gain immortality. But he gains something else instead, returning to Uruk with the story that Uta-napishti told him. The sage tells the story of the Flood to explain why Gilgamesh cannot be immortal: the gods gathered to decree eternal life for Uta-napishti under extraordinary circumstances, circumstances that not even the desperate Gilgamesh would want to re-create. But the story is not only an explanation of Uta-napishti's immortality. It is also a precious discovery, and the prologue trumpets that discovery as Gilgamesh's greatest triumph, introducing him as the hero who "brought home a story from before the Flood."[32] Gilgamesh's victories in battle, the killing of Humbaba and the Bull of Heaven, are comparatively worthless. It is the story of the Flood that matters. When we read the epic today, its ending seems like a tragic failure, as Gilgamesh returns to Uruk empty-handed, having lost his chance at immortality. Yet according to the prologue, that same ending represents a victory, for Gilgamesh brings home a story from before the Flood. But how can the one make up for the other? How can a story stand in for eternal life?

We must understand that for the Babylonians the tale of the Flood was a story unlike any other, and not only because it explained the necessity of omens and offerings. Uta-napishti makes clear from the outset that this is no campfire yarn but a secret kept hidden by the gods themselves, no doubt because it exposed the biggest mistake of their endless lives.[33] But the story of the Flood was also extraordinary because it was seen as the outermost limit of history.

In the Babylonian worldview, time was split in two: there was a time before the Flood (*lām abūbi*) and a time after the Flood (*arki abūbi*), and even an ancient king like Gilgamesh belonged to the latter. What made the Flood special was that the destruction it wrought was all-englobing. Everything was destroyed and everyone not on Uta-napishti's ship killed, so the time before the Flood could not be known in any way: the storm had erased all records, monuments, and witnesses of the past. Observing the catastrophe, Belet-ili cries out, "All the past has turned to clay!"[34] Everything and everyone was transformed by the Flood into a malleable mass with no form or face—just like a lump of wet clay.

To the ancient scribes, the metaphor would have been particularly poignant, because clay was the material on which they wrote their texts and on which they could read stories from the past. But clay is also water soluble, and the Flood turned all texts back into their original form, a shapeless mix of earth and water that bore no trace of the past.[35] And since the survivors who might have remembered that past were long dead, the Flood was the ultimate limit of history: by studying ancient records, one could reach far back in time, but never farther than the Flood.[36]

In fact, the only possible way of knowing anything about the time before the Flood was to find its sole remaining survivors, Uta-napishti and his wife. So when Gilgamesh brought home a story "from before the Flood" (*lām abūbi*), he was carrying out a feat of epic proportions, realizing his desire to do what no one had done before. If death is the limit of human life, the Flood was the limit of human history: the story told by Uta-napishti explains why Gilgamesh cannot cross the former, but it also allows him to cross the latter, reaching back into a past that was otherwise impossible to access.

As he hears this precious story, Gilgamesh also learns something else: the value of stories in general. By telling the tale of the Flood, Uta-napishti shows the hero three things at once. He shows him why he cannot become immortal, he shows him a way across the greatest threshold of history, and he shows him why stories matter. It is the last lesson that will make all the difference to Gilgamesh as he comes home to Uruk and starts to tell his own story.

The Assyriologist Piotr Michalowski argues that Uta-napishti's account of how he gained eternal life is itself a kind of life.[37] The sage lives with his wife in an impossibly distant exile, and we can debate whether they are even alive in this world in any meaningful sense. Despite Uta-napishti's immortality, his only existence in the land of the living is through the stories that people tell about him. Gilgamesh calls him "the faraway Uta-napishti, of whom people talk," neatly summarizing his ambiguous position: he is distant but famous, faraway in body but still present as a story.[38] The tale of the Flood is the only life he has outside the island, where nothing ever happens. Michalowski concludes that "this story within a story points to nothing else but narrative: the flood survivor and his wife live in separation from the rest of humanity and their only reality is their own story."[39]

The account of the Flood was not composed for *Gilgamesh* but seems to have been copied from an older epic known as *Atra-hasis*.[40] The first part of

Atra-hasis tells of how humanity was created, the second of how it was destroyed by the Flood; it is this second part that was woven into the Standard Babylonian *Gilgamesh*. The allusion adds a further layer to the epic. When Gilgamesh says that "people talk" of Uta-napishti, Babylonian scribes knew that to be true from their own experience: they would probably have heard the epic of *Atra-hasis* and its story of the man who survived the Flood.

Since Uta-napishti essentially lives on as a story, he does his utmost to make that story memorable. In the tale he recounts, he displays a dazzling control of narrative. The story brims with subtle ironies, as Uta-napishti plays with the hidden meanings of words. Take the unfortunate shipwright who is made to seal the ship from outside, saving those inside it but consigning himself to death: "I gave my palace and all its treasure to Puzur-Enlil, the shipwright who caulked the hatch from outside."[41] There is a double irony here. First, Puzur-Enlil will not have long to enjoy his newfound wealth: he will soon die in the Flood that only Uta-napishti knows to be coming.[42] Second, his name literally means "Protection of Enlil," but it was Enlil who unleashed the Flood that is about to kill him. "Nomen omen, indeed," writes Michalowski; "his fate was inscribed ironically in his name, for the god who would send him to his death was his protector."[43]

A similar irony is at play with the elaborate puns described above, in which Ea's words can be read as either a promise of abundance or a warning of disaster. Again, the double meaning creates a distance between the narrator and the characters of the story, between Uta-napishti and the citizens of Shuruppak. The secret that Ea tells to Uta-napishti places him in a privileged position because he knows what is about to happen, and so he can be alert to the grim ironies of the events unfolding around him, while Puzur-Enlil and the Shuruppakeans take them at face value. That is the privilege of storytellers, who know the full story in advance, unlike characters, who must figure it all out as it happens.

Uta-napishti also displays his command over words in what he chooses *not* to say. As Worthington notes, the sage's story paints him as "an enigmatic, even sinister figure."[44] There is much that his account leaves unclear. Did he realize the double meaning of the message he passed on from Ea to the people of Shuruppak? Did he know that he was consigning them all to death, even as they toiled away on the ship that would save him? Or was he as confused as they were? Even his status in Shuruppak is left unstated: Was he a king, a priest, or both, or neither? All these questions and more swirl around Uta-napishti, again revealing the power of the storyteller, who can choose what to hide and what to reveal.

Perhaps the most pressing question, which again goes unanswered, is why Ea chose to reveal the secret of the coming Flood to him, of all people. Before he gained the name Uta-napishti (He Found Life) he was called Atra-hasis, "He Is Very Wise," or, literally, "He Is Extraordinarily Listening." According to the Babylonians, intelligence resided not in the brain, the heart, or the eyes but in the ears. To understand the world was to hear it, to be alert to its subtler notes and echoes. The first part of *Atra-hasis* describes how, in creating humankind, the gods gave us the gift of intelligence and hearing; the second part describes how Atra-hasis used his gift to hear Ea's whispered words and decipher their double meaning.[45] Atra-hasis is a superhero not because he is particularly strong or brave but because he has a "wide ear" in the Babylonian idiom (*uznu rapaštu*): he is clever, he listens, and he speaks better than anyone.

Uta-napishti's story reveals him to be a master of words, and we are made to understand that he gained immortality exactly because he was attentive to the workings of language. The story that Gilgamesh hears from him demonstrates the power of narrative, which the hero will go on to employ for himself as he composes the epic. Storytelling will be Gilgamesh's last recourse when he fails to gain eternal life, for as Michalowski reminds us, "history, remembrance, and story are, after all, the only forms of immortality."[46]

When Gilgamesh tells the story of his life to Shiduri, Ur-shanabi, and Uta-napishti, he tells the same story each time, but it is a confused and mixed-up tale. The Assyriologist Nathan Wasserman points out that in this miniature autobiography Gilgamesh reverses the order of events. He tells of how he and Enkidu killed Humbaba and the Bull of Heaven, but he "consistently mentions these two scenes in inverted order."[47] When asking him about it, Shiduri gets the chronology right, so the confusion is confined to Gilgamesh's speech. In addition, Gilgamesh does not distinguish between what he did with Enkidu and what he did alone after Enkidu's death, inserting into the list of their joint adventures that they "butchered lions in the mountain passes," though Enkidu was dead by the time Gilgamesh did this.[48] The grieving Gilgamesh is like a broken record, stuck telling the same jumbled tale over and over again, unsure of what he did when and with whom.

It is against this background that Uta-napishti's narrative mastery unfolds in the following Tablet, all the more striking in contrast to Gilgamesh's muddled attempt at autobiography. As Uta-napishti knows, a well-told story is the only thing that can give him the eternal fame he wants: "Gilgamesh must understand the power inherent in the control of discourse, and so the story within the story is told," Michalowski writes.[49] At first, we are left uncertain whether Gilgamesh has understood the message, since he seems to be as restless and dissatisfied as ever. But in the last lines of the text, the realization dawns on us that the entire epic has been nothing but Gilgamesh's prolonged compliance with Uta-napishti's lesson. We are reminded that the epic is in fact the king's story of himself, "an autobiography that mimics the one told to Gilgamesh by Utanapishtim."[50]

There are many echoes between the epic and the epic inside the epic. Both begin by describing a city: Uta-napishti's story begins in Shuruppak, Gilgamesh's in Uruk. Both begin by announcing that they contain a secret: Uta-napishti says he will reveal a secret of the gods, while the prologue tells the reader to find the tablet box and "open the door to its secrets."[51] And both use the phrase "six days and seven nights" to highlight the transformation at the heart of the story: the disastrous Flood in Uta-napishti's story and the movement back and forth across the border of humanity in Gilgamesh's.

In short, by failing to become immortal, Gilgamesh learns to tell stories. His other major failure in the epic also holds a bittersweet reward for him. Gilgamesh plunges into the depths to find the plant of youth, making his way to the Apsû, the mythical underground sea, and returning triumphant with plant in hand. His ambition is again foiled when he loses it to a snake, but there is a victory beneath his apparent failure. The Apsû is not a sea like any other, but the home of Ea—the god of wisdom. Although it is not made explicit in the text, Gilgamesh's contact with the Apsû seems to be one reason why the young and foolish hero becomes the wise sage described in the prologue, "who knew the ways and learned all things." And again, we had been warned of this by Ninsun, who says that Gilgamesh will "grow wise with Ea in the Apsû."[52]

Gilgamesh loses life and youth but gains insight and the skill of storytelling, and that, according to the prologue, is all that matters.[53] The prologue directs our attention not to Gilgamesh's battles and victories, or even to his great love and grief, but to the themes of wisdom, secrecy, stories, history, and depth. To be a hero, according to the Standard Babylonian version, a man need not fight and kill and die; he must listen, observe, travel, and read. In the Old Babylonian version, the story began with the words "He surpassed all kings," *šūtur eli šarrī*, but the mortal audience of the epic has not the slightest chance of surpassing Gilgamesh, so we can admire the hero of this version only from afar. The Standard Babylonian version, however, begins with the words "Who saw the deep," *ša naqba īmuru*, a far more inclusive opening. By reading Gilgamesh's story and seeing the world through his eyes, we too can become as wise as he was.[54] His triumph was to bring home a secret from before the Flood, and he uncovered that secret through brutal hard work. But having done that, he gave it to others—to us. When we finish reading the epic, we know the secret too. By reading his tale, we too have become *ša naqba īmuru*, those "who saw the deep."

This is the logic of the mise en abîme, the story within the story. Recursion works both ways. If there can be a story inside the story, and a story inside *that* story, and so on, zooming forever in, then it might be possible to zoom out too. Gilgamesh learns from Uta-napishti's story, and we can learn from Gilgamesh's story. Gilgamesh becomes a little more like Uta-napishti by listening to his tale, molding his own autobiography after Uta-napishti's, and so we, by listening to Gilgamesh's tale, become a little more like him, a little more like heroes who saw the deep.

In one very obvious sense, Gilgamesh's story grants him immortality: eternal life of the literary kind, as his memory will be carried through the ages by his epic tale. But how unsatisfying! This is immortality in the most abstract sense, not the actual, flesh-and-bones life that Gilgamesh was hoping for. But, as shown by Keith Dickson, Gilgamesh *does* also get life of the more blood-pumping kind, though again, it is not quite what he hoped for.[55] He does not achieve immortality, but he comes closer to immortal life than the dry pages of a book—or the dry surface of a tablet, for that matter. But to understand that life, we must first understand the difference between Enkidu's statue and Enkidu's corpse.

The statue is a lavish accomplishment. Gilgamesh spares no expense of gold, silver, or precious stones, and the craftsmen of Uruk turn those riches into a glorious image of the dead hero. The statue reminds us again of the alluring *kuzbu* of Enkidu's body, with what Walls describes as its "sensuous concentration upon Enkidu's masculine form in anatomical detail," though the passage is too fragmentary to let us enjoy that detail for long.[56] The passage may be fragmentary, but the statue is not. It is made of imperishable materials such as metal and stone, meant to display the magnificent beauty of Enkidu forever. Beautiful as it may be, the statue does little to soothe Gilgamesh's grief. It is made of materials like gold and lapis lazuli that, while imperishable, cannot house life. Dickson notes that for all its sumptuousness, "the material of the statue remains nonetheless as inert as the corpse it is meant to replace. It does not live, as Gilgamesh would ardently want it to."[57] Meanwhile, Enkidu's corpse has the opposite problem. The stuff of his flesh *can* house life, but unlike lapis lazuli, it cannot last forever.

According to the creation story in *Atra-hasis,* humans were made out of clay which had been imbued with a divine spark of life.[58] When a person died, the spark disappeared and left behind the clay. In the same way, Enkidu's life story is framed by clay. The goddess Aruru creates him by taking "a lump of clay" and throwing it into the wild, and when he dies, Gilgamesh says that he has "turned to clay."[59] Just like the records of the past destroyed by the Flood, Enkidu has returned to the shapeless material from which he was formed.

Clay is a perfect metaphor for impermanence: always ready to be reshaped and, when dry, always prone to breaking. A precious stone like lapis lazuli is the opposite, shining with its own inexhaustible brilliance. It does not break but will forever carry a sheen of timeless light—timeless, but also lifeless. The clay corpse and the jeweled statue represent with perfect clarity the dilemma that runs through the epic: lasting or living?[60] If Gilgamesh is to live forever, he will need an object that is both, but the material world of the epic is ruled by a strict binary logic. Statues last, bodies live—nothing does both.

Except the garden of Jeweled Trees. These trees pose all sorts of troubling questions, because they conflate some of the most fundamental oppositions of human culture: the living and the lifeless, the vegetable and the mineral, things that grow and things that endure. "What is this strange garden?" asks Dickson. "How is such fruit grown? From what seeds? By what weird agronomy? And perhaps most important of all: What kind of being can pluck and eat and somehow incorporate this jewelled stuff—*abashmu*-stone, lapis lazuli, agate—into the stuff of its own flesh?"[61] Not Gilgamesh, that's for sure. The carob he touches remains alien to him, because the "weird, even scandalous fruit" does the impossible: it lives and lasts.[62]

In short, the garden appears in the epic as a proof of principle. What was supposed to be impossible turns out to be—not easy—but not undoable either. When Gilgamesh walks through the garden on his way to Uta-napishti, he still has much to learn, and one thing that he will learn is how he might be able to copy its tricks.

Babylonian scribes knew from personal and prolonged experience how brittle clay is. Every day they would handle clay, shaping it into tablets and reshaping it again whenever they needed to. Add a little water, and even the most carefully copied composition can be wiped clean and reshaped. The scribes lived with clay, forever reading and molding a material that they, at least in a mythical sense, believed themselves to be made of. The perishability of clay is further reinforced by the story of the Flood. A well-stored tablet could last much longer than a human lifespan, but even the most durable clay tablet could someday turn back into mud. No wonder, then, that Gilgamesh inscribed his tale on a tablet of lapis lazuli: having heard the story from Uta-napishti, he knows what happened during the Flood, and so opts for a stone that might stand the test of time, unlike the clay dissolved by the Flood. But as the epic has made emphatically clear, the choice of lapis lazuli has its own problems. It may be durable, but it cannot hold life. So how does Gilgamesh expect to find eternal life with a story if that story is told on lifeless matter? Or as Dickson puts it, "How is it exactly that heroes 'live on' in the narrative and the narration of their deeds?"[63]

In fact, the lapis lazuli tablet is only one part of the equation. The other is the reader. The prologue tells us to "take up the tablet of lapis lazuli and read aloud: read of all that Gilgamesh went through, read of all his suffering!"[64] The tablet cannot move; it lies inert in a box. It is readers who bring it to life, picking it up and reading it out, animating the dead words with our voice. Lapis lazuli alone cannot grant immortality, but it allows us to read the text in a way that might. Gilgamesh failed to turn his own body into something that could both live and last, but perhaps, Dickson surmises, "what cannot be accomplished everlastingly once and for all may still be achieved in serial fashion."[65] That "serial fashion" is the repetition of the epic itself, as reading after reading brings it to new life.

Immortality is not to be found in either clay or gems; it lies in the rhythm of performance and permanence. The performance of our voices brings the story to life for another short moment, but when one voice stops, the permanence of the tablet allows the story to survive for the next reader. The written text and the reading voice depend on each other, writing and reading are "collaborative events."[66] Neither voice nor dry text can work on its own, but their combination will bring the hero back to life.

As we read about Gilgamesh, we come to resemble him. The reading of the text makes us, in our own way, into heroes "who saw the deep," since we peer into the depth of time. The prologue brings the similarity home by having us re-create the movements of the hero in our mind.[67] Just as Gilgamesh traveled restlessly around the edge of the world, so are we to walk around the wall of Uruk. Just as Gilgamesh journeyed down to the Apsû, so are we to survey the foundation of the wall. We are to find the tablet box and discover the secret that Gilgamesh revealed, learn what he learned, and copy the words he wrote, either by writing them onto a new tablet or by turning them into sound. It becomes increasingly clear that the epic is trying to recruit us and make us resemble Gilgamesh himself.

The splendid statue of Enkidu could not bring him back to life because the dead matter of which it was made lacked the spark of living things. But where the statue failed, the epic succeeds, by enlisting the readers and the spark that comes with them. By lending our voice and body to the text, and repeating the movement of its hero in our mind, we become a living, walking statue of Gilgamesh.

The epic thus manages in its own way to give him something that resembles eternal life. But the trick comes at a price. To live forever, Gilgamesh must stop moving. The prologue tells us that he was "exhausted but at peace, as he set down all his trials on a slab of stone," so it would seem that when the epic is written, the storm of his heart—that powerful and obscure desire that had been raging inside him all his life—will finally end. Gilgamesh is at peace, his journey has ended. Andrew George notes that the verbs for "was exhausted," "was given peace," and "set down" are all in the stative form, marking the end of Gilgamesh's travels: "After so long in motion, now he has arrived at a condition of stasis. . . . The journey has come to a halt."[68] But what respite does Gilgamesh find in writing down the story?

Remember that death and the knowledge of death is a specifically human problem, one that defines who we are as human beings. It follows that, to make peace with death, the hero must become somehow inhuman. Gilgamesh must become *Gilgamesh*. He cannot live on as a body, so he must live on as a story that is told and retold, lending him a new lease on life each time. But stories are not people. Gilgamesh does live on in one form, but part of his living self is lost. As he sets down his story, he becomes *fixed* in writing. He no longer walks around or burns with desire; he lies motionless, waiting for us to pick him up. He surrenders himself to the voice and goodwill of the readers.

The literary critic Mikhail Bakhtin notes that, unlike the main character of a novel, the hero of an epic is usually "a fully finished and completed being." In most epics, the hero has a fixed fate and an equally fixed personality throughout the story. Heroes merely move through epic adventures; they are not changed by them. That, for Bakhtin, is the aesthetic flaw of the epic hero: "What is complete is also something hopelessly ready-made; he is all there, from beginning to end he coincides with himself, he is absolutely equal to himself."[69] If a story must have this kind of hero to qualify as an epic, then *Gilgamesh* is not an epic. Gilgamesh is always beside himself, always restless and changing, moved and moving, unsatisfied and unfinished. Readers experience him as a person and not as an epic hero precisely because he persistently refuses to be "equal to himself." He wants more, always more.

Until, that is, he tells his story. At that moment, he becomes precisely what Bakhtin describes. He stops moving. He is completed, he is captured in the text, he is at peace and fully made. He becomes, literally, *ša naqba īmuru*, one "who saw the deep": he becomes the story of his life. In Bakhtin's words, he "coincides with himself," he is nothing but words on a tablet—and that is the price of immortality. To live forever, Gilgamesh must become something that is not quite human and not quite living: he must become epic.

Kings, Women, Monsters

In the last lines of the epic, Gilgamesh tells Ur-shanabi to look beyond the wall of Uruk and into the city itself. The lines show a shift in Gilgamesh's gaze: once desperate and self-centered, his eyes are now outbound and calm. Gilgamesh's words redirect the readers' attention from his own travails to the community of Uruk.[1] Gilgamesh has not stopped caring about himself; rather, as I discussed in the previous essay, he has realized that he cannot achieve immortality alone. He needs others to carry his name through time. But who are those others? I have spoken loosely of "readers" who are to bring Gilgamesh back to life each time they pick up his story, but which readers would he have expected to reach? What community does he see when he lifts his eyes and looks at Uruk?

The moment Gilgamesh comes home is the moment he surrenders to his city, leaving his story in the care of others and giving the last word to Uruk:

> Two thousand acres for the city,
> two thousand acres for the orchards,
> two thousand acres for the pits of clay,
> and one thousand acres for the temple of Ishtar.
> Seven thousand acres is the size of Uruk.[2]

As noted in my introduction, my translation here deviates from the compact structure of the Akkadian text. The original has two lines and a total of fourteen words. My translation has thirty-seven words, which I have broken into five lines to emphasize the shift in format, from the normal symmetry of half-lines to a rigid list. But there is something beautiful about the poem's use of measurements. Having spent eleven Tablets telling the story of two men, the text ends by measuring out an entire community. It is a different way of looking at the city—not through the story of its king, but through the size of its population. Many people and many life stories are subsumed under the word *šār*, "two thousand acres." Tellingly, the word is written with the sign ŠAR$_2$, which can also mean "totality" or "whole."

Andrew George argues that in these lines Gilgamesh's "preoccupation with his personal existential crisis gives way to an impersonal topic, in which suddenly self-reference is completely lacking."[3] To George, the list shows an abandonment of personality. No matter how great a person is, that person is but a single individual in an acre, one part of the whole. "The ending of the poem, then, abrupt and anticlimactic though it is, makes a grand statement about man and mankind. Essentially it subordinates the concerns of man the individual to those of man the collective."[4]

These two perspectives—personal and collective—are defined by two different kinds of time. The personal perspective has the time of stories: brief, exciting, finite, full of ups and downs. The collective perspective has the time of cities: slow, endless, gradual, full of repetitions. The two kinds of time are set against each other in Uta-napishti's monologue on death, which I unpacked in the previous essay. The story of the family that builds a house, founds a home, and is torn apart by an inheritance feud brings together the time of the single person, who lives and dies, and the time of the community, in which that story unfolds again and again: "one day . . . one day . . . one day . . . one day . . ." The moral, George concludes, is that though a single man may die, "men endure forever through the cycle of generations."[5]

The story ends with the couplet "One day, the river rose and brought high water, a mayfly (*kulīlu*) drifting down the river." In evoking the image of mayflies being carried by the annual flooding of the Tigris, writes George, Uta-napishti "restates the same contrast between man and men as a metaphor, in which the brief-lived insect *kulīlu* symbolizes the individual and the eternal river stands, as elsewhere, for the current of time."[6] The mayfly lives for a day, the river flows forever, flooding anew each spring.

The two kinds of time are different in every way, but they are linked by death. Death is a temporal mediator, robbing us of our individual perspective to inscribe us in the larger flow of time. In death, we become a statistic: our life story is made part of an immensely bigger cycle of seasons and currents. That is what Gilgamesh resists in his struggle against death; he clings to his own exceptional life in the face of normal mortality.[7] However, though we never hear him accept death explicitly, in the end he seems at least to accept that all individuals must find their place in a broader community—and turns to Uruk.

The theme of surrendering to one's community was made even clearer by the new fragment discovered in 2018, which showed that Enkidu and Shamhat had sex not just for seven nights but for two full weeks, and enabled us to trace the stages of Enkidu's humanization in more detail. After the first week of sex, Shamhat invites Enkidu to Uruk and describes it as a place "where Gilgamesh is superb in strength, overbearing like an aurochs among the young men." Enkidu picks up on the animal metaphor and responds in animal fashion: he will challenge Gilgamesh and usurp his position as alpha male. But after the second week, as Enkidu becomes more human, "he forgot the wild of his youth." When Shamhat again invites him to Uruk, she describes it as a place "where all men can ply their trade: you too, human as you are, will find a place for yourself."[8] Enkidu agrees. He no longer wishes for power and raw animal strength; now he wants to find a suitable role in a city of workers and dutiful citizens.

George argues that the scene reflects a development in Enkidu's psychology, one that pits two different perspectives on the community against each other.[9] Is the society defined by strength and power or by work and duty? The epic shows that to become fully human, Enkidu must adopt the second perspective. He must abandon his alpha-male instincts and surrender to the city, becoming one cog in the collective, one person in the acre.

To join the city, Enkidu must find out what his role in the community will be. Everyone has a role, even Gilgamesh, though his is different from everyone else's. The fact that Gilgamesh surrenders to the perspective of his city at the end of the epic does not make him equal to the citizens of Uruk—he is still their king. But what did it mean to be a king in ancient Iraq? What duties and prerogatives did kingship entail? Gilgamesh helpfully illustrates the norms and expectations that applied to Babylonian kings by exceeding or falling short of them all.[10]

The epic makes clear that it will reflect on the nature and limitations of kingship in Tablet II through the story of Gilgamesh's foiled attempt to have sex with another man's bride on her wedding night. This practice is generally known as "droit du seigneur" or "ius primae noctis"; Michael Schmidt more aptly terms it "first-night rights."[11] Modern readers might receive the impression that this was an actual Babylonian custom, but they must remember that Babylonian readers saw Gilgamesh as a figure of the distant past. As noted by the Assyriologist Gonzalo Rubio, first-night rights were probably never a historical custom; it was a myth created to illuminate the cruel ways of a bygone time. Today, readers are not sensitive to that anachronism, and often take Gilgamesh's era and the Babylonian era to be one and the same.[12] But in fact the epic shows Enkidu putting an end to the custom: the first-night rights would be no more.

When Enkidu blocks the door to the wedding house, he effectively draws a line for kingship. Babylonian kings may have wielded autocratic power, but the epic implicitly argues that some things even they were not supposed to do, and demanding first-night rights was one of them. The scene sets the tone for the epic, which will repeatedly reflect on the norms that Gilgamesh comes up against and those he pushes to a breaking point. Over the course of the epic, Gilgamesh does five tasks that were typical of Babylonian kings: he builds a wall around the city, he goes on a military campaign, he communicates with the god of his city, he interacts with the city assembly, and he leaves behind a commemorative inscription to preserve his memory. But in all five, Gilgamesh deviates from the ideal, by either overdoing or undermining his duty.

Take the last of the five tasks, the commemorative inscription. All kings made their inscriptions as impressive as possible, but Gilgamesh's inscription, we are given to understand, is the epic itself, a complex literary masterpiece that is three thousand lines long and begins with the words "He surpassed all kings." This is how Gilgamesh approaches kingship in general. In every aspect of his royal character, as in every other aspect of his life, Gilgamesh is excessive, going above and beyond normal expectations—but often doing more damage than good in the process.

The wall of Uruk is a case in point. In ancient Iraq, a central element in the relation between the king and his subjects was corvée, or unpaid labor.[13] Essentially, this was a form of tax. Free male citizens would work for the king a certain number of days each year or employ servants to do so for them. In return, they received basic rights that the kings ideally had to respect, such as the right to own private property. One could say that corvée represented the mutual obligation of state and subject, and so the king was expected to use this unpaid labor to accomplish projects that benefited the entire community: building temples to worship the gods, digging canals to water the fields, or, as in *Gilgamesh*, building walls to protect the city. As the Assyriologist Eva van Dassow points out, the performance of corvée became synonymous with citizenship, in the same way "taxpayer" is today used as another word for "citizen."[14]

The wall of Uruk is many things in *Gilgamesh*. It is a metaphor for the epic itself, a threshold between the urban and the natural world, and, most concretely, a monument that was built by a king using corvée. The statement that Gilgamesh "built the wall around Uruk" reflects not just an epic feat, but also a particular exercise of state power, a particular use of his citizens' time and labor. As a royal building project, it was expected to benefit the Urukeans by protecting them from wild beasts and enemy raids. The wall is a potent metaphor for the state. It defines the limits of the city and protects those it includes from those it excludes. Just as important, it is the civil pride of Uruk: as the epic makes abundantly clear, the wall is majestic and unrivaled. The prominence of the wall in the urban landscape would have been a constant reminder of the city's greatness.

However, the wall could also represent Gilgamesh's excessive use of corvée, and more broadly his abuse of the Urukean citizens. The exact nature of Gilgamesh's oppression of Uruk is left ambiguous, but one possibility is that he was remembered as a tyrant because he was said to have built the wall of Uruk.[15] The greater the building project, the harder the labor it required. A king could not demand endless amounts of corvée from his subjects: revolts against excessive requests of labor are known from both myths and administrative records.[16] In short, the wall captures both sides of Gilgamesh's excess. He goes beyond what is expected of him, building a wall that is nothing short of legendary, but he also perverts his royal duty, asking too much of his exhausted subjects—who must turn to the gods for relief.

One of the king's most important duties was to secure a good relationship between the city and its gods.[17] The king was effectively the main priest of his city, and he was expected to build temples, give offerings, obey omens, hold festivals, and perform regular rituals to keep the gods well-disposed. If the relationship between city and god was damaged, the consequences would be catastrophic. At worst, the god could decide to abandon the city and so surrender it to obliteration.

The degree to which Gilgamesh mismanages Uruk's relationship with Ishtar makes it the most egregious of his royal crimes. Not only does he fail to pay homage to Ishtar; he insults her bitterly. His crime is not simply turning down a marriage proposal; Gilgamesh endangers the entire city with his insults. Ishtar reacts by unleashing the Bull of Heaven, and had the heroes not managed to kill it, it would probably have laid waste to Uruk. Gilgamesh's behavior is the opposite of what was expected of a responsible ruler.

That is not the only occasion that Gilgamesh puts his own desires over the relations between Uruk and its gods. When he goes on his expedition against Humbaba, he says that he will be unable to perform the *akītu*, the New Year's festival, which was the most important religious ritual in the Babylonian calendar. Instead, he promises to hold the festival twice a year from then on. The episode is meant to explain why Uruk, unlike other Babylonian cities, had an *akītu* in the spring and another in the fall, but it is also a neat example of Gilgamesh's style of kingship: first he fails to do his duty, then he does twice as much as he is he supposed to.[18]

The quest against Humbaba, although it interrupts his religious obligations, was in itself a duty that Gilgamesh was expected to carry out. The Babylonian and Assyrian kings were not supposed to strive for peace but to go on campaigns and conquer far-off lands. If the kings wanted to build large palaces and temples—and they absolutely did want that—they had to go on campaigns. Iraqi soil is poor in timber, and the small trees that grow there cannot be used for the large beams that are needed to build a great hall. The Babylonian kings often turned their eyes to Lebanon, which was covered by mighty cedar trees, and Gilgamesh's quest against Humbaba can be seen as a mythical mirror of those campaigns.[19]

But if this is the case, the expedition reflects poorly on its real-life counterparts. The quest against Humbaba becomes morally suspect as it nears completion. At first justified by Shamash's hatred of Humbaba, the quest turns out to be an insult to the gods, who had installed Humbaba as a holy protector of the Cedar Forest. As Humbaba pleads for his life, the campaigns carried out by Babylonian and Assyrian rulers might start to seem dubious too. Tracy Davenport concludes that the epic can be read as a statement against the violence of imperialism. "The implications of this episode for imperialist powers are clear: expansion should not be approached with a view to dominating others with unnecessary force."[20] Gilgamesh's crime is not that he defeats Humbaba but that he turns down Humbaba's offer to remain in the Cedar Forest and act as his vassal. Humbaba promises to supply Gilgamesh with all the timber he could wish for, but Gilgamesh kills him regardless and turns the forest into a wasteland. Military success is all well and good, but the epic condemns unnecessary murder and devastation—in the mythical world and so, implicitly, in the real one too. As always, Gilgamesh surpasses all other kings, and the result is predictably disastrous.

Indeed, he had been warned that it would be disastrous. Before embarking on the quest, Gilgamesh presents his plan to the elders of Uruk, who advise against it in no uncertain terms. Their response illustrates another fundamental element of the relation between kings and cities, namely the role of the assembly. The states of the ancient Near East were not democratic, but their citizens were not entirely powerless, either. We have evidence from many periods, especially from the early second millennium BCE, that the most influential citizens gathered in a city assembly, called the *puḫru*, to discuss social, juridical, and economic issues.[21] Unfortunately, they did not keep minutes (or at least, none have turned up in excavations), so we know next to nothing about how these worked. It seems that they had a large influence on state administration but were ultimately subject to the decisions of the king: the assemblies advised but did not legislate.

In *Gilgamesh and Akka*, one of the five Sumerian poems about the hero, Gilgamesh goes to the assembly of elders and presents his plans for an expedition against the city of Kish. The elders promptly turn him down. Gilgamesh then goes to the assembly of young men, who are much more belligerent and so approve the plan. According to a now outmoded but still thought-provoking suggestion by Thorkild Jacobsen, the episode suggests that the king needed the support of his citizens to rule and also that he had room for political maneuvering to secure that support.[22] The episode is not included in the Standard Babylonian version, not least because society had changed considerably in the millennium that separates the two texts. In the Akkadian epic, Gilgamesh again has trouble convincing the elders that a military excursion is a good idea, but he simply ignores their objections. The assembly can advise, lecture, and even chide its king, but it cannot change the stubborn mind of an autocratic ruler. The assembly does not take the king's wish as law, instead debating the matter with him and opposing his decision, but it cannot impose its will if the king fails to listen.

However, the epic also shows that the assembly could easily do without a king. When Gilgamesh departs for the Cedar Forest, he seems to put in place no royal steward to care for Uruk in his absence, confidently leaving the state administration in the hands of his officials (though note that a major section of Tablet III is missing). Conversely, the elders tell Enkidu that they place their king in his care and that he is to ensure Gilgamesh's safe return, portraying the king as a precious property that may be lent out but that ultimately belongs to the assembly. In short, there is a mutual if not symmetrical relation of power and trust between the king and his council.

In the end, things turn out just as the elders had predicted: the quest against Humbaba is an apparent success, but it quickly leads to tragedy. As we have seen, the epic repeatedly shows that kingship can turn catastrophic if it is not kept in check by the advice of wise counselors.[23] In the story of the Flood, Ea berates Enlil for having acted so thoughtlessly, asking, "How could you cause the Flood, acting without counsel?"[24] The word for "counsel," Akkadian *milku*, implies an extended process of deliberation and debate—precisely what an assembly would give the king. Without the right *milku*, there were no limits to the disasters that kings could cause.

So much for those who speak in the city assembly. But what about those who do not? The epic also dwells on people and places outside the male, urban community of Uruk, specifically women and the natural world beyond the city wall.

Simply put, not everyone got to speak in the seat of power, and in ancient Iraq, as has been the awful tendency throughout human history, women had little or no access to political decision making.[25] When giving lectures on the epic, I am often asked "how patriarchal" the cultures of ancient Iraq were, but I have no good answer to give. One reason is that these cultures were not a single entity: their social structures differed from one another and changed radically from one period to the next. The other reason is that there is no universal scale of patriarchy-ness. That being said, a rough answer might be: "more than ancient Rome but less than ancient Greece."[26] Generally speaking, women could leave the house, own and inherit property, bring lawsuits, make contracts, join business ventures, divorce their husbands, and learn to read and write, though all those rights were subject to restrictions depending on the given period, culture, and social class.[27]

But it is unlikely that women would have been allowed a voice in the assemblies.[28] As Mary Beard argues in her "manifesto" *Women and Power,* the exclusion of women in antiquity still casts a shadow on modern society. Beard is focused on Classical antiquity, but the same could be said about the ancient Near East: what she calls "the mechanisms that silence women, that refuse to take them seriously, and that sever them . . . from the centres of power" were at work in Uruk too.[29] But though practically universal, the silencing of women's speech is not a simple matter. It can have counterintuitive and ironic effects, as is the case in *Gilgamesh*. In a nutshell, male anxiety about women's speech, and the patriarchal belief that women should not speak at all, leads to a literary fantasy of women's speech being extremely influential.

The epic is a story that was told *by* men *to* men *about* men, with "women functioning as supporting and subsidiary characters in the cast," in the words of the Assyriologist Rivkah Harris.[30] Women stand at the outer edges of the epic, but ironically, those edges can be a powerful place to be. Precisely because women are excluded from the male sphere of decisions, they hold a strange power over it. This is the logic of an anxious male privilege. To maintain an exclusive grasp on power, men restrict the speech of women and so come to imagine that if it were not restricted, women's speech would hold great danger. That fear in turn becomes a reason to curtail their speech all the more.[31] In *Gilgamesh*, the few women who speak do so to great effect. This is not because the epic is feminist, but, I believe, because it rests on the cultural assumption that women's speech is a rare, dire, and dominant force, which can change the lives of men and so must be treated with constant suspicion.

A clear example of this dynamic is found in the three wives who appear in the epic: the wives of Uta-napishti, Shamash, and the scorpion man. All three talk back to their husbands and change their minds—and when they do, the course of Gilgamesh's journey changes as well. The wife of Uta-napishti speaks to her husband when Gilgamesh sleeps, urging him to wake up the hero, and again when Gilgamesh has left the island, chiding Uta-napishti for his lack of hospitality and persuading him to tell Gilgamesh about the plant of youth. Crucially, she speaks to her husband only when Gilgamesh cannot hear her, perhaps because wives were expected to be silent in the company of other men. But although she does not speak in Gilgamesh's presence, it is she who launches him on his final quest, giving him his last chance to regain youth.

Aya, the goddess of the dawn, is not shown speaking directly, but her words are evoked by Ninsun in her prayer to Shamash. "May Aya, your bride, not fear to remind you: 'When Gilgamesh and Enkidu face off with Humbaba, unleash, Shamash, your mighty storms against him.'" It is chilling that Ninsun must pray for Aya not to be afraid when speaking to her husband.[32] But she also assumes that if Aya does speak up, Shamash will listen and follow her advice, and that is precisely what happens: Shamash unleashes his storms and clinches the battle. Ninsun and Aya are excluded from this all-male melee, but it is they who, acting together, determine its outcome. Though she appears only indirectly, the epic gives Aya the power to change the course of the story.

The third wife, the scorpion woman, also talks back to her husband: she repeats and reverses the words of the narrator, who said that Gilgamesh is "two-thirds god and only one-third human."[33] When the scorpion woman speaks back to her husband, she gives those words new meaning. Her husband had said that Gilgamesh had the flesh of gods in his body, but she points out that this is not all he has. The conversation that follows is badly broken, so it is unclear if the scorpion woman, like her fellow wives, changes the mind of her husband and the journey of Gilgamesh.[34]

The examples illustrate the ambiguous position of women in the epic. Their speech is restricted, but the patriarchal logic behind the text also assumes that it will be effective—which is why it has to be restricted in the first place. But if the role of the wives is ambiguous, that of the epic's unmarried women is even more fraught.

Rivkah Harris argues that women in *Gilgamesh* are portrayed through a "symbolic inversion"—that is, they reverse the stereotypes associated with their roles. Harris claims that Shiduri, the innkeeper of the gods, is "depicted in ways that are very unlike the actual tavernkeeper."[35] Perhaps, but we know very little about what "the actual tavernkeeper" would have been like in Babylonian culture.[36] If we assume that taverns were places of lewd and base reputation, Shiduri is indeed an exception. She speaks wise words, acts with restraint, and helps Gilgamesh on his journey. But perhaps that is the way ancient innkeepers were expected to behave: as wise women offering guidance to their troubled customers. With so little information about ancient taverns to go on, we cannot gauge whether Shiduri is to be understood as exceptional or typical.

A similar problem applies to Shamhat and her profession. She is a *ḫarimtu*, which has traditionally been understood as a sex worker employed by Ishtar's temple. Many translators opt for the word "harlot," but as an increasing number of philologists are pointing out, older studies of the term *harimtu* are plagued by numerous shortcomings, so we cannot be sure that they were sex workers.[37] In cuneiform literature, *harimtu*s were clearly thought to be sexually promiscuous, but this does not make them prostitutes. In *Gilgamesh*, Shamhat is said to receive gifts from her lovers, but that, too, is not necessarily the same as payment for sex.

Part of the problem is that the longest and most detailed description of a *harimtu* is found in *Gilgamesh* itself, but the epic is a literary fiction, not a real-life report.[38] Deducing facts about *harimtu*s from the epic and then applying those conclusions to Shamhat is a circular argument. And in any case, the text is highly ambiguous when it comes to Shamhat's social status. For example, are we to take the curses and blessings laid on her by Enkidu as depictions of the actual social standing of *harimtu*s or as rhetorical flourishes about the fate of this one character? At present, we cannot know, and it would be foolish to claim certainty on such meager grounds.

Shamhat is a wise and outspoken woman who makes conscious use of her sexual appeal. Labeling such a woman a prostitute is, to put it mildly, not ideal, unless the claim is backed up by solid philological evidence, which is not currently available. In my translation, I have opted for a compromise. One thing all scholars agree on is that *harimtu*s were employed by temples and participated in religious rituals, and in *Gilgamesh*, Ishtar summons the *harimtu*s to perform a ritual mourning over the Bull of Heaven. Regardless of whatever else she might be, a woman engaged in the service of a temple and performing religious rituals for a deity is a priestess. So Shamhat is, in my translation, a priestess.

Either way, like Shiduri, Shamhat occupies an exceptional position in the social world of the epic. All other women are defined by their legal relation to a man, as wives, mothers, or unmarried daughters. But innkeepers, *harimtu*s, and other kinds of priestess were the exception.[39] They supported themselves by their own labor, whatever the nature of that labor was. But even as they seem to be exceptional, their status follows the logic described above: The women have some degree of freedom from a male-governed household, but as a result they are relegated to the margins of society. Shiduri lives at the edge of the world, and Shamhat is likewise linked to the outside of society. Enkidu's curse is that she will have no house or home, and even when he blesses her, she is still destined to disrupt family life by seducing a rich man away from his wife and children.

This position at the threshold of society makes Shamhat the ideal candidate to bring Enkidu across the border of culture. The ḫarimtus stand outside the social order of patriarchal households, but they are also the image of urban luxury. When Shamhat tells Enkidu about the wonders of Uruk, she dwells on the ravishing ḫarimtus, with "their faces full of charm and hearts full of joy."[40] Central but also marginal to urban society, the ḫarimtu is ideally suited to help Enkidu bridge the threshold between the outside and inside of the culture.

In short, women in *Gilgamesh* stand at the edge of power. Silenced but still speaking, they are viewed with both awe and anxiety by the male protagonists of the epic, and time and again it is women who decide the fate of the male heroes. This is the paradox of female power in *Gilgamesh,* and nobody represents that paradox better than Ishtar.

Like her priestesses, Ishtar was both central and marginal. She is the most important Akkadian goddess, but also constantly associated with all that is unusual, disruptive, and immoral. According to Zainab Bahrani, Ishtar is a divine embodiment of cultural exclusion.[41] Societies define themselves by what they are not—by excluding unwanted elements and setting up boundaries for what cannot be permitted. But those norms are often invisible and implicit, and this is why, according to Bahrani, societies need a figure like Ishtar. She breaks every rule and crosses every boundary, and so makes them visible: again, norms are clearest when they are being broken.

The stories about Ishtar make the outlines of Babylonian culture easier to see, as we follow her violating its rules. In this sense, Ishtar is a lot like Gilgamesh, who has the same instinct for breaking every boundary he bumps into. Like Gilgamesh, Ishtar is constantly excessive, short-sighted, and destructive. We might reasonably assume that they would be a well-matched pair—but the epic makes us think again.[42] Gilgamesh refuses Ishtar's offer of marriage with gusto and malice, and in return she sends the Bull to kill him. So much for romance.

The scene is deceptively simple—proposal, refusal, revenge—but many cultural tensions are at stake in this exchange. First is the issue of female agency. Ishtar's marriage proposal is often read as assertive, even aggressive, because it is made by a woman, though here again the distance between reality and fiction can be difficult to gauge.[43] This could well be another instance of "symbolic inversion," a reversal of the expected gender roles. But the only other preserved instance of a marriage proposal in

Akkadian literature also comes from a goddess—Ishtar's sister Ereshkigal, queen of the underworld, who proposes marriage to the god of disease, Nergal—so who knows?[44]

We should also consider the question of the female gaze.[45] Earlier I described the logic of *kuzbu*, which explains the magnetic pull that Gilgamesh's body exerts on Ishtar: she is drawn to him the moment she sees him. And when she approaches him, she expects that he will immediately give himself to her. But strangely, the object of her desire fails to be attracted by her—by Ishtar, the most beautiful and enticing of all cuneiform goddesses! In the scene, female agency is thus both asserted and undermined. Ishtar is free to make the first move and state her desire, but she does so only to be rejected.

It is not wholly clear why Gilgamesh refuses her, and, as noted earlier, many interpretations have been proposed. Regardless, Gilgamesh's denial leads to a now familiar pattern. Ishtar is excluded from—and for that very reason decisive to—the male community of the epic. The two heroes rebuff her attempt to get between them, and Enkidu throws the Bull's member at her. The symbolism could hardly be clearer: the phallic meat marks her expulsion from their male intimacy. But as a direct result of that expulsion, she seals their fate, crying out, "Woe to Gilgamesh!"[46] Her wish comes true the next day.

The encounter between Gilgamesh and Ishtar realizes in miniature format what seems to be the overall logic of the epic. Male spheres of power are created by the violent exclusion of women, but as a result, women become an eternal threat to those spheres. The epic indulges in the literary fantasy that every time a woman speaks, she decides the fate of men, perhaps to justify why women must be silenced.

Gilgamesh's rejection of Ishtar also illustrates another aspect of the epic's world—namely, the borderland between nature and culture, which is a constant obsession in the story.[47] Time and again the epic returns to the relations among animals, humans, and gods—strikingly so in the account of Ishtar's exes. The goddess is said to have loved a bird, a lion, and a horse, in a provocative sequence of transspecies flings. Meanwhile, her human lovers were turned into animals, with the shepherd becoming a wolf: "now his own shepherd boys chase him away and his own sheepdogs bite his thighs."[48] The irony is grim. The shepherd used to be like the boys who now chase him, and he is now like the dogs that bite him.[49] He is not quite this and not quite that. The epic revels in this kind of slippery, double relation between humans and animals, using similarities and metamorphoses to explore the borderland between nature and society.

As noted by Keith Dickson, *Gilgamesh* "unfolds within the space between two trees."[50] At either end of the epic's world stands a forest. The forest of Humbaba is the noisy, aromatic, and tangled land of animals. The garden of Jeweled Trees is the silent, luminous, and everlasting land of gods. Between them stands Uruk, land of humans. Humans live in this in-between state: they are not gods, but they are not-gods in a way that is not animal either. Unlike gods, humans are mortal; unlike animals, they are aware of their mortality. Unlike animals, humans are sentient; unlike gods, they are not all-knowing.

To be human is to inhabit this mirror room of double differences. Throughout the epic, humans are defined as being not quite this and not quite that. Uruk is both not the Cedar Forest and not the Jeweled Trees, just as the shepherd turned wolf is both not a boy and not a dog. In the world of the epic, all creatures are linked by a similar string of dichotomies, and by the possibility of being transformed from one to the other. The epic explores the in-between states of its world, by following Enkidu, the animal who became human, and Gilgamesh, the human who tried to become a god.

As described in the introduction, cities were the centers of cuneiform culture. In the general Babylonian view of things, cities were places of life and luxury, and the world outside was a dangerous wasteland. The natural world of the hills, steppes, mountains, and deserts is often portrayed in cuneiform sources as a place of danger, death, lions, wolves, brigands, and witches, where travelers fared at their own risk.[51] But the epic goes against that trend by giving us a more ambiguous image of the world outside the city and of the animals that live there.[52]

It is not the case, as in many cuneiform texts, that the wilderness is evil and the city safe, but it is not exactly the other way around, either. As noted by the Assyriologists Aage Westenholz and Ulla Koch, the ambiguity is best captured by Enkidu's journey.[53] The wilderness we see through Enkidu's eyes is almost paradisiac: he frolics with the animals and frees them from snares. But the epic does not fully abandon the mainstream view of the wilderness as dangerous. When Enkidu is humanized, the first thing he does is to defend the shepherds' camp against raving wolves. And when he gets to the city, we find a similar ambiguity. At first, the not fully civilized Enkidu is horrified by the customs of the city and stands up against Gilgamesh's attempt to use his first-night rights. As highlighted by Westenholz and Koch, the depiction of Enkidu as a noble savage who is morally superior to the ways of the city is exceptional in the hyper-urban world of ancient Iraq. But though his first impression of the city is negative, he soon becomes part of the urban world and is literally adopted into it by Ninsun. When he returns to the wild, he does so as an invader bringing death and destruction to the Cedar Forest. His journey from wilderness to city casts both places in an ambivalent light, muddling the usually clear-cut contrast between good cities and dangerous steppes.

Again, the epic displays its interest in the changes that lead from one state of being to another. As Enkidu moves from animal to human, he goes from eating flesh to prepared food, from drinking spring water to manmade beer, from bathing in pools to shaving his hair and smearing himself with oil. In short, he moves from the raw to the reworked. As noted by Martin Worthington, Gilgamesh's two dreams can be seen as a metaphor for this process.[54] In the first dream, Enkidu is represented as a meteorite, in the second as an ax. In the Bronze Age, meteorites were a source of iron, which was used to make weapons that were sturdier than bronze. The meteorite and the ax are a raw and reworked version of the same material—iron in its natural form, iron hammered into a weapon—symbolizing Enkidu's journey from brute to urbanite.

Whereas Enkidu moves across the borderland of culture, he and Gilgamesh encounter creatures who live in that borderland: they are the monsters of the epic. Monsters are composite creatures who straddle the thresholds that structure a culture, mixing incompatible elements into one body.[55] Monsters frighten us because they join things that should not be joined—such as a human head with animal appendages—violating the normal order of things.

The scorpion people are a clear example. They protect the sun as it moves through the gate of the Twin Peaks at dusk and dawn. The gate is a symbolic threshold in all sorts of ways—between humans and gods, night and day, light and darkness—and the mountains themselves reach up to the heavens and down to the underworld. Who better to guard this gate than two creatures who are themselves a mix of beings, half human and half animal? As with all monsters, that mixture of categories makes the scorpion people terrifying to behold: "When Gilgamesh saw them, his face went dark with dread."[56]

The same logic also makes Humbaba a monster. He is never described directly, only through metaphors: "his howl is a flood, his voice is fire, his breath is death."[57] But we get a sense of what he looks like from an Old Babylonian terracotta plaque now in the British Museum, which probably depicts Humbaba's face.[58] The plaque shows a monstrous visage of winding coils—long labyrinthine wrinkles that form his teeth, nose, chin, curls, cheeks, and jowls. Like the shepherd turned wolf, Humbaba is caught in the dichotomies that define the relation between humans and others. His forest is less like the lair of a monster and more like the court of a king.[59] The air is scented by resin oozing from the cedars and filled by the music of birds and beasts. But these similarities only make Humbaba and his home all the more monstrous by creating a state of near-resemblance, with monkeys as musicians and natural scents instead of artificial censers. The uncanny rift between animals and humans is what makes Humbaba a monster, and his forest a dark mirror of Uruk.

The unusually ambiguous image of the natural world allows the epic to play with our expectation of the Cedar Forest. The forest is first described as a dangerous and unsettling place, the lair of a menacing monster: "in the home of Humbaba, all hope is lost."[60] But when the heroes arrive at the forest, we find, as Andrew George and Farouk al-Rawi put it, "one of the rare passages of Babylonian narrative poetry that is given over to the description of nature."[61] It is a rich and riotous place, full of music and aromas, so when the heroes turn this lush jungle into a wasteland, the epic offers the closest Babylonian literature comes to an ecological critique.[62] Because the natural world is portrayed with unusual sensitivity and detail, it follows that wreaking violence on it is also morally suspect, and punishable by death.

Humbaba mixes animal and human traits, making him both and so neither. His moral position is similarly unclear: he is the evil creature that Shamash hates, and a sacred protector installed by Enlil. But precisely because of that ambiguous mixture, he can act as a kind of monstrous border guard, protecting the world of animals against human incursions, and thereby shoring up the boundaries that define the cultural order. When the heroes kill him, they violate this order. The crime is especially grave on Enkidu's part, because he had crossed that boundary once already, when he became human. The Assyriologists Ulla Koch and Laura Feldt argue that with Enkidu's death, the epic reaffirms the basic fabric of its world, drawing a clear line between humans and nature, and warning us to be wary of crossing it.[63]

The other great monster of the epic, whose murder is the other crime that leads to Enkidu's death, is the Bull of Heaven.[64] Like the scorpion people and Humbaba, the Bull is a monster because it traverses cultural boundaries in impossible ways, as made clear by its name: the Bull of Heaven (Sumerian gu_4 an-na) is both animal and divine, celestial and wild. The Bull is literally to be understood as the constellation we know today as Taurus (Latin for "bull"). Because it belongs to another dimension, its presence on earth disturbs the natural elements: "When it reached the land of Uruk, the forest, marsh, and canebrake dried up."[65] Like Humbaba, the Bull meets an unhappy fate, and again the heroes' treatment of it is shown to be morally ambiguous. Not only do they kill it, they dismember it, giving its heart to Shamash, hurling its member at Ishtar, and turning its horns into lavish containers for ceremonial oil. The heroes' approach to the Bull is the same as their approach to the Cedar Forest: they kill the monster and then go about extracting whatever precious materials they can find. Despite Enkidu's soul-searching after razing the forest, the heroes have learned nothing. They still see the natural world only in terms of what resources they can take from it.[66]

But while Gilgamesh gathers his craftsmen to turn the body of the Bull into a commodity, Ishtar gathers her priestesses to mourn its death. Once more, the creation of a male community depends on the exclusion of women, but in this scene the excluded women form their own community. Though it is founded on grief, it provides an occasion for female companionship. It is a brief and touching moment of melancholy solidarity, and that solidarity extends to the animal slaughtered by the male heroes. The women and the wilderness are brought together, joined by the heroes' double defeat of a woman and an animal, Ishtar and the Bull. Together, the women mourn the murder of an animal, standing on the wall between the wilderness and the city.

And so we return once more to where we began—the wall of Uruk. I promised to pick up the epic's invitation to study the metaphorical brickwork of the wall, and as we have seen, we can find an almost impossibly large number of meanings built into it. The wall marks the circular and symmetrical structure of the epic, the ambiguous borderland between city and wilderness, the complex relationships of genders, and more. The wall is where Gilgamesh surrenders to his community—the community that built the wall to protect and define itself—and it is where he begins to tell his story, bringing peace to the storm of his heart and becoming, in his own way, immortal. Like the epic, the wall can signify endlessly. The readings presented in this book are just a sample of what philologists have teased out of the poem in the 150 years since its rediscovery, but as always with *Gilgamesh*, new eyes will see new ideas in it. Crucially, our understanding of the epic's women and wilderness is inevitably shaped by our current concerns over gender equality and the climate crisis, so as those concerns develop, our understanding of the epic will change with them. *Gilgamesh* is adept at adapting to the passing of time. The brickwork is laid so tightly and with such precision that, one feels, an infinite number of meanings has been built into the text, ready for each new reader to uncover.

NOTES

Unless otherwise specified, all translations are my own.

INTRODUCTION

1. Rilke and Kippenberg, *Briefwechsel*, 191.

2. Schmidt, *Gilgamesh*, xv.

3. Rilke and Kippenberg, *Briefwechsel*, 192.

4. Smith, "Gold from the Old."

5. On *Gilgamesh* and Star Trek, see Miller, "He Who Saw the Stars." Darwish refers to *Gilgamesh* in "Horse for the Stranger," 1151. On Jung's relation to the epic, see Ziolkowski, *Gilgamesh Among Us*, 29–30. Wilhelm II wrote on *Gilgamesh* in *Königtum im alten Mesopotamien*, 4. On insomnia, see Deagon, "Twelve Double-Hours."

6. I use the term "philosophy" here in the general sense of "intellectual reflections on the nature of existence." For the question of whether Babylonians also had a philosophy in the stricter sense of the word—as a tradition of systematic, rational investigations into the world and its knowability—see van de Mieroop, *Philosophy Before the Greeks*.

7. I 9–10.

8. For an introduction to cuneiform cultures in general, see van de Mieroop, *History of the Ancient Near East*; and Foster and Foster, *Civilizations of Ancient Iraq*. Another good starting point is the essays collected in Radner and Robson, *Oxford Handbook of Cuneiform Culture*; and Frahm, *Companion to Assyria*. See also the recent *Oxford History of the Ancient Near East*, edited by Radner, Moeller, and Potts, whose first volume (of a planned five) appeared in 2020. The best anthology of Akkadian literature is Foster, *Before the Muses*; for Sumerian literature, it is Black et al., *Literature of Ancient Sumer*; see also Lenzi, *Introduction to Akkadian Literature*.

9. For an introduction to the cuneiform script, see Finkel and Taylor, *Cuneiform*; and Charpin, *Reading and Writing*.

10. On the spread of cuneiform literature through the ancient Near East, see, for example, Cohen, *Wisdom from the Late Bronze Age*, chap. 3. Van de Mieroop has coined the term "Babylonian cosmopolis" in an article of the same name, but it would be just as accurate (and more alliterative) to speak of a "cuneiform cosmopolis." For the literary effects of cuneiform's spread in a comparative perspective, see Damrosch, "Scriptworlds."

11. On the earliest stages of cuneiform—and its uses in accountancy—see Nissen, Damerow, and Englund, *Archaic Bookkeeping.* The invention of writing remains a difficult topic; for alternative approaches, see Schmandt-Besserat, *Before Writing;* and Glassner, *Invention of Cuneiform.* I take this occasion to remember the great Terry Jones, who in *The Story of One* called chartered accountancy "Sumer's great gift to the world."

12. Geller, "Last Wedge."

13. The go-to handbook for cuneiform signs and their readings is Borger, *Mesopotamisches Zeichenlexikon.*

14. On the creativity that cuneiform affords, see for example Finkel, "Strange Byways"; on its inherent potential for interpretation and hermeneutic engagement, see Frahm, *Babylonian and Assyrian Text Commentaries,* chap. 5; and for a particularly noteworthy case of the latter, see Bottéro, "Les noms de Marduk." On the wider significance of cuneiform polysemy for the intellectual culture of the ancient world, see Bottéro, *Mesopotamia,* chaps. 5 and 6; Bahrani, *Graven Image,* chaps. 4 and 5; and van de Mieroop, *Philosophy Before the Greeks.*

15. Streck, "Großes Fach Altorientalistik."

16. An overview of the archaeology of the ancient Near East can be found in Potts, *Companion to the Archaeology of the Ancient Near East.*

17. To see which manuscripts supply which parts of the text, go to the synoptic edition that Andrew George has made freely available at soas.ac.uk/gilgamesh/standard/, where all the manuscripts are transliterated individually.

18. For an introduction to the Akkadian language, see Huehnergard, *Grammar of Akkadian.* Sumerian is a more difficult matter—a much-repeated joke among specialists is that there are as many grammars of Sumerian as there are Sumerologists—but a good introduction for beginners is Michalowski, "Sumerian."

19. On the difficult question of when Sumerian died out, see Woods, "Bilingualism, Scribal Learning, and the Death of Sumerian"; Michalowski, "Lives of the Sumerian Language."

20. It is unclear how this "emphatic" sound was achieved. There are two main options: the consonants may have been pharyngealized, as in Arabic, or glottalized, as in Ge'ez. Scholars currently favor the latter option—see Kouwenberg, "Evidence for Post-Glottalized Consonants."

21. Readers wishing to compare the different versions can consult the edition by Andrew George, *Babylonian Gilgamesh Epic,* to which I return below. For the differences between the versions and the developments that led from one to the next, see the seminal study by Tigay, *Evolution of the Gilgamesh Epic.*

22. On the library, see Fincke, "Assyrian Scholarship and Scribal Culture"; and Finkel, "Assurbanipal's Library"; with references to further reading.

23. For cuneiform colophons, see Leichty, "Colophon"; and the catalogue assembled by Hunger, *Babylonische und assyrische Kolophone.*

24. On alliteration in Akkadian epics, see Hecker, *Untersuchungen zur akkadischen Epik,* 139–41; and Helle, "Rhythm and Expression," 65–66. On the stylistics of Akkadian literature more generally, see Wasserman, *Style and Form;* and the essays collected in Vogelzang and Vanstiphout, *Mesopotamian Poetic Language.*

25. I 7–8.

26. George, *Babylonian Gilgamesh Epic,* 162–65, summarizes what may be called the traditional view of Akkadian prosody, which distinguishes between verses that have four "semantic beats" and verses that have three; George illustrates this system of scansion with examples from the Old Babylonian version of *Gilgamesh.* For alternatives to this view, see Helle, "Rhythm and Expression"; and Wisnom, "Stress Patterns."

27. Landsberger, "Eigenbegrifflichkeit der babylonischen Welt," 371; for the prevalence of the trochaic ending see also Lambert, *Babylonian Creation Myths,* 18–20. For the scansion of Gilgamesh's name, see George, *Babylonian Gilgamesh Epic,* 89–90.

28. The exact nature of the game that Gilgamesh plays and the ball he loses is unclear. See Edzard, "mekkû, pukku und"; and George, *Babylonian Gilgamesh Epic,* 898–900.

29. For various perspectives on Tablet XII's relation to the rest of the epic, see Jacobsen, *Treasures of Darkness,* 215, who sees it as an incongruent addition; Tigay, *Evolution of the Gilgamesh Epic,* 105–7, who sees it as an external but crucial complement; Vulpe, "Irony and Unity," who sees it as an integral part of the text; and George, *Babylonian Gilgamesh Epic,* 47–49, who sees it as an appendix. My own view is closest to the latter.

30. I return to the question of genre in cuneiform literature in a later chapter, but see George, "*The Epic of Gilgameš:* Thoughts on Genre and Meaning"; Vanstiphout, "Some Thoughts on Genre" and "Use(s) of Genre." For the genre of epics more generally, see Hainsworth, *The Idea of Epic;* Bates, *Cambridge Companion to Epic;* and the essays collected in the recent volumes by Reitz and Finkman, *Structures of Epic Poetry.* For a convincing argument that *Gilgamesh* does qualify as an epic, see Vanstiphout, "Craftmanship of *Sîn-leqi-unninnī,*" 68–71.

31. I have adapted the definition of "extra" from the blog *Rachel's English:* rachelsenglish .com/american-slang-extra-cringey-basic/.

32. For an up-to-date introduction to the Uruk period, see Selz, "Uruk Phenomenon."

33. See for example Leick, *Mesopotamia,* which tells the story of cuneiform cultures entirely through a sequence of cities, from Eridu to Babylon.

34. For a lively and comprehensive introduction to the Old Akkadian Empire, see Foster, *Age of Agade.*

35. Barjamovic, "Mesopotamian Empires," 123–24.

36. According to another metrological system, a *šār* would be the equivalent of 960 acres. For the size of a *šār*, see Powell, "Maße und Gewichte," 480–81; and George, *Babylonian Gilgamesh Epic*, 782. On *Gilgamesh*'s use of numbers in general, see Robson, *Mathematics in Ancient Iraq*, 177–81.

37. For the broader literary significance of Uruk's measurements, see George, "Mayfly on the River."

38. On this fascinating goddess, see especially Harris, "Inanna-Ishtar as Paradox"; Bahrani, *Women of Babylon*, chap. 7; Pryke, *Ishtar*; and the list of further reading provided in Heffron, "Inana/Ištar."

39. For an example of a hymn depicting Ishtar as a naive young girl in love with Dumuzi, see Black, "Babylonian Ballads." Ishtar—or rather Inana, her Sumerian counterpart—is depicted as eating the corpses of her enemies in Enheduana's *Exaltation of Inana*, l. 128; see the translation in Foster, *Age of Agade*, 335. For Inana as doing everything that should not be done and nothing of what should be done, see *Enki and the World Order*, l. 446; a translation of which is given in Black et al., *Literature of Ancient Sumer*, 225.

40. For the association between Uruk and otherwise taboo rituals, see the description of the city in *Erra and Ishum*, IV 52–62; a translation of which can be found in Foster, *Before the Muses*, 904.

41. Tigay, *Evolution of the Gilgamesh Epic*, 108–109.

42. Worthington, *Ea's Duplicity*, chap. 20.

43. Apart from the Flood story, Ea's most notable appearances in Akkadian literature include *Ishtar's Descent*, in which he extricates Ishtar from death itself; *Anzu*, in which he helps the young god Ninurta recover the Tablet of Destinies; the first part of *Atra-hasis*, in which he creates humankind; *Enuma Elish*, in which he appears as Marduk's father, cleverly guiding his son to universal kingship; and *Adapa*, in which his role is particularly ambiguous: does he save Adapa or keep him from gaining immortality? Translations of all these can be found in Foster, *Before the Muses*. In Sumerian literature, where he is known as Enki, he establishes the universal order (and the chaos integral to that order) in *Enki and the World Order*; creates humans and disabilities in *Enki and Ninmah*; and is outwitted, for once, in *Enki and Inana*. Finally, *Enki and Ninhursanga* describes how Ea made the land of Dilmun fertile through a combination of incest, agriculture, and clever naming. Translations of these texts can be found in Black et al., *Literature of Ancient Sumer*.

44. George, *Babylonian Gilgamesh Epic*, 444–45.

45. Worthington, *Ea's Duplicity*, 323–24.

46. The fraction is mentioned in lines I 48, V 12, IX 51, and XI 80. On Ur-shanabi's name, see Fink, "How Gilgameš Became a Two-Thirds God"; and George, *Babylonian Gilgamesh Epic*, 150.

47. Worthington, *Ea's Duplicity*, 319–20. For the use of numbers to represent gods in Akkadian scholarship, see Röllig, "Götterzahlen."

48. For a comprehensive study of the Flood story in cuneiform cultures, especially its emergence and literary treatments, see Chen, *Primeval Flood Catastrophe*.

49. The epic is edited in Lambert and Millard, *Atra-ḫasīs;* see also Shehata, *Annotierte Bibliographie* and the translation in Foster, *Before the Muses*, 227–80. There is a long history of scholarship on *Atra-hasis,* which I condense in my summary. For readings of the epic that focus on human-divine relations, see especially Moran, "Creation of Man" and "Some Considerations of Form and Interpretation"; Wilcke, "Weltuntergang als Anfang"; von Soden, "Konflikte und ihre Bewältigung"; and more recently Gabriel, "Exemplificational Critique of Violence"; as well as the overview in Pryke, "Religion and Humanity," 7–9.

50. On the name change from Atra-hasis to Uta-napishti, and the meaning of the latter, see George, *Babylonian Gilgamesh Epic*, 152–53; and Worthington, *Ea's Duplicity*, xxxi and 262.

51. See Worthington, *Ea's Duplicity;* and my summary of Worthington's analysis in "Study the Brickwork," below.

52. On the ship's shape and construction, as well as many other fascinating details about the Flood hero and his ark, see Finkel, *Ark Before Noah.*

53. It is worth noting that in the Old Babylonian *Atra-hasis,* the introduction of the main character emphasizes his ability to speak directly with Ea: "He spoke with his god and his god with him spoke" (I 366–67), linking the two through a symmetrical exchange of words. In my reading, *Atra-hasis* shows how this mutual and direct form of communication was undone by the Flood, to be replaced by the system of divination. Of course, as *Gilgamesh* shows, it remained possible for gods to address humans directly, as both Ishtar and Shamash speak to the heroes without having recourse to omens, but these are, I believe, to be taken as rare deviations from the normal system of human-divine communication whose existence *Atra-hasis* explains. However, neither *Atra-hasis* nor *Gilgamesh* explicitly specifies that the oath of silence which preceded the Flood was meant to last forever, so the interpretation of Ea's message as an etiology of omens remains one possibility among many. Gösta Gabriel and Annette Zgoll are preparing a new study of how the Flood marks a shift in human-divine communication, which may clarify some of these questions. On the relation between the Flood story and divination, see also George, "Sign of the Flood"; and Worthington, *Ea's Duplicity*, 97.

54. Only half the series has been published—in Freedman, *If a City Is Set.* For omens concerning human behavior, see Guinan, "Human Behavioral Omens" and "Erotomancy."

55. For an introduction to cuneiform divination, see Koch, *Mesopotamian Divination Texts.*

56. Tellingly, the one time that Gilgamesh sleeps without dreaming is when he sleeps for six days and seven nights, and so loses his shot at immortality.

57. For dreams in *Gilgamesh,* see Noegel, *Nocturnal Ciphers,* chap. 2. The English word *analyze* also means "to unknot": it comes from Greek *aná,* "up," and *lúō,* "loosen."

58. For the implicit logic of Babylonian medicine, see Heeßel, *Babylonisch-assyrische Diagnostik.*

59. Fincke, "The British Museum's Ashurbanipal Library Project," gives an overview of the tablets held at Nineveh written in the Babylonian script, which constitute about a seventh of the entire library. Of the 3,680 Babylonian texts found at Nineveh, 2,459 can be identified, and 1,128 of these are legal or administrative documents. The remaining 1,331 texts can be divided into several genres: divination, medicine, religious texts (including prayers, ritual instructions, incantations, and lamentations), epic and myths, lexical lists, historical texts, and mathematics. The first three groups, which all directly relate to human-divine communication, account for 1,269 or about 95.3 percent of the scholarly Babylonian texts found at Nineveh (again, this is not the complete library, but a representative subset). The epics and myths account for 19 of the texts, but, as *Gilgamesh* shows, even these could be related to the system of human-divine communication.

60. George, *Babylonian Gilgamesh Epic,* 379.

61. George, *Babylonian Gilgamesh Epic,* 418–19.

62. New pieces of the epic have been published in George, "Civilizing of Ea-Enkidu"; George, "Gilgameš Epic at Ugarit"; George, *Babylonian Literary Texts,* 29–41; George, "Enkidu and the Harlot"; George and al-Rawi, "Back to the Cedar Forest"; Cavigneaux, "Oiseaux de l'arche"; Jiménez, "New Fragments of Gilgameš"; Jiménez et al., "From the Electronic Babylonian Literature Lab," no. 1, 76–77. Some newly discovered pieces of the epic have not yet been published but are available in the German translation by Maul, *Gilgamesch-Epos.* A fragment that, while not belonging to *Gilgamesh,* sheds important new light on the story of the Flood was published in Finkel, *Ark Before Noah.*

63. Jiménez, "In the Spotlight"; Jiménez et al., "From the Electronic Babylonian Literature Lab," 75–76.

64. George, "Enkidu and the Harlot."

65. Whipple, "Ancient Sex Saga."

66. Jiménez et al., "From the Electronic Babylonian Literature Lab," no. 1, 76–77.

67. Karen Emmerich, in *Literary Translation,* argues that *Gilgamesh* is merely an extreme case of a much more widespread phenomenon: more often than not, literary translations

lead the reader to believe that the original is a single stable text, when it is in fact a composite and fluctuating construct, changing shape even as translators work on it.

68. X 290–96.

69. The interview with Komunyakaa can be viewed at learner.org/series/invitation-to -world-literature/the-epic-of-gilgamesh/ (20:17).

70. For archaeological looting in Iraq, see E. C. Stone, "Update on the Looting of Archaeological Sites in Iraq." For a concise statement of what is lost when an object is brought to light through looting rather than scientific excavation, see Hanson, "Why Does Archaeological Context Matter?"

71. III 65–66.

72. George, *Babylonian Gilgamesh Epic*.

73. George, *Babylonian Gilgamesh Epic*; George, *Epic of Gilgamesh*; Foster, *Epic of Gilgamesh*.

74. Ferry, *Gilgamesh*; Lewis, *Gilgamesh Retold*; Sandars, *Epic of Gilgamesh*; Mitchell, *Gilgamesh*.

75. OB II 108–109. In one extreme case, a single Akkadian word, *lūšibakkum* (SB V 175), literally "let me dwell for you," becomes seven words in my translation: "Let me stay here, in your service."

76. *šumma šamma šâsu ikaššada qātaka*, XI 285. For the system of scansion employed here, see Helle, "Rhythm and Expression."

77. On this reading of the line, see Nemirovskaya, "lú as a logogram for *mamma*."

78. See George, *Babylonian Gilgamesh Epic*, 538–39, including the notes on 778–82. See also the synoptic edition that George has made available at soas.ac.uk/gilgamesh/standard/, where the text of the manuscripts is given in individual lines.

79. More significant discrepancies are found elsewhere in the text. One example is VIII 56, where Gilgamesh speaks to Enkidu's corpse. In one of the two manuscripts that preserve the first word of this line, Gilgamesh says, "you have become unconscious," or literally, "you have become obscure to me" (*ta"adram-ma*). In my translation, I opt for the variant reading given in the other manuscript: "You, come back!" (*atta tūram-ma*). Though this second manuscript contains more mistakes in general, here it preserves a more visceral, desperate exclamation, which I find more forceful in the context. Another notable variant comes from Uta-napishti's monologue on death, which I discuss in detail in "Dying to Be Read," below. Line X 318, which I translate as "no one has ever greeted a dead man," is rendered by another manuscript as "the human being is imprisoned. After they blessed me . . ." See George, *Babylonian Gilgamesh Epic*, 876–77.

80. George, "Gilgameš Epic at Ugarit," 238–48.

81. On the ambiguity of *naqbu*, see Castillo, "*Nagbu:* Totality or Abyss"; George, *Babylonian Gilgamesh Epic,* 444–45. For its further meaning as one of Ea's names, see Worthington, *Ea's Duplicity,* 324.

82. On this difficult line, see George, *Babylonian Gilgamesh Epic,* 780–81; Nurullin, "Philological Notes on the First Tablet," 194–96. See also Nurullin's comments on the ambiguity of the sign ^{giš}KUN₄ as either "staircase" or "threshold," and on the relation between the Eana, Uruk, and the wall (189–93).

83. I translate the phrase as an active construction—"he set"—but as noted in George, "Mayfly on the River," 230, the verb is in the stative form, "the hardships were set": "It is not he who places his story on the tablet of lapis lazuli," George writes; "that is done for him." That may be so, and I do appreciate George's point about the literary effect of Gilgamesh's inaction in the prologue (see the ending of "Dying to Be Read" and the beginning of "Kings, Women, Monsters," below). But it is worth noting that the couplet lists three statives in quick succession—*anih, šupšuh, šakin*—that together describe Gilgamesh's condition on arriving home: tired, rested, writing. To mimic this triple description, and the grammatical linking between the three words, I found it best to insert an active subject in the last verb: "exhausted but at peace, as he set down . . ."

84. George, "Gilgameš Epic at Ugarit," 246, takes *parakku* as denoting "the centres of mortal power, divine power or both," but rebuffs the idea that it might refer to Gilgamesh's visits to Humbaba and Uta-napishti, since "neither is truly a place where political or cosmic power was wielded." I disagree: the Cedar Forest is explicitly described as *parak Irnini,* "throne-dais of goddesses," and Uta-napishti can easily be seen as, if not explicitly a king or god, then at least a deified person of special importance, whose home could well be described as a *parakku.* The qualification of these visits as *mitharis,* "matching," could then refer to the position of the two locations at opposite ends of the earth; see Helle, "Two-Act Structure."

GILGAMESH

1. The aurochs ("*Ur*-ox") is a now extinct breed of wild oxen. Larger and stronger than domesticated cattle, they must have been a formidable sight.

2. The nature of the bat-and-ball game that Gilgamesh plays here—and with which Tablet XII begins—is unclear. See Edzard, "mekkû, pukku und"; and George, *Babylonian Gilgamesh Epic,* 898–900.

3. In the Bronze Age, meteorites were a rare source of iron, a much harder material than bronze. See George, *Babylonian Gilgamesh Epic,* 793.

4. It is not fully clear whether it is Shamhat or Enkidu who is compared to a god here; see George, *Babylonian Gilgamesh Epic,* 167. Gods leading their worshippers by the hand were

a popular motif in ancient Near Eastern art, so the metaphor might be comparing Shamhat to a god (not a goddess?). Likewise, priests sometimes led the statues of gods by the hand on a ritual procession, so the metaphor could also apply to Enkidu.

5. It is unclear whether this is a sign of victory or defeat; see George, *Babylonian Gilgamesh Epic*, 191–92.

6. This one line is restored from the Old Babylonian version.

7. The Anunnaki were a group of gods, but their role shifted over time. In the third and early second millennium BCE, the term denoted the highest gods of the pantheon: Anu, Enlil, Ea, and so on. Later, however, it came to refer to the gods of the underworld, as opposed to the Igigi, who were the gods of heaven. It is not fully clear which of the two senses is used in *Gilgamesh*. In this line, the mountainous Cedar Forest is referred to as the "home of the Anunnaki," which implies that the high gods of heaven are meant. But later, in connection with Enkidu's funeral, there is a reference to the "judge of the Anunnaki," suggesting that the underworld gods are meant. For an overview of these and other problems related to the Anunnaki, see Brisch, "Anunna."

8. There must be some confusion in the Old Babylonian measurement of the heroes' weapons. The axes and swords are measured in talents, Akkadian *biltu*, a unit of weight corresponding to approximately 30 kilograms (66 pounds)—see Powell, "Maße und Gewichte," 510. The text states that the axes weighed three talents, the blades of the swords two talents, and their cross-guards and hilts half a talent each. But the text then concludes that the heroes were loaded with ten talents each, and that does not add up: no matter how you calculate it, the sum of the previous weights is not ten. The solution to this mathematical conundrum can be found in the new manuscript of Tablet V, in line 309, which states that the heroes' axes weighed *two* talents each, not three. The Old Babylonian and Standard Babylonian versions do not always give the same measurements, but the latter invariably makes things bigger, longer, and heavier than its precursor, so we can safely amend the weight of the axes in the Old Babylonian version to two talents. And, callooh callay, the math adds up: $(2 + 2 + \frac{1}{2} + \frac{1}{2}) \times 2 = 10$.

9. Gods, demons, and monsters were surrounded by an awe-inspiring light called *melammu*; the classic study of this phenomenon remains Cassin, *La splendeur divine*. Humbaba has seven such auras, which later turn out to be named living creatures and in fact the sons of Humbaba; see George and al-Rawi, "Back to the Cedar Forest," 74–75.

10. The melee is so intense that it creates the ten-mile-wide Beqaa valley, which today separates Lebanon's two main mountain ranges.

11. The Akkadian cry, *kappī*, sounds just like the call of the roller bird. Another possible identification of the *allallu* bird, as it is called in Akkadian, is with the hoopoe. I prefer the Indian roller because it really is *bitrumu*, "multicolored": its plumage is a stunning sequence

of azure, pale peach, streaks of black and orange, and sudden dots of violet. See Salonen, *Vögel und Vogelfang,* s.v. *allallu;* George, *Babylonian Gilgamesh Epic,* 834.

12. As noted by George, *Babylonian Gilgamesh Epic,* 854, the word *ḫīqu* in this context likely refers to a dairy product diluted with water, perhaps like the beverage today known as *doogh* in Farsi and *ayran* in Turkish: a refreshing drink made by mixing yogurt with water and salt.

13. Gilgamesh provides Enkidu with funerary gifts for the underworld gods, to make his life in the hereafter more comfortable. Note that the passage contrasts the bright blue of lapis lazuli with the dull red of carnelian.

14. According to legend, Gilgamesh and Enkidu were buried underneath the Euphrates river; see Cavigneaux and al-Rawi, *Gilgameš et la Mort,* 5–11. On the term "Anunnaki" in this context, see note 7 above.

15. Older studies identified the Stone Ones, which allow Ur-shanabi to cross the Waters of Death, as amulets or pieces of equipment on the boat, but following George, *Babylonian Gilgamesh Epic,* 501–502, I interpret them as stone golems crewing Ur-shanabi's ship. This is also made clear by the Hittite version of the epic, in which they are identified as stone statues.

16. Ea's words can be read in two ways at once: as a promise and a warning. See the discussion of this passage in "Study the Brickwork," below.

17. Uta-napishti here refers to himself as Atra-hasis. Worthington, in *Ea's Duplicity,* xxxi, argues that Atra-hasis ("He Is Very Wise") was the sage's original name, and Uta-napishti ("He Found Life") a title he gained upon achieving immortality.

18. Moorings and dikes usually marked the border between land and water—but in the Flood, all overflows. As pointed out to me by Selena Wisnom, Ninurta was also the inventor of irrigation, so he is here shown destroying his own creation.

19. The name of the mountain is traditionally read Nimush; see George, *Babylonian Gilgamesh Epic,* 516. But the way it is spelled in cuneiform also allows one to read Niṣir, which recalls the word *niṣirtu,* "secret"; see Finkel, *Ark Before Noah,* 280. Even if the mountain's name was pronounced Nimuš, this spelling is surely significant, given the importance of the word *secret* to Uta-napishti's story: "I will tell you a secret, Gilgamesh, and reveal what the gods keep hidden . . ." (XI 9–10). I have chosen to render its name as "Mountain of Secrets" to highlight that connection.

20. The iridescent wings of the mythical flies, arranged in a semicircle around Belet-ili's neck, become the rainbow; see Kilmer, "Symbolism of the Flies," 179.

21. On the term "Igigi," see note 7 above.

22. On the nature of the game, see note 2 above.

23. Children provided their deceased parents with offerings in the underworld, and a greater number of children meant a more secure source of food and water.

24. Note that the Akkadian translation and the Sumerian original present the exchanges in different orders. The preserved ending of the Standard Babylonian version—given below—contains lines that are dispersed across the Sumerian text. Further, different Sumerian manuscripts do not have the same order—the line numbers given here are based on the translation in Gadotti, *"Gilgamesh, Enkidu and the Netherworld,"* 154–60.

25. The Sumerian version ends here. Death by fire was the worst possible fate because it led not just to death, but to nonexistence.

A POEM FOR THE AGES

1. To delve deeper into the world of *Gilgamesh,* I recommend first reading alternative translations of the epic, especially the one by Foster, *Epic of Gilgamesh* (an updated version of which will be made freely available through the Electronic Babylonian Literature website); the one accompanying the edition in George, *Babylonian Gilgamesh Epic* (chap. 11); and, if possible, the German translation by Stefan Maul, *Gilgamesch-Epos,* and the French by Jean Bottéro, *L'Épopée de Gilgameš.* I would then read the introductions by Pryke, *Gilgamesh,* and Sallaberger, *Gilgamesch-Epos,* then chaps. 1, 3, 4, and 10 in George, *Babylonian Gilgamesh Epic.* Finally, I would turn to the recent and detailed study by Worthington, *Ea's Duplicity,* which presents many new ideas about the epic in its wide-ranging discussions, while also summarizing its long history of interpretation. Another crucial, if now somewhat dated, work is Tigay, *Evolution of the Gilgamesh Epic,* which traces the epic's history of development in the ancient world.

For an introduction to the world of Assyriology more generally, see van de Mieroop, *History of the Ancient Near East;* and Foster and Foster, *Civilizations of Ancient Iraq;* as well as the essays collected in Radner and Robson, *Oxford Handbook of Cuneiform Cultures,* and Frahm, *Companion to Assyria.* Another crucial sourcebook is the anthology of Akkadian literature in Foster, *Before the Muses;* and that of Sumerian literature in Black et al., *Literature of Ancient Sumer;* see also the introduction by Lenzi, *Introduction to Akkadian Literature.*

A good place to begin a search for an Assyriological topic is the *Reallexikon der Assyriologie,* whose entries provide quick overviews and references for follow up (an electronic version of the lexicon is available at publikationen.badw.de/de/rla/index). Readers looking for a specific Akkadian word should consult the *Chicago Assyrian Dictionary* (which can be freely downloaded through the Oriental Institute's website, oi.uchicago.edu) and Wolfram von Soden's *Akkadisches Handwörterbuch.* Web resources include the Cuneiform Digital Library Initiative (CDLI), a digital archive of cuneiform text that also has a helpful wiki (cdli.ox.ac

.uk/wiki); and the Openly Richly Annotated Cuneiform Corpus (ORACC), an umbrella site that covers various corpora of cuneiform texts, as well as useful guides such as "Ancient Mesopotamian Gods and Goddesses" and the wiki that was made for the "Geography of Knowledge" project (oracc.museum.upenn.edu/projectlist.html). Finally, two other digital archives of cuneiform poetry are available: the Electronic Text Corpus of Sumerian Literature (ETCSL, etcsl.orinst.ox.ac.uk) and the Electronic Babylonian Literature project (eBL, available in fall 2021).

2. On the current state of the discipline of philology, see Pollock, "Future Philology?" and "Introduction."

3. Aidt, *Har døden taget*, 88, translation mine.

4. On the concept of "world literature," see Damrosch, *What Is World Literature?*, whose first chapter is on *Gilgamesh*.

5. For *Gilgamesh*'s modern reception, see especially Damrosch, *Buried Book*; Ziolkowski, *Gilgamesh Among Us*; Cregan-Reid, *Discovering Gilgamesh*; Pryke, *Gilgamesh*, chap. 7; and the essays collected in Maier, *Gilgamesh*, part 2. Michael Schmidt invited a range of contemporary poets to respond to the epic, presenting their comments in Schmidt, *Gilgamesh*.

6. On "Project Gilgamesh," see Harari, *Sapiens*, chap. 14.

7. For the NSA's Gilgamesh software, see Sullivan, "Did a Drone Carrying NSA Tech Crash in Yemen?"; and Scahill and Greenwald, "The NSA's Secret Role in the U.S. Assassination Program."

8. For *Atra-hasis*, see Lambert and Millard, *Atra-ḫasīs*; for the *Cycle of Aratta*, see Vanstiphout, *Epics of Sumerian Kings*; on whether the latter can be termed an epic, see Michalowski, "Maybe Epic." It is difficult to say for sure what the oldest recorded poem is, but one candidate is the *Instructions of Shuruppak*, whose earliest preserved manuscripts date to the twenty-sixth century BCE; see Alster, *Instructions of Suruppak*. Personally, I would argue that *Gilgamesh* is not even the first literary masterpiece, as I would reserve that title for the poems of Enheduana, high priestess of Ur and the first known author—but that is a story for another time. On Enheduana, see Zgoll, *Rechtsfall der En-ḫedu-Ana*; Foster, *Age of Agade*, 206–208 and appendix II; and Konstantopoulos, "Many Lives of Enheduana."

9. For the ancient literary history of *Gilgamesh*, see Tigay, *Evolution of the Gilgamesh Epic*; Sallaberger, *Gilgamesch-Epos*; George, *Babylonian Gilgamesh Epic*, part 1; and the summary in George, "Shattered Tablets." See also the alternative account proposed in Fleming and Milstein, *Buried Foundation*.

10. A new edition of the *Sumerian King List* is being prepared by Gösta Gabriel.

11. XI 11–14.

12. On the earliest manuscripts of *Gilgamesh* poems and their connection with Shulgi, see Michalowski, "Maybe Epic," 20–21; and George, *Babylonian Gilgamesh Epic*, 7. Shulgi's

father, Ur-Nammu, also claimed to be Gilgamesh's brother; see George, *Babylonian Gilgamesh Epic*, 108–12. One of the Ur III tablets of the Sumerian *Gilgamesh* cycle was published in Cavigneaux and al-Rawi, "Gilgameš et Taureau de Ciel," 101–3; two others await publication by Gonzalo Rubio.

13. Tigay, in *Evolution of the Gilgamesh Epic*, 13, speaks confidently of a historical Gilgamesh who lived in the Early Dynastic Period (c. 2700–2500 BCE), but today the majority view holds that Gilgamesh is a literary invention. An early argument in that direction is Lambert, "Gilgameš in Religious, Historical and Omen Texts." Of course, we cannot prove a negative, but at present no convincing evidence clinches the case for Gilgamesh's historical existence.

14. A persuasive argument against Enmebaragesi's historicity is given in Michalowski, "A Man Called Enmebaragesi."

15. On the order of the poems in the cycle, see Gadotti, "*Gilgamesh, Enkidu and the Netherworld*." For the Sumerian Gilgamesh cycle, see Edzard, "Gilgameš und Huwawa"; Cavigneaux and al-Rawi, "Gilgameš et Taureau de Ciel"; Katz, *Gilgamesh and Akka;* Cavigneaux and al-Rawi, *Gilgameš et la Mort;* and especially Gadotti, "*Gilgamesh, Enkidu and the Netherworld*." For the stories of Lugalbanda and Enmerkar, see Vanstiphout, *Epics of Sumerian Kings.* Gilgamesh's name in Sumerian was previously read "Bilgames," but as shown by Rubio, "Reading Sumerian Names," he was Gilgamesh in Sumerian too.

16. For the Old Babylonian school system, see Tinney, "On the Curricular Setting"; Veldhuis, *Religion, Literature, and Scholarship;* and Robson, "Tablet House."

17. For the school system after the Old Babylonian period, see Gesche, *Schulunterricht in Babylonien.*

18. It is not certain that the Old Babylonian version was a single epic, as we have not recovered the entire composition. The Old Babylonian manuscripts of *Gilgamesh* may yet turn out to have been separate poems that were brought together to form a single text in the eleventh century BCE. Fleming and Milstein, in *Buried Foundation,* argue that the preserved Old Babylonian manuscripts of *Gilgamesh* are not internally consistent, suggesting that they belong to separate stories, but this argument has not gained widespread traction in the field.

19. Tigay, *Evolution of the Gilgamesh Epic,* chap. 2; see also his summary on 242–43.

20. On the use of Akkadian in the wider Near East, see Nett, "Akkadian as Lingua Franca"; on the cultural significance of that distribution, see van de Mieroop, "Babylonian Cosmopolis."

21. George, "Civilizing of Ea-Enkidu." The tablet giving Gilgamesh's and Enkidu's names as Sîn and Ea was smuggled illegally into the United States, and in May 2020 it became the object of an unusual lawsuit. When attorneys in New York sought to return the tablet to Iraq, they employed what is known as an *in rem* forfeiture case—in which the

government files a lawsuit against an inanimate object in order to seize that object from the person who is thought to be holding it illegally. This legal maneuver led to the amazing case name *United States of America v. One Cuneiform Tablet Known as the "Gilgamesh Dream Tablet."*

22. For the "serialization" of cuneiform literature, as this process is called, see Heeßel, "Sieben Tafeln," with references to previous literature on the topic.

23. For Esagil-kin-apli's claim, see Schmidtchen, "Esagil-kīn-apli's Catalogue"; for its parallel with *Gilgamesh,* see George, "Shattered Tablets."

24. For the Standard Babylonian serialization of *Gilgamesh* and the changes described below, see Tigay, *Evolution of the Gilgamesh Epic,* chaps. 6–12; and George, *Babylonian Gilgamesh Epic,* 39–47.

25. On the monotony of the Standard Babylonian version, see Cooper, "Gilgamesh Dreams of Enkidu"; Tigay, *Evolution of the Gilgamesh Epic,* 244; and Gilbert, "Repetition and the Death Drive."

26. I take the idea of the Standard Babylonian version as a more "philosophical" work from George, *Babylonian Gilgamesh Epic,* 32–33, 47; see also Jacobsen, "Gilgamesh Epic: Romantic and Tragic Vision."

27. Lambert's edition of *Enuma Elish* includes 181 manuscripts; see Lambert, *Babylonian Creation Myths,* 3–4. George's edition of the Standard Babylonian *Gilgamesh* includes 116 manuscripts; see George, *Babylonian Gilgamesh Epic,* 379.

28. Object no. AO 19862, available at louvre.fr/en/oeuvre-notices/hero-overpowering -lion.

29. For an introduction to Sargon's reign, see Elayi, *Sargon II.*

30. Annus, "Louvre Gilgamesh." The measurements are lost in both Babylonian versions but can be reconstructed from the Hittite and Ugaritic versions. For other artistic depictions of Gilgamesh, see Steymans, *Gilgamesch.* The relief is object no. AO 19861, available at cartelfr.louvre.fr/cartelfr/visite?srv=car_not_frame&idNotice=17557.

31. On intertextual allusions in the Assyrian royal inscriptions, see Bach, *Untersuchungen zur Transtextuellen Poetik.*

32. TCL 3, l. 19. A new edition of Sargon's inscriptions is being prepared by Grant Frame; an analysis of this specific intertextual connection is given in Bach, *Untersuchungen zur Transtextuellen Poetik,* 247–54.

33. A fascinating study of Sargon's death and its intellectual repercussions at the Assyrian court is given in Tadmor, Landsberger, and Parpola, "Sin of Sargon."

34. Frahm, "Nabû-zuqup-kēnu, das Gilgameš-Epos und der Tod Sargons II."

35. XII 148–53.

36. For an introduction to the turbulence of the Sargonid dynasty, see the succinct overview in Frahm, "Neo-Assyrian Period."

37. A summary of the debate on Ashurbanipal's literacy can be found in Livingstone, "Ashurbanipal: Literate or Not?"

38. On the library at Nineveh, see Fincke, "Assyrian Scholarship and Scribal Culture"; and Finkel, "Assurbanipal's Library"; with references to further reading.

39. Wells, *Outline of History*, 246.

40. Hunger, *Babylonische und assyrische Kolophone*, 98; for Ashurbanipal's intellectual ambitions, see Frahm, "Keeping Company with Men of Learning."

41. For the first-millennium education of Babylonian scribes, see Gesche, *Schulunterricht in Babylonien;* for *Gilgamesh's* place in it, see George, *Babylonian Gilgamesh Epic,* 35–39.

42. I 7–8. For the epic's role in the creation of scribal identities, see Lenzi, "Advertising Secrecy."

43. For sage advisers moderating the intemperance of kings in *Gilgamesh,* see Sonik, "Gilgamesh and Emotional Excess." For the scholars' own perception of their relation to the king in the first millennium, see Beaulieu, "Social and Intellectual Setting"; Frahm, "Keeping Company with Men of Learning," 517–20; and Pongratz-Leisten, "All the King's Men." For other critiques of royal power in cuneiform literature, see Finn, *Much Ado About Marduk.* For the world of cuneiform scholars in the first millennium more generally, see the recent study by Robson, *Ancient Knowledge Networks.*

44. Lambert, "Catalogue of Texts and Authors"; Michalowski, "Sailing to Babylon," 186–87; Helle, "Literary Heritage." The development of authorial attributions in cuneiform cultures was the subject of my Ph.D. thesis, "The First Authors: Narratives of Authorship in Ancient Iraq" (Aarhus University, 2020).

45. For Sîn-leqi-unnenni's profession, see Jiménez, *Babylonian Disputation Poems,* 112–13; for the connection between that profession and the epic, see Beaulieu, "Social and Intellectual Setting."

46. On the *Uruk List of Kings and Sages,* see Lenzi, "Uruk List"; and Helle, "Role of Authors."

47. On the Sîn-leqi-unnenni family, see Beaulieu, "Descendants of Sîn-lēqi-unninni." On the practice of claiming descent from an illustrious ancestor more generally, see Lambert, "Ancestors, Authors, and Canonicity"; Nielsen, *Sons and Descendants;* and Helle, "Literary Heritage."

48. For ancient literary compositions referring to Gilgamesh, see George, *Babylonian Gilgamesh Epic,* chap. 3; Wasserman, "Distant Voice of Gilgameš," 4–9; Jiménez, *Babylonian Disputation Poems,* 83–84; and Wisnom, *Weapons of Words,* chap. 6.

49. George, *Babylonian Gilgamesh Epic,* 112.

50. For the *Gilgamesh Letter,* see Kraus, "Brief des Gilgameš"; and the translation in Foster, *Before the Muses,* 1017–19.

51. For the *Ballad of Early Rulers*, see Alster, *Wisdom of Ancient Sumer*, 288–322.

52. For the *Dialogue of Pessimism*, see Lambert, *Babylonian Wisdom Literature*, chap. 6. For the relation between the two texts, see Wasserman, "Distant Voice of Gilgameš," 7–9; Buccellati, "Dialogo del pessimismo"; and Helle, "Babylonian Perspectives," 216–19.

53. Respectively, the *Dialogue* l. 60 and *Gilgamesh* XI 116.

54. Respectively, the *Dialogue* l. 33 and *Gilgamesh* IX 51; see Wasserman, "Distant Voice of Gilgameš," 9.

55. Respectively, the *Dialogue* ll. 76–78 and *Gilgamesh* I 18. For the *Dialogue*'s allusion to the wall of Uruk, see Wasserman, "Distant Voice of Gilgameš," 8–9; George, *Babylonian Gilgamesh Epic*, 526; and Metcalf, "Babylonian Perspectives," 263. For the phrase "the poor and the great," see below, note 62 of "The Storm of His Heart."

56. The word "skull," *gulgullu*, even echoes the name *Gilgāmeš*, having a similar syllable and stress structure. Especially in the context of so patent an allusion to the epic, this may well have been intentional.

57. The idea that scripts can determine the extent of literary circulation was put forward by David Damrosch in "Scriptworlds," 196–203, who uses *Gilgamesh* as a key example. George, in *Babylonian Gilgamesh Epic*, 70, argues persuasively that the epic died with its script. However, it should be noted that cuneiform is much more likely to survive than other ancient writings because it was mainly written on clay. It is fully possible that a version of *Gilgamesh* was written with Aramaic script on a parchment roll that did not survive the passing of time. I have adapted the term "cuneiform cosmopolis" from van de Mieroop, "Babylonian Cosmopolis."

58. See for example Dalley, "Gilgamesh in the Arabian Nights," for the suggestion that the epic survived long enough to influence the Arabic tale of Buluqiya; and the cogent dismissal of that argument in George, *Babylonian Gilgamesh Epic*, 65–68.

59. On the epic's post-cuneiform history, see the overviews in George, *Babylonian Gilgamesh Epic*, 60–61; Tigay, *Evolution of the Gilgamesh Epic*, 253–55. On the *Book of Giants*, see Cooley, "Book of Giants and the Greek Gilgamesh," with references to previous literature.

60. A good introduction to the relation between *Gilgamesh* and the Hebrew Bible, and to the complex history of the scholarship on this question, is given in Pryke, *Gilgamesh*, 190–97; see also the references provided in Worthington, *Ea's Duplicity*, 403–10.

61. For arguments in favor of a direct connection between *Gilgamesh* and the Homeric poems, the classic study is West, *East Face of Helicon*; more recent approaches include Currie, "The *Iliad*, *Gilgamesh*, and Neoanalysis"; Haubold, *Greece and Mesopotamia*; and López-Ruiz, Karahashi, and Ziemann, "*They Who Saw the Deep*." For a contrary perspective see George, *Babylonian Gilgamesh Epic*, 55–57.

My favorite parallel between the *Iliad* and *Gilgamesh* is that both contain a double description of walls. In the *Iliad*, the flashforward to Poseidon and Apollo's destruction of the wall around the Greek camp in 12.1–37 is matched by the flashback to the same gods' creation of the wall around Troy in 21.441–57. As in *Gilgamesh*, walls are used to encircle and delineate the plot (here marking the beginning and end of the war, but in reverse order). But then again, the same might be said of another story, which is entirely unconnected to *Gilgamesh:* John le Carré's *The Spy Who Came In from the Cold.* Just like *Gilgamesh*, it begins at a wall—in this case, the Berlin Wall. Our protagonist then travels westward, passes the wall again midway through the story, travels eastward, and comes back to the wall for the finale, dying as he scales it (figuratively in Gilgamesh's case, literally in Leaman's). Despite the similarities, I am unconvinced that Homer or his hypostases ever read *Gilgamesh*—but I'm less sure about le Carré.

62. Budge, *Rise of Assyriology*, 152–53.

63. I owe this suggestion to Frederik Stjernfeldt. Finkel, *Ark Before Noah*, 3, suggests that Smith's undress may have been due to an epileptic seizure.

64. Gladstone's words are quoted in a report by the *Times:* "Chaldean History of the Deluge," 7; see also Damrosch, *Buried Book*, 33–34. The paper was published as Smith, "Chaldean Account of the Deluge."

65. Smith also compares the adventures of Gilgamesh to Greek myths throughout his paper, including those of Hercules ("Chaldean Account of the Deluge," 215).

66. On Smith's involvement with the *Daily Telegraph*, see Damrosch, *Buried Book*, 34–48; on his death see chapter 2 in the same book.

67. See Damrosch, *Buried Book*; and Larsen, *Conquest of Assyria*. On the reception of these discoveries in Europe, see Bohrer, *Orientalism and Visual Culture*.

68. See Cathcart, "Earliest Contributions to the Decipherment."

69. Rawlinson et al., *Inscription of Tiglath Pileser I*, 3–16.

70. Cregan-Reid, *Discovering Gilgamesh*.

71. Arnold and Weisberg, "Centennial Review."

72. Wilhelm II, *Königtum im alten Mesopotamien*, 4.

73. Pinches, "Exit Gištubar!" 264. In the original article, the word "GILGAMEŠ" is indented and centered for even more dramatic effect. Pinches dryly adds: "Assyriologists may congratulate themselves on having been, mostly, practically right with regard to one syllable out of the three."

74. George, "Shattered Tablets," 8.

75. Rilke and Kippenberg, *Briefwechsel*, 191–92, 194–95, and 198. On Rilke's relation to the epic, see Moran, "Rilke and the Gilgamesh Epic"; and Schmidt, *Gilgamesh*, 104. The editor,

Katharina Kippenberg, asked Rilke whether he might be interested in writing a new German version, but Rilke refused: "Oh no, Gilgamesh I will never recount any way but orally, for in so doing I discover more expression every time." Reading Stefan Zweig's description of how Rilke told stories, in *The World of Yesterday*, we begin to see why: "He spoke naturally and simply, like a mother telling a fairy tale to her child, and just as lovingly; it was wonderful how, listening to him, even the most insignificant subject became picturesque and important. . . . Every movement, every gesture was soft" (115). But what is loving and light in speech can easily become imposing and authoritative in script, which may be what Rilke wanted to avoid. Still, it is striking that a version of *Gilgamesh* made four millennia ago survives, while that told by Rilke a little over a century ago is lost.

76. For Ted Hughes's unfinished adaptation, see Schmidt, *Gilgamesh*, 28.

77. Ziolkowski, *Gilgamesh Among Us*, 189.

78. Ziolkowski, *Gilgamesh Among Us*, 197.

79. Ziolkowski, *Gilgamesh Among Us*, 191.

80. Jung, *Symbols of Transformation*, 196, 200, 298, and passim.

81. Ziolkowski, *Gilgamesh Among Us*, 33 and 38.

82. See, respectively, Bjelke, *Saturn* and *To mænd*; Uçar-Özbirinci, "A Woman Playwright's Revision"; and Mielke, *Gilgamesch, König von Uruk*.

83. On the imperialism of early Mesopotamian archaeology, I recommend Bohrer, *Orientalism and Visual Culture*; Malley, "Layard Enterprise"; Bahrani, "Review of *The Conquest of Assyria*"; and the recent volume by Melman, *Empires of Antiquities*.

84. Rothfield, *Rape of Mesopotamia*; see also Stone and Farchakh Bajjaly, *Destruction of Cultural Heritage*.

85. I thank Zainab Bahrani for helping me navigate the epic's Iraqi reception.

86. Bahrani and Shabout, *Modernism and Iraq*, 16.

87. Bahrani, "Dia al-Azzawi's Modern Antiquity."

88. For the complex history of secularism, nationalism, and cultural heritage in Iraq, see Baram, "A Case of Imported Identity."

89. On Kadhim's play, see al-Azraki and al-Shamma, "General Introduction," xv.

90. Iskander, *Gilgamesh's Snake*. For the connection between Siti's work, *Gilgamesh*, and migration, see walidsiti.com/mona-kriegler.

91. Kubba's *The Path Ahead* is now in a private collection, but it can still be viewed, with the artist's commentary, at ayagallery.co.uk/4666.html. Kubba states that while one of the figures was meant to represent Gilgamesh, "subconsciously I changed him into a woman"—just as another Iraqi artist, Suad al-Attar, did in her painting *Gilgamesh and Enkidu* (2001), as discussed in "The Storm of His Heart," below.

92. Thal, "Are the Iraqis 'Waiting for Gilgamesh'?"

93. Jacobsen, "Mesopotamia," 212.

STUDY THE BRICKWORK

1. XI 323–24.

2. Zgoll, "monumentum aere perennius"; see also Dickson, "Wall of Uruk"; and Vanstiphout, "Craftmanship of *Sîn-leqi-unninnī*," 66–67 (I assume that "city of Uruk" in the last line of 66 is a mistake for "wall of Uruk").

3. Zgoll, "monumentum aere perennius," 464.

4. In addition to Jacobsen, whose protests against the epic's ending are quoted in the previous essay, see Ray, "Gilgamesh Epic," 316–17; Gresseth, "Gilgamesh Epic and Homer," 2–3; and George, "Mayfly on the River," 230.

5. I 10.

6. On *Gilgamesh* as a third-person autobiography, see Walker, "Second Tablet of *ṭupšenna pitema*"; Michalowski, "Commemoration, Writing, and Genre," 80–82, and "Sailing to Babylon," 187–88; George, *Babylonian Gilgamesh Epic*, 32 and 445–46; and Vanstiphout, "Craftmanship of *Sîn-leqi-unninnī*," 67.

7. Westenholz, *Legends of the Kings of Akkade*, chap. 10. The parallel between the two texts has often been noted, but see especially Michalowski, "Commemoration, Writing, and Genre," 80–82. Note also that the two kings are listed next to each other in the *Uruk List of Kings and Sages*, in ll. 12 and 13 (at least according to my reconstruction of the text), showing that the ancient scribes thought of them as closely related—see Helle, "Role of Authors," 233.

8. L. 1, see Westenholz, *Legends of the Kings of Akkade*, 300–1.

9. The term "*narû* literature" was coined in 1934 by Hans Güterbock in "Die historische Tradition," 15; on this genre, see Longman, *Fictional Akkadian Autobiography*.

10. Walker, "Second Tablet of *ṭupšenna pitema*," 194. Walker also notes that the stele in the box could be understood as a foundation inscription: it was common for kings to deposit an inscription commemorating their deeds in the foundation of a building they had commissioned, and such an inscription could indeed be described as a *narû* kept in a box (192). George, in *Babylonian Gilgamesh Epic*, 446, concludes that "very probably the poet is evoking a fictional scene in which an inscription left by Gilgameš himself, when he built the wall of Uruk, is discovered. The tablet of lapis lazuli (1.27) which the audience is invited to read is evidently to be identified with the stone monument on which he set in writing his adventures (1.10)." This is certainly a possibility, but not the only one: the *narû* of lapis lazuli on which the epic is written, left by Gilgamesh in a cedarwood box, is not explicitly

said to have been deposited beneath Uruk's wall (which, as George concedes, would already have been built by the time Gilgamesh returned to Uruk). I acknowledge that the prologue makes many suggestive references to foundations, but perhaps the epic is being deliberately ambiguous on this point, alluding to several scenarios at once.

11. It is a common feature of cuneiform narratives that they describe their own creation; see Foster, "On Authorship." Foster deals only with Akkadian literature, but the same motif is also found in Sumerian literature: see for example Enheduana's *Exaltation of Inana* or the tale of *Inana and Shukaletuda*, both of which end by describing how they came into being.

12. The symmetrical structure of the epic has been noted by, among others, Vanstiphout, "Craftmanship of *Sîn-leqi-unninnī*," 48–53; George, *Babylonian Gilgamesh Epic*, 48; Foster, *Epic of Gilgamesh*, xvi–xvii; Feldt and Koch, "Life's Journey," 112; Wolff, "Gilgamesh, Enkidu, and the Heroic Life," 392. In Helle, "Two-Act Structure," I argue that this same symmetrical structure is found in a number of other Babylonian epics: *Atra-hasis, Enuma Elish, Etana, Ereshkigal and Nergal,* and more.

13. It is not certain that the two journeys are to be understood as westward and east-ward, respectively. Here I assume that the Cedar Forest is a mythical image of Lebanon's cedar-covered mountains, northwest of Uruk, and that the Tunnel of Darkness lies in the mountainous region east of the Iraqi floodplain. But neither assumption is beyond chal-lenge, in part because they are mythical places that cannot be mapped directly onto a mod-ern understanding of geography, as noted in Konstantopoulos, "Disciplines of Geography"; and in part because the location of the mythical Cedar Forest seems to have shifted over time, from the Zagros mountains in the Sumerian cycle to Lebanon in the Akkadian ver-sion: see Klein and Abraham, "Problems of Geography in the Gilgameš Epics." Gilgamesh is said to travel "toward sunrise," east, in his journey to Uta-napishti (see for example line I 40), but confusingly, the Sun God seems both to set and rise through the same gate (IX 45), muddying the picture.

14. On the contrast between Ishtar and Shiduri, see Walls, *Desire, Discord, and Death,* 70; and the extended discussion in Abusch, *Male and Female,* chaps. 1–3.

15. I 100 and VIII 212.

16. On the expansion of the second act, see Vanstiphout, "Craftmanship of *Sîn-leqi-unninnī*," 53–56. In Helle, "Two-Act Structure," I argue that the expansion of the second act is a common feature of many Babylonian epics.

17. VI 153.

18. It is not certain that the word *imittu* refers to the Bull's penis; George, in *Babylonian Gilgamesh Epic*, 843, takes it to be the top part of the rear leg, translating it as "haunch." The word literally means "right hand," but as noted by George, its identification as a euphemism for the Bull's penis goes all the way back to George Smith in 1873. I am unconvinced by

George's counterargument that it cannot be a penis because Enkidu says to Ishtar: "I would do the same to you, if only I could catch you" (VI 156). True, Enkidu cannot tear off Ishtar's penis, but threatening to tear off her leg is no great taunt either. Either Enkidu means that he would kill Ishtar as he killed the Bull, or we are to understand that Enkidu *does* imply, if only sarcastically and rhetorically, that Ishtar has a penis, perhaps as a way of chiding her for her aggressive and "masculine" behavior. I do not mean to suggest that Ishtar was perceived as being transgender or intersex (as argued by Groneberg, "Die sumerisch-akkadische Inanna/Ištar," though see the rebuttal in Bahrani, *Women in Babylon*, 143–48), only that Enkidu might be willfully implying that she had a penis in order to insult her.

19. VI 159, *bikīta iškun;* and 179, *ištakan ḥidūtu.*

20. VI 182–83. The following passage is based on Helle, "Tablets as Narrative Episodes."

21. For ancient archives holding only select tablets, see Robson, "Production and Dissemination," 570. As with most cuneiform compositions, Tablet I was generally overrepresented; see Oppenheim, *Ancient Mesopotamia*, 243.

22. X 1. The elders' speech at the end of Tablet III (215–27) is followed by fourteen more lines, but these are largely lost. On the relation between narrative content and the structure of individual Tablets in cuneiform poetry, see also Kilmer, "Visualizing Texts."

23. Hess, "Songs of Clay."

24. V 146, see Lambert, *Babylonian Creation Myths*, 132–33.

25. It was long thought that readers in the ancient world *only* read aloud, never silently, but that idea has been dismissed by Gavrilov in "Techniques of Reading"; see also Worthington, *Principles of Akkadian Textual Criticism*, 260 and 290.

26. On the orality and aurality of cuneiform literature, see the essays and the bibliography collected in Vogelzang and Vanstiphout, *Mesopotamian Epic Literature;* as well as the more recent arguments by Worthington, *Ea's Duplicity*, 250–52; Wisnom, "Dynamics of Repetition"; Delnero, "Texts and Performance"; and Wasserman, "Lists and Chains," 70–72. For musicians in the cuneiform world, see Shehata, *Musiker und ihr vokales Repertoire.*

27. A tentative reconstruction of Akkadian phonology is given in Huehnergard and Woods, "Akkadian and Eblaite," 230–41.

28. On the stultifying effects of repetition, see Gilbert, "Repetition and the Death Drive"; and Cooper, "Symmetry and Repetition."

29. Wisnom, "Dynamics of Repetition."

30. For the incantatory effects of poetic repetition, see Culler, *Theory of the Lyric,* chap. 4.

31. Stein, *Lectures in America*, 168.

32. On Akkadian literary style in general, see Hecker, *Untersuchungen zur akkadischen Epik;* Wasserman, *Style and Form;* and the essays collected in Vogelzang and Vanstiphout, *Mesopotamian Poetic Language.*

33. XI 168–69. According to George, *Babylonian Gilgamesh Epic*, 891, the alliteration suggests "that the mother goddess uttered her words in a kind of ululation." For other examples of alliteration in *Gilgamesh*, see George, 185 (OB II 98), 271 (OB IM 22), 817 (SB IV 214), 879 (SB XI 21–22), 892 (SB XI 200), and 894 (SB XI 254).

34. *ša šadû šumāšu mašū-ma* IX 37. This case is admittedly uncertain, because the manuscript that preserves the line is corrupt at this point, giving *še-mu-šu₂*; see the discussion in George, *Babylonian Gilgamesh Epic*, 863. Emending *šemu* to *šumu* is hardly problematic, but I would further suggest that the word was originally set in the dual form, *šumāšu*. The dual is an archaic and rarely used nominal form, but its usage is not impossible in a Standard Babylonian literary text, especially if it were used to describe a pair of mountains: the Twin Peaks. Still, the suggestion should be taken with a grain of salt. For the system of scansion employed here, see Helle, "Rhythm and Expression."

35. On puns in *Gilgamesh*, see among others, Hurowitz, "Finding New Life in Old Words"; Kilmer, "Note on an Overlooked Word-Play"; Noegel, *Nocturnal Ciphers,* chap. 2; and Worthington, *Ea's Duplicity,* chap. 4.

36. VI 68–69. In fact, Ishtar refers to herself in the plural: *ḫurdatna,* "our vagina." This appears to be a common convention in cuneiform love poetry; see J. G. Westenholz, "Forgotten Love Song," 417. Shalom Paul coined the delightful term "plural of ecstasy" to describe the phenomenon.

37. The equation of *ḫurdatu* with *ḫurri dādu* is made in 11N-T3, ll. 42–43, published in Civil, "Medical Commentaries from Nippur," 332; explained in Cavigneaux, "Aux sources du Midrash," 255; and translated into English by Jiménez at ccp.yale.edu/P459066. On *ḫurdatu* as relating to trees, see von Soden, *Akkadisches Handwörterbuch,* s.v. *ḫurdatānu* and *ḫurdatu.* Von Soden translates the word as "Querbalken," "crossbeam," since it also refers to a part of chariots and houses. For a sample of different views on Ishtar's exchange with Ishullanu, see George, *Babylonian Gilgamesh Epic,* 473–74 and 836–38; Oppenheim, "Mesopotamian Mythology II," 37; Abusch, *Male and Female,* chap. 1; Walls, *Desire, Discord, and Death,* 38–39; and Pryke, *Ishtar,* 147–48.

38. It is not clear what Ishullanu is turned into—see the discussion and overview of previous suggestions in George, *Babylonian Gilgamesh Epic,* 835–38, notes to lines 64 and 76. Ishullanu is turned into a *dallalu,* but the word is a hapax legomenon, so its meaning is unclear. George argues that it means "dwarf," because the Akkadian words *šullānu* and *dallu* both refer to something of diminutive size, but I would argue that an insect or a worm is also diminutive. As I see it, the word must refer to something tiny and voracious that afflicts orchards, matching both the shepherd's transformation into a wolf and Ishullanu's refusal to eat. The obvious solution is a garden pest, as several other scholars have argued before me—see the references collected by George. I have chosen "weevil" because it begins with

"wee," just as *dallalu* begins with *dallu*, "puny," but the normal Akkadian word for a weevil is *kalmatu*, so another garden pest must be meant.

39. XI 26-27.

40. For this pun, see Wasserman, *The Flood*, 121; and Noegel, "Janus Parallelism in the Gilgamesh Flood Story." For the epic's many puns on the word *napištu*, "life," see Hurowitz, "Finding New Life in Old Words," 69-70 and 74-77.

41. XI 35; Worthington, *Ea's Duplicity*, 276-78.

42. Worthington, *Ea's Duplicity*. The puzzle of this passage leads Worthington to consider countless other *Gilgamesh*-related matters as well, and I highly recommend delving into his insightful discussions.

43. Worthington, *Ea's Duplicity*, 159; referring to an earlier suggestion by Simoons-Vermeer, "Mesopotamian Floodstories," 22.

44. XI 46-47 and passim. Note that no preserved manuscript actually presents the rhyming couplet as a couplet: it is either written as one long line or broken in two after *ina šēr kukkī*. For the structure of the couplet, and the possibility that this rare rhyme suggests the sound of a magical incantation, see Worthington, *Ea's Duplicity*, 228-29. Note also that I here transcribe the passage according to its positive meaning—the negative meanings are written the same way in cuneiform but would be rendered differently in modern transcription: see the various transcriptions in Worthington, *Ea's Duplicity*, 234-36.

45. This overview is a simplification of the analysis presented in Worthington, *Ea's Duplicity*, for which see especially the recapitulation on 234-36. Crucially, Worthington's scheme allows for more combinatorial possibilities. I here split the negative senses into two main meanings, but the double connotations of each word could be put together in different ways, for example by joining the sense of "darkness" with the "death of wheat," and so on.

46. Worthington, *Ea's Duplicity*, 233. As Worthington notes, Uta-napishti has just used the image of reed stalks to symbolize human lives in X 301, so the association would probably be present in the audience's mind. Different as reed canes and wheat stalks are, they both take the form of a thin stalk that is easily snapped, which is how Uta-napishti views human mortality.

47. Worthington, *Ea's Duplicity*, 252.

48. V 14. The root of the word is *la'ābu*, normally "to infect"; for its connection with skin lesions, see George and al-Rawi, "Back to the Cedar Forest," 83; and Scurlock and Andersen, *Diagnoses in Assyrian and Babylonian Medicine*, 30. George and al-Rawi translate the line as "the cedar was scabbed with lumps (of resin)" (77), taking the adjectival form *la'bu* as a metaphorical description of "the scabby blisters that form where resin seeps through a cedar's bark" (83). This is one possibility, but I prefer to see *la'bu* as denoting scar tissue, which can look just like creepers growing on trees, especially when the creepers have lost

their leaves and become encrusted in the trunk. But no matter how one understands the metaphor, it is significant that a medical terminology of skin disfiguration is here applied to the appearance of the trees.

49. V 26 and II 271.

50. V 42–43. The two contrasting perspectives on the Cedar Forest were presented at the 63rd Rencontre Assyriologique Internationale, at a workshop titled "How to Tell a Story—Theoretical Approaches to Mesopotamian Literature," whose proceedings will appear in a volume edited by Dahlia Shehata, Karen Sonik, and Frauke Weiershäuser.

51. George, *The Epic of Gilgameš:* Thoughts on Genre and Meaning," 52–53. On genre in Akkadian literature more generally, see Vanstiphout, "Some Thoughts on Genre" and "Use(s) of Genre," with references to further reading. Here I follow George's analysis of the epic as an anthology of genres (see Tigay, *Evolution of the Gilgamesh Epic,* chap. 8, for a similar view), but I am also guided by Mikhail Bakhtin's response to Vissarion Belinsky's characterization of Pushkin's *Eugene Onegin* as an "encyclopedia of Russian life." This is true, Bakhtin notes, but it is not a static encyclopedia or a mere compendium of different voices: language is "represented precisely as a living mix of varied and opposing voices, developing and renewing itself"; see Bakhtin, *Dialogic Imagination,* 49.

52. For literary genres as "horizons of expectations," see Jauss, "Theory of Genres"; see also the other essays collected in Duff, *Modern Genre Theory,* for an overview of genre theory in general. The example of the unsolved murder is taken from Pia Juul's *Mordet på Halland,* which plays with the generic expectation that murder mysteries will be resolved by starting out as a detective novel and blending into a realist novel along the way.

53. VII 61–63. For the lines as a reversal of the conventional prayers in building inscriptions, see Foster, "Gilgamesh: Sex, Love, and the Ascent of Knowledge," 37; and George, *Babylonian Gilgamesh Epic,* 478.

54. For the narrative irony in the parallel between Ishullanu's and Gilgamesh's stories, see Abusch, *Male and Female,* 33–41.

55. On the structure and implicit logic of cuneiform prayers—exchanging sacrifices and praise for divine favors—see Zgoll, "Audienz."

56. III 100. Yet another example of the epic's ironic use of genre is the proverbs quoted by the characters. In "The Storm of His Heart," below, I describe how the epic uses the saying "Go first and you help an ally" (III 4) in surprising ways, first undermining and then reaffirming the proverb's wisdom. Likewise, the phrase "all men are fated for marriage" (OB II 150–51), which has the ring of a proverb, appears to be ironic in an epic about two men who have no intention of getting married, preferring each other's company instead.

57. Foster, *Epic of Gilgamesh*, xix. On Ishtar's speech as crude, see also George, *Babylonian Gilgamesh Epic*, 837.

58. I 48 and IX 51; see Helle, "Contrast," 160. In my translation, I have added the word "only" to the first and the second part of the line, respectively, to bring out the difference between them more clearly, but the word does not appear in the original Akkadian.

59. See Foster, *Epic of Gilgamesh*, xv.

60. Dickson, "Wall of Uruk," 30, n. 11.

61. IX 1–3.

62. For Gilgamesh's transition from grieving for Enkidu to fearing for his own life, see Dickson, "Jeweled Trees," 200; Hawthorn, "'You Are Just Like Me,'" 461; and Rendu, "Cri ou silence," 212.

63. See Worthington, "*mamma(n) . . . ul*," on negative rhetorical questions in Akkadian literature.

64. X 40–52 and passim.

65. VI 173, 175 and XI 7. Note that in the case of the servant girls, Foster, in *Epic of Gilgamesh*, 55 takes Gilgamesh as the speaker of both the question and the answer, casting doubt on even this rare exception to the rule. Another possible exception comes in II 186–91, when Gilgamesh asks Enkidu why he is crying and weakened, to which Enkidu replies that he is sad and that terror has entered his heart. This seems to me to leave a central question unanswered—"So why are you sad?"—but the context is fragmentary, so the case is uncertain.

66. Bakhtin, *Problems of Dostoevsky's Poetics*.

67. Note that both Enkidu and the Sun God pun on Shamhat's name, which literally means "flourishing, luxuriant, lush"; when applied to moods, it means something like "merry." Enkidu says that Shamhat's life will lack "merry feasts," or, literally, "the setting of the table, the people's merriment (*šamuḫ nišī*)" (VII 114): in other words, the priestess will not have the joy her name implies. In his reply, the Sun God says that Gilgamesh will honor Enkidu after his death, and that "the merry (people) (*šamḫati nišī*) he will fill with misery for you" (VII 145). The god picks up on Enkidu's pun and reverses it, making Shamhat's name a promise rather than a curse. For other puns on Shamhat's name, see Hurowitz, "Finding New Life in Old Words," 68–69.

68. A similar point is made in another Babylonian epic, *Enuma Elish*, in which the birth of the god Marduk is also placed in two different story arcs at once, giving it both a positive and a negative meaning; see Helle, "Tablets as Narrative Episodes." *Enuma Elish* makes this reflection on actions and their multiple consequences explicit in II 66–67; for which see Lambert, *Babylonian Creation Myths*, 66–67, and the analysis in Haubold, "From Text

to Reading," 231–36. Here, Ea is accused of having driven Tiamat to evil by murdering her husband, Apsû. Ea argues that killing Apsû was the best course of action available at the time, and that the negative consequences of that action could not have been predicted: his actions should thus be read as positive *in their proper narrative context.*

69. Jacobsen, "Mesopotamia," 212.

THE STORM OF HIS HEART

1. The scene in question is X 180–83. On Gilgamesh's invention of sailing, see George, *Babylonian Gilgamesh Epic,* 502–3; and Dalley, "What Did Ut-napišti Say." This essay is based on my MA thesis, "Emotions in *Gilgamesh:* Desire, Grief, and Identity in the Standard Babylonian *Epic of Gilgamesh*" (University of Copenhagen, 2016).

2. I 97.

3. On Gilgamesh's excessive feelings, see Sonik, "Gilgamesh and Emotional Excess"; and Foster, "Similes in the Gilgamesh Epic," 321, and "Review of Ackerman, *When Heroes Love,*" 542.

4. On this genealogically unusual condition, see Fink, "How Gilgameš Became a Two-Thirds God," including his overview of previous suggestions.

5. The debate on how Gilgamesh abused the citizens of Uruk has a long history; here I give just a sample of opinions: Jacobsen, in "How Did Gilgamesh Oppress Uruk?" suggests sexual abuse; Cooper, in "Buddies in Babylonia," emphasizes athletic contests; Tigay, in *Evolution of the Gilgamesh Epic,* chap. 9, links athletic contests with Gilgamesh's abuse of newlywed brides (the *ius primae noctis*), rejecting corvée (unpaid labor); Klein, in "New Look at the 'Oppression of Uruk,'" argues for a mixture of abuses, including corvée but excluding sexual abuse.

6. George, in *Babylonian Gilgamesh Epic,* 456, notes that Gilgamesh proposes the quest "perhaps to distract Enkidu from his misery"; Foster, in *Epic of Gilgamesh,* 18, suggests that he does so "perhaps to legitimize their friendship"; Tigay, in *Evolution of the Gilgamesh Epic,* 77, stresses Gilgamesh's desire "to leave an enduring name after he dies" but notes that this motive is first supplemented and later replaced by Shamash's desire to destroy the evil Humbaba; Bailey, in "Male, Female and the Pursuit of Immortality," 444, proposes a more psychological explanation, rooted in the heroes' instinct for violence. On the unclarity of motives in *Gilgamesh* more generally, see Helle, "Chronotope of the Threshold," 193–97.

7. See George, *Babylonian Gilgamesh Epic,* 456.

8. II 262 and III 24.

9. II 46–48.

10. Tigay, in *Evolution of the Gilgamesh Epic,* 81, suggests that this confusion came about through a gradual increase in Shamash's role in the quest against Humbaba, from an ally in

the Old Babylonian version to an instigator in the Standard Babylonian version. That may be, but regardless of how it came about, the unreconciled double explanation of Gilgamesh's quest remains a literary feature of great force.

11. V 200–1.

12. V 303–6.

13. X 40–52 and passim.

14. On Gilgamesh's constant movement, and how it is eventually brought to an end, see George, "Mayfly on the River," 230; on the connection between wandering and grief in ancient Near Eastern literature, see Barré, "'Wandering About' as a Topos of Depression."

15. XI 243–46.

16. II 289–90.

17. I 213–14 and 220. On the confusion of motives, see Walls, *Desire, Discord, and Death*, 52; on Enkidu's animal instincts in this scene, see George, "Enkidu and the Harlot."

18. Dickson, "Looking at the Other," 175. On journeys in Gilgamesh as transformative, see also Feldt and Koch, "Life's Journey"; and Helle, "Chronotope of the Threshold."

19. X 43 and passim.

20. Feldt and Koch, in "Life's Journey," 117–18, argue that both Gilgamesh and Enkidu are eventually destroyed by their journeys across culturally established borders.

21. XI 5.

22. On Gilgamesh's instinctive hostility, see Sonik, "Gilgamesh and Emotional Excess."

23. X 156.

24. For various accounts of Gilgamesh's rejection of Ishtar, see Harris, "Images of Women," 226–28, who connects it with Ishtar's reversal of typically gendered behavior; Frymer-Kensky, *In the Wake of the Goddesses*, chap. 7, who views it in light of a more general denigration of goddesses in the second millennium BCE; Bahrani, *Women of Babylon*, 153–54, who argues that Gilgamesh's rejection expresses a latent anxiety about the destructive force of female sexuality; Walls, *Desire, Discord, and Death*, 37–49, who reads the exchange as a reflex of Gilgamesh's homoerotic relation to Enkidu; George, *Babylonian Gilgamesh Epic*, 472–73, who stresses that Ishtar is unable to conform to a patriarchal household; Abusch, *Male and Female*, chap. 1, who argues that Ishtar's proposal contains a veiled death threat; and the overview of the debate in Vanstiphout, "Craftmanship of Sîn-leqi-unninnī," 48, n. 13.

25. See Walls, *Desire, Discord, and Death*, 58–59; see also Bailey, "Male, Female and the Pursuit of Immortality."

26. XI 121.

27. For the parallel between Gilgamesh and Enlil, see Sonik, "Gilgamesh and Emotional Excess," 393–94, 402–3. It is worth noting that although the episodes are presented to the audience in this order—first the destruction of the Cedar Forest, then the story of

the Flood—chronologically the events come the other way around. The Flood took place millennia before Gilgamesh and Uruk laid waste to the Cedar Forest, so if there is an ethical analogy to be drawn between the two scenes, it also points to a hypocrisy on Enlil's part: he puts Enkidu to death for a crime that he himself committed long ago, one that had even more catastrophic consequences.

28. XI 170.

29. Sonik, "Gilgamesh and Emotional Excess."

30. For Gilgamesh as excessively emotional, see Sonik, "Gilgamesh and Emotional Excess"; Foster, "Similes in the Gilgamesh Epic," 321, and "Review of Ackerman, *When Heroes Love*," 542.

31. Worthington, "On Names and Artistic Unity," 404–6.

32. I 256 and passim, X 55 and passim.

33. Jacobsen, "How Did Gilgamesh Oppress Uruk?" 70; for the historical context of Jacobsen's argument, see Guinan and Morris, "Mesopotamia Before and After Sodom," 150. In fact, Jacobsen's proposal was preceded by an even earlier, if much subtler suggestion from 1904 in Küchler, *Beiträge zur Kenntnis der assyrisch-babylonischen Medizin*, 124.

34. Notable entries in this debate include Kilmer, "Note on an Overlooked Word-Play"; Walls, *Desire, Discord, and Death*, chap. 1; Cooper, "Buddies in Babylonia"; Nissinen, *Homoeroticism in the Biblical World*; Ackerman, *When Heroes Love*, pt. 1; and Nardelli, *Homosexuality and Liminality*. For studies of the friendship between the heroes that does not focus on its erotic dimension, see Furlani, "L'*Epopea di Gilgames*"; von Weiher, "Gilgameš und Enkidu"; and Dietrich, "Von der Freundschaft."

35. XII 96.

36. On the inapplicability of the term *homosexuality* to cuneiform cultures, see Walls, *Desire, Discord, and Death*, esp. 13; and Nissinen, "Are There Homosexuals in Mesopotamian Literature?" The example of the masturbator is taken from Sedgwick, "Jane Austen and the Masturbating Girl."

37. Helle, "Marduk's Penis," 67.

38. Westenholz, "Metaphorical Language in the Poetry of Love," 381.

39. Walls, *Desire, Discord, and Death*, 14–15.

40. Walls, *Desire, Discord, and Death*, 17–18; I 183; on *kuzbu* in general, see Walls, *Desire, Discord, and Death*, 17–23.

41. I 234–237.

42. VI 6. On the *kuzbu* of male bodies, see also Winter, "Sex, Rhetoric, and the Public Monument."

43. Walls, *Desire, Discord, and Death*, 58.

44. II 113 and 182. The scene of the fight is badly preserved in the Standard Babylonian version, so in the translation, I follow the Old Babylonian version, where the word *iṣṣabtū* also occurs, in II 218 and 223.

45. II 113–14; the pun is noted in Glassner, "Polygynie ou prostitution," 162. In the Old Babylonian version, only one part of the pun, *rēbit māti*, has been preserved (II 214); it is unclear whether the phrase *bit emūti* was used in one of the preceding, fragmentary lines, or whether the pun was introduced in the Standard Babylonian version.

46. Bailey, "Male, Female and the Pursuit of Immortality," 444.

47. Walls, *Desire, Discord, and Death*, 61.

48. The episode is recounted in Graves, *Good-Bye to All That*, 308.

49. Damrosch, *Narrative Covenant*, 96–97.

50. Guinan and Morris, "Mesopotamia Before and After Sodom." Here I quote from a preliminary draft of the article, kindly made available to me by the authors.

51. Respectively, I 97, I 258 and passim, II 40, I 60 and 107, and VII 95. Note that in I 97, the word *ma-ḫ[ir]* is fragmentary and could also be restored *ma-š[il]*; George, *Babylonian Gilgamesh Epic*, 788. On the similarity between the two heroes, see especially Hawthorn, "'You Are Just Like Me'"; and Dietrich, "Von der Freundschaft," 42.

52. OB II 193–95.

53. For the link with mythological battles, see George, *Babylonian Gilgamesh Epic*, 190, note to ll. 192–95. For the scene's allusion to the Sacred Marriage ritual, see Tigay, *Evolution of the Gilgamesh Epic*, 176. The Sacred Marriage is a ritual depicted in some Sumerian literary sources, such as *Iddin-Dagan A*, but it is unclear if it was ever practiced and if so, how. See Nissinen and Uro, *Sacred Marriages*; Renger, "Heilige Hochzeit A"; and Cooper, "Heilige Hochzeit B," and "Sacred Marriage and Popular Cult." See also Streck, "Beiträge zum akkadischen Gilgameš-Epos," 407, for an entirely different view of this scene, taking *meḫru* as "offering." Note that there is another, similarly ambiguous comparison of characters with a god in II 36, where it is unclear whether the simile "like a god" applies to Shamhat or Enkidu—see note 4 to the translation above.

54. Guinan and Morris, "Mesopotamia Before and After Sodom," 168. On love between male equals as a deviation from social norms in cuneiform cultures, see also Ackerman, *When Heroes Love*, esp. 77; but see the rejoinder to this view in Nardelli, *Homosexuality and Liminality*, 12–15.

55. Guinan and Morris, "Mesopotamia Before and After Sodom," 160. The omen is *Shumma Alu*, Tablet 104, omen 13; on this tablet, see also Guinan, "Auguries of Hegemony" and "Erotomancy."

56. Guinan and Morris, "Mesopotamia Before and After Sodom," 168.

57. II 4–6 and 218–20.

58. George and al-Rawi, "Back to the Cedar Forest," 84, note to ll. 35–50.

59. V 45.

60. Leick, in *Sex and Eroticism*, 268, writes about the quest against Humbaba that "at this stage, the heroes become 'one,' their differences in opinion, sexual preference and social status blur, and the common quest unites them."

61. Guinan and Morris, "Mesopotamia Before and After Sodom," 168.

62. VIII 62. There may be a reference to the trope of "going behind and in front" in the comical *Aluzinnu* text, in which a jester satirizes the conventions of cuneiform scholarship. Unfortunately, the text is difficult to understand and badly in need of a new edition—for now, see Foster, "Humor and Cuneiform Literature," 74–79. At one point, the jester seems to refer to his male lover, saying that "he will keep turning around, in front of him and behind him" (*ana panīšu u arkīšu*, l. ii 24). Might this be an allusion to *Gilgamesh*? See also the *Dialogue of Pessimism*, l. 77, which, in a passage about the skulls on ruin mounds that clearly alludes to *Gilgamesh* (see my discussion in "Poem for the Ages," above), uses the words *arkûti u panûti*, "those behind and in front," seemingly in the sense "those of high and low (status)," or "the poor and the great." Perhaps this phrase was in some way associated with *Gilgamesh*?

63. VIII 1–3. See Worthington, "On Names and Artistic Unity," 406; and Guinan and Morris, "Mesopotamia Before and After Sodom," 169.

64. For analyses of Gilgamesh's grief, see especially Müller, "Gilgameschs Trauergesang"; Abusch, *Male and Female*, chap. 4; Anderson, *Time to Mourn*, 74–80; and Couto-Ferreira, "It Is the Same for a Man."

65. Walls, *Desire, Discord, and Death*, 68.

66. IX 3.

67. On Gilgamesh's quest for immortality as a narcissistic interruption of his mourning, see Dickson, "Jeweled Trees," 200; Hawthorn, "'You Are Just Like Me,'" 461; and Rendu, "Cri ou silence," 212.

68. This view of mourning, as the rebuilding of a self outside a relation in which that self had been constituted, is taken from Butler, *Precarious Life*, 20–22.

69. For the feral nature of Gilgamesh's grief, see Anderson, *Time to Mourn*, 74; Dickson, "Jeweled Trees," 200; and Pryke, *Gilgamesh*, 108–12.

70. X 45 and passim.

71. For the shift in Gilgamesh's ambition toward the divine, see Moran, "Gilgamesh Epic," 2329.

72. Feldt and Koch, in "Life's Journey," argue that the world of the epic can be divided into three distinct ontological spheres, which they term Culture, Nature, and Supernature: the world of men, animals, and gods, respectively.

73. VIII 45, 61, and 59.

74. On the feminine connotations of grief in cuneiform cultures, see Cooper, "Genre, Gender and the Sumerian Lamentation"; Foster, "Review of *When Heroes Love*," 542, and "Similes in the Gilgamesh Epic," 318, 321. See also Leick, *Sex and Eroticism*, 269, who argues that in his grief, Gilgamesh "speaks like the bereaved goddesses in the Lamentations."

75. Suad al-Attar's painting can be viewed at: arthistoryarchive.com/arthistory/arabic/Iraqi-Artists.html.

76. Nippurian version ll. v 17–20; see also Cavigneaux and Al-Rawi, *Gilgameš et la Mort*, 16–17.

77. On death as a specifically human problem in cuneiform cultures, especially in relation to gods and animals, see Foster, "The Person in Mesopotamian Thought," 119. On cuneiform notions of death more generally, see the essays by Jacobsen, Bottéro, and Lambert in Alster, *Death in Mesopotamia*.

78. OB II 108–11. Note that the word *mutu* in this context can also be understood as "warrior"; George, in *Babylonian Gilgamesh Epic*, 177, opts for this translation, presumably because it fits well with the following lines, where Enkidu is shown fighting lions and wolves. However, the word could easily convey several meanings at once—"husband," "warrior," and the latent meaning "death."

79. The same pun is also found elsewhere in cuneiform literature, such as the epic poem *Ereshkigal and Nergal*. As noted by Jean Bottéro in *Mesopotamia*, 245, Ereshkigal first summons Nergal to put him to death (*mūtu*), but he ends up becoming her husband (*mutu*).

DYING TO BE READ

1. Moran, "Gilgamesh Epic," 2328–29. The phrase occurs in I 194, OB II 49, XI 209, and XI 225–30.

2. XI 230.

3. XI 128–29.

4. X 301–22. The following reading of the monologue is based on Helle, "Babylonian Perspectives." For other approaches to this passage, see George, "Mayfly on the River," 237–39; and Lambert, "Theology of Death," 54–57.

5. Specifically, Uta-napishti says that the "lines" of humanity snap like reed. The Akkadian word *šumu* literally means "name," but it also has a range of other connotations that are better captured by the word "line" in English: it can mean the name that one passes on to one's children (a "family line"), as well as the "line" of a text. Intriguingly, all three senses of the word were thought to be an extension of a person's presence: see Radner, *Macht des Namens*; and Bahrani, *Graven Image*. In Babylonian culture, people were thought to exist in several ways at once, as a collection of physical manifestations—their bodies, their children,

their visual depictions (such as statues), and their names, whether inscribed on texts or carried through time by storytelling. When Uta-napishti says that a person's "line" can snap with frightening ease, he refers to all these forms of existence at once: life, descendants, and textual records. All are brittle; all can be claimed by death.

6. On *zērūtu* as "feuds" see George, *Babylonian Gilgamesh Epic*, 875.

7. The spring flood carrying glittering mayflies is described in George, "Mayfly on the River," 238, with references to previous literature.

8. George, "Mayfly on the River," 239.

9. The line has been understood differently by other commentators. Lambert, in "Theology of Death," 55, translates "suddenly there is nothing," commenting that the line describes how the mayflies "disappear for ever under an eddy" (57).

10. On these contrasting perspectives see Metcalf, "Babylonian Perspectives"; and Helle, "Babylonian Perspectives."

11. For the epic as offering a variety of perspectives on death, see the brief communication by Jacobsen, "Death in Mesopotamia"; and the overview in Pryke, *Gilgamesh*, chap. 6.

12. V 47 and 41. Compare the nature of names described in note 5 of this essay with the statement in OB III 148–49: "If I die, I will only have made a name for myself: 'Gilgamesh battled the brutal Humbaba!'" The lines encapsulate the logic of names in cuneiform cultures: names are a miniature story, an extended presence through which we can live on after death.

13. XI 244–46.

14. See the Church of Siduri website: churchofsiduri.webs.com.

15. OB VA+BM iii 1–14. For a close reading of Siduri's reply to Gilgamesh, see Abusch, *Male and Female*, chap. 3.

16. See Walls, *Desire, Discord, and Death*, 70.

17. The idea of the meaninglessness of life as an occasion for pleasure is a common trope in cuneiform wisdom literature. Cohen, in *Wisdom from the Late Bronze Age*, 15, terms it the "negative" mode of wisdom literature, arguing that it "expresses two intertwined notions: 1) nothing is of value, hence 2) enjoy life while you can before eternal death." A similar view is presented by Alster, in *Wisdom of Ancient Sumer*, 26, who labels the trope "critical wisdom" and splits it into "the vanity theme" and "the carpe diem theme," again noting that they are often conjoined: "Since no material things are of lasting value, the best one can do is to enjoy the present life as much as one can."

18. III 101–6.

19. On Gilgamesh's role as a judge in the underworld, see George, *Babylonian Gilgamesh Epic*, 127–35.

20. The poem is edited in Cavigneaux and al-Rawi, *Gilgameš et la Mort*. The relevant lines are 78–83 in the Meturan version; see the translation in George, *Babylonian Gilgamesh Epic*, 128.

21. On the narrative irony created by this revelation, see Vulpe, "Irony and the Unity of the Gilgamesh Epic"; on divine foreshadowing in cuneiform literature more generally, see Pryke, "Unreliable Foreshadowing in Divine Predictions."

22. On cuneiform notions of the afterlife, see Bottéro, "Mythologie de la mort"; Scurlock, "Death and the Afterlife"; and Wilcke, "Der Tod im Leben der Babylonier."

23. VII 162. Note that another major description of the afterlife in cuneiform literature, *The Underworld Vision of an Assyrian Prince*—for which see Livingstone, *Court Poetry*, 68–76—is also undercut by the madness of its narrator: the vision drives the prince who receives it to insanity. Perhaps this was a recurrent trope, meant to underscore the ultimate unknowability of the afterlife. On the other hand, Enkidu's vision has many exact parallels in *Ishtar's Descent* and *Nergal and Ereshkigal*, where the description is given by the narrator with no hint of doubt.

24. On Enkidu's account of the underworld, see the analyses and references to previous literature in Gadotti, *"Gilgamesh, Enkidu and the Netherworld,"* chap. 8.

25. On the importance of lists for cuneiform scholarship, see, among many others, Hilgert, "Von 'Listenwissenschaft'"; Civil, "Ancient Mesopotamian Lexicography"; Bottéro, *Mesopotamia*, 29–39; and Mieroop, *Philosophy Before the Greeks*. On the importance of lists for cuneiform belles lettres, see Rubio, "Early Sumerian Literature"; Wasserman, "Lists and Chains"; and Civil, "Feeding Dumuzi's Sheep."

26. See, respectively, Moren, "Lost 'Omen' Tablet," 66–68, l. 23; *Hammurabi's Code* §22 in Roth, *Law Collections from Mesopotamia*, 85; and *Sagig* III C obv. 51 in Scurlock and Andersen, *Diagnoses in Assyrian and Babylonian Medicine*, 27. The technical term for the two parts of the sentence are the protasis ("if") and apodosis ("then").

27. The term "Listenwissenschaft" was coined by von Soden, "Leistung und Grenze"; for a critique of von Soden's formulation, see Hilgert, "Von 'Listenwissenschaft.'"

28. On abstract reflection being expressed differently in (rather than absent from) cuneiform cultures, see Michalowski, "Presence at the Creation," 387.

29. See Guinan, "Left/Right Symbolism." An intriguing exception to this trend is *Multabiltu*, which does spell out some of the overarching principles of liver divination—see Koch, *Secrets of Extispicy*.

30. Frahm, "Nabû-zuqup-kēnu, das Gilgameš-Epos und der Tod Sargons II," 79.

31. Gadotti, in *"Gilgamesh, Enkidu and the Netherworld,"* 110, emphasizes that the Sumerian poem should not be understood as "a canonical document about what awaited mankind

in the afterlife," since different cuneiform sources, and even different manuscripts of the same Sumerian poem, offer different perspectives on this question. I agree, and I am not arguing that Tablet XII presented a universally accepted account of the underworld; I am merely noting that its format reflects a specifically cuneiform mode of textual authorization. On cuneiform strategies for textual authorization more generally, see Cancik-Kirschbaum and Wagensonner, "Abschrift, Offenbarung, Sukzession."

32. I 8.

33. On the theme of the gods' secrecy in cuneiform culture, see Lenzi, *Secrecy and the Gods.*

34. XI 119.

35. On the symbolic connection between clay, death, and the real-life scribes who copied the poem, see Gilbert, "Repetition and the Death Drive," 163–64.

36. Later accounts suggest that the antediluvian past could be accessed by other means: Ashurbanipal, for example, claims in his inscriptions to have "examined stone inscriptions from before the Flood," emphasizing the extreme difficulty of this task; see Livingstone, "Ashurbanipal: Literate or Not?" 100–1. But the idea of stone inscriptions having survived the Flood seems to postdate *Gilgamesh*, which stresses that the story of the Flood was, until Gilgamesh brought it back to Uruk, a secret known only to the gods and Uta-napishti.

37. Michalowski, "Sailing to Babylon," 188.

38. X 250.

39. Michalowski, "Commemoration, Writing, and Genre," 80.

40. See Lambert and Millard, *Atra-ḫasīs;* for the relation between the two accounts of the Flood, see Tigay, *Evolution of the Gilgamesh Epic,* chap. 12; Chen, *Primeval Flood Catastrophe;* and the detailed notes in Wasserman, *The Flood.*

41. XI 95–96.

42. See Worthington, *Ea's Duplicity,* 358–63, who finds a number of hidden word-plays in the Puzur-Enlil scene. Worthington suggests that the scene can be read as Uta-napishti's revenge on the boatman for a theft of oil—assuming that in XI 70 the boatman "stowed" (Akkadian *puzzuru*) the oil away in the sense of stealing it, not storing it safely in the ship.

43. Michalowski, "Sailing to Babylon," 189.

44. Worthington, *Ea's Duplicity,* 364. The questions listed in this paragraph are discussed in chapter 21 of the same book. Worthington further stresses that Ea is just as duplicitous a figure as Uta-napishti, likewise shrouded in unanswered questions. The inscrutability of these two figures is, according to Worthington, central to the epic's literary effect: "With so much about Ea being hermeneutically unstable, we are left reflecting on meaning, what it is, who controls it, and how it is communicated" (339).

45. In *Atra-hasis*, the god Wê-ila, ringleader of a rebellion against the elder gods, is sacrificed so that his blood can be used to make human beings, and it is said that his *eṭemmu*, "spirit," was passed on from his body to the humans (I 215 and passim). Crucially, the word *eṭemmu* recalls *ṭēmu*, "plan, forethought," which is also used to describe Wê-ila: he is chosen for the sacrifice precisely because "he had the *ṭēmu*" (I 223), meaning both intellect in general and the idea for the rebellion. Further, Wê-ila's name begins with the sign PI, which can represent the Akkadian word *uznu*, "ear" or "intelligence." The first part of *Atra-hasis* is thus, among many other things, an explanation of how humans came to have consciousness. See especially Moran, "Creation of Man"; and Abusch, "Ghost and God."

46. Michalowski, "Commemoration, Writing, and Genre," 80; see also Altes, "Gilgamesh and the Power of Narration."

47. Wasserman, "Rhetoric of Time Inversion," 29.

48. X 34 and passim; see the notes in George, *Babylonian Gilgamesh Epic*, 869.

49. Michalowski, "Sailing to Babylon," 190.

50. Michalowski, "Commemoration, Writing, and Genre," 80.

51. I 26.

52. I 2 and III 104; for Gilgamesh's sojourn in the Apsû as a source of his wisdom, see George, *Babylonian Gilgamesh Epic*, 444–45.

53. On the addition of the prologue to the Standard Babylonian version, and how it shifted the emphasis of the poem toward the themes of wisdom and storytelling, see George, *Babylonian Gilgamesh Epic*, 32–33; and Tigay, *Evolution of the Gilgamesh Epic*, 149.

54. For the audience's identification with Gilgamesh in the Standard Babylonian prologue, see Dickson, "Wall of Uruk," 45–46.

55. The following reading is a summary of Dickson's arguments in "Wall of Uruk" and "Jeweled Trees."

56. Walls, *Desire, Discord, and Death*, 65.

57. Dickson, "Jeweled Trees," 205.

58. See the summary of the epic in note 45 of this essay.

59. I 102 and X 68 and passim. As noted by Polinger Foster, "Well-Tempered Words," in cuneiform poetry more generally, ceramic metaphors often connote creation, destruction, or both.

60. See Dickson, "Wall of Uruk," 40–42.

61. Dickson, "Jeweled Trees," 204; see also Dickson, "Wall of Uruk," 42.

62. Dickson, "Wall of Uruk," 42.

63. Dickson, "Wall of Uruk," 38.

64. I 27–28.

65. Dickson, "Wall of Uruk," 44.

66. Dickson, "Wall of Uruk," 28.

67. See Dickson, "Wall of Uruk," 45–46.

68. George, "Mayfly on the River," 230.

69. Bakhtin, *Dialogic Imagination,* 34.

KINGS, WOMEN, MONSTERS

1. For Gilgamesh's shift from a personal to a collective perspective on life, see George, "Mayfly on the River."

2. XI 327–28.

3. George, "Mayfly on the River," 232–33.

4. George, "Mayfly on the River," 235.

5. George, "Mayfly on the River," 238.

6. X 313; George, "Mayfly on the River," 238.

7. See Helle, "Babylonian Perspectives," 214.

8. SB 211–12, OB II 47, and OB II 61–62.

9. For this development of Enkidu's psychology, see George, "Enkidu and the Harlot," 19–20.

10. For cuneiform ideals of kingship, see the essays by Brisch, Frahm, and Waerzeggers in Radner and Robson, *Oxford Handbook of Cuneiform Culture,* all with references to further reading. For kingship in *Gilgamesh,* see the overview in Pryke, *Gilgamesh,* chap. 1, again with further references.

11. Schmidt, *Gilgamesh,* 11.

12. For the "droit du seigneur" as a myth of former, crueler times—not only in ancient Babylonia but in medieval Europe too—see Rubio, "Gilgamesh and the *ius primae noctis.*" The problem of modern readers not recognizing "which parts were *supposed* to sound old" is neatly captured in the webcomic XKCD by Randall Munroe, no. 1491: xkcd.com/1491/. *Gilgamesh* can be found in the lower left corner of the graph.

13. On corvée as representing the mutual relation between states and individuals, see van Dassow, "Freedom in Ancient Near Eastern Societies," 211–14; and Steinkeller, "Employment of Labor on National Building Projects."

14. Van Dassow, "Freedom in Ancient Near Eastern Societies," 213.

15. For the suggestion that Gilgamesh was seen as a tyrant because he built the wall of Uruk, see the references collected in Tigay, *Evolution of the Gilgamesh Epic,* 181–82. Tigay disagrees with this suggestion, since the epic does not use any of the common terms for corvée, such as *ilku*—but surely, an abuse of corvée could be implied without being stated explicitly. For an argument in favor of corvée as among Gilgamesh's ways of oppressing his subjects, see Klein, "New Look at the 'Oppression of Uruk.'"

16. On revolts against excessive demands of corvée, see van Dassow, "Freedom in Ancient Near Eastern Societies," 212.

17. See Waerzeggers, "Pious King," with references to further reading.

18. On the double *akītu* of Uruk, see Linssen, *Cults of Uruk and Babylon,* 72-78. On the *akītu* in general, see Bidmead, *The Akitu Festival.*

19. See Davenport, "Anti-Imperialist Twist."

20. Davenport, "Anti-Imperialist Twist," 14; see also Konstantopoulos, "Gods in the Margins."

21. On collective governance in cuneiform cultures, see Fleming, *Democracy's Ancient Ancestors;* van de Mieroop, "Government of an Ancient Mesopotamian City"; Barjamovic, "Civic Institutions"; Worthington, *Ea's Duplicity,* 287-99; and the outdated but still thought-provoking Jacobsen, "Primitive Democracy."

22. Jacobsen, "Primitive Democracy," 166. Later scholars have questioned this interpretation; see especially Ridley, "Saga of an Epic."

23. See Sonik, "Gilgamesh and Emotional Excess."

24. XI 184.

25. There are of course exceptions to this trend: women who achieved great political influence. One route to power was through the royal family, as described in Svärd, *Women and Power in Neo-Assyrian Palaces.* A famous example is the Neo-Assyrian queen Naqia, wife of Sennacherib and mother of Esarhaddon, who seems to have gained tremendous power at the Assyrian court; see Melville, *Role of Naqia/Zakutu in Sargonid Politics.* Another route to power was through the office of the priestess, especially the high priestess, who not only commanded religious respect but was also responsible for administering the temple's large holdings of wealth and land. A notable group of priestesses were the *nadītu*s, who became an economic force to be reckoned with in Old Babylonian Sippar; see the succinct overview in Jeyes, "Nadītu Women of Sippar."

26. I first heard this excellent line from Gina Konstantopoulos, but I've heard it from a few other people since, so I'm not sure who first came up with it. Its quality resides not least in highlighting how intensely patriarchal the supposedly democratic city-states of ancient Greece were.

27. Much has been written about women in ancient Iraq; see the exhaustive bibliography compiled by Asher-Greve and Wogec, "Women and Gender in Ancient Near Eastern Cultures." An easily accessible introduction to the topic can be found in Lassen and Wagensonner, *Women at the Dawn of History.* The volumes published in connection with the biannual conference "Gender, Methodology and the Ancient Near East" give a fair idea of the current state of the field: see Svärd and Garcia-Ventura, *Studying Gender in the Ancient Near East;* and Budin et al., *Gender and Methodology in the Ancient Near East.*

28. On whether women could speak in the city assemblies, see Worthington, *Ea's Duplicity,* 293, n. 1176, and 372, n. 1444.

29. Beard, *Women and Power,* xiii.

30. Harris, "Images of Women," 220.

31. In Helle, "Marduk's Penis," I describe a similar dynamic at work in *Enuma Elish,* where Tiamat's motherly and monstrous body has to be constantly, violently suppressed to allow for the creation of an all-male sphere of discourse.

32. III 86–88. The translation in Foster, *Epic of Gilgamesh,* 25, underplays the chilling effect of this scene by rendering it: "May Aya your bride not hesitate to remind you."

33. I 48 and IX 51.

34. See Harris, "Images of Women," 225–26.

35. Harris, "Images of Women," 224–25.

36. On the status of tavern keepers in cuneiform cultures, see Worthington, "Schankwirt(in)"; but see the dissenting voices on the question of prostitution in the next note.

37. See, e.g., Budin, *Myth of Sacred Prostitution,* chap. 2; Brisch, "Šamhat: Deconstructing Temple Prostitution"; Assante, "kar.kid/ḫarimtu"; Pryke, *Ishtar,* 20–24. The "traditional" view on the *ḫarimtu* and similar terms as denoting sex workers is best summarized in Cooper, "Prostitution."

38. See Brisch, "Šamhat: Deconstructing Temple Prostitution." My understanding of Shamhat's role owes much to my discussions with Nicole Brisch and Laura Feldt, and I would like to thank them both.

39. Crucially, Assante, "kar.kid/ḫarimtu," suggests that this is how the position of the *ḫarimtu* is to be understood: she argues that *ḫarimtu*s were women who stood outside the patriarchal household, which led to their being seen as outsiders and as sexually promiscuous.

40. I 231. My understanding of the relations among wilderness, culture, wisdom, and sex in *Gilgamesh* is based on the studies by Laura Feldt; see especially "Sex, visdom og magtens ambivalens."

41. Bahrani, *Women of Babylon,* chap. 7. On Ishtar's character, see Harris, "Inanna-Ishtar as Paradox"; Pryke, *Ishtar;* and the list of further reading provided in Heffron, "Inana/Ištar."

42. See Pryke, *Ishtar,* 133–34; for the parallel between Gilgamesh and Ishtar see also Sonik, "Gilgamesh and Emotional Excess," 403–4.

43. For Ishtar as assuming "an active, aggressive posture" when she proposes to Gilgamesh, see Harris, "Images of Women," 227.

44. See Greengus, "Old Babylonian Marriage Contract," 516-17, who places the literary scenes from *Gilgamesh* and *Ereshkigal* in the context of real-life marriage contracts and formulas.

45. See Walls, *Desire, Discord, and Death,* 34-50.

46. VI 153.

47. For movements across cultural borders in *Gilgamesh,* see Feldt and Koch, "Life's Journey"; for metamorphoses in cuneiform literature more generally, see Sonik, "Breaching the Boundaries of Being."

48. VI 62-63.

49. See Abusch, *Male and Female,* 43.

50. Dickson, "Jeweled Trees," 193. For the tripartite structure of the epic's world, see Feldt and Koch, "Life's Journey," who refer to the three "worlds" of the epic as Culture, Nature, and Super nature.

51. On the generally negative view of the natural world in cuneiform sources, see for example A. Westenholz and Koch, "Enkidu—the Noble Savage?" 443-44.

52. The ambiguity of the natural world in *Gilgamesh* is well illustrated by Pryke, who in "Bull of Heaven" shows that lions are depicted as both lethal killers and pitiful prey; and A. Westenholz and Koch, who in "Enkidu—the Noble Savage?" argue that Enkidu is neither a stereotypical brute nor a noble savage. For animals and the natural world in *Gilgamesh* more generally, see Pryke, *Gilgamesh,* chap. 3; for more examples of the wilderness as an ambiguous space in cuneiform literature, see Feldt, "Religion, Nature, and Ambiguous Space." Gina Konstantopoulos is preparing a new study of exotic landscapes in the cuneiform imaginary.

53. A. Westenholz and Koch, "Enkidu—the Noble Savage?"

54. Worthington, *Principles of Akkadian Textual Criticism,* 204-9. The cultural distinction between "raw" and "reworked" was explored in Lévi-Strauss, *Le cru et le cuit,* a foundational book in structuralist anthropology. For the connection between Enkidu's movement from the wilderness to the city and his transformation along the way, see also Feldt and Koch, "Life's Journey"; and Dickson, "Looking at the Other."

55. On monsters in cuneiform cultures, see Feldt and Koch, "Life's Journey," 112-15; Verderame, "Osservazioni a margine dei concetti"; Sonik, "Mesopotamian Conceptions of the Supernatural"; and Konstantopoulos, *They Are Seven.*

56. IX 46; see Pryke, *Gilgamesh,* 103-4.

57. II 221-22 and passim.

58. Object no. BM 116624, available at britishmuseum.org/collection/object/W_1883-0118 -AH-2598. On this plaque and its relation to entrails in cuneiform omens and medicine, see Geller, "Divination or Medicine?"

59. See George and al-Rawi, "Back to the Cedar Forest," 74; and Konstantopoulos, "Gods in the Margins."

60. OB III 115–16.

61. George and al-Rawi, "Back to the Cedar Forest," 69. The epic highlights the ambiguity of the Cedar Forest through a play of shadows. The description of the entrance begins with the "pleasant, joyful shades" of the cedar trees but ends on a very different note—"a cedar cast its shadow and terror fell on Gilgamesh" (V 9 and 27–28)—thereby framing the forest in an alluring half-light of joy and horror.

62. On Humbaba's ambiguity and the "ecological outlook" articulated in *Gilgamesh*, see Azize, "Wrestling as a Symbol," 4–5 and 22; and Pryke, *Gilgamesh*, chap. 3.

63. See Feldt and Koch, "Life's Journey," 117–18.

64. See Pryke, "Bull of Heaven."

65. VI 117.

66. As noted by Pryke, in *Gilgamesh*, 104–5, Gilgamesh later changes his ways when he arrives at the Jeweled Trees: here he leaves the trees and their valuable gems unravished, in a striking reversal of his earlier behavior, as his mind is now fully set on the pursuit of immortality.

BIBLIOGRAPHY

Abusch, Tzvi. "Ghost and God: Some Observations on a Babylonian Understanding of Human Nature." In *Self, Soul and Body in Religious Experience*, edited by Albert I. Baumgarten, Jan Assmann, and Guy G. Stroumsa, 363–83. Numen 78. Leiden: Brill, 1998.

———. *Male and Female in the Epic of Gilgamesh: Encounters, Literary History, and Interpretation.* Winona Lake, Ind.: Eisenbrauns, 2015.

Ackerman, Susan. *When Heroes Love: The Ambiguity of Eros in the Stories of Gilgamesh and David.* New York: Columbia University Press, 2005.

Aidt, Naja Marie. *Har døden taget noget fra dig så giv det tilbage.* Copenhagen: Gyldendal, 2017.

Al-Azraki, Amir, and James al-Shamma. "General Introduction." In *Contemporary Plays from Iraq,* edited by Amir al-Azraki and James al-Shamma, i–xvii. London: Bloomsbury, 2017.

Alster, Bendt. *The Instructions of Suruppak: A Sumerian Proverb Collection.* Mesopotamia 2. Copenhagen: Akademisk Forlag, 1974.

———. *Wisdom of Ancient Sumer.* Winona Lake, Ind.: Eisenbrauns, 2005.

Alster, Bendt, ed. *Death in Mesopotamia.* Compte rendu de la Rencontre Assyriologique Internationale 26, Mesopotamia 8. Copenhagen: Akademisk Forlag, 1980.

Altes, Liesbeth Korthals. "Gilgamesh and the Power of Narration." *Journal of the American Oriental Society* 127, no. 2 (2007): 183–93.

Anderson, Gary A. *A Time to Mourn, a Time to Dance: The Expression of Grief and Joy in Israelite Religion.* University Park: Pennsylvania State University Press, 1991.

Annus, Amar. "Louvre Gilgamesh (AO 19862) Is Depicted in Life Size." *Nouvelles assyriologiques brèves et utilitaires* 2012, no. 2 (2012): 44–45.

Arnold, Bill T., and David B. Weisberg. "A Centennial Review of Friedrich Delitzsch's 'Babel und Bibel' Lectures." *Journal of Biblical Literature* 121, no. 3 (2002): 441–57.

Asher-Greve, Julia M., and Mary Frances Wogec. "Women and Gender in Ancient Near Eastern Cultures: Bibliography 1885 to 2001 AD." *NIN* 3 (2001): 33–114.

Assante, Julia. "The kar.kid/*harimtu*, Prostitute or Single Woman? A Critical Review of the Evidence." *Ugarit-Forschungen* 30 (1998): 5–96.

Azize, Joseph. "Wrestling as a Symbol for Maintaining the Order of Nature in Ancient Mesopotamia." *Journal of Ancient Near Eastern Religions* 2 (2002): 1–26.

Bach, Johannes. *Untersuchungen zur Transtextuellen Poetik: Assyrischer Herrschaftlich-Narrativen Texte.* State Archives of Assyria Studies 30. Helsinki: Neo-Assyrian Text Corpus Project, 2020.

Bahrani, Zainab. "Dia al-Azzawi's Modern Antiquity." In *Dia al-Azzawi: A Retrospective, from 1963 until Tomorrow,* edited by Catherine David, 12–17. Milan: Silvana Editoriale, 2017.

———. *The Graven Image: Representation in Babylonia and Assyria.* Philadelphia: University of Pennsylvania Press, 2003.

———. "Review of *The Conquest of Assyria,* by Mogens Trolle Larsen." *Journal of the American Oriental Society* 118, no. 4 (1998): 573–74.

———. *Women of Babylon: Gender and Representation in Mesopotamia.* London: Routledge, 2001.

Bahrani, Zainab, and Nada M. Shabout. *Modernism and Iraq.* New York: Wallach Art Gallery, 2009.

Bailey, John A. "Male, Female and the Pursuit of Immortality in the Gilgamesh Epic." *La parola del passato* 171 (1976): 433–57.

Bakhtin, Mikhail M. *The Dialogic Imagination: Four Essays.* Translated by Caryl Emerson and Michael Holquist. Austin: University of Texas Press, 1981.

———. *Problems of Dostoevsky's Poetics.* Translated by Caryl Emerson. Theory and History of Literature 8. Minneapolis: University of Minnesota Press, 1984.

Baram, Amatzia. "A Case of Imported Identity: The Modernizing Secular Ruling Elites of Iraq and the Concept of Mesopotamian-Inspired Territorial Nationalism, 1922–1992." *Poetics Today* 15, no. 2 (1994): 279–319.

Barjamovic, Gojko. "Civic Institutions and Self-Government in Southern Mesopotamia in the Mid-First Millennium BC." In *Assyria and Beyond: Studies Presented to Mogens Trolle Larsen,* edited by Jan Gerrit Dercksen, 47–98. Publications de l'Institut historique-archéologique néerlandais de Stamboul (PIHANS) 100. Leiden: Nederlands Instituut voor het Nabije Oosten, 2004.

———. "Mesopotamian Empires." In *The Oxford Handbook of the State in the Ancient Near East and the Mediterranean,* edited by Peter Fibiger Bang and Walter Scheidel, 120–60. Oxford: Oxford University Press, 2013.

Barré, Michael L. "'Wandering About' as a *Topos* of Depression in Ancient Near Eastern Literature and in the Bible." *Journal of Near Eastern Studies* 60, no. 3 (2001): 177–87.

Bates, Catherine, ed. *The Cambridge Companion to the Epic.* Cambridge: Cambridge University Press, 2010.

Beard, Mary. *Women and Power: A Manifesto.* Updated version. London: Profile, 2018.

Beaulieu, Paul-Alain. "The Descendants of Sîn-lēqi-unninni." In *Assyriologica et Semitica: Festschrift für Joachim Oelsner anläßlich seines 65. Geburtstages am 18. Februar 1997,* edited by Joachim Marzahn and Hans Neumann, 1–16. Alter Orient und Altes Testament 252. Münster: Ugarit-Verlag, 2000.

———. "The Social and Intellectual Setting of Babylonian Wisdom Literature." In *Wisdom Literature in Mesopotamia and Israel,* edited by Richard J. Clifford, 3–19. Society of Biblical Literature Symposium Series 36. Atlanta: Society of Biblical Literature, 2007.

Bidmead, Julye. *The Akītu Festival: Religious Continuity and Royal Legitimation in Mesopotamia.* Piscataway, N.J.: Gorgias Press, 2002.

Biggs, Robert D., John A. Brinkman, Miguel Civil, Walter Farber, Ignace J. Gelb, A. Leo Oppenheim, Erica Reiner, Martha T. Roth, and Matthew W. Stolper, eds. *The Assyrian Dictionary of the Oriental Institute of the University of Chicago (Chicago Assyrian Dictionary).* 26 vols. Chicago: Oriental Institute of the University of Chicago, 1956–2010.

Bjelke, Henrik. *Saturn.* Viborg: Arena, 1974.

———. *To mænd, eller, Hvad ingen skrev om Gilgamesh og Enkidu.* Risskov: Jorinde and Joringel, 1982.

Black, Jeremy A. "Babylonian Ballads: A New Genre." *Journal of the American Oriental Society* 103, no. 1 (1983): 25–34.

Black, Jeremy A., Graham Cunningham, Eleanor Robson, and Gábor Zólyomi, eds. *The Literature of Ancient Sumer.* Oxford: Oxford University Press, 2004.

Bohrer, Frederick N. *Orientalism and Visual Culture: Imagining Mesopotamia in Nineteenth-Century Europe.* Cambridge: Cambridge University Press, 2003.

Borger, Rykle. *Mesopotamisches Zeichenlexikon.* Alter Orient und Altes Testament 305. Second edition. Münster: Ugarit-Verlag.

Bottéro, Jean. *L'Épopée de Gilgameš: Le grand homme qui ne voulait pas mourir.* Paris: Gallimard, 1992.

———. *Mesopotamia: Writing, Reasoning, and the Gods.* Translated by Zainab Bahrani and Marc van de Mieroop. Chicago: University of Chicago Press, 1987.

———. "La mythologie de la mort en Mésopotamie ancienne." In *Death in Mesopotamia,* edited by Bendt Alster, 25–52. Compte rendu de la Rencontre Assyriologique Internationale 26, Mesopotamia 8. Copenhagen: Akademisk Forlag, 1980.

———. "Les noms de Marduk, l'écriture et la 'logique' en Mésopotamie ancienne." In *Essays on the Ancient Near East in Memory of Jacob Joel Finkelstein,* edited by Maria deJong Ellis, 5–27. Memoirs of the Connecticut Academy of Arts and Sciences 19. Hamden: Archon, 1977.

Brisch, Nicole. "Anunna (Anunnaku, Anunnaki)." Ancient Mesopotamian Gods and Goddesses, 2016. http://oracc.museum.upenn.edu/amgg/listofdeities/anunna/.

———. "Changing Images of Kingship in Sumerian Literature." In *The Oxford Handbook of
Cuneiform Culture,* edited by Karen Radner and Eleanor Robson, 706–24. Oxford: Oxford
University Press, 2011.

———. "Šamḫat: Deconstructing Temple Prostitution One Woman at a Time." In *Powerful
Women in the Ancient World: Perception and (Self)Presentation,* edited by Sebastian Fink
and Kerstin Droß-Krüpe, 77–90. Melammu Workshops and Monographs 4. Münster:
Zaphon, 2021.

Buccellati, Giorgio. "Il Dialogo del Pessimismo: la scienza degli opposti come ideale sapien-
ziale." *Oriens Antiquus* 11 (1972): 81–100.

———. "On Poetry—Theirs and Ours." In *Lingering over Words: Studies in Ancient Near Eastern
Literature in Honor of William L. Moran,* edited by Tzvi Abusch, John Huehnergard, and
Piotr Steinkeller, 105–34. Harvard Semitic Studies 37. Atlanta: Scholars', 1990.

Budge, E. A. Wallis. *The Rise and Progress of Assyriology.* London: Martin Hopkinson, 1925.

Budin, Stephanie Lynn. *The Myth of Sacred Prostitution in Antiquity.* Cambridge: Cambridge
University Press, 2008.

Budin, Stephanie Lynn, Megan Cifarelli, Agnès Garcia-Ventura, and Adelina Millet Albà,
eds. *Gender and Methodology in the Ancient Near East: Approaches from Assyriology and
Beyond.* Barcino 10. Barcelona: Universitat de Barcelona Edicions, 2018.

Butler, Judith. *Precarious Life: The Powers of Mourning and Violence.* London: Verso, 2004.

Cancik-Kirschbaum, Eva, and Klaus Wagensonner. "Abschrift, Offenbarung, Sukzession:
Autoritätsnarrative in der Textkultur Mesopotamiens." In *Sukzession in Religionen: Au-
torisierung, Legitimierung, Wissenstransfer,* edited by Almut-Barbara Renger and Markus
Witte, 33–54. Berlin: De Gruyter, 2017.

Cassin, Elena. *La splendeur divine: Introduction à l'étude de la mentalité mésopotamienne.* Paris:
Mouton, 1968.

Castillo, Jorge Silva. "*Nagbu:* Totality or Abyss in the First Verse of Gilgamesh." *Iraq* 60
(1998): 219–21.

Cathcart, Kevin J. "The Earliest Contributions to the Decipherment of Sumerian and Akkadian." *Cuneiform Digital Library Journal* 2011, no. 1 (2011): 1–12.

Cavigneaux, Antoine. "Aux sources du Midrash: L'herméneutique babylonienne." *Aula
Orientalis* 5 (1987): 243–55.

———. "Les oiseaux de l'arche." *Aula Orientalis* 25, no. 2 (2007): 319–20.

Cavigneaux, Antoine, and Farouk N. H. Al-Rawi. *Gilgameš et la Mort: Textes de Tell Haddad VI, avec un appendice sur les textes funéraires sumériens.* Cuneiform Monographs 19.
Groningen: Styx, 2000.

———. "Gilgameš et Taureau de Ciel (šul-mè-kam) (textes de Tell Haddad IV)." *Revue d'Assyriologie* 87, no. 2 (1993): 97–129.

"Chaldean History of the Deluge." *The Times.* December 4, 1872.

Charpin, Dominique. *Reading and Writing in Babylon.* Translated by Jane Marie Todd. Cambridge: Harvard University Press, 2010.

Chen, Y. S. *The Primeval Flood Catastrophe: Origins and Development in Mesopotamian Traditions.* Oxford: Oxford University Press, 2013.

Civil, Miguel. "Ancient Mesopotamian Lexicography." In *Civilizations of the Ancient Near East,* volume 4, edited by Jack M. Sasson, 2305–14. New York: Scribner's, 1995.

———. "Feeding Dumuzi's Sheep: The Lexicon as a Source of Literary Inspiration." In *Language, Literature, and History: Philological and Historical Studies Presented to Erica Reiner,* edited by Francesca Rochberg, 37–56. American Oriental Series 67. New Haven, Conn.: American Oriental Society, 1987.

———. "Medical Commentaries from Nippur." *Journal of Near Eastern Studies* 33, no. 3 (1974): 329–38.

Cohen, Yoram. *Wisdom from the Late Bronze Age.* Writings from the Ancient World 34. Atlanta: Society of Biblical Literature, 2013.

Cooley, Jeffrey L. "The Book of Giants and the Greek Gilgamesh." In *Windows to the Ancient World of the Hebrew Bible: Essays in Honor of Samuel Greengus,* edited by Bill T. Arnold, Nancy Erickson, and John H. Walton, 67–79. Winona Lake, Ind.: Eisenbrauns, 2014.

Cooper, Jerrold S. "Buddies in Babylonia: Gilgamesh, Enkidu, and Mesopotamian Homosexuality." In *Riches Hidden in Secret Places: Ancient Near Eastern Studies in Memory of Thorkild Jacobsen,* edited by Tzvi Abusch, 73–85. Winona Lake, Ind.: Eisenbrauns, 2002.

———. "Genre, Gender, and the Sumerian Lamentation." *Journal of Cuneiform Studies* 58 (2006): 39–47.

———. "Gilgamesh Dreams of Enkidu: The Evolution and Dilution of Narrative." In *Essays on the Ancient Near East in Memory of Jacob Joel Finkelstein,* edited by Maria deJong Ellis, 39–44. Memoirs of the Connecticut Academy of Arts and Sciences 19. Hamden: Archon, 1977.

———. "Heilige Hochzeit, B, Archäologisch." *Reallexikon der Assyriologie* 4 (1972): 259–69.

———. "Prostitution." *Reallexikon der Assyriologie* 11 (2008): 12–21.

———. "Sacred Marriage and Popular Cult in Early Mesopotamia." In *Official Cult and Popular Religion in the Ancient Near East,* edited by Eiko Matsushima, 81–96. Heidelberg: Universitätsverlag C. Winter, 1993.

———. "Symmetry and Repetition in Akkadian Narrative." *Journal of the American Oriental Society* 97, no. 4 (1977): 508–12.

Couto-Ferreira, Erica. "It Is the Same for a Man and a Woman: Melancholy and Lovesickness in Ancient Mesopotamia." *Quaderni di studi indo-mediterranei* 3 (2010): 21–39.

Cregan-Reid, Vybarr. *Discovering Gilgamesh: Geology, Narrative, and the Historical Sublime in Victorian Culture.* Manchester: Manchester University Press, 2013.

Culler, Jonathan. *Theory of the Lyric.* Cambridge: Harvard University Press, 2015.

Currie, Bruno. "The *Iliad, Gilgamesh,* and Neoanalysis." In *Homeric Contexts: Neoanalysis and the Interpretation of Oral Poetry,* edited by Franco Montanari, Antonios Rengakos, and Christos Tsagalis, 543–80. Trends in Classics Supplementary Volumes 12. Berlin: De Gruyter, 2012.

Dalley, Stephanie. "Gilgamesh in the Arabian Nights." *Journal of the Royal Asiatic Society* 1, no. 1 (1991): 1–17.

———. "What Did Ut-napišti Say When He First Caught Sight of Gilgamesh?" *Revue d'Assyriologie* 106 (2012): 101–2.

Damrosch, David. *The Buried Book: The Loss and Rediscovery of the Great Epic of Gilgamesh.* New York: Holt, 2007.

———. *The Narrative Covenant: Transformations of Genre in the Growth of Biblical Literature.* San Francisco: Harper and Row, 1987.

———. "Scriptworlds: Writing Systems and the Formation of World Literature." *Modern Language Quarterly* 68, no. 2 (2007): 195–219.

———. *What Is World Literature?* Princeton: Princeton University Press, 2003.

Darwish, Mahmoud. "A Horse for the Stranger." Translated by Fady Joudah. *Callaloo* 32, no. 4 (2009): 1150–52.

Dassow, Eva van. "Freedom in Ancient Near Eastern Societies." In *The Oxford Handbook of Cuneiform Culture,* edited by Karen Radner and Eleanor Robson, 205–27. Oxford: Oxford University Press, 2011.

Davenport, Tracy. "An Anti-Imperialist Twist to 'The Gilgameš Epic.'" In *Gilgameš and the World of Assyria,* edited by Joseph Azize and Noel Weeks, 1–23. Ancient Near Eastern Studies 21. Leuven: Peeters, 2007.

Deagon, Andrea. "The Twelve Double-Hours of the Night: Insomnia and Transformation in *Gilgamesh.*" *Soundings* 81, nos. 3–4 (1998): 461–89.

Delnero, Paul. "Texts and Performance: The Materiality and Function of the Sumerian Liturgical Corpus." In *Texts and Contexts: The Circulation and Transmission of Cuneiform Texts in Social Space,* edited by Paul Delnero and Jacob Lauinger, 87–118. Studies in Ancient Near Eastern Records 9. Berlin: De Gruyter, 2015.

Dickson, Keith. "The Jeweled Trees: Alterity in *Gilgamesh.*" *Comparative Literature* 59, no. 3 (2007): 193–208.

———. "Looking at the Other in 'Gilgamesh.'" *Journal of the American Oriental Society* 127, no. 2 (2007): 171–82.

———. "The Wall of Uruk: Iconicities in *Gilgamesh*." *Journal of Ancient Near Eastern Religions* 9, no. 1 (2009): 25–50.

Dietrich, Jan. "Von der Freundschaft im Alten Testament und Alten Orient." *Welt des Orients* 44, no. 1 (2014): 37–56.

Duff, David, ed. *Modern Genre Theory.* London: Pearson Longman, 2000.

Edzard, Dietz-Otto. "Gilgameš und Huwawa A. I. Teil." *Zeitschrift für Assyriologie* 80 (1990): 165–203.

———. "Gilgameš und Huwawa A. II. Teil." *Zeitschrift für Assyriologie* 81 (1991): 165–233.

———. "mekkû, pukku und." *Reallexikon der Assyriologie* 8 (1997): 34.

Elayi, Josette. *Sargon II, King of Assyria.* Archaeology and Biblical Studies 22. Atlanta: Society of Biblical Literature, 2017.

Emmerich, Karen. *Literary Translation and the Making of Originals.* London: Bloomsbury, 2017.

Feldt, Laura. "Religion, Nature, and Ambiguous Space in Ancient Mesopotamia: The Mountain Wilderness in Old Babylonian Religious Narratives." *Numen* 63, no. 4 (2016): 347–82.

———. "Sex, visdom og magtens ambivalens i oldtidens Babylon: Kvinder og køn i Gilgamesh-eposset." In *Venus, Lucie og Margrethe: Kvindehistorier i kultur, religion og politik,* edited by Sissel Bjerrum Fossat and Lone Kølle Martinsen, 132–53. Odense: University Press of Southern Denmark, 2018.

Feldt, Laura, and Ulla Susanne Koch. "A Life's Journey—Reflections on Death in the Gilgamesh Epic." In *Akkade Is King: A Collection of Papers by Friends and Colleagues Presented to Aage Westenholz on the Occasion of His 70th Birthday 15th of May 2009,* edited by Gojko Barjamovic, Jacob L. Dahl, Ulla Susanne Koch, Walter Sommerfeld, and Joan Goodnick Westenholz, 111–26. Publications de l'Institut historique-archéologique néerlandais de Stamboul (PIHANS) 118. Leiden: Nederlands Instituut voor het Nabije Oosten, 2011.

Ferry, David. *Gilgamesh: A New Rendering in English Verse.* New York: Farrar, Straus and Giroux, 1993.

Fincke, Jeanette C. "Assyrian Scholarship and Scribal Culture in Kalḫu and Nineveh." In *A Companion to Assyria,* edited by Eckart Frahm, 378–97. Chichester: Wiley-Blackwell, 2017.

———. "The British Museum's Ashurbanipal Library Project." *Iraq* 66 (2004): 55–60.

Fink, Sebastian. "How Gilgameš Became a Two-Thirds God: It Was the Ferryman." *State Archives of Assyria Bulletin* 20 (2014): 73–78.

Finkel, Irving L. *The Ark Before Noah: Decoding the Story of the Flood.* London: Hodder and Stoughton, 2014.

———. "Assurbanipal's Library: An Overview." In *Libraries Before Alexandria: Ancient Near Eastern Traditions*, edited by Kim Ryholt and Gojko Barjamovic, 367–89. Oxford: Oxford University Press, 2019.

———. "Strange Byways in Cuneiform Writing." In *The Idea of Writing*. Volume 1: *Play and Complexity*, edited by Alex de Voogt and Irving L. Finkel, 7–25. Leiden: Brill, 2009.

Finkel, Irving L., and Jonathan Taylor. *Cuneiform*. London: British Museum Press, 2015.

Finn, Jennifer. *Much Ado About Marduk: Questioning Discourses of Royalty in First Millennium Mesopotamian Literature*. Studies in Ancient Near Eastern Records 16. Berlin: De Gruyter, 2017.

Fleming, Daniel E. *Democracy's Ancient Ancestors: Mari and Early Collective Governance*. Cambridge: Cambridge University Press, 2004.

Fleming, Daniel E., and Sara J. Milstein. *The Buried Foundation of the Gilgamesh Epic: The Akkadian Huwawa Narrative*. Cuneiform Monographs 39. Leiden: Brill, 2010.

Foster, Benjamin R. *The Age of Agade: Inventing Empire in Ancient Mesopotamia.* London: Routledge, 2016.

———. *Before the Muses: An Anthology of Akkadian Literature*. Third edition. Bethesda: CDL Press, 2005.

———. *The Epic of Gilgamesh*. Second edition. New York: Norton, 2019.

———. "Gilgamesh: Sex, Love and the Ascent of Knowledge." In *Love and Death in the Ancient Near East: Essays in Honor of Marvin H. Pope*, edited by John H. Marks and Robert M. Good, 21–42. Guildford: Four Quarters, 1987.

———. "Humor and Cuneiform Literature." *Journal of the Ancient Near Eastern Society* 6 (1974): 69–85.

———. "On Authorship in Akkadian Literature." *Annali dell'Università degli Studi di Napoli L'Orientale* 51 (1991): 17–32.

———. "The Person in Mesopotamian Thought." In *The Oxford Handbook of Cuneiform Culture*, edited by Karen Radner and Eleanor Robson, 117–39. Oxford: Oxford University Press, 2011.

———. "Review of *When Heroes Love*, by Susan Ackerman." *Journal of the American Oriental Society* 125, no. 4 (2005): 539–43.

———. "Similes in the Gilgamesh Epic." In *Proceedings of the 53e Rencontre Assyriologique Internationale*. Volume 1: *Language in the Ancient Near East*, edited by Leonid E. Kogan, Natalia Koslova, Sergey Loesov, and Serguei Tishchenko, 313–21. Compte rendu de la Rencontre Assyriologique Internationale 53, Babel und Bibel 4. Winona Lake, Ind.: Eisenbrauns, 2010.

Foster, Benjamin R., and Karen Polinger Foster. *Civilizations of Ancient Iraq*. Princeton: Princeton University Press, 2011.

Frahm, Eckart. *Babylonian and Assyrian Text Commentaries: Origins of Interpretation.* Guides to the Mesopotamian Textual Record 5. Münster: Ugarit-Verlag.

———. "Keeping Company with Men of Learning: The King as Scholar." In *The Oxford Handbook of Cuneiform Culture,* edited by Karen Radner and Eleanor Robson, 508–32. Oxford: Oxford University Press, 2011.

———. "Nabû-zuqup-kēnu, das Gilgameš-Epos und der Tod Sargons II." *Journal of Cuneiform Studies* 51 (1999): 73–90.

———. "The Neo-Assyrian Period." In *A Companion to Assyria,* edited by Eckart Frahm, 161–208. Chichester: Wiley-Blackwell, 2017.

Frahm, Eckart, ed. *A Companion to Assyria.* Chichester: Wiley-Blackwell, 2017.

Freedman, Sally M. *If a City Is Set on a Height: The Akkadian Omen Series Šumma Alu ina Mēlê Šakin.* Volume 1: *Tablets 1–21.* Occasional Publications of the Samuel Noah Kramer Fund 17. Philadelphia: University of Pennsylvania Museum, 1998.

———. *If a City Is Set on a Height: The Akkadian Omen Series Šumma Alu ina Mēlê Šakin.* Volume 2: *Tablets 22–40.* Occasional Publications of the Samuel Noah Kramer Fund 19. Philadelphia: University of Pennsylvania Museum, 2006.

———. *If a City Is Set on a Height: The Akkadian Omen Series Šumma Alu ina Mēlê Šakin.* Volume 3: *Tablets 41–63.* Occasional Publications of the Samuel Noah Kramer Fund 20. Winona Lake, Ind.: Eisenbrauns, 2017.

Frymer-Kensky, Tikva. *In the Wake of the Goddesses: Women, Culture, and the Biblical Transformation of Pagan Myth.* New York: Free Press, 1992.

Furlani, Giuseppe. "L'*Epopea di Gilgames* come inno all'amicizia." *Belfagor* 1 (1946): 577–89.

Gabriel, Gösta Ingvar. "An Exemplificational Critique of Violence: Re-Reading the Old Babylonian Epic *Inūma ilū awīlum* (a.k.a. *Epic of Atramḫasīs*)." *Journal of Ancient Near Eastern History* 5 (2018): 179–213.

Gadotti, Alhena. *"Gilgamesh, Enkidu and the Netherworld" and the Sumerian Gilgamesh Cycle.* Untersuchungen zur Assyriologie und vorderasiatischen Archäologie 10. Berlin: De Gruyter, 2014.

Gavrilov, A. K. "Techniques of Reading in Classical Antiquity." *Classical Quarterly* 47, no. 1 (1997): 56–73.

Geller, Markham J. "Divination or Medicine?" In *Ancient Near Eastern Studies in Memory of Blahoslav Hruška,* edited by Luděk Vacín, 91–96. Dresden: Islet, 2011.

———. "The Last Wedge." *Zeitschrift für Assyriologie* 87 (1997): 43–95.

George, Andrew R. *The Babylonian Gilgamesh Epic: Introduction, Critical Edition, and Cuneiform Texts.* 2 vols. Oxford: Oxford University Press, 2003.

———. *Babylonian Literary Texts in the Schøyen Collection.* Cornell University Studies in Assyriology and Sumerology 10. Bethesda: CDL Press, 2009.

———. "The Civilizing of Ea-Enkidu: An Unusual Tablet of the Babylonian Gilgameš Epic." *Revue d'Assyriologie* 101 (2007): 59–80.

———. "Enkidu and the Harlot: Another Fragment of Old Babylonian Gilgamesh." *Zeitschrift für Assyriologie* 108, no. 1 (2018): 10–21.

———. *The Epic of Gilgamesh: The Babylonian Epic Poem and Other Texts in Akkadian and Sumerian.* Penguin Classics. London: Penguin, 1999.

———. "*The Epic of Gilgameš:* Thoughts on Genre and Meaning." In *Gilgameš and the World of Assyria,* edited by Joseph Azize and Noel Weeks, 37–66. Ancient Near Eastern Studies 21. Leuven: Peeters, 2007.

———. "The Gilgameš Epic at Ugarit." *Aula Orientalis* 25, no. 2 (2007): 237–54.

———. "The Mayfly on the River: Individual and Collective Destiny in the Epic of Gilgamesh." *Kaskal* 9 (2012): 227–42.

———. "Shattered Tablets and Tangled Threads: Editing Gilgamesh, Then and Now." *Aramazd* 3, no. 1 (2008): 7–30.

———. "The Sign of the Flood and the Language of Signs in Babylonian Omen Literature." In *Proceedings of the 53e Rencontre Assyriologique Internationale.* Volume 1: *Language in the Ancient Near East,* edited by Leonid E. Kogan, Natalia Koslova, Sergey Loesov, and Serguei Tishchenko, 323–35. Compte rendu de la Rencontre Assyriologique Internationale 53, Babel und Bibel 4. Winona Lake, Ind.: Eisenbrauns, 2010.

George, Andrew R., and Farouk N. H. al-Rawi. "Back to the Cedar Forest: The Beginning and End of Tablet V of the Standard Babylonian Epic of Gilgameš." *Journal of Cuneiform Studies* 66 (2014): 69–90.

Gesche, Petra D. *Schulunterricht in Babylonien im ersten Jahrtausend v. Chr.* Alter Orient und Altes Testament 275. Münster: Ugarit-Verlag, 2000.

Gilbert, Jane. "Repetition and the Death Drive in *Gilgamesh* and Medieval French Literature." *Kaskal* 9 (2012): 157–75.

Glassner, Jean-Jacques. *The Invention of Cuneiform: Writing in Sumer.* Translated by Zainab Bahrani and Marc van de Mieroop. Baltimore: Johns Hopkins University Press, 2003.

———. "Polygynie ou prostitution: Une approche comparative de la sexualité masculine." In *Sex and Gender in the Ancient Near East,* vol. 1, edited by Simo Parpola and Robert M. Whiting, 151–64. Compte rendu de la Rencontre Assyriologique Internationale 47. Helsinki: Neo-Assyrian Text Corpus Project, 2002.

Graves, Robert. *Good-Bye to All That.* London: Jonathan Cape, 1929.

Greengus, Samuel. "The Old Babylonian Marriage Contract." *Journal of the American Oriental Society* 89, no. 3 (1969): 505–32.

Gresseth, Gerald K. "The Gilgamesh Epic and Homer." *Classical Journal* 70, no. 4 (1975): 1–18.

Groneberg, Brigitte. "Die sumerisch-akkadische Inanna/Ištar: Hermaphroditos?" *Welt des Orients* 17 (1986): 25–46.

Guinan, Ann K. "Auguries of Hegemony: The Sex Omens of Mesopotamia." *Gender and History* 9, no. 3 (1997): 462–79.

———. "Erotomancy: Scripting the Erotic." In *Sex and Gender in the Ancient Near East*, vol. 1, edited by Simo Parpola and Robert M. Whiting, 185–201. Compte rendu de la Rencontre Assyriologique Internationale 47. Helsinki: Neo-Assyrian Text Corpus Project, 2002.

———. "The Human Behavioral Omens: On the Threshold of Psychological Inquiry." *Bulletin of the Canadian Society for Mesopotamian Studies* 19 (1990): 9–14.

———. "Left/Right Symbolism in Mesopotamian Divination." *State Archives of Assyria Bulletin* 10, no. 1 (1996): 5–10.

Guinan, Ann K., and Peter Morris. "Mesopotamia Before and After Sodom: Colleagues, Crack Troops, Comrades-in-Arms." In *Being a Man: Negotiating Ancient Constructs of Masculinity*, edited by Ilona Zsolnay, 150–75. London: Routledge, 2017.

Güterbock, Hans-Gustav. "Die historische Tradition und ihre literarische Gestaltung bei Babyloniern und Hethitern bis 1200. I. Teil: Babylonier." *Zeitschrift für Assyriologie* 42 (1934): 1–91.

Hainsworth, John Bryan. *The Idea of Epic.* Berkeley: University of California Press, 1991.

Hanson, Katharyn. "Why Does Archaeological Context Matter?" In *Catastrophe! The Looting and Destruction of Iraq's Past*, edited by Geoff Emberling and Katharyn Hanson, 45–50. Oriental Institute Museum Publications 28. Chicago: Oriental Institute of the University of Chicago, 2008.

Harari, Yuval Noah. *Sapiens: A Brief History of Humankind.* Translated by Yuval Noah Harari, John Purcell, and Haim Watzman. London: Harvill Secker, 2014.

Harris, Rivkah. "Images of Women in the Gilgamesh Epic." In *Lingering over Words: Studies in Ancient Near Eastern Literature in Honor of William L. Moran*, edited by Tzvi Abusch, John Huehnergard, and Piotr Steinkeller, 219–30. Harvard Semitic Studies 37. Atlanta: Scholars', 1990.

———. "Inanna-Ishtar as Paradox and a Coincidence of Opposites." *History of Religions* 30, no. 3 (1991): 261–78.

Haubold, Johannes. "From Text to Reading in *Enūma Eliš*." *Journal of Cuneiform Studies* 69 (2017): 221–46.

———. *Greece and Mesopotamia: Dialogues in Literature.* Cambridge: Cambridge University Press, 2020.

Hawthorn, Ainsley. "'You Are Just Like Me': The Motif of the Double in the Epic of Gilgamesh and the Agushaya Poem." *Kaskal* 12 (2015): 451–66.

Hecker, Karl. *Untersuchungen zur akkadischen Epik.* Alter Orient und Altes Testament 8. Neukirchen-Vluyn: Neukirchener Verlag, 1974.

Heeßel, Nils P. *Babylonisch-assyrische Diagnostik.* Alter Orient und Altes Testament 43. Münster: Ugarit-Verlag, 2000.

———. "'Sieben Tafeln aus sieben Städten': Überlegungen zum Prozess der Serialisierung von Texten in Babylonien in der zweiten Hälfte des zweiten Jahrtausends v. Chr." In *Babylon: Wissenskultur in Orient und Okzident,* edited by Eva Cancik-Kirschbaum, Margarete van Ess, and Joachim Marzahn, 171–95. Topoi 1. Berlin: De Gruyter, 2011.

Heffron, Yağmur. "Inana/Ištar." Ancient Mesopotamian Gods and Goddesses, 2016. http://oracc.museum.upenn.edu/amgg/listofdeities/inanaitar/.

Helle, Sophus. "Babylonian Perspectives on the Uncertainty of Death: SB *Gilgamesh* 301–21." *Kaskal* 14 (2017): 211–19.

———. "The Chronotope of the Threshold in *Gilgamesh.*" *Journal of the American Oriental Society* 141, no. 1 (2021): 185–200.

———. "Contrast Through Ironic Self-Citation in *Atra-ḫasīs.*" *Nouvelles assyriologiques brèves et utilitaires* 2015, no. 4 (2015): 158–60.

———. "A Literary Heritage: Authorship in the Neo-Assyrian Period." *Kaskal* 16 (2019): 349–71.

———. "Marduk's Penis: Queering *Enūma Eliš.*" *Distant Worlds Journal* 4 (2020): 63–77.

———. "Rhythm and Expression in Akkadian Poetry." *Zeitschrift für Assyriologie* 104, no. 1 (2014): 56–73.

———. "The Role of Authors in the 'Uruk List of Kings and Sages': Canonization and Cultural Contact." *Journal of Near Eastern Studies* 77, no. 2 (2018): 219–34.

———. "Tablets as Narrative Episodes in Babylonian Poetry." In *The Shape of Stories: Narrative Structures in Cuneiform Literature,* edited by Sophus Helle and Gina Konstantopoulos. Cuneiform Monographs. Leiden: Brill, forthcoming.

———. "The Two-Act Structure: A Narrative Device in Akkadian Epics." *Journal of Ancient Near Eastern Religions* 20, no. 2 (2020): 190–224.

Hess, Christian W. "Songs of Clay: Materiality and Poetics in Early Akkadian Epic." In *Texts and Contexts: The Circulation and Transmission of Cuneiform Texts in Social Space,* edited by Paul Delnero and Jacob Lauinger, 251–84. Studies in Ancient Near Eastern Records 9. Berlin: De Gruyter, 2015.

Hilgert, Markus. "Von 'Listenwissenschaft' und 'epistemischen Dingen': Konzeptuelle Annäherungen an altorientalische Wissenspraktiken." *Zeitschrift für allgemeine Wissenschaftstheorie* 40, no. 2 (2009): 277–309.

Huehnergard, John. *A Grammar of Akkadian.* Third edition. Harvard Semitic Studies 45. Leiden: Brill, 2011.

Huehnergard, John, and Christopher Woods. "Akkadian and Eblaite." In *The Cambridge Encyclopedia of the World's Ancient Languages,* edited by Roger D. Woodard, 218–87. Cambridge: Cambridge University Press, 2004.

Hunger, Hermann. *Babylonische und assyrische Kolophone.* Alter Orient und Altes Testament 2. Neukirchen-Vluyn: Neukirchener Verlag, 1968.

Hurowitz, Victor A. "Finding New Life in Old Words: Word Play in the *Gilgameš Epic.*" In *Gilgameš and the World of Assyria,* edited by Joseph Azize and Noel Weeks, 67–78. Ancient Near Eastern Studies 21. Leuven: Peeters, 2007.

Iskander, Ghareeb. *Gilgamesh's Snake and Other Poems: Bilingual Edition.* Translated by John Glenday. Syracuse, N.Y.: Syracuse University Press, 2016.

Jacobsen, Thorkild. "Death in Mesopotamia." In *Death in Mesopotamia,* edited by Bendt Alster, 19–24. Compte rendu de la Rencontre Assyriologique Internationale 26, Mesopotamia 8. Copenhagen: Akademisk Forlag, 1980.

———. "The Gilgamesh Epic: Romantic and Tragic Vision." In *Lingering over Words: Studies in Ancient Near Eastern Literature in Honor of William L. Moran,* edited by Tzvi Abusch, John Huehnergard, and Piotr Steinkeller, 231–49. Harvard Semitic Studies 37. Atlanta: Scholars', 1990.

———. "How Did Gilgamesh Oppress Uruk?" *Acta Orientalia* 8 (1930): 62–74.

———. "Mesopotamia." In *The Intellectual Adventure of Ancient Man: An Essay on Speculative Thought in the Ancient Near East,* edited by Henri Frankfort, Henriette A. Groenewegen-Frankfort, John A. Wilson, Thorkild Jacobsen, and William A. Irwin, 125–222. Chicago: University of Chicago Press, 1946.

———. "Primitive Democracy in Ancient Mesopotamia." *Journal of Near Eastern Studies* 2, no. 3 (1943): 159–72.

———. *The Treasures of Darkness: A History of Mesopotamian Religion.* New Haven: Yale University Press, 1976.

Jauss, Hans Robert. "Theory of Genres and Medieval Literature." In *Modern Genre Theory,* edited by David Duff, 127–47. London: Pearson Longman, 2000.

Jeyes, Ulla. "The Nadītu Women of Sippar." In *Images of Women in Antiquity,* edited by Averil Cameron and Amélie Kuhrt, 260–72. Revised edition. Detroit: Wayne State University Press, 1993.

Jiménez, Enrique. *The Babylonian Disputation Poems: With Editions of the Series of the Poplar, Palm and Vine, the Series of the Spider, and the Story of the Poor, Forlorn Wren.* Culture and History of the Ancient Near East 87. Leiden: Brill, 2017.

———. "In the Spotlight: The Electronic Babylonian Literature Project." *Mar Shiprim.* February 18, 2020. iaassyriology.com/in-the-spotlight-the-electronic-babylonian-literature-project/.

————. "New Fragments of Gilgameš and Other Literary Texts from Kuyunik." *Iraq* 76 (2014): 99–121.

Jiménez, Enrique, Aino Hätinen, Zsombor J. Földi, Adrian C. Heinrich, and Tonio Mitto. "From the Electronic Babylonian Literature Lab 1–7." *Kaskal* 16 (2019): 75–94.

Jung, Carl G. *Symbols of Transformation: An Analysis of the Prelude to a Case of Schizophrenia.* Translated by R. F. C. Hull. Bollingen Series 20. Princeton: Princeton University Press, 1956.

Juul, Pia. *Mordet på Halland.* Copenhagen: Tiderne Skifter, 2009.

Katz, Dina. *Gilgamesh and Akka.* Library of Oriental Texts 1. Groningen: Styx, 1993.

Kilmer, Ann D. "A Note on an Overlooked Word-Play in the Akkadian Gilgamesh." In *Zikir Šumim: Assyriological Studies Presented to F. R. Kraus on the Occasion of His Seventieth Birthday,* edited by Govert van Driel, Theo J. H. Krispijn, Marten Stol, and Klaas R. Veenhof, 264–68. Leiden: Brill, 1982.

————. "The Symbolism of the Flies in the Mesopotamian Flood Myth and Some Further Implications." In *Language, Literature, and History: Philological and Historical Studies Presented to Erica Reiner,* edited by Francesca Rochberg, 175–80. American Oriental Series 67. New Haven: American Oriental Society, 1987.

————. "Visualizing Texts: Schematic Patterns in Akkadian Poetry." In *If a Man Builds a Joyful House: Assyriological Studies in Honor of Erle Verdun Leichty,* edited by Ann Guinan, Maria deJong Ellis, A. J. Ferrara, Sally Freedman, Matthew Rutz, Leonhard Sassmannshausen, Stephen Tinney, and Matthew Waters, 209–21. Cuneiform Monographs 31. Leiden: Brill, 2006.

Klein, Jacob. "A New Look at the 'Oppression of Uruk' Episode in the Gilgameš Epic." In *Riches Hidden in Secret Places: Ancient Near Eastern Studies in Memory of Thorkild Jacobsen,* edited by Tzvi Abusch, 187–201. Winona Lake, Ind.: Eisenbrauns, 2002.

Klein, Jacob, and Kathleen Abraham. "Problems of Geography in the Gilgameš Epics: The Journey to the 'Cedar Forest.'" In *Landscapes: Territories, Frontiers and Horizons in the Ancient Near East,* volume 3, edited by Lucio Milano, Stefano De Martino, Frederick Mario Fales, and Giovanni B. Lanfranchi, 63–73. Compte rendu de la Rencontre Assyriologique Internationale 44, History of the Ancient Near East 3. Padua: Sargon Editrice, 2000.

Koch, Ulla Susanne. *Mesopotamian Divination Texts: Conversing with the Gods, Sources from the First Millennium BCE.* Guides to the Mesopotamian Textual Record 7. Münster: Ugarit-Verlag, 2015.

————. *Secrets of Extispicy: The Chapter Multābiltu of the Babylonian Extispicy Series and Niṣirti Bārûti Texts Mainly from Aššurbanipal's Library.* Alter Orient und Altes Testament 326. Münster: Ugarit-Verlag, 2005.

Konstantopoulos, Gina. "The Disciplines of Geography: Constructing Space in the Ancient World." *Journal of Ancient Near Eastern History* 4 (2017): 1–18.

———. "Gods in the Margins: Religion, Kingship, and the Fictionalized Frontier." In *As Above, So Below: Religion and Geography,* edited by Gina Konstantopoulos and Shana Zaia. Winona Lake, Ind.: Eisenbrauns, 2021.

———. "The Many Lives of Enheduana: Identity, Authorship, and the 'World's First Poet.'" In *Powerful Women in the Ancient World: Perception and (Self)Presentation,* edited by Sebastian Fink and Kerstin Droß-Krüpe, 57–76. Melammu Workshops and Monographs 4. Münster: Zaphon, 2021.

———. *They Are Seven: Demons and Monsters in the Mesopotamian Textual and Artistic Tradition.* Ancient Magic and Divination. Leiden: Brill, 2021.

Kouwenberg, Bert N. J. C. "Evidence for Post-Glottalized Consonants in Assyrian." *Journal of Cuneiform Studies* 55 (2003): 75–86.

Kraus, F. R. "Der Brief des Gilgameš." *Anatolian Studies* 30 (1980): 109–21.

Küchler, Friedrich. *Beiträge zur Kenntnis der assyrisch-babylonischen Medizin: Texte mit Umschrift, Übersetzung und Kommentar.* Assyriologische Bibliothek 18. Leipzig: J. C. Hinrichs Buchhandlung, 1904.

Lambert, Wilfred G. "Ancestors, Authors, and Canonicity." *Journal of Cuneiform Studies* 11, no. 1 (1957): 1–14.

———. *Babylonian Creation Myths.* Mesopotamian Civilizations 16. Winona Lake, Ind.: Eisenbrauns, 2013.

———. *Babylonian Wisdom Literature.* Winona Lake, Ind.: Eisenbrauns, 1996.

———. "A Catalogue of Texts and Authors." *Journal of Cuneiform Studies* 16, no. 3 (1962): 59–77.

———. "Gilgameš in Religious, Historical and Omen Texts and the Historicity of Gilgameš." In *Gilgameš et sa légende,* edited by Paul Garelli, 39–56. Compte rendu de la Rencontre Assyriologique Internationale 7. Paris: Klincksieck, 1960.

———. "The Theology of Death." In *Death in Mesopotamia,* edited by Bendt Alster, 53–66. Compte rendu de la Rencontre Assyriologique Internationale 26, Mesopotamia 8. Copenhagen: Akademisk Forlag, 1980.

Lambert, Wilfred G., and Alan R. Millard. *Atra-ḫasīs: The Babylonian Story of the Flood.* Oxford: Clarendon, 1969.

Landsberger, Benno. "Die Eigenbegrifflichkeit der babylonischen Welt: Ein Vortrag." *Islamica* 2 (1926): 355–72.

Larsen, Mogens Trolle. *The Conquest of Assyria: Excavations in an Antique Land.* London: Routledge, 1996.

Lassen, Agnete K., and Klaus Wagensonner, eds. *Women at the Dawn of History.* New Haven: Yale Babylonian Collection, 2020.

Le Carré, John. *The Spy Who Came In from the Cold*. London: Pan, 1963.

Leichty, Erle V. "The Colophon." In *Studies Presented to A. Leo Oppenheim*, edited by Robert D. Biggs and John A. Brinkman, 147–54. Chicago: Oriental Institute of the University of Chicago, 1964.

Leick, Gwendolyn. *Mesopotamia: The Invention of the City*. London: Penguin, 2002.

———. *Sex and Eroticism in Mesopotamian Literature*. London: Routledge, 1994.

Lenzi, Alan. "Advertising Secrecy, Creating Power in Ancient Mesopotamia: How Scholars Used Secrecy in Scribal Education to Bolster and Perpetuate Their Social Prestige and Power." *Antiguo Oriente* 11 (2013): 13–42.

———. *Introduction to Akkadian Literature: Contexts and Content*. Winona Lake, Ind.: Eisenbrauns, 2019.

———. *Secrecy and the Gods: Secret Knowledge in Ancient Mesopotamia and Biblical Israel*. State Archives of Assyria Studies 19. Helsinki: Neo-Assyrian Text Corpus Project, 2008.

———. "The Uruk List of Kings and Sages and Late Mesopotamian Scholarship." *Journal of Ancient Near Eastern Religions* 8, no. 2 (2008): 137–69.

Lévi-Strauss, Claude. *Mythologique*. Volume 1: *Le cru et le cuit*. Paris: Plon, 1964.

Lewis, Jenny. *Gilgamesh Retold: A Response to the Ancient Epic*. Manchester: Carcanet Classics, 2018.

Linssen, Marc J. H. *The Cults of Uruk and Babylon: The Temple Ritual Texts as Evidence for Hellenistic Cult Practice*. Cuneiform Monographs 25. Leiden: Brill, 2004.

Livingstone, Alasdair. "Ashurbanipal: Literate or Not?" *Zeitschrift für Assyriologie* 97, no. 1 (2007): 98–118.

———. *Court Poetry and Literary Miscellanea*. State Archives of Assyria 3. Helsinki: Helsinki University Press, 1989.

Longman, Tremper, III. *Fictional Akkadian Autobiography: A Generic and Comparative Study*. Winona Lake, Ind.: Eisenbrauns, 1991.

López-Ruiz, Carolina, Fumi Karahashi, and Marcus Ziemann. "*They Who Saw the Deep*: Achilles, Gilgamesh, and the Underworld." *Kaskal* 15 (2018): 85–107.

Maier, John R., ed. *Gilgamesh: A Reader*. Wauconda, Ill.: Bolchazy-Carducci, 1997.

Malley, Shawn. "Layard Enterprise: Victorian Archaeology and Informal Imperialism in Mesopotamia." *International Journal of Middle East Studies* 40, no. 4 (2008): 623–46.

Maul, Stefan M. *Das Gilgamesch-Epos: Neu übersetzt und kommentiert*. Munich: C. H. Beck Verlag, 2005.

Melman, Billie. *Empires of Antiquities: Modernity and the Rediscovery of the Ancient Near East, 1914–1950*. Oxford: Oxford University Press, 2020.

Melville, Sarah C. *The Role of Naqia/Zakutu in Sargonid Politics*. State Archives of Assyria Studies 9. Helsinki: Neo-Assyrian Text Corpus Project, 1999.

Metcalf, Christopher. "Babylonian Perspectives on the Certainty of Death." *Kaskal* 10 (2013): 256–67.

Michalowski, Piotr. "Commemoration, Writing, and Genre in Ancient Mesopotamia." In *The Limits of Historiography: Genre and Narrative in Ancient Historical Texts,* edited by Christina S. Kraus, 69–90. Leiden: Brill, 1999.

———. "The Lives of the Sumerian Language." In *Margins of Writing, Origins of Culture,* edited by Seth L. Sanders, 163–88. Oriental Institute Seminars 2. Chicago: Oriental Institute of the University of Chicago, 2006.

———. "A Man Called Enmebaragesi." In *Literatur, Politik und Recht in Mesopotamien: Festschrift für Claus Wilcke,* edited by Walther Sallaberger, Konrad Volk, and Annette Zgoll, 195–208. Wiesbaden: Harrassowitz Verlag, 2003.

———. "Maybe Epic: The Origins and Reception of Sumerian Heroic Poetry." In *Epic and History,* edited by David Konstan and Kurt A. Raaflaub, 7–25. Chichester: Wiley-Blackwell, 2010.

———. "Presence at the Creation." In *Lingering over Words: Studies in Ancient Near Eastern Literature in Honor of William L. Moran,* edited by Tzvi Abusch, John Huehnergard, and Piotr Steinkeller, 381–96. Harvard Semitic Studies 37. Atlanta: Scholars', 1990.

———. "Sailing to Babylon, Reading the Dark Side of the Moon." In *The Study of the Ancient Near East in the Twenty-First Century: The William Foxwell Albright Centennial Conference,* edited by Jerrold S. Cooper and Glenn M. Schwartz, 177–93. Winona Lake, Ind.: Eisenbrauns, 1996.

———. "Sumerian." In *The Cambridge Encyclopedia of the World's Ancient Languages,* edited by Roger D. Woodard, 19–59. Cambridge: Cambridge University Press, 2004.

Mielke, Thomas R. P. *Gilgamesch, König von Uruk.* Munich: Schneekluth, 1989.

Mieroop, Marc van de. "A Babylonian Cosmopolis." In *Problems of Canonicity and Identity Formation in Ancient Egypt and Mesopotamia,* edited by Kim Ryholt and Gojko Barjamovic, 259–70. Copenhagen: Museum Tusculanum Press, 2016.

———. "The Government of an Ancient Mesopotamian City: What We Know and Why We Know So Little." In *Priests and Officials in the Ancient Near East,* edited by Kazuko Watanabe, 139–61. Heidelberg: Universitätsverlag C. Winter, 1998.

———. *A History of the Ancient Near East, ca. 3000–323 BC.* Third edition. Chichester: Wiley-Blackwell, 2015.

———. *Philosophy Before the Greeks: The Pursuit of Truth in Ancient Babylonia.* Princeton: Princeton University Press, 2016.

Miller, Eva. "He Who Saw the Stars: Retelling Gilgamesh in *Star Trek: The Next Generation.*" In *Receptions of the Ancient Near East in Popular Culture and Beyond,* edited by Lorenzo Verderame and Agnès Garcia-Ventura, 141–58. Atlanta: Lockwood, 2020.

Mitchell, Stephen. *Gilgamesh: A New English Version.* New York: Free Press, 2004.

Moran, William L. "The Creation of Man in Atrahasis I 192–248." *Bulletin of the American Schools of Oriental Research* 200 (1970): 48–56.

———. "The Gilgamesh Epic: A Masterpiece from Ancient Mesopotamia." In *Civilizations of the Ancient Near East,* volume 4, edited by Jack M. Sasson, 2327–36. New York: Scribner's, 1995.

———. "Rilke and the Gilgamesh Epic." *Journal of Cuneiform Studies* 32, no. 4 (1980): 208–10.

———. "Some Considerations of Form and Interpretation in *Atra-ḫasīs.*" In *Language, Literature, and History: Philological and Historical Studies Presented to Erica Reiner,* edited by Frances Rochberg, 245–55. American Oriental Series 67. New Haven: American Oriental Society, 1987.

Moren, Sally M. "A Lost 'Omen' Tablet." *Journal of Cuneiform Studies* 29, no. 2 (1977): 65–72.

Müller, Hans-Peter. "Gilgameschs Trauergesang um Enkidu und die Gattung der Totenklage." *Zeitschrift für Assyriologie* 68, no. 2 (1978): 233–50.

Nardelli, Jean-Fabrice. *Homosexuality and Liminality in the "Gilgameš" and "Samuel."* Classical and Byzantine Monographs 64. Amsterdam: A. M. Hakkert, 2007.

Nemirovskaya, Adel V. "lú as a Logogram for *mamma* in the Standard Babylonian Epic of Gilgamesh." *Nouvelles assyriologiques brèves et utilitaires* 2008, no. 4 (2008): 110–12.

Nett, Seraina. "Akkadian as Lingua Franca: A Sociolinguistic Analysis of the Form, Function, and Use of Akkadian in the Western Mesopotamian Periphery, 2450–1200 BC." Ph.D. diss. Copenhagen: University of Copenhagen, 2012.

Nielsen, John P. *Sons and Descendants: A Social History of Kin Groups and Family Names in the Early Neo-Babylonian Period, 747–626 B.C.* Culture and History of the Ancient Near East 43. Leiden: Brill, 2011.

Nissen, Hans J., Peter Damerow, and Robert K. Englund. *Archaic Bookkeeping: Early Writing and Techniques of Economic Administration in the Ancient Near East.* Chicago: University of Chicago Press, 1993.

Nissinen, Martti. "Are There Homosexuals in Mesopotamian Literature?" *Journal of the American Oriental Society* 31, no. 1 (2010): 73–77.

———. *Homoeroticism in the Biblical World: A Historical Perspective.* Translated by Kirsi Stjerna. Minneapolis: Fortress, 2004.

Nissinen, Martti, and Risto Uro, eds. *Sacred Marriages: The Divine-Human Sexual Metaphor from Sumer to Early Christianity.* Winona Lake, Ind.: Eisenbrauns, 2008.

Noegel, Scott B. "A Janus Parallelism in the Gilgamesh Flood Story." *Acta Sumerologica* 13 (1991): 419–21.

———. *Nocturnal Ciphers: The Allusive Language of Dreams in the Ancient Near East.* American Oriental Society 89. New Haven: American Oriental Society, 2007.

Nurullin, Rim. "Philological Notes on the First Tablet of the Standard Babylonian Gilgameš Epic." *Babel und Bibel* 6 (2012): 189–208.

Oppenheim, A. Leo. *Ancient Mesopotamia: Portrait of a Dead Civilization.* Revised by Erica Reiner. Chicago: University of Chicago Press, 1977.

———. "Mesopotamian Mythology II." *Orientalia Nova Series* 17, no. 1 (1948): 17–58.

Paul, Shalom M. "The 'Plural of Ecstasy' in Mesopotamia and Biblical Love Poetry." In *Solving Riddles and Untying Knots: Biblical, Epigraphic, and Semitic Studies in Honor of Jonas C. Greenfield,* edited by Ziony Zevit, Seymour Gitin, and Michael Sokoloff, 585–97. Winona Lake, Ind.: Eisenbrauns, 1995.

Pinches, Theophilus. "Exit Gištubar!" *Babylonian and Oriental Record* 4 (1890): 264.

Polinger Foster, Karen. "Well-Tempered Words: Ceramic Metaphors in Cuneiform Literature." In *Opening the Tablet Box: Near Eastern Studies in Honor of Benjamin R. Foster,* edited by Sarah Melville and Alice Slotsky, 141–53. Culture and History of the Ancient Near East 42. Leiden: Brill, 2010.

Pollock, Sheldon. "Future Philology? The Fate of a Soft Science in a Hard World." *Critical Inquiry* 35, no. 4 (2009): 931–61.

———. "Introduction." In *World Philology,* edited by Sheldon Pollock, Benjamin A. Elman, and Ku-ming Kevin Chang, 1–24. Cambridge: Harvard University Press, 2015.

Pongratz-Leisten, Beate. "All the King's Men: Authority, Kingship, and the Rise of the Elites in Assyria." In *Experiencing Power, Generating Authority: Cosmos, Politics, and the Ideology of Kingship in Ancient Egypt and Mesopotamia,* edited by Jane A. Hill, Philip Jones, and Antonio J. Morales, 285–310. Philadelphia: University of Pennsylvania Press, 2013.

Potts, Daniel T., ed. *A Companion to the Archaeology of the Ancient Near East.* Chichester: Wiley-Blackwell, 2012.

Powell, Marvin A. "Maße und Gewichte." *Reallexikon der Assyriologie* 7 (1990): 457–517.

Pryke, Louise M. "The Bull of Heaven: Animality and Astronomy in Tablet VI of the *Gilgamesh Epic.*" *Aram* 29 (2017): 161–68.

———. *Gilgamesh.* Gods and Heroes of the Ancient World. London: Routledge, 2019.

———. *Ishtar.* Gods and Heroes of the Ancient World. London: Routledge, 2017.

———. "Religion and Humanity in Mesopotamian Myth and Epic." In *Oxford Research Encyclopedia of Religion,* edited by Julia Kostova, 1–30. Oxford: Oxford University Press, 2016.

———. "Unreliable Foreshadowing in Divine Predictions." In *The Shape of Stories: Narrative Structures in Cuneiform Literature,* edited by Sophus Helle and Gina Konstantopoulos. Cuneiform Monographs. Leiden: Brill, forthcoming.

Radner, Karen. *Die Macht des Namens: Altorientalische Strategien zur Selbsterhaltung.* Santag 8. Wiesbaden: Harrassowitz Verlag, 2005.

Radner, Karen, Nadine Moeller, and D. T. Potts, eds. *The Oxford History of the Ancient Near East.* Volume 1: *From the Beginnings to Old Kingdom Egypt and the Dynasty of Akkad.* Oxford: Oxford University Press, 2020.

Radner, Karen, and Eleanor Robson, eds. *The Oxford Handbook of Cuneiform Culture.* Oxford: Oxford University Press, 2011.

Rawlinson, Sir Henry C., William Henry Fox Talbot, Edward Hincks, and Julius Oppert. *Inscription of Tiglath Pileser I., King of Assyria, B.C. 1150.* London: J. W. Parker and Son, 1857.

Ray, Benjamin Caleb. "The Gilgamesh Epic: Myth and Meaning." In *Myth and Method,* edited by Laurie L. Patton and Wendy Doniger, 300–326. Charlottesville: University Press of Virginia, 1996.

Reitz, Christiane, and Simone Finkmann. *Structures of Epic Poetry.* 3 volumes. Berlin: De Gruyter, 2019.

Rendu, Anne-Caroline. "Cri ou silence: Deuil des dieux et des héros dans la littérature mésopotamienne." *Revue de l'histoire des religions* 225, no. 2 (2008): 199–221.

Renger, Johannes. "Heilige Hochzeit, A, Philologisch." *Reallexikon der Assyriologie* 4 (1972): 251–59.

Ridley, Ronald T. "The Saga of an Epic: Gilgamesh and the Constitution of Uruk." *Orientalia* 69 (2000): 341–67.

Rilke, Rainer Maria, and Katharina Kippenberg. *Briefwechsel.* Leipzig: Insel Verlag, 1954.

Robson, Eleanor. *Ancient Knowledge Networks: A Social Geography of Cuneiform Scholarship in First-Millennium Assyria and Babylonia.* London: UCL Press, 2019.

———. *Mathematics in Ancient Iraq: A Social History.* Princeton: Princeton University Press, 2009.

———. "The Production and Dissemination of Scholarly Knowledge." In *The Oxford Handbook of Cuneiform Culture,* edited by Karen Radner and Eleanor Robson, 557–76. Oxford: Oxford University Press, 2011.

———. "The Tablet House: A Scribal School in Old Babylonian Nippur." *Revue d'Assyriologie* 93, no. 1 (2001): 39–66.

Röllig, Wolfgang. "Götterzahlen." *Reallexikon der Assyriologie* 3 (1957–1971): 499–500.

Roth, Martha T. *Law Collections from Mesopotamia and Asia Minor.* Second edition. Atlanta: Scholars', 1997.

Rothfield, Lawrence. *The Rape of Mesopotamia: Behind the Looting of the Iraq Museum.* Chicago: University of Chicago Press, 2009.

Rubio, Gonzalo. "Early Sumerian Literature: Enumerating the Whole." In *De la tablilla a la inteligencia artificial: Homenaje al Prof. Jesús-Luis Cunchillos en su 65 aniversario,* volume 1, edited by Antonino González Blanco and Jesús-Luis Cunchillos, 131–42. Zaragoza: Instituto de Estudios Islámicos y del Oriente Próximo, 2004.

———. "Gilgamesh and the *ius primae noctis.*" In *Extraction and Control: Studies in Honor of Matthew W. Stolper,* edited by Michael Kozuh, Wouter F. M. Henkelman, Charles E. Jones, and Christopher Woods, 229–32. Studies in Ancient Oriental Civilization 68. Chicago: Oriental Institute of the University of Chicago, 2014.

———. "Reading Sumerian Names, II: Gilgameš." *Journal of Cuneiform Studies* 64 (2012): 3–16.

Sallaberger, Walther. *Das Gilgamesch-Epos: Mythos, Werk und Tradition.* Munich: C. H. Beck, 2013.

Salonen, Armas. *Vögel und Vogelfang im alten Mesopotamiaen.* Annales Academiae Scientiarum Fennicae Series B 208. Helsinki: Academia Scientiarum Fennica, 1973.

Sandars, N. K. *The Epic of Gilgamesh.* London: Penguin, 1960.

Scahill, Jeremy, and Glenn Greenwald. "The NSA's Secret Role in the U.S. Assassination Program." *The Intercept.* October 2, 2014. https://theintercept.com/2014/02/10/the-nsas -secret-role/.

Schmandt-Besserat, Denise. *Before Writing.* Volume 1: *From Counting to Cuneiform.* Austin: University of Texas Press, 1992.

Schmidt, Michael. *Gilgamesh: The Life of a Poem.* Princeton: Princeton University Press, 2019.

Schmidtchen, Eric. "The Edition of Esagil-kīn-apli's Catalogue of the Series *Sakikkû* (SA. GIG) and *Alamdimmû.*" In *Assyrian and Babylonian Scholarly Text Catalogues: Medicine, Magic and Divination,* edited by Ulrike Steinert, 313–33. Die babylonisch-assyrische Medizin in Texten und Untersuchungen 9. Berlin: De Gruyter, 2018.

Scurlock, JoAnn. "Death and the Afterlife in Ancient Mesopotamian Thought." In *Civilizations of the Ancient Near East,* volume 3, edited by Jack M. Sasson, 1883–93. New York: Scribner's, 1995.

Scurlock, JoAnn, and Burton R. Andersen. *Diagnoses in Assyrian and Babylonian Medicine: Ancient Sources, Translations, and Modern Medical Analyses.* Urbana: University of Illinois Press, 2005.

Sedgwick, Eve Kosofsky. "Jane Austen and the Masturbating Girl." *Critical Inquiry* 17, no. 4 (1991): 818–37.

Selz, Gerhard J. "The Uruk Phenomenon." In *The Oxford History of the Ancient Near East: From the Beginnings to Old Kingdom Egypt and the Dynasty of Akkad,* edited by Karen Radner, Nadine Moeller, and D. T. Potts, 163–244. Oxford: Oxford University Press, 2020.

Shehata, Dahlia. *Annotierte Bibliographie zum altbabylonischen Atramḫasīs-Mythos: inūma ilū awīlum.* Göttinger Arbeitshefte zur altorientalischen Literatur 3. Göttingen: Göttingen University Press, 2001.

———. *Musiker und ihr vokales Repertoire: Untersuchungen zu Inhalt und Organisation von Musikerberufen und Liedgattungen in altbabylonischer Zeit.* Göttinger Beiträge zum Alten Orient 3. Göttingen: Göttingen University Press, 2009.

Simoons-Vermeer, Ruth E. "The Mesopotamian Floodstories: A Comparison and Interpretation." *Numen* 21, no. 1 (1974): 17–34.

Smith, Ali. "Gold from the Old." *The Guardian.* January 14, 2006. https://www.theguardian.com/books/2006/jan/14/poetry.alismith.

Smith, George. "The Chaldean Account of the Deluge." *Transactions of the Society of Biblical Archaeology* 2 (1873): 213–34.

Soden, Wolfram von. *Akkadisches Handwörterbuch.* 3 vols. Wiesbaden: Harrasowitz, 1959.

———. "Konflikte und ihre Bewältigung in babylonischen Schöpfungs- und Fluterzählungen: Mit einer Teil-Übersetzung des Atramḫasīs-Mythus." *Mitteilungen der Deutschen Orient-Gesellschaft* 11 (1979): 1–33.

———. "Leistung und Grenze sumerischer und babylonischer Wissenschaft." *Die Welt als Geschichte* 2 (1936): 411–64, 509–57.

Sonik, Karen. "Breaching the Boundaries of Being: Metamorphoses in the Mesopotamian Literary Texts." *Journal of the American Oriental Society* 132, no. 3 (2012): 385–93.

———. "Gilgamesh and Emotional Excess: The King Without Counsel in the SB *Gilgamesh Epic*." In *The Expression of Emotions in Ancient Egypt and Mesopotamia*, edited by Shih-Wei Hsu and Jaume Llop Raduà, 390–409. Culture and History of the Ancient Near East 116. Leiden: Brill, 2020.

———. "Mesopotamian Conceptions of the Supernatural: A Taxonomy of *Zwischenwesen*." *Archiv für Religionsgeschichte* 14 (2013): 103–16.

Stein, Gertrude. *Lectures in America.* Reprint. Boston: Beacon, 1957.

Steinkeller, Piotr. "The Employment of Labor on National Building Projects in the Ur III Period." In *Labor in the Ancient World*, edited by Piotr Steinkeller and Michael Hudson, 137–236. Dresden: Islet Verlag, 2015.

Steymans, Hans Ulrich, ed. *Gilgamesch: Ikonographie eines Helden.* Orbis Biblicus et Orientalis 245. Fribourg: Academic Press Fribourg, 2010.

Stone, Elizabeth C. "An Update on the Looting of Archaeological Sites in Iraq." *Near Eastern Archaeology* 78, no. 3 (2015): 178–86.

Stone, Peter G., and Joanne Farchakh Bajjaly, eds. *The Destruction of Cultural Heritage in Iraq.* Woodbridge: Boydell, 2008.

Streck, Michael P. "Beiträge zum akkadischen Gilgameš-Epos." *Orientalia Nova Series* 76, no. 4 (2007): 404–23.

———. "Großes Fach Altorientalistik: Der Umfang des keilschriftlichen Textkorpus." *Mitteilungen der Deutschen Orient-Gesellschaft* 142 (2010): 35–58.

Sullivan, Ben. "Did a Drone Carrying NSA Tech Crash in Yemen?" *Vice News.* February 17, 2017. https://www.vice.com/en_us/article/d7578q/did-a-drone-carrying-nsa-tech-crash-in-yemen.

Svärd, Saana. *Women and Power in Neo-Assyrian Palaces.* State Archives of Assyria Studies 23. Helsinki: Neo-Assyrian Text Corpus Project, 2015.

Svärd, Saana, and Agnès Garcia-Ventura, eds. *Studying Gender in the Ancient Near East.* Winona Lake, Ind.: Eisenbrauns, 2018.

Tadmor, Hayim, Benno Landsberger, and Simo Parpola. "The Sin of Sargon and Sennacherib's Last Will." *State Archives of Assyria Bulletin* 3 (1989): 3–52.

Thal, Ian. "Are the Iraqis 'Waiting for Gilgamesh'?" *The Arts Fuse*, July 9, 2014. http://artsfuse.org/110067/fuse-theater-review-are-the-iraqis-waiting-for-gilgamesh/.

Tigay, Jeffrey H. *The Evolution of the Gilgamesh Epic.* Reprint. Wauconda, Ill.: Bolchazy-Carducci, 1997.

Tinney, Steve. "On the Curricular Setting of Sumerian Literature." *Iraq* 61 (1999): 159–72.

Uçar-Özbirinci, Pürnur. "A Woman Playwright's Revision of a Legendary Epic: Zeynep Avcı's *Gilgamesh.*" *Tulsa Studies in Women's Literature* 29, no. 1 (2010): 107–23.

Vanstiphout, Herman L. J. "The Craftmanship of *Sîn-leqi-unninnī.*" *Orientalia Lovaniensia Periodica* 21 (1990): 45–79.

———. *Epics of Sumerian Kings: The Matter of Aratta.* Edited by Jerrold S. Cooper. Writings from the Ancient World 20. Atlanta: Society of Biblical Literature, 2003.

———. "Some Thoughts on Genre in Mesopotamian Literature." In *Keilschriftliche Literaturen,* edited by Karl Hecker and Walter Sommerfeld, 1–11. Compte rendu de la Rencontre Assyriologique Internationale 32, Berliner Beiträge zum vorderen Orient 6. Berlin: D. Reimer Verlag, 1986.

———. "The Use(s) of Genre in Mesopotamian Literature: An Afterthought." *Archiv Orientální* 67, no. 4 (1999): 703–17.

Veldhuis, Niek. *Religion, Literature, and Scholarship: The Sumerian Composition "Nanše and the Birds."* Cuneiform Monographs 22. Leiden: Brill, 2004.

Verderame, Lorenzo. "Osservazioni a margine dei concetti di 'ibrido' e 'mostro' in Mesopotamia." In *Monstra: Costruzione e percezione delle entità ibride e mostruose nel Mediterraneo antico,* volume 1, edited by Igor Baglioni, 160–72. Rome: Edizione Quasar, 2013.

Vogelzang, Marianna E., and Herman L. J. Vanstiphout, eds. *Mesopotamian Epic Literature: Oral or Aural?* Lewiston, N.Y.: Edwin Mellen Press, 1992.

———. *Mesopotamian Poetic Language: Sumerian and Akkadian.* Cuneiform Monographs 6. Groningen: Styx, 1996.

Vulpe, Nicola. "Irony and the Unity of the Gilgamesh Epic." *Journal of Near Eastern Studies* 53, no. 4 (1994): 275–83.

Waerzeggers, Caroline. "The Pious King: Royal Patronage of Temples." In *The Oxford Handbook of Cuneiform Culture,* edited by Karen Radner and Eleanor Robson, 725–51. Oxford: Oxford University Press, 2011.

Walker, Christopher B. F. "The Second Tablet of *ṭupšenna pitema*, an Old Babylonian Naram-Sin Legend?" *Journal of Cuneiform Studies* 33, nos. 3-4 (1981): 191-95.

Walls, Neal H. *Desire, Discord, and Death: Approaches to Ancient Near Eastern Myth.* American Schools of Oriental Research Books 8. Boston: American Schools of Oriental Research, 2001.

Wasserman, Nathan. "The Distant Voice of Gilgameš: The Circulation and Reception of the Babylonian Gilgameš Epic in Ancient Mesopotamia." *Archiv für Orientforschung* 52 (2011): 1-14.

———. *The Flood: The Akkadian Sources—A New Edition, Commentary, and a Literary Discussion.* Orbis Biblicus et Orientalis 290. Leuven: Peeters, 2020.

———. "Lists and Chains: Enumeration in Akkadian Literary Texts." In *Lists and Catalogues in Ancient Literature and Beyond: Towards a Poetics of Enumeration,* edited by Rebecca Lämmle, Cédric Scheidegger Lämmle, and Katharina Wesselmann, 57-80. Trends in Classics Supplementary Volumes 107. Berlin: De Gruyter, 2021.

———. "The Rhetoric of Time Inversion: *Hysteron-Proteron* and the 'Back to Creation' Theme in Old Babylonian Literary Texts." In *Genesis and Regeneration: Essays on Conceptions of Origins,* edited by Shaul Shaked, 13-30. Jerusalem: Israel Academy of Sciences and Humanities, 2005.

———. *Style and Form in Old-Babylonian Literary Texts.* Cuneiform Monographs 27. Leiden: Brill, 2003.

Weiher, Egbert von. "Gilgameš und Enkidu: Die Idee einer Freundschaft." *Baghdader Mitteilungen* 11 (1980): 106-19.

Wells, H. G. *The Outline of History: Being a Plain History of Life and Mankind.* Edited by Ernest Barker. London: Macmillan, 1920.

West, Martin L. *The East Face of Helicon: West Asiatic Elements in Greek Poetry and Myth.* Oxford: Clarendon, 1997.

Westenholz, Aage, and Ulla Susanne Koch. "Enkidu—the Noble Savage?" In *Wisdom, Gods and Literature: Studies in Assyriology in Honour of W. G. Lambert,* edited by Andrew R. George and Irving L. Finkel, 437-51. Winona Lake, Ind.: Eisenbrauns, 2000.

Westenholz, Joan Goodnick. "A Forgotten Love Song." In *Language, Literature, and History: Philological and Historical Studies Presented to Erica Reiner,* edited by Frances Rochberg, 415-25. American Oriental Series 67. New Haven: American Oriental Society, 1987.

———. *Legends of the Kings of Akkade: The Texts.* Mesopotamian Civilizations 7. Winona Lake, Ind.: Eisenbrauns, 1997.

———. "Metaphorical Language in the Poetry of Love in the Ancient Near East." In *La circulation des biens, des personnes et des idées dans le Proche-Orient ancien,* edited by Dominique

Charpin and Frances Joannès, 381–87. Compte rendu de la Rencontre Assyriologique Internationale 38. Paris: Éditions recherche sur les civilisations, 1992.

Whipple, Tom. "Ancient Sex Saga Now Twice as Epic." *The Times.* November 19, 2018. https://www.thetimes.co.uk/article/ancient-sex-saga-now-twice-as-epic-ng03tblxh.

Wilcke, Claus. "Der Tod im Leben der Babylonier." In *Tod, Jenseits und Identität: Perspektiven einer kulturwissenschaftlichen Thanatologie,* edited by Jan Assmann and Rolf Trauzettel, 252–66. Veröffentlichungen des Instituts für historische Anthropologie 7. Freiburg: Karl Alber Verlag, 2002.

———. "Weltuntergang als Anfang: Theologische, anthropologische, politisch-historische und ästhetische Ebenen der Interpretation der Sintflutgeschichte im babylonischen Atramhasīs-Epos." In *Weltende: Beiträge zur Kultur- und Religionswissenschaft,* edited by Adam Jones, 63–112. Wiesbaden: Harrasowitz Verlag, 1999.

Wilhelm II. *Das Königtum im alten Mesopotamien.* Berlin: De Gruyter, 1938.

Winter, Irene. "Sex, Rhetoric, and the Public Monument: The Alluring Body of Naram-Sîn of Agade." In *Sexuality in Ancient Art: Near East, Egypt, Greece, and Italy,* edited by Natalie Kampen, 11–26. Cambridge: Cambridge University Press, 1996.

Wisnom, Selena. "The Dynamics of Repetition in Akkadian Literature." In *The Shape of Stories: Narrative Structures in Cuneiform Literature,* edited by Sophus Helle and Gina Konstantopoulos. Cuneiform Monographs. Leiden: Brill, forthcoming.

———. "Stress Patterns in *Enūma Eliš:* A Comparative Study." *Kaskal* 12 (2015): 485–502.

———. *Weapons of Words: Intertextual Competition in Babylonian Poetry.* Culture and History of the Ancient Near East 106. Leiden: Brill, 2019.

Wolff, Hope Nash. "Gilgamesh, Enkidu, and the Heroic Life." *Journal of the American Oriental Society* 89, no. 2 (1969): 392–98.

Woods, Christopher. "Bilingualism, Scribal Learning, and the Death of Sumerian." In *Margins of Writing, Origins of Culture,* edited by Seth L. Sanders, 95–124. Oriental Institute Seminars 2. Chicago: Oriental Institute of the University of Chicago, 2006.

Worthington, Martin. *Ea's Duplicity in the Gilgamesh Flood Story.* London: Routledge, 2019.

———. "*mamma(n)* . . . *ul* and Its Alternatives in Babylonian Literature." *Kaskal* 7 (2010): 123–42.

———. "On Names and Artistic Unity in the Standard Version of the Babylonian Gilgamesh Epic." *Journal of the Royal Asiatic Society* 21, no. 4 (2011): 403–20.

———. *Principles of Akkadian Textual Criticism.* Studies in Ancient Near Eastern Records 1. Berlin: De Gruyter, 2012.

———. "Schankwirt(in)." *Reallexikon der Assyriologie* 12 (2011): 132–34.

Zgoll, Annette. "Audienz: Ein Modell zum Verständnis mesopotamischer Handerhebungs-rituale, mit einer Deutung der Novelle vom Armen Mann von Nippur." *Baghdader Mitteilungen* 34 (2003): 181–203.

———. "monumentum aere perennius—Maerring und Ringkomposition im Gilgameš-Epos." In *Von Göttern und Menschen: Beiträge zu Literatur und Geschichte des Alten Orients—Festschrift für Brigitte Groneberg*, edited by Dahlia Shehata, Frauke Weiershäuser, and Kamran V. Zand, 443–70. Cuneiform Monographs 41. Leiden: Brill, 2010.

———. *Der Rechtsfall der En-ḫedu-Ana im Lied nin-me-šara*. Alter Orient und Altes Testament 246. Münster: Ugarit-Verlag, 1997.

Ziolkowski, Theodore. *Gilgamesh Among Us: Modern Encounters with the Ancient Epic*. Ithaca: Cornell University Press, 2011.

Zweig, Stefan. *The World of Yesterday*. Translated by Benjamin W. Huebsch and Helmut Ripperger. London: Cassell, 1943.

ACKNOWLEDGMENTS

This book is the result of a long labor of love, and I am grateful beyond words to all who helped me complete it. There are so many delightful people to thank, more than these pages (or my memory) can easily accommodate. I have been reading, thinking, and writing about *Gilgamesh* for eight years now, and for all that time I have gushed about the epic to friends, family, and colleagues, who, in each their own way, have shaped my thoughts on the text: thank you all. I think the first to lend an ear to my enthusiasm was Viktor Blichfeldt, and Alexandra O'Sullivan Freltoft did so more than most—for that and for everything else, thank you both. The English translation could not have been made without two people in particular. Aya Labanieh worked with me every step of the way, from the first sample pages to the final text, and many of my most fortuitous phrases I owe to her. Without her support, this book would not be. My father, Morten Søndergaard, with whom I spent a year translating the epic into Danish, gave me the courage and the fresh perspective I needed to attempt an English translation too. My understanding of Akkadian poetry has been shaped and sharpened by countless discussions with Selena Wisnom, Gina Konstantopoulos, Omar N'Shea, Ann Guinan, and Nicole Brisch, for which I am extremely grateful. Selena, Martin Worthington, Louise Pryke, Frank Simons, Julia Levenson, Evelyne Koubkova, Claudio Sansone, and Laura Feldt all made invaluable comments on earlier drafts of the manuscript, as did my mother, Merete Pryds Helle. I would also like to thank Johannes Haubold, Gösta Gabriel, Theodore Ziolkowski, Johannes Bach, Eva Miller, and Karen Sonik as well as Martin, Louise, Ann, Selena, Gina, and Nicole for sharing unpublished work with me. The arguments presented in these essays build on articles I have published on the epic, and I would like to thank the editors and reviewers of the journals in which those articles appeared for honing my ideas. The essay "The Storm of His Heart" is based on my MA thesis, which was supervised by Nicole Brisch—the most supportive adviser anyone could wish for. In connection with the Danish translation of *Gilgamesh*, I have given about forty interviews and public lectures on the epic, and the audiences at those events have helped me better understand which aspects of the epic were exciting, which they could relate to, and which needed to be explained. Their encouragement (and merciful laughter at my bad jokes) has been a crucial source of support in this project. The book would never have seen the light of day had it not been for the combined efforts of Ann, Michael Coogan, and my editor Jennifer Banks—thank you so much! Working with my copyeditor Susan Laity was a rare delight; her reading of the book was both brilliant and kind-hearted. My stay in London, where I carried out the translation at the peak of the Covid-19 lockdown, was made possible by the generous support of the C. L. David Foundation and Collection. Finally, there are the people who helped in ways big and small, who know how they helped me and who know how very grateful I am: Mads Rosendahl Thomsen, David Damrosch, Marshall Brown, Mons Bissenbakker, Nils Heeßel, Nell Hawley, Berit Kjærulff, Maja Bak Herrie, Jana Matuszak, Rune Rattenborg, and Nikoline Sauer.